UNDER
the
SAME
BLUE SKY

Also by Pamela Schoenewaldt

*Swimming in the Moon*
*When We Were Strangers*

# UNDER
## the
# SAME
# BLUE SKY

## Pamela Schoenewaldt

WILLIAM MORROW
*An Imprint of* HarperCollins*Publishers*

P.S.™ is a trademark of HarperCollins Publishers.

HarperCollins books may be purchased for educational, business, or sales promotional use. For information please e-mail the Special Markets Department at SPsales@harpercollins.com.

FIRST EDITION

*Designed by Diahann Sturge*

Library of Congress Cataloging-in-Publication Data has been applied for.

ISBN 978-0-06-232663-8

15 16 17 18 19    OV/RRD    10 9 8 7 6 5 4 3 2 1

*For Silvia*

# Contents

# UNDER
## the
# SAME
# BLUE SKY

Yes; quaint and curious war is!
You shoot a fellow down
You'd treat, if met where any bar is,
Or help to half a crown.

*Thomas Hardy*
*from "The Man He Killed"*

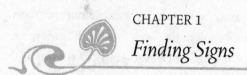

## CHAPTER 1

# *Finding Signs*

"See? Here are the men in scarlet jackets with gold braid, the grand stairway with rainbow light, the hall of mirrors where I played. And look, here's someone carrying me through gardens." I turned the sketchbook pages of my earliest memories, carefully rendered in watercolors. I was eighteen and sure that my art would convince her.

My mother had just spread a rectangle of sweet dough with melted butter, chopped nuts, and cinnamon sugar. "No, those were *dreams*, Hazel. You've always dreamed and you're always drawing. But dreams aren't real. We never had a garden. Look around this flat. Do you see rainbow light? Men in scarlet jackets with gold braid? Mirror halls? This is *Pittsburgh*."

She was right that in 1914, in our German-American enclave of East Ohio Street, men didn't wear scarlet jackets. My father's hardware store dealt in silvers, grays, bronze, and brass. No rainbow light ever pierced the narrow stairway to our flat. Black smoke from the city's steel mills smeared our skies, our clothes, and the faces of men who spent their days stoking coal fires. Yet how could I deny memories as real as my own life? "Musicians played while people ate," I insisted as she rolled the dough in a neat log.

"Now *that's* impossible. We only have a Victrola." She wet a finger to seal the roll, adding loyally: "Of course your father's hammer makes a kind of music." A kind of music, yes. Every night after dinner he tapped scenes of his beloved Heidelberg into tin plates for other heart-torn immigrants. "You were so young when we came to America," she persisted, cutting the log into slices she'd set to rise near our coal stove. "You can't possibly remember Germany, and we certainly weren't rich there. Do you remember the storm at sea or that terrible bread?"

"No."

"Or changing your name from Hilde to Hazel to make you more American?"

"No."

"Well then? All that scarlet and gold must be a dream."

Whether memories or dreams, the men in scarlet jackets were real to me, but as distant as the marvelous lands I read about beyond the constant stain of Pittsburgh's smokestacks: "It was a beautiful blue day . . . The sparkling waters . . . A cloudless morning greeted them with sweet, clear air." I filled private sketchbooks with green fields hugging a white schoolhouse, forests mirrored in lakes, and bright skies over Paris, Rome, and Venice. Meanwhile, the windows of our flat looked over rolling waves of smoke. Rain sprayed grit against the glass I washed each week, leaning precariously over the street. Factory dust sieved into the four rooms, fading the wallpaper and filming the copper pots my mother scrubbed back to ruddy suns. With equal care, she swept our hardware store, polished counters, and kept the front windows sparkling. She even washed meat from Mr. Schmidt's butcher shop and vegetables from Mr. Hesse's grocery. Our cabbage sometimes harbored whiffs of soap. I began each school day in starched clothes and polished shoes, as if my American citizenship must be confirmed with unfailing cleanliness and order.

Yet no matter how hard my mother and her neighbors worked, they could only clean their private realms of Pittsburgh. The Monongahela River was a black swill. Trudging home in midafternoon gloom, we schoolchildren wrote our names in dust that settled everywhere. We stomped off soot and shook our coats before coming indoors. Everyone coughed, for there was no cleaning the lungs. Those who worked in foundries and mills coughed most of all. Pneumonia and dysentery raged through families housed in soggy ravines with open sewers. In the steady gloom, children's bones grew crooked. In cheap boardinghouses, men slept in dank rooms, in beds warm from those in the shifts before them. When millworkers' funerals wound through the streets, my parents and their friends were grateful to be shopkeepers, butchers, brewers, cabinetmakers, bookkeepers, and tailors.

Thanks to my good grades and their careful savings, I could enter "the professions," my mother boasted. Of course I would be successful. "That goes without saying." But she *did* say it, to my teachers, for example, while I squirmed in embarrassment. She announced my remarkable future in shops and outside our Lutheran church, where we gathered after Sunday services. Their great friends—I called them my Uncle Willy and Tante Elise—heard in exquisite detail every sign of my extraordinary destiny. At the least, I'd be a lawyer, a professor, or doctor and have a fine home in Pittsburgh's elegant Shadyside neighborhood.

"Or an artist," I suggested. "Like Father with his tins."

Uncomfortable silence spread around our table. "The tins are a *pastime*," my mother clarified. "They're not what he *does*. With your advantages, you could rise above."

"Like Brunnhilde the Valkyrie?" I suggested. Encouraged by my father's twitch of a smile, I threw a wider net: "Or Boudica, the warrior queen?"

"Laugh if you want, but *I've* known from the first that you were destined to be extraordinary. Even," she conceded, "an extraordinary teacher. I've seen signs." Here all jesting stopped, for her signs were not to be contradicted. They were as much a fixture of our flat as boiled potatoes.

"Well then," my father said, "are there signs of sauerbraten? Could we eat before Hazel achieves her destiny?" When he touched my mother's hand as she passed the serving bowl, the blues of their eyes melted together.

In *my* future dreams, the "extraordinary" meant travel, sketching, painting, meeting great artists, and passing golden hours in a storied café, funding these adventures through teaching and tutoring. It went without saying that my parents weren't delighted. They were only modestly pleased when, at sixteen, I began working at our pastor's Saturday school, teaching American-born children to read and write German. Yes, it was good to preserve our *Kultur*, the language of Goethe, and pride in the Fatherland, but not as preparation for "a gypsy life."

"What do you expect, Hazel? You're their only child," my friend Luisa demanded. She was right: I was the vessel for all my parents' ambitions, fierce love, and claim to the Renner family's success in America. I knew my mother's pain that there was no child after me, no baby for the cradle my father had hopefully carved, and then tactfully stored away. I knew about the patent medicines she bought with money squeezed from small economies and the Russian herb woman she surreptitiously visited. I saw how hungrily she looked at babies on the street, her tense smiles when neighbors' bellies bulged, and heavy silences after baptisms in our church. "Don't cry, Katarina," my father whispered in their bedroom when they thought I was asleep.

"But a *son*, Johannes. Don't you want a good American son?"

"We're happy. We have a good American daughter. She'll be extraordinary, just as you say. Meanwhile, we have our health, our friends, and the store's doing well. Best of all, I have you. Come close, come close, my little darling." Their voices softened into murmurs and I crept back to my room.

Yes, I was my parents' "real American," while they'd be forever branded as foreigners the instant they opened their mouths. Every bungled *th* or *w* betrayed them. The very cadence of their voices, even the studied perfection of my father's grammar labeled him as a foreigner who tried too hard. Because I had no accent, shopkeepers didn't speak loudly and slowly to me as if I were deaf or dull-witted.

I ached for my parents as their fingers crept down tight columns of the *Pittsburgh Post*, or they delivered careful thanks to my teachers each June. In German, they never halted or stammered, searching for words. Even their laughter was different, freer and more rolling. They told stories and jokes. They sang. Americans couldn't imagine how their tongues loosened at home like stout women unlacing corsets, relating their day, the store business, my mother's shopping, my school grades, and news from Germany in Pittsburgh's *Volksblatt* newspaper.

Still they struggled on in English. My mother and I crawled through books from the public library. I'd read one page of *Little Women*, and then she'd do the next, earnestly mimicking my accent. We worked through *The Red Badge of Courage*, *The Adventures of Tom Sawyer*, and her favorite: Edgar Allan Poe's *Tales of Terror*, until she could read by herself with a dictionary at her side.

"You're already a citizen," I reminded her. "You don't have to do this."

"Yes I do."

Perhaps she was right. Everywhere one heard how our country was polluted by "hyphenated Americans": German-Americans, Hungarian-Americans, Polish-Americans, Greek- and Italian-Americans. Everything "ethnic" was an unpleasant mold that must be removed. President Woodrow Wilson himself had warned the foreign-born: "You cannot become thorough Americans if you think of yourself in groups." Each month, fewer children came to German Saturday school. They wanted to be Americans. More and more, their parents let them play baseball, stickball, or marbles on Saturday, or gave them nickels to see the Keystone Cops, Fatty Arbuckle, and Charlie Chaplin.

My father began introducing himself as John Renner. He stocked *Popular Mechanics, Scientific American,* and Uncle Sam piggy banks for children. But when my mother began preparing American meals suggested by *Good Housekeeping,* he revolted. "In the privacy of my own home, I'd like decent food." Why the "ridiculous" green of parsley butter? Why tomato bisque when potato soup was clearly better? Jell-O repulsed him. "Is this alive?" he demanded, bouncing his spoon on a crimson square. He refused grapefruit at breakfast, was suspicious of store mayonnaise, and would not substitute cottage cheese for *quark.*

"You could try it," my mother argued. "Don't you like experiments?"

"Not with food." For Sunday dinners with Uncle Willy and Tante Elise, we did have "normal" meals: sauerbraten, green beans, spaetzle, and rye bread. "Come more often, Willy," my father pleaded, "and save me from *Good Housekeeping.*" As belts and tongues loosened and the men moved from beer to schnapps, talk turned to Europe's troubles: Kaiser Wilhelm's bluster and blunders, unrest in Serbia, and outrageous French demands for the return of Alsace-Lorraine, which was clearly German territory.

I eased from the table to the window seat and took out my colors. The Kaiser meant nothing to me; I had many Serbian friends and didn't care about Alsace-Lorraine. Sometimes my parents felt as far away as

Europe, still locked in kingdom struggles. Better to tackle the persistent puzzle of my life: the splendid rooms I shouldn't remember. Where did those memories come from? Was there another Hazel besides this one on East Ohio Street? And another mystery: Why did I always draw the *same* little blue house in the country, in the same avidly imagined detail, with two vague figures on the porch step? One might be me. And the other?

And why were my dreams so ungrateful, so bent to my own pleasure? If I went to medical school and became a doctor as my mother often suggested, I could buy my parents a house with a big kitchen, separate dining room, garden, and a workroom for my father's tins and projects. I could take them back to Heidelberg. We could walk along the Neckar River, visit old relatives, see the church where they were married, and eat white asparagus that was nowhere finer than in the stalls along the Marktplatz. Didn't they deserve these pleasures?

"Wouldn't you like to be a doctor, Hazel?" my mother might let fall while shaping rolls or pressing out *butterplätzchen,* the butter cookies so beloved at our church dinners. "After all, you have the healing touch." So many times I'd heard the story, the telling as solemn as any liturgy: "When you were just five years old, you cooled your hands in ice water, climbed on a stool, and rubbed your father's headache away. You knew what to do! Wasn't that a sign?"

"I'm not sure."

"But you should be sure. You make my shoulder better in the morning just by rubbing it."

"Dr. Edson says arthritis is always worse in the morning. Rubbing just feels good; it doesn't heal anything." No, she insisted, I'd be an extraordinary doctor. There were signs. Apparently, school prizes in drawing weren't signs of an art career. An award for memorizing Bible verses was merely admirable. Having my own class in the German Saturday school wasn't a sign for a teaching career. First place in the girls' fifty-yard dash wasn't a sign of anything at all. "Why are only *her* signs real?" I asked Luisa as we sat in Katz's, sharing a chocolate milkshake.

"I don't know, but the only signs *my* mother sees are that I'll be in trouble if I don't hurry up and marry a sober, hardworking man with a good job. Your parents want more for you. You should be grateful."

"You're right," I admitted. How many shoeshine and messenger boys would rather be in school? Girls my age ironed for hours in steaming laundries or scrubbed for rich people. Children of millworkers played with lumps of coal, their only toys. Nobody took them to Carnegie Library on their sixth birthday for their own borrowing card.

"Well then? Will you think about medicine?" Luisa demanded.

"Yes." But not today. I persuaded Luisa to come with me to the Carnegie Institute to see great art: Grecian gods and goddesses, English landscapes, and French women wearing clouds of lace, swinging in sylvan glades. "Those ladies never cook," Luisa said. "I have to go now and help my mother make tortellini." I lingered, entranced by the skill of artists whose skill soared over mine. *They* were extraordinary.

On my way home, Mr. Schmidt the butcher stopped me. "Hazel, we've been looking everywhere for you."

"What happened?" A fire in our flat? Sickness? A robbery in the store? Were my parents hit by a streetcar?

"You know how they always walk together to the newsstand for the *Volksblatt*?"

I nodded. Mr. Schmidt could not be hurried in carving meat or telling stories, but now I wanted to shake him. "What happened? Are they hurt?"

"Well, they were coming home, passing my store. Your father was reading the headlines to your mother, as he always does. They waved to me, and I waved back. I was trimming ribs."

"Yes, and—"

"So he was reading the headlines. Then two hoodlum boys shoved them, ripped the *Volksblatt* from his hands and threw it in the gutter. They said real Americans read American newspapers."

"But nobody was hurt."

"I don't think so."

I thanked Mr. Schmidt and ran home. My father wouldn't discuss the incident or speak to the boys' parents, who were his customers. "Next time, I'll buy a *Pittsburgh Post* and fold the *Volksblatt* inside it."

"You shouldn't have to."

"But it's better that way. Now look at the fine apple strudel your mother made." As I walked down East Ohio Street in the next week, I studied every passing pair of boys. Were they the ones who insulted my parents? What had they heard at home that made them want to do such things?

"*Next* Sunday," my mother announced, "we're having a picnic at Raccoon Creek Park." She'd already determined the streetcar routes that would take us there, the picnic menu, and that we would not say a single word about the Kaiser, Serbia, Alsace-Lorraine, or anything in the newspapers.

"Well, Hazel," my father said, "I see signs that our Sunday is planned." So we went. The air at Raccoon Creek was silky soft, as clean as fresh linen. Green lawns surrounded a placid lake under a tender blue sky. I helped spread our gingham tablecloth over springy grass and set out a plate of rye bread. My father lay down with a sigh. My mother opened her mending basket. I sketched willow trees bent over the lake. From the corner of my eye, I saw my father's arm arching back and forth, pulling off chunks of bread he dropped in his mouth. "Don't spoil your appetite," my mother muttered, bent over a sock.

"Bread is life," he answered dreamily.

Suddenly an unearthly gag ripped the quiet. My father was on all fours, shoulders heaving. Then he collapsed like a house of cards, his face a sickly gray.

My mother shrieked and for the first time used his Christian name in my presence: "Johannes!"

*Not possible, not possible,* I thought wildly. Not on a green lawn by Raccoon Creek Park, under this blue sky. When I yanked him up to sitting, he was limp as a rag doll. Picnickers came running with suggestions.

"Hit him on the back!"

"Lift his arms!"

"Shake him!"

"He's dead," my mother sobbed.

"He's not!" I don't know why I thought of a child's popgun. With a surge of strength, I squeezed hard under his ribs. *Pop the cork.* I squeezed again, even harder. A wad of bread flew out of his mouth, landing on my mother's skirt. She shrieked again. He heaved, weakly breaking my grip as a red curtain rose up his face. Inside that gorgeous scarlet, blue eyes flew open, looking back at me. My chest heaved in exhaustion and relief.

"Johannes!" my mother cried, flinging her arms around him. She'd never done this in public before, ever.

He coughed and gasped: "What were you doing, Hazel, squeezing me to death?"

"No, pal, squeezing you to *life,*" said a spectator.

My mother seized the loaf and—another first—threw away perfectly good food. The loaf made a wide arc and plopped into the lake.

"Great pitch."

"Throw that sucker!"

"You should play for the Pittsburgh Pirates, lady! What an arm!"

"Hazel, you saved him. He was *dead* and you brought him back," one cried.

No, no, both things were impossible, first that *my* father could die and so absurdly, for a bit of bread. Second, that I, plain Hazel, could bring back the dead. "Now, now," my father said reasonably. "Maybe I skipped some breaths, but let's not be dramatic. I *am* thirsty, though. I'd like a beer, Mother."

"Of course." She fumbled for a bottle. "But Hazel, isn't this a sign that you were meant to be a doctor? After all, you knew just what to do. You saved—"

My father wiped his mouth. "Enough. We're grateful that Hazel was with us and thought quickly. Let's just enjoy—"

"But she saved—" The blue glaze caught hers and she fell silent, brushing crumbs from the tablecloth. In the next days, her wondering, adoring eyes on me, her heaping my plate with the choicest sausage, and exquisite care in ironing my clothes, all repeated one certainty: I had miraculously saved her treasure on earth. "If you really don't want to be a doctor," she conceded, "you could at least be a nurse. I'm sure the picnic was a sign."

"Mother, not *everything* is a sign." Perhaps not, but signs filled her world. Chimney sweeps were good signs; seeing anyone walk between two old ladies was very bad, like a song before breakfast. A knife received as a present was a sign of coming misfortune. After an Italian friend announced that 17 was even more unlucky than 13, the 17th of many months brought her sick headaches. A husband nearly killed by rye bread and saved by his daughter, how could that *not* be a sign?

*Was it?* The question rolled in my mind at night. My future swirled. Perhaps I was as wrong about my dreams of travel and drawing as I was about the scarlet jackets. Why *not* do good in this obvious way? I'd helped my father; I could help others. *Were* there really signs that I had been called to a life of art and not of healing? Was I being arrogant—or simply wrong? If I went to museums, shouldn't I at least see where doctors trained?

I took a streetcar to the University of Pittsburgh Medical School, mounted the broad steps, and wandered through hallways smelling of alcohol, formaldehyde, and oiled wood. Neatly labeled displays lined the halls. In an amphitheater, a professor questioned a one-armed millworker about phantom pain. Students in white jackets discussed a pneumonia case. "Atypical," said one. "Fascinating," said another. A young woman was among them, wearing a white coat like theirs, an equal. They might welcome me. But could I share their fascination, their dedication? Would I be a fraud, or worse, if I tended the sick by rote or duty? "Can I help you, miss?" one of the young men asked. "Are you looking for someone?"

"No, just—looking around." He turned back to his colleagues. I hurried away. I *had* been looking for someone: Dr. Hazel Renner. But she wasn't here.

I went to Dr. Edson's office and waited until the last patient left. "So, Hazel," he began as he always did, "what brings you here?"

I wasn't sick, I explained, only curious: "When did you decide to be a doctor?"

"I didn't decide. I always wanted this life." He studied me, the mild eyes and soft questions drawing out every symptom of distress. I explained how I'd helped my father at the picnic, my good grades, my mother's plans for my future, and my uncertainty. "I see. You think you *ought* to want to be a doctor because it's an honorable profession, but you aren't sure it's the right path for you. Is that it?" I nodded. Dr. Edson studied his stethoscope, as he often did, so intently that when I was small I imagined it held all the world's medical knowledge. "You know, Hazel, there are *many* honorable professions." The old eyes twinkled. "Plumbing, for instance. Running a hardware store, teaching, or art. You must find *your* honorable profession, the place where you can do good. If not, if you choose wrong, some damage might be done, don't you think?"

"Perhaps."

"Almost certainly." He tucked the stethoscope into its wooden box for the night. "I hear good reports from your Saturday school class."

"Some children have stopped coming."

"They'll be back. This unpleasant idea that true Americans must forget their father's culture will surely pass." He fumbled for his Homburg hat. I helped him with the tweed jacket he'd worn forever. "Thank you, my dear. Mrs. Edson is waiting for me, as your parents are waiting for you, I'm sure." He opened the office door for me and led me to the street, where he bowed slightly and started home, stopping often to greet his many patients.

I passed the next days in a haze of anxiety until on a grimy morning like any other. I made my choice, or rather, seized the choice that had hovered over me for months like a gauzy dream. Not medicine and not travel yet. By next year I could be qualified for teaching in a one-room country school. In a green and quiet place outside the city, I'd draw and paint, capturing light in color. Children would drink knowledge like water. I'd live frugally, save money, and then begin my great adventures.

I laid out this plan to my parents, Uncle Willy, and Tante Elise at our next Sunday dinner, noting that the city's finest normal school for teacher training was only a streetcar ride away. I could even get a scholarship. "It's *much* cheaper than studying medicine," I finished hopefully.

My mother set down our potato spoon. "Teaching in a *country* school," she repeated. I knew what she was thinking, that there was no "extraordinary" in this plan.

"Teaching is a respectable profession," Uncle Willy observed, spearing a potato.

"And honorable," I said, but so softly that nobody heard me over the tapping of my father's fork on the tablecloth like his hammer on tin.

"It might not be forever," Tante Elise added. "You could stop, like Cousin Ludwig. He taught school for a while and then—" She trailed off, having once again offered a poor example. Ludwig embezzled school funds to pay off gambling debts, left town, and drifted south to New Orleans, where he died penniless.

Uncle Willy buttered a roll thoughtfully. "It *is* the American way for young people to decide their own futures."

"That's true," my father agreed, rubbing out the fork marks my mother so disliked. "Well then, our Hazel will be the finest teacher in—western Pennsylvania. You *will* stay close for now, won't you?"

"Yes, for now."

"So," Uncle Willy said loudly, "it's settled." We toasted my future with schnapps and *prinzregententorte,* the chocolate cake that my father claimed could bring back the dead.

"Hazel is restless; it's in her blood," Tante Elise observed as my mother poured schnapps. A fork clattered on a plate. Her hand wavered; my father had to chase the stream of schnapps with his shot glass. "I mean," stammered Tante Elise, "that you both left Heidelberg even though your families wanted you to stay."

"Exactly," added Uncle Willy. "Crossing the ocean with a crazy *tinsmith.*" He clapped my father on the back. "Remember what Katarina's father said? 'That Johannes wouldn't keep a roof over her head and he'll break her heart besides.' Now there's a fine store, and twenty years later you still can't take your eyes off her." My mother blushed as my father squeezed her thickening waist. Once again he told how he'd first seen Katrina Brandt studying confections in a bakery window, comparing them to her own. Uncle Willy told how he met Tante Elise at a butcher shop and followed her home, carrying her meat. In years to come, I'd think often of that Sunday dinner when the shock of my revelation rolled into memories of the Old Country, the berry-picking parties and hikes, open-air concerts, and river walks in the long days of summer. That dinner was the last time America let us forget we were hyphenates.

SIX DAYS LATER, on June 27, 1914, peace blew out of our world like air from a pinpricked balloon. *Pittsburgh Post* extras blared the news: Archduke Franz Ferdinand of Austria, heir to the Austro-Hungarian throne, had been shot on a bridge in Sarajevo. I knew Sarajevo from geography class as a staid, minor city in a shrinking empire. Who could have predicted that shots fired on a bridge there would ricochet as far as East Ohio Street?

"What's one archduke more or less?" I heard the next morning on a streetcar. "Thank God it's not our problem."

But that night my father hunched over a map of Europe, making lists of countries that might stand for or against the Austro-Hungarians. "So many enemies," he said. "We're trapped in the middle."

"The middle of *what*?" I demanded. "They caught the assassin, didn't they? He'll have a trial. There'll be another archduke. It's simple."

My father ran his hand down my arm. "Hazel, Hazel, you're so American sometimes. *Nothing's* that simple in Europe. Watch. You'll see."

## CHAPTER 2
## *War Games*

Within days, I saw. Germany declared her support of Austria-Hungary against the Serbian rebels. Russia began mobilizing along her western front against possible Austro-Hungarian aggressions. "Ha!" my father snorted. "Russia wants Prussia. *They'll* be doing the aggression."

"Let them fight it out. It's what Europe does best," Luisa said. "*We* have the Atlantic Ocean." The *Post* praised America's happy freedom from entangling alliances. "It'll be over by Christmas," my teachers predicted. But each week brought more alliances, outraged diplomatic letters, and another ultimatum refused. Meanwhile local companies jockeyed for munitions contracts; steel mills hired new workers, and every company supplying the mills rejoiced. Our mayor predicted golden times for Pittsburgh, with good jobs for every able-bodied man. Luisa's father, a master mechanic, was jubilant: "This madness will make us rich!"

I watched in horror as Europe's war spread to the empty lot by our store. Herman, the tailor's lisping son, donned a cut-down military jacket and set a troop of neighborhood boys to digging trenches they fortified with wood scraps. At first the sides were Germany and Austria-

Hungary against an equal set of Russians and Serbs. In late afternoons, the belligerents shared nickel sodas and planned the next day's battle before reverting to familiar games of marbles and mumblety-peg. Peter played Russia, declaring "deathless" loyalty to Tsar Nicholas II. Artie claimed Austria-Hungary. But roles expanded with the war. Max was Serbia and sometimes France. Cheerful, limping Davy played England unless Herman needed him for Germany. Other boys were Ottomans, Italians, Poles, or Belgians, sure that these countries would soon join the fray. Lars, recently arrived from Sweden, predicted his country's neutrality, so he'd change sides as he pleased. Walking to summer classes, I watched with sickening fascination as boys replayed the archduke's death with screaming tumbles from a little red wagon followed by wild chases after the assassin.

"They're too serious about this," I reported to my teacher. "I'm afraid for them." This was overreacting, I was told. War play is a natural human sport. As the great psychologist G. Stanley Hall explained, children are born as savages, to be civilized by education and discipline. When I pointed out that these boys were imitating the brutality of "civilized adults," it was suggested that we move on to the day's lessons. But my mind kept flying back to the empty lot. What could we expect if boys played in the shadows of munitions plants?

In late August, Uncle Willy's nephew wrote from an army hospital: "I was a soldier for one week before I lost my leg. Will Clara want me now?"

Fighting in the Battle of Tannenberg, my father's youngest brother, Wilhelm, wrote: "Dear Johannes, You can't imagine what it's like in the trenches; they destroy all that's human in a man. We live like rats, burrowed in dirt. When we come over the top, out of the trenches, shells are whizzing like bees all around. Imagine your own men behind you, bayonets fixed, as you run between bomb craters toward great coils of barbed wire. Enemy guns fire from their trenches. Everywhere explosions and men shrieking. Our first wave cut the wire just before they were slaughtered. I was in the second wave. We almost reached the Russian line before they beat us back. I put a bayonet in a man's gut. I shot another in the face. Johannes, they looked like us, just in different uniforms. Retreating to our trenches, I ran past comrades screaming in pain. I couldn't help them. We lost forty-three men in fifteen minutes. All that night, I saw their faces; I heard their screams. The bombs and shells and rain never stopped. How can a man sleep? By dawn we were to our knees in mud and water. The officers said—" Here my father squeezed his eyes shut and then opened them to read aloud: "They made us lay the bodies of our dead at the bottom of the trenches and stand on them to fight. Dear brother, if I live, which I doubt, who will I be? Not the Wilhelm you know."

My mother gently pulled the letter from his hands, set it on the table, and led him to their bedroom. "Good night, Hazel," she said softly, closing the door behind her. A week later, "by the grace of God," my father said, Wilhelm lost an arm and was sent home to Heidelberg.

Germany won the Battle of Tannenberg, devastating the Russian Second Army, but the cost on both sides was staggering: nearly one hundred thousand casualties. In German shops along our street, men and women bent over the newspaper accounts, stunned. Meanwhile, boys played "Tannenberg" with sticks and popguns. "You're my prisoner!" one voice would cry, then "No, you're mine. *I'm* Russia now."

"Hazel," my father announced one evening, "when you're teaching mathematics, ask your students to figure how many blocks of East Ohio Street one hundred thousand bodies would fill."

My mother slammed down a plate of spaetzle. "She's *not* asking children such questions. And why must we keep talking about war at the table?"

"Because one talks at the table. That's what tables are *for*." Silence. My father noted the sag of her mouth, adjusted his fork, and took a deep breath. "You're right, my dear. Why ruin good spaetzle?" And he launched into a funny tale of how a Swede and a Hungarian who happened to be in the store together helped him puzzle out a Greek customer's plumbing problem. "He didn't speak a word of English, and not one of us knew each other's languages, but you should have heard the Swede imitating plumbing sounds while the Hungarian brought out tools and mimed how to use them. I said we'd make a great vaudeville troupe. We got to laughing our heads off, complete strangers." My father dug into his spaetzle. "Countries should be like that. *Everything* can be solved if you work together." No, I thought, kings and ministers should be like Johannes Renner, who treated any man's need for a washer, screw, or particular length of chain as a sacred trust. In his little world, peace reigned.

My mother beamed. "You see? Good things *are* happening."

For the next few weeks, as the war churned on, we followed my mother's new rule: "no war talk at the table." I brought home teaching ideas from classes; we talked about how children could and couldn't be educated, and we played word games in German and English. We even briefly discussed closing the store for two weeks and renting a cabin on Lake Erie. Here was the happy warmth I remembered from the time before Archduke Franz Ferdinand was shot.

Our peace didn't last. At one Sunday dinner, Tante Elise cited H. G. Wells, who had said that this would be the war to end all wars. "You'll see," she announced. "Serbia will be punished. Germany will get Alsace again, and the Russians will go back to their farms."

My father shook his head, slowly spooning beef chunks on egg noodles. "Have you seen what those bombs do to the land? How can it be farmed again? The war is spreading all over the world, like a great stain." Yes, that was true. Japan and South Africa had joined the Allies, as if one archduke dead in Sarajevo, thousands of miles away, threatened their peace.

"Any time now," my father predicted, "America will join. Then *we'll* be the enemy."

"President Wilson doesn't want war and if he's pushed to it, America will side with Germany. Count on it," Uncle Willy declared, banging the table so hard that our beer steins jumped. "There are so many of us. In Pittsburgh, New York, Cincinnati, and Milwaukee, what language do you hear on the street? German! Remember, Americans fought England in their own revolution."

"That was a long time ago," my father countered. "It was a family fight. Americans and English understand each other. They buy German bread and meat; we build their houses, run their shops and brew their beer, but they don't understand us. Hazel, who did you read in high school, Shakespeare or Friedrich Schiller?"

"Shakespeare."

"Dickens or Johann von Goethe?"

"Dickens."

"You see? They don't care about our culture."

"If America joins the Allies, will we be safe?" my mother asked nervously. I'd wondered this myself. Would my classmates turn against us? Would worse happen to my parents than a German newspaper pulled from their hands?

"Of course we'll be safe, Katarina," Tante Elise declared. "They need us; we're so useful. Look around. Like Willy said, there are Germans everywhere: in banks, businesses, shops, schools, hospitals, everywhere." This was true enough, but the history I'd teach was an endless march of wars with intervals of peace, like lulls between waves. In all these wars, useful people had been slaughtered.

"Listen to this," said Uncle Willy, unfolding a letter from his cousin Oskar: "We've made a great killing machine. This war crushes men as boys stamp out ants, never caring who they are or what they could be. Those not killed are lost to madness." Oskar was right. We would learn of a new kind of insanity called "shell shock" when Davy's uncle was sent home twitching like a mis-strung marionette. His mother wrote that he screamed and dove under tables at any innocent noise, a pot lid falling or a baby's cry.

Uncle Willy continued reading: "Rats the size of big cats eat bodies in No Man's Land between the trenches. Arms and legs hang on trees like fruit. They throw limbs in coffins, enough to make a whole man. Sometimes parts are left over, or the living are buried in rubble. We can't find them."

"Please, Willy, stop," said Tante Elise.

*Yes, stop. Stop! Stop!* The bread was a dry lump in my mouth. I saw rats. I saw bodies on trees. My father brought out his map. Already pins marking the shifting front lines had turned whole patches of Germany into paper lace. I excused myself to fetch paper and charcoals. "I'm taking classes at the Carnegie Institute," I explained. "Rendering shape with shadow."

"Oh," said my mother, "well then." She and Tante Elise took out their mending. I went to the window seat and sketched a splash of light from our hanging lamp on the anxious faces and soft slope of shoulders, Tante Elise's frown as she studied a seam, and the drape of our tablecloth. But when the fabric folds became trenches and the table was No Man's Land, I started drawing children at play in a schoolyard far from Pittsburgh.

How could children "play" in this city? We lived in the clanging heart of a killing machine. Under a constant gray sky, the air pulsed with pounding. Factories churned out cannons, armor plate, and thousands on thousands of shells. Westinghouse built a new munitions plant in twenty-nine days. We made howitzers and casings, locomotive parts for Russia, and grenades for Italy and France. "We're arming the Allies," owners said, but one heard of shipments quietly diverted to Germany or middlemen who played to the best offer, sometimes splitting a shipment.

Everyone profited from war, as if our faces were stamped on each howitzer. All able-bodied, willing men had work, and many women. Wages rose; union power grew. Business at our store was brisk. At home we ate more chicken, fruit, and chocolate. My mother bought me a fine wool skirt in coral and cream, a suit with a vaguely military jacket, and kidskin shoes more delicate than any she would have considered before. "It's the American fashion," she said, surely thinking: *Dressed so well for the city, why move to the country?*

But Pittsburgh was strangling me. Only wandering in Carnegie Institute, studying the lines and shadings of the masters, gave a little calm—until a battle scene reminded me that Mr. Carnegie's companies grew fatter with war contracts. I stopped going to picture shows, for each began with newsreels of Allied soldiers kissing mothers and sweethearts good-bye, battlefield heroics, or maps of Europe jigsaw-cut with new front lines. My school friends were German, English, Russian, Italian, Greek, and Polish. Each week brought word from "over there" of men dead, maimed, shell-shocked, taken prisoner, or missing, homes destroyed, and towns blasted away. Like my father, I began picturing East Ohio Street lined with corpses. Life before the war was a pretty fairy tale. Who could see peace through the gritty dust that burned our eyes?

THOSE WHO HAD predicted peace by Christmas were wrong. The killing had no end. Thousands on thousands died in battles that moved front lines a few yards or not at all. Who were *my* allies now, when Americans praised Britain's blockade of Germany? Winston Churchill, First Lord of the Admiralty, admitted blandly that the blockade's goal was to starve both soldiers and civilians, that one must not be squeamish in combating evil. "The hideous policy of indiscriminate brutality has placed the German race outside of the pale. The only way to restore peace in the world and shatter the brutal menace is to carry the war throughout the length and breadth of Germany."

Uncle Willy read these words in the *Post* and slammed the paper on our table, thundering: "Russians slaughtered their way across Prussia. The British crucified a German prisoner; Belgians gouged out eyes, strung up our men on trees, and set bodies on fire. Isn't *that* 'indiscriminate brutality'?"

"Willy, please," my mother said quietly, "the neighbors." Yes, we had begun to live like secret traitors, careful not to speak publicly about the war lest someone suspect us of "helping the Kaiser," to keep silent as our people starved and died.

After winter retreated to a bearable chill, neighborhood boys came out again to play. Now the games were laced with name-calling, spiked with vengeance for their families' losses. They came filled with talk of the Kaiser's blood-mad Huns, vicious English drinking tea after killing babies, merciless French and Italians, and barbarous Russians, worse than Cossacks. The boys' grim faces frightened me. With a plate of my mother's *butterplätzchen,* I lured them from trenches on a Saturday afternoon.

"Listen," I began as they munched cookies. "If you *must* play war, why not one from the history books?" One that's long over, I meant, with deaths they needn't revenge. "How about the American Revolution?"

"We don't have red coats," Artie complained.

"Do you really need them?"

"My ma has red ribbons," Peter offered.

"If she has brown ones, they can be for Americans," Davy said.

"Wonderful! And since they didn't use trenches back then, maybe you could—"

"Fill them in!" the boys announced, thrilled with the new enterprise.

The de-trenching and construction of costumes took days. For what was grandly termed the "inauguration," I was brought to see Davy play Patrick Henry, perched on a rock with a three-corner cardboard hat. "Gentlemen may cry peace, peace," he declaimed, "but there is no peace." The shrill voice rose: "I know not what course others may take, but as for me, give me liberty or give me death!" The boys cheered. The speech was such a success that others made it, then a King George responded. I suggested Paul Revere's Ride, the Boston Tea Party, Washington crossing the Delaware, Swamp Fox eluding the Redcoats, and Nathan Hale's heroic last words: "I only regret that I have but one life to give for my country." Squatting on a filled-in trench, the boys spent hours in loud but peaceful planning. I brought history books and helped them search out other stories: freezing camps at Valley Forge, Lafayette training the troops, Cornwallis surrendering at Yorktown. "They aren't angry anymore," I bragged in my pedagogy class. "They're just playing." I began believing my mother: I *would* be extraordinary in my field.

Then the American Revolution ended. Coming home one afternoon in late April, I found the boys filthy and exhausted between remade trenches. With difficulty, I coaxed them to the sidewalk for a game of marbles from the time we simply called "before." They played awhile to please me, but then Davy sat back on his heels and announced: "Hazel, the problem is, marbles just aren't *fun* anymore."

Why had I been so confident? Fortunately, dense storm clouds were rolling over the daily gray. "It's going to rain," I said. "You better get home. Your mothers don't like muddy shoes." With this much in common, they scampered away. For a week, rain kept the boys inside as their trenches filled with filthy water. I'd never been so grateful for rain, as if Nature worked to my purposes.

THAT MONTH, HELEN Keller came to town. My entire normal school class went to hear the toneless, mechanical voice interpreted by her great teacher and companion, Anne Sullivan. Miss Keller described her childhood, blind and deaf, and how she had been released from darkness by the light of learning. The audience cheered wildly but turned grimly silent when Miss Keller spoke of public matters: "War is the particular business of a few men." I leaned forward, now understanding her perfectly. "Some of the ablest press agents of the world are hired to promote preparedness. But peace is everybody's business, and no one attends to it."

"What the heck does Helen Keller know about anybody's business? She's blind and deaf, for God's sake," someone said in the lobby.

*I* would attend to peace. *I* would teach the merits of peace to country schoolchildren. *My* students would not play war games. Perhaps peace could even come to East Ohio Street. But as my father could have told me, these hopes were simple and sanguine. The rains ceased and warm days dried the empty lot. A few boys now worked as messengers in munitions plants, but Davy and Artie commandeered the others to find abandoned baby carriages they would transform into armored tanks.

May 17 brought new disaster. The RMS *Lusitania*, a British passenger ship with 128 Americans on board, was torpedoed by a German U-boat and sank. The German embassy was unrepentant: the *Lusitania* was carrying more than four thousand cases of ammunition destined for the Allies. Clear warnings had been placed in New York papers that she'd be a legitimate target.

Anxious clumps of German-Americans in shops and homes argued in whispers that the loss of life was regrettable but justified. Far more than 128 of *our* women and children had starved to death from the British blockade. But American newspapers exploded against the Huns, the barbarous killer of innocent civilians. In this web of fury and accusation, where was justice, reason, or sanity? I said nothing about the war in class and stopped reading newspapers on streetcars, afraid the very movements of my eyes would betray me.

"What will they do to us?" my mother fretted.

"Nothing," my father soothed. "We've lived here for years. People know us. That's the important thing." It's true that the boys of the *Volksblatt* incident had apologized. Their families owed money at our store. "I know you'll pay me when you can," my father always said. They'd remembered this. My mother's ministrations were equally known: blankets and warm bread for a family burned out of their home at night, money collected for a crippled steelworker, healing soups for the sick, and cakes donated for charity bake sales. Besides, my father argued, President Wilson knew very well that the *Lusitania* was armed. *He* didn't want war, and Congress knew all the advantages of neutrality.

But the boys weren't neutral. The next Sunday, after church services and masses, they poured back to the empty lot. I heard them fighting about the *Lusitania* and hurried over. "You killed civilians!" Davy was shrieking at Herman. "My father said so."

"She was a warship!" Herman screamed back. "Every passenger knew that."

"We'll get you for Tannenberg," Peter said. "My uncle was saving his friend, and you Krauts killed him."

The small, contorted faces were hardly recognizable. "Boys! Boys!" I pleaded. "You're not enemies." How does one instant become an eternity? How are the particulars of space and gesture recalled with such horrible clarity? Even today, I can draw Davy, Peter, Artie, Herman, Max, Lars, and all the others in their places. I see Davy pick up a rock. His knuckles clench. I hear my scream as the rock leaves his hand. It turns in the air. I'm running, holding up my own hand as if to pluck it down before it drives into Herman's eye. Red erupts.

I send Artie, the fastest runner, to Dr. Edson's office. The other boys stand stricken. I'm holding Herman, my hand over the streaming eye, repeating: "The doctor's coming, the doctor's coming." I want to scream to all of Pittsburgh: *Stop the factories! Stop the newspapers! Take us back to "before"!*

Dr. Edson arrives, gasping: "I called an ambulance." He covers the eye with gauze.

"Will he live?" Davy whispers. Dr. Edson nods. "And his eye?" No answer.

Herman lost the eye. It was a miracle, everyone said, that the damage wasn't worse. Davy ceased eating, so stricken and comfortless that his family moved to a different neighborhood, more "American," and not so "mixed."

My father, Uncle Willy, and Mr. Schmidt filled in the trenches while Mr. Hess and I rigged a fence around the lot. Older boys stopped to watch. "This wouldn't have happened to the kid if Germany hadn't started the war."

"It wasn't Germany," Uncle Willy said quietly. "A Serb shot the arch-duke."

"Serbs, Krauts, same thing."

## CHAPTER 3
### *Shell Shock*

In the days after Herman lost his eye, I feared I was losing myself. To have held a child and been so helpless was an agony. Suppose I'd left our flat earlier or run faster? Suppose I'd found better ways to move the boys back to marbles and stickball? Suppose I wasn't meant to be a teacher? "Suppose the war hadn't started?" my friend Luisa countered. "Hazel, you can't control everything. The good thing is, nobody's using the lot anymore, and the boys *are* playing stickball now. They could get hurt at stickball. Would *that* be your fault?"

No, I admitted, I couldn't avert every tragedy, but I was realizing that doing the business of peace, even among children, was far more difficult than I'd imagined. Here in a city where so many nationalities chafed together, where so many families' food was paid by munitions contracts, and the air itself was thick with the throb of war work, what teacher could work the miracle I intended?

But surely far from Pittsburgh, under placid blue skies, Europe's troubles would feel far away. "Let's *all* move," I urged my parents. "There must be many towns that need hardware stores." Blank stares answered me. This was home, the trench they'd defend. I loved them, but more and more I was becoming a foreigner on East Ohio Street. My dreams perplexed them, and the habits that brought them comfort made me restless.

The rains returned, thick streaming walls of gray, until the sidewalks ran with mud and ash, a filthy mix my mother would not allow in the house or even on the steps to our flat. It was Friday. I'd just heard that the small town of Galway, two hours south of Pittsburgh, might need a teacher for their one-room school. I took off my wet shoes at the base of the stairway and started up in stocking feet, thinking of Galway.

Walking softly, I heard my mother and Tante Elise speaking of me. "I'm worried about her," my mother was saying. "She thinks every-thing will be different somewhere else. My sister Margit was the same at her age. She couldn't stand Heidelberg."

"But Hazel doesn't even remember your sister. She thinks you and Johannes are—"

"Yes," my mother said sharply. "But suppose this restlessness is in the blood? Margit was *sure* she'd be happy in New Jersey, but she wasn't. Then, no, having a baby, *that* would make her happy, and then no, living in New York City without her baby, but she wasn't happy there, either."

"It doesn't matter what Margit did or what was in her blood. You and Johannes raised Hazel."

I gripped the banister. *Raised Hazel.* Not birthed me? Rain pounded outside, washing away my world. The step beneath my feet sagged. Margit Brandt, that flitting name in family stories, the shadowy figure who died young in New York, *that* woman was my mother? Were the men in scarlet jackets true but the man in a faded work apron, his face as familiar as my own, *that* man was not my father? The voice behind the door was not my mother's? Was I myself not Hazel, then, but some-one else?

"Margit never fit in Heidelberg and Hazel doesn't seem to fit in Pittsburgh either. She's always drawing, always dreaming," my mother was saying. "She— What's that sound?" Had she heard my thumping heart?

"Nothing. But, Katarina, this is your very best *kirschenplotzer*. Could I have more?" As talk turned to cherry cake, I made my way downstairs, put on my shoes, and walked on wooden legs to our store, shell-shocked. After the loss of a certainty I'd never thought to doubt: that I was Hazel Renner, born in Heidelberg to Johannes and Katarina. So I'd been lied to, lovingly, but lied to. The ground shook beneath me, as if battered by bombs. And in the future, what else that I fervently, fondly thought was true, told by those who claimed to love me, might be revealed as false?

In the store, a tall man known to all as Johannes Renner, was listening intently to Mr. Goldstein speaking Yiddish and answering him in German as they puzzled out malfunctions in a stove. When Mr. Goldstein left, I opened my mouth, closed it, and finally tried again: "I was on the stairs. Mother and Tante Elise were talking about Margit's baby." The store clock boomed. A mouse scrabbled behind a wall. "She didn't keep the baby, did she? Was it me?"

He—this man, my uncle, my father—walked slowly to the door and turned the "Open" sign to "Closed." Then he put his arm lightly on my shoulder and led me to his desk. "Yes, Hazel, you were that baby."

"So I wasn't born in Heidelberg? It was in New Jersey, to Margit Brandt. Why didn't she keep me? And why didn't you tell me, all this time?"

His hand hovered over a hinge, touched it, turned it, and moved it back. When he finally looked up, the slightest shift of face and voice announced that we would now speak as adults. "Sit down, Hazel." He pointed to the stool that once was my high perch. "I knew you'd find out someday. But we hoped it would be later, when you're settled. So it's now."

"Yes. It's now."

He took a breath. "Katarina's sister Margit came to America first. She was younger than Katarina, and her parents wanted her to wait so we could all go together, but she insisted. She was unhappy in Heidelberg and there was someone in New Jersey who'd sponsor her, a woman named Anna. She said New Jersey was the place for her, in a town called Dogwood."

"But my mo— Margit wasn't happy there, either."

"No. That's what worried Katrina, that she couldn't be happy."

"And my father?"

"I never saw him. I understood that he was German. They worked together in Dogwood, but he left before you were born."

"And Margit wasn't happy with me."

"I don't know why. She met us in New York when we arrived. She brought you with her and we went to a restaurant. Everything you did annoyed her. And you were so dear. Anyone would have wanted you, but Margit was sure she'd be happier in a big city."

"Without me?"

He pushed the hinge away. "Yes. In fact, she'd already moved to New York and left you behind in Dogwood. When she knew we were coming, she went back to get you and a little bundle of clothes. She'd even had someone make a false birth certificate naming us as your parents. When I said we'd be your family, you—" His voice caught. "You said 'good.' So we took you on the train with us to Pittsburgh. We changed your name to Hazel, and you seemed to like that. You never spoke of Margit again. You were so little that we thought, we hoped, you'd forget her. We loved you. It all seemed so simple."

"What about Margit after she gave me away?"

"A few months later, we got a telegram that Margit had died."

"How?"

"We don't know. We wrote, but we never got an answer."

There wasn't much sorrow in me for her death. As mother or aunt, Margit Brandt had been less real than the men in scarlet jackets. The new grief was that she'd borne me, known me, and chose New York over me. The "who" I used to be—the natural daughter of Johannes and Katarina Renner—didn't exist. The "who" I truly was had been created in a New York restaurant by a forged certificate. "You never told me."

This man moving a hinge back and forth was my uncle. Is that what I should call him? He brushed back sandy hair, now tinged with silver. "Katarina made me promise I wouldn't. Hazel, a man's vows to his wife can't be broken. You didn't seem to remember Margit or mourn her. We never wanted you to feel abandoned. Perhaps we made a terrible mistake. It's been a weight on me. Often I lie in bed wondering if we'd hurt you. We never wanted to do that. I'm actually glad you know the truth now. Were we wrong? Can you forgive us?"

The blue eyes turned to mine, a warmer blue than any sky or sea. I've loved that blue all my life. Johannes and Katarina Renner had lied; this much was true. Yet it was equally true that they chose me and loved me from the first. And I loved them. These three truths clashed like cymbals. With the fixity of purpose that defined their lives, they'd kept faith with their secret until today's rain washed it out. Margit Brandt had abandoned me, but here was my father; upstairs was my mother. We would not un-choose each other now, and I could not un-choose my life as Hazel Renner.

My mind jolted to another, more tangible question: "So the grand rooms I remember might be real?"

He shrugged. "We knew Margit worked for a wealthy man, but she never spoke of him, and you were describing a *palace*. How could that be in New Jersey? You might have been dreaming. We couldn't pretend we'd lived such a life in Germany."

"You never saw Dogwood?"

"No, we came straight here. Someone there might remember her. You could write, I suppose, and try to find out more."

"No, not yet." I didn't need particulars of how I was objectionable or extraneous, carelessly housed until Margit found a respectable alternative. Men in scarlet jackets didn't matter now. I had to look to my own future: where Hazel-Hilda would begin the next stage of her life.

My father, *yes, my father,* opened the jar where he kept caramels, inviting little children to choose "the best and juiciest" for themselves. "Now Hazel," he said, "shall we choose a caramel?"

"I'm too old for that."

"Are you?" he asked mildly, searching for the biggest, the juiciest caramel and slipping it in my mouth. "Come." He folded me in his arms. Years ago, in a nameless New York restaurant, an uncle became a father; an aunt became a mother. This was a mystery, dark as the melting caramel. "The rain stopped. You take a walk, Hazel. I have to speak with Katarina."

I walked for blocks, thinking of New York, of a place called Dogwood, where I wasn't wanted, and of Galway, where I might be needed. When I came home, anxious eyes studied me. "You heard."

"Yes, Mother."

She looked into a bowl of potatoes, squeezing her eyes shut for a minute. "Can you help me with these, Hazel?"

"Yes, Mother." We peeled a mountain of potatoes. When we finished, we hugged each other, our hands sticky with starch. Yes, here was my home, my family, but Katarina Renner's nagging fear was mine

as well. Peace might elude me as it had eluded Margit Brandt, always
somewhere *over there*. Like her, I'd have to search it out.

I WROTE TO Galway for particulars of the post. The matter of Margit
had only increased my restlessness on East Ohio Street. Every head-
line, every casualty report in the *Volksblatt* and editorial in the *Post*
blasting the Central Powers' aggression made me want to leave. In a
small town, I'd be plain Hazel Renner, the schoolteacher, not a hyphenated American or a wanderer's illegitimate offspring. Galway's
people might not have families in Europe writing about the atrocities
of war. Children wouldn't hear these horrors at the dining room table,
or reenact them in schoolyards. Boys would farm with their fathers.
They wouldn't be stoning each other.

Two weeks later, I received an offer of a teaching post at sixty dollars a month, including "a small furnished house with a tight roof and
abundant wood for winter." This was exceptional. Most small towns
boarded out teachers to the lowest bidder. Some were shunted to un-
heated rooms barely larger than closets. I'd have space for my art and
even paid work in the summer. A local judge needed tutoring for his
invalid daughter.

"When would you leave?" my mother asked the carrots she was
chopping.

"In early July, for the tutoring."

"I see. Well then."

I'd mentioned Galway before, but now my mother's knife missed
the carrots. "Suppose your father chokes again?"

"That only happened once," he said. "I've had my bad-luck rye bread.
It sounds like a good post. And it's not far, is it, Hazel?"

"Just two hours by train."

"Two hours," my mother repeated. And then, "Coffee?" So we wouldn't speak of Galway that evening, or the next day or the next, until Uncle Willy and Tante Elise came on Sunday and my plans were formally announced.

"Well," said Uncle Willy, "we all left home when we were about Hazel's age. Now it's Hazel's turn. Isn't that right, Katarina?" No answer.

"Another letter, Willy?" my father asked in the silence, pointing to the white edge of an envelope. Yes, another letter from the front. *Don't read it,* I wanted to scream, but he did. The poison waves of war talk rolled over us again. Later that evening, my father beat out a new tin: an imagined face of Uncle Willy's childhood friend, now buried alive in No Man's Land when a bomb fell beside him.

"We have to distract him, Hazel," my mother said. We did, gathering commissions from friends and neighbors for tins of peaceful scenes and portraits. Within a week we had generated enough work to last the summer. To our delight, my father seemed almost relieved. He bought new tins and in the long June evenings we sketched scenes together while my mother did her baking. She and I were so hopeful.

On an early July morning, my parents took me to Union Station. "I'll write you this afternoon from my new house," I promised.

"We'll visit as soon as you're settled," they said.

"I'll be back for Christmas. Perhaps we'll have peace then."

"Peace at Christmastime," my father said wistfully. "That would be a miracle." He handed me a neat package. "For your new house." The keen edge of tins poked through paper wrappings. "Scenes from Germany before the war. But tell people it's America. That's safer." We hugged in public, as we'd never done before, and stood close together until the train came roaring in.

On board, I watched the city's stain melt into green. In Europe, millions of men were blasting their old world away. Perhaps the shock of bullets fired in Sarajevo would even reach Galway. I'd have to work hard to shore up the blessings of peace there, to keep the boys from **digging** trenches. I opened my copy of John Dewey's *The School and Social Progress*, intending to read until my whistle-stop at Galway Station.

But the train was slow and the carriage hot, melting away my confidence. *What was I doing? Was I even remotely ready for a one-room schoolhouse?* In Saturday school, I'd had an easy group of eight-year-olds. In the aisle across from me sat two gangly boys, a head taller than I was, debating the prospects for the World Series. Why would they listen to me? What could I tell them about baseball? I'd never even seen a game. A little girl quarreling with her mother ripped a picture book and had to be chased down the aisle. Could I make her sit still for hours on a wooden bench? A boy stared glumly out the window. Could I capture him with the parts of speech? And how could I possibly fashion lessons that would engage all four at once? "The first months will be difficult," our teachers had warned. I'd ignored them. Had I even pictured myself alone in a schoolhouse, facing ranks of children, waiting for me to fascinate them?

Sweat coursed under my new shirtwaist. What was my mother thinking with her signs that I'd be extraordinary, that I'd rise above? Did Margit have this same shaking fear when her ship approached New York? Did she want to cry out to the captain: "Stop. Go back. I'm not ready. I made a huge mistake!" But we had reached Galway Station. A squeal of brakes and piercing whistle scorched the air. I gathered my bags and hurried off the train.

## CHAPTER 4

## *Why Not Blue?*

Henry McFee cut me easily from the other passengers because, he said, I "looked like a stranger." He was a tall, rangy man in his forties with stooped shoulders and a wheezing cough. "I manage the school, fire, and water departments," he announced. "I hope you like small towns."

"I do." If men didn't pore over newspapers studying casualty counts, I liked small towns. "Thank you for meeting the train, Mr. McFee."

"Call me Henry. Well, you probably want to see your house. Isn't fancy, like maybe you had in *Pittsburgh*, but it's yours." He helped me into a dusty Model T.

"I'm sure it's lovely."

He coughed. "Like I said, it's yours." We turned on a dirt road through fields and orchards. He grimaced as we jounced. "Bum shoulder. These ruts make it worse. And today's worse than usual." A sharp look declared that he'd come out on this bad day for me. We bounced along until I thought to end the silence by asking what farmers grew in Galway. "Apples, corn, hay, milk, butter, cheese, and eggs for Pittsburgh. Folks have to haul their produce to Galway Station, that's outside of town," he added bitterly. "We were bamboozled by a city slicker who took us for hicks." He glanced at me, another city slicker. "Can you make sure our kids don't grow up bamboozled?" We lurched in a rut so deep that I struck my head on the roof. "Damn," he muttered, rubbing his shoulder.

"I'll do my best, Henry."

"We hope so. Well, here's Galway." White frame houses hugged Main Street. Marigolds and roses grew in small front yards. White curtains fluttered, never grayed by coal dust. Yes, here was where I wanted to be. Women gathered outside Burnett's Grocery shouted: "Is that the new schoolmarm, Henry?"

"Sure is," he shouted back. "Miss Hazel Renner. I'm taking her home."

"Hope she stays," a voice trailed after us.

"You have a sweetheart?" Henry asked suddenly.

"No."

"Good. Mildred Clay up and got married, so we had to let her go. Can't have married schoolmarms. You know that, don't you, Hazel?"

"Yes. I do."

"Folks said I should have seen it coming since he was from around here. They'd been stepping out on the sly. This time we thought we'd try a city teacher. She might concentrate more on the job. But maybe you'll say the country's too quiet."

"Quiet is good," I said quickly. But where was the country warmth I'd read about in books? Between ruts, Henry studied me like a specimen: city teacher. Still, I was determined to love Galway. On dusty streets, boys chased cart hoops. Others played marbles. Circles of little girls under shade trees were busy with jacks and dolls. I nearly laughed out loud. This could be 1913, an age ago, before the trouble started. Did people even follow the war news here? "You've heard about the *Lusitania*?" I hazarded.

"Sure did. Alfred Vanderbilt went down. One less millionaire in the world, I say. As for the rest of them in Europe, let 'em blow their heads off. It's not our problem. We're Americans from way back, before the first war." Henry clarified, as if to a backward schoolchild: "With England, the revolution."

"Ah."

"It's good, rich land. Here, feel it." Stopping the car with a jolt, he jumped down, coughing, scooped up a handful of dirt and pressed it in my hand. "Finest soil this side of the Mississippi." I held the clod until we swerved around a wagonload of chicken crates and I could toss it out a window. Henry coughed into a bandanna pulled from his pocket. "Arthritis and this blasted cough. Young folks like you don't know what I'm talking about. You can't appreciate good health." Unsure how to respond, I said nothing.

"Well, Hazel, you know the rules, don't you? You'll need to come an hour early to start the stove if it's cold out, bring in a pail of water and one of coal, sweep twice a day, wash down the blackboard, and keep the schoolyard clean. There's Christmas and spring pageants to put on; folks appreciate a good show. County tests twice a year. We need better scores than Mildred got. You should have twenty-six students, but not all of them come. Or they come and don't stay."

"I'll try to convince them all to stay."

"Hum. Well—lots of schoolmarms try. Here's your house." He rattled to a stop by a small frame house of unpainted boards in a weedy patch of green. A jolt ran through me at the sight of the porch. It was exactly as I'd imagined: a perfect place to sit and draw. The steps were swept and the windows freshly washed, yet the house had an air of loneliness, as if it had stood empty for years. In fact, it had. "Might as well tell you the truth about this place, Hazel, so you can leave now if you want to."

I met Henry's challenging eye. "Tell me."

"All right then. The young couple that built this place five years ago, Oliver and Ethel Harding, disappeared on their wedding night. Everyone suspected John Foster, who was sweet on Ethel, especially when he left town the next day. We found their bodies over there." He pointed to a thicket. "After that, people said the house was spooked and maybe John was coming back. Nobody wanted to live here. So we figured we'd offer it along with the salary because somebody from outside wouldn't be as scary as Galway folks."

"Scary?"

"Get scared for no reason," he translated. I wasn't "scary" at that moment. John's quarrel was with Oliver and Ethel, not with me, and certainly not with the house.

"Can we go inside?"

"Sure." He stopped on the porch to cough. "You know, John was a good boy before, preacher's kid. Never a lick of trouble. His family moved away after what happened, and of course John never came back. A shame, the whole thing. He always wanted to be a doctor. He had the touch." Henry opened the door. "My wife and some of the ladies cleaned up for you. They thought if they didn't, you'd be on the next train to Pittsburgh, scary or not."

Sunlight poured through sparkling windows. I had an inside bathroom, two electric lights, iron bed, oak table, four straight chairs and a rocking chair, storage trunk, reading lamp, clock, fresh linens, two towels, a neat row of clothes hooks, and a simple kitchen with a woodstove, water pump and sink, dishes, pots, pans, an old-fashioned pie safe, and a washbasin.

"No icebox, but the root cellar keeps things pretty cool. Jim Burnett, the grocer, sent over some provisions." The kitchen table held a basket of onions, beans and early potatoes, a bag of flour, slab of bacon, loaf of bread, and small block of cheese.

"Please tell everyone that I'm very grateful."

"Well, just trying to be hospitable. Let's get your things."

Outside, Henry's eyes followed mine to the bare sideboards of the house. "Never did get it painted after what happened, with nobody living here and all."

"It could be painted now," I said. "Something bright, like blue."

"*Blue?* Folks here have white houses. They're blue in Pittsburgh?"

"No, I just like blue."

"Hum, well. We'll see." The women's few hours of work had cost him nothing. Painting houses was different. We stood uncomfortably by his car. I asked to see the school, *the white school,* I nearly added.

"Sure." At a movement in the woods, he barked: "You leave the schoolteacher alone, Ben!" I turned to catch a pale, lined face peering at us from a thicket. Then the whole of the man appeared: thin, of indeterminate age with rheumy eyes, scratching himself mercilessly.

"Stop scratching!" The man stopped, clenching his fists. "That's Ben Robinson. He's harmless," Henry explained, as if the man were deaf. "He claims he was with Roosevelt's Rough Riders in '98 for the Spanish-American War. He showed up in town a few years ago, half crazy and scratching, like you see. Folks give him odd jobs, but sometimes he just disappears for days. Don't you, Ben?"

Ben was edging closer, as if fascinated by his own story. "Yes, ma'am, I saw things in Cuba. I hear voices and then I go to the woods. I don't hurt nobody."

"Uh-huh. Well, you don't bother her. Maybe she'll have some work for you, maybe she won't, but one word of trouble and you'll be out of town with this boot in your backside. Understand?"

"Yes," he said softly.

"Yes what?"

"Yes, Mr. McFee."

"Good. So get along now." Ben limped back into the woods, scratching.

"Where does he live?"

"He's got a little shack behind Burnett's Grocery, and there's talk that he built a camp over Red Gorge," Henry said with distaste. "Nobody's seen it. But never mind Ben. Come on. I'll show you the schoolhouse. It's down the road." It was indeed white, with a well, outhouse, and bare patch of playground. Half the windows were broken. Inside, rows of battered desks faced a torn world map and cracked blackboard. "Slate," said Henry proudly, "not just wood painted black like in some schools."

"The windows will be fixed?"

"Soon as we get the glass." He pointed to a stack of aging McGuffey Readers. "You asked for those new readers, but we've got these. Might as well keep them." Useless to lecture that modern pedagogy rejected the rote memorization of the McGuffey series. Henry might counter that pedagogy was a city concern. "Well, you'll want to be settling in. Judge Ashton expects you tomorrow morning for tutoring Susanna. You'll like her, everybody does," he said with sudden warmth. "She was sick all spring. Weak heart, folks say. You can't miss the house. It's the big white one about a mile down the road. Two big oak trees and a circle drive. You can walk home from here?" I nodded and he climbed into his Model T. "Then good afternoon, Hazel, and welcome to Galway."

*Was* I welcome, a city slicker with an unaccountable preference for blue? I'd have to earn my welcome and prove that I'd fit in. "Confidence and pride," my teachers had advised. "Demand them of yourself as well as your students." I would. I'd start now. By calling up confidence and pride, perhaps I could beat back a nagging fear that, like Margit, I'd merely found another place I'd soon want to leave.

I reached the house that would be mine, small and gray as it was. But I looked at its charms: good light, a porch, space to hang my drawings, all the furnishings I'd need, even a vase to hold wildflowers blooming outside my door. My house. My kitchen. I made toasted cheese and bread: my first meal in Galway. Delicious. I unpacked clothes and hung up my father's new tins. One showed the Old Bridge of Heidelberg over the River Neckar. In the other, fairy spires of a distant castle peeked over pine trees. Hung by my bed, they caught the silver sheen of afternoon light. I wrote a quick and happy account of the day and walked into town to post my first letter home.

All along Main Street, people already knew who I was; many greeted me by name. Yet at every step I was studied, as if my dress, the twists of my hair, and my very way of walking were notable and strange. Where was the welcome? *It will come. I'll be their finest teacher, and they'll appreciate me for their children's sake.* Meanwhile, there was no factory stench in the bright, clear air. Those whose families came here before the American Revolution would have no cousins, brothers, or nephews dead, shell-shocked, or sent home with limbs hacked off, and thus no reason to hate their neighbors. They might not even know that I was a hyphenate.

In the grocery store, I thanked Mr. Burnett for his provisions and bought green beans, carrots, coffee, soap, butter, and eggs. "Call me Jim, and my wife's Ellen. We hope you're happy here." I nearly leaned across the counter to hug him. A black-haired girl about nine years old watched me from a doorway, clutching a book. When I waved, she ducked away.

"That's our Alice. She'll be in your school," he said loudly.

"Wonderful. I see she's a reader."

"She is." He glanced over his shoulder and motioned me closer.

"Alice has epilepsy. When she has fits at school, boys torment her. Miss Clay, the last schoolmarm, switched them."

"I don't believe in switching children, but I won't allow tormenting."

"Well, I hope you can stop them some other way." Could I? The wave of confidence I'd ridden an hour ago collapsed in doubt. Could I even promise *one* child that she'd be safe? The store filled and I slipped out. Everything in Galway looked different now. The falling sun sent shadow bars across the road. Back at my house, knotholes in the bare siding looked out like baleful eyes. I'd never slept alone before. There was always my parents' good-night kiss and their murmured voices before sleep. Tonight even the pound of distant factories would be comforting.

I contrived to be busy. With the last light, I fashioned bookshelves from planks and bricks piled outside my house. I made soup, heated water for a bath, and planned the next day's lessons for Susanna, starting at each hooting owl and breaking branch. Could a scuffle near my house be John Foster coming back or Ben, the scratching, twitching man? Finally I curled in bed. Moonlight glazed my father's tins. I'd never imagined what courage the night could need. Was Margit afraid her first night in Dogwood? She'd been my age, exactly. Did she watch through a window as stars caught and freed themselves in leafy branches? Did she wait for daylight, wondering if she'd made a mistake in coming to this new place?

THE NEXT MORNING was crisp and bright. "Confidence and pride," I repeated aloud until my spirits lifted. Tutoring one child would be simple and build my confidence for the schoolroom. Buoyed by the pleasure of learning, the sickly Susanna might gain strength like the invalid Clara in *Heidi*. Why not, on warm days in such beautiful country? Lilies and daisies lined the mile to Judge Ashton's stately, columned white home.

Mrs. Ashton hurried down the broad porch steps and earnestly pressed my hand between her thin ones as if I'd brought a magical healing salve. "Hazel, we're so glad you're here. But poor Susanna was excited about your coming and slept badly last night. So we'll have a short day. She's only nine, remember."

"Well, let's see how she does."

"We can't have her overtired. On nicer days, when she's stronger, you can meet in the gazebo." What day could be "nicer" than this one? "She's in the parlor. Come." I was shown to a room heavy with giant ferns in waist-high vases, tasseled velvet curtains, Tiffany lamps, antimacassars on padded wing chairs, and a globe in an ornate frame. In the exact center, a slender child bundled in a cashmere shawl on a velvet divan regarded me with avid eyes. Here was someone new and different in her world. When a breeze ruffled her damp curls, she opened her mouth, tasting the air. A white hand emerged from the cashmere. "Thank you for coming, Miss Renner. I got behind in school."

"We'll catch up, Susanna. Don't worry."

Mrs. Ashton hurried to close the window. As I set books, paper, pen, a small slate, and chalk on the lacquered table, she brought in tea, crackers, cups, sugar, cream, and water glasses in separate bustling trips until I interrupted: "Thank you, ma'am, we'll be fine now." She retreated but left the parlor door open, passing often to listen.

Instructions from Judge Ashton had specified beginning each session with the poetry of Tennyson. "It's boring," Susanna complained. "Even arithmetic is better." So I had her find percentages of vowels, articles, and adjectives in each stanza and mentally figure the life spans of Victorian poets from their birth and death dates. As we moved into Bible study, and then history, Mrs. Ashton revealed a preternatural ability to appear whenever Susanna yawned, sweeping in to fluff pillows, adjust the shawl, or anxiously suggest "a little rest."

"We're doing well, ma'am," I assured her each time. The warm, stuffy room would make anyone yawn. I had to get the child moving. The polished brass armature of the globe suggested a geography game. The parlor would represent Europe. The divan was France. Moving around the room, Susanna would "visit" the British Isles, Prussia, Sicily, Hungary or Greece and tell me what she knew of each country, which was an astonishing amount. "I like to read about other places," she confessed.

"Careful!" Mrs. Ashton warned as Susanna traveled down "the Danube," a strip of oak flooring, reciting the cities she'd pass. Weakened by hours of forced idleness, she did bump a glass-topped end table. Afraid our lesson would be ended, I bundled her back on the divan for penmanship practice before Judge Ashton returned. He paid me the agreed $1.20 for three hours of tutoring.

"Susanna looks flushed," he said. "She mustn't be overtired. Come at ten tomorrow, Miss Renner. We'll just do two hours a day for a while." I had to agree, even if Susanna needed more time for review, and I needed the full three hours' pay until my regular school salary began.

As I walked home in the warm pour of sunshine, a soft crackle of dry leaves trailed me in the woods. A raccoon, a badger, or a deer? I'd seen none of them outside of zoos or picture books. A wolf? A bear? Should I freeze or run? A human shape appeared in the shadows. "Ben?" I hazarded nervously. It was Ben Robinson, bare arms scratched to bleeding, with a package wrapped in leaves. Coming closer as I stepped back, he smelled of moss, ferns, and sweat. "It's for you, ma'am." Folding back the green, I found wild strawberries: tiny, tart, and delicious. He wouldn't take any but asked as I ate: "You were teaching Miss Susanna?"

"Yes. How do you know?"

He shook his head and scratched. "She's been sick. Can you make her better?"

"I don't think so, but I'm helping with her schoolwork."

"Well, the berries grow back there." He pointed into the woods. "In a meadow by the pines. You can find them." Before I could thank him, he melted away, so quickly and cleanly that if not for the leafy package, I might have conjured him. I took a pot to the meadow, gathered berries, and made a passable jam. Then I planned the next day's lessons. My own teachers had never addressed the problem of a mother's hovering care. This would be my challenge, the first of many. Perhaps in facing them, I could achieve what Margit couldn't: a useful, even happy life in a new land.

On Saturday, I walked into town. Families from the country would be there. I'd introduce myself to parents and ensure they'd keep their children in my school. Men in overalls and women in faded print dresses listened politely, looking over my shoulder, or at the ground, or across the street as I spoke. "Yes, miss," they said. "We'll send them."

In two hot hours on Main Street, I told Jim Burnett proudly, I'd accounted for thirteen children. With those from town, every bench would be filled. "Well, let's hope they stay that way, Hazel," he said.

As WE MOVED through the summer, my hours with Susanna grew longer. We could sometimes take our lessons in the gazebo, a delicious nest of honeysuckle and roses. By folding Bible study into history; poetry into spelling, penmanship, and mathematics; and alternating natural science with recitations, I postponed the yawns that drew Mrs. Ashton scurrying from the house with her terrible word *overtired*.

"I'm fine, Mother," might wrest us more time, in which Susanna unfailingly requested geography. "Do you think I'll ever see the world?" she always asked. I always answered, "Of course." Then she'd look away, as if searching for herself on the Amazon, in Bombay, or even Arizona.

Often, coming home from tutoring, I found gifts on my porch steps: wild onions, dandelion greens, daylily roots, or edible mushrooms. When I bent to get them, Ben would come melting out of the woods. To be thanked set him to scratching, but he readily explained where he'd found these offerings and how to prepare them.

"Now you let me know if Crazy Ben is bothersome. I can make him stay away," Henry regularly offered.

"He's no bother, and he knows so much about the woods."

"I'm not surprised. Some say he's half Indian. The crazy half." Ignoring this, I asked again when my house might be painted. "You're still wanting *blue*?"

"Yes, I'd like that."

"Well, we'll see." So I'd get no paint. City folks want strange things, he might be thinking. And they don't mind a crazy man.

It was true that I'd ceased being troubled by Ben's matted hair, ravaged skin, sometimes-vacant eyes when his voices called, his twitches, and sudden comings and disappearances. The common term *friendship* fit our bond as poorly as cast-off clothes fit his spindly limbs. He listened with quiet patience when I spoke of my plans and fears for teaching, the cities I hoped to see, and my mother's anxious letters: "All he talks about now are casualties and every night he's working on those tins."

"I don't know much about this war," Ben said, "but I saw the other one."

"In Cuba, with the Rough Riders?"

"Yes, that one." He spoke often of Cuba, or rather, shared wisps of memories: the bright birds, shimmering heat over tobacco fields, fine ladies' promenades by the sea, and hills where "bad things happened." Of these "things" he'd offer only: "You can't get blood off your skin. It's always there forever."

"Is that why you scratch?"

He didn't answer, only noting that he knew where to find more blackberries. Then he was silent. I asked if I could sketch him and he nodded. No model was more patient, or more difficult. I had to wait out his jerks, twitches, and scratching, but he'd pose for hours. I drew him as he was now and as he might have been before Cuba, with smooth skin in a crisp uniform. I drew Susanna for him, and the Burnett family, who were good to him. For myself, I drew children bent over their slates in the schoolhouse. Ben never came inside my house and took no pay for the wild foods he brought or the firewood he chopped. He did accept coffee and some meals on the porch and sometimes let me patch his clothes. Only one fact was troubling: his constant questions about Susanna and our lessons.

"Ben, do you ever watch us from the woods?"

"The judge said: 'Stay away from my house.'"

"Do you?"

"They keep her inside too much. That makes her sick. Outside, the bad things go away. Look, Miss Hazel, the night's first firefly." So we looked, as tiny lights filled the ragged lawn. I put down my pencil and let the outside fill me.

With each week, I was growing more at ease in Galway. I'd begun attending church. Parents smiled and nodded as we gathered for coffee after services. Some children shyly asked if I was strict, if I switched "the bad ones," how long they'd have for recess, what we'd do for the Christmas program, and if I could teach them how to draw, for word had spread that I could do this.

Several mothers politely said they'd heard from Mrs. Ashton that Susanna enjoyed her lessons. Judge Ashton, always formal in a wool jacket and waistcoat despite the heat, pulled me aside to admit that he'd tested Susanna and found her progressing well.

"Thank you, Judge."

He cleared his throat. "However, please do not expose our daughter to diseases."

"Sir?"

"I'm talking about Crazy Ben. I've heard he—visits at your house." Had Henry told him this?

I bristled. "Ben Robinson has a mental condition. It's in no way contagious." The bushy eyebrows pulled together.

"He scratches like a dog with fleas."

"It's a mental condition," I repeated, managing a wide smile as Mrs. Ashton came to remind me of the ice cream social that afternoon.

"Susanna is still too delicate for school," she said, "but we do hope to send her soon, don't we, Edgar?" The judge nodded, gave me a chill handshake, and moved away.

That evening I wrote home about the social and the square dance that followed. "Everyone is very nice. Come visit soon and see." I'd asked Henry once again when the house would be painted. My parents would be troubled by the dreary, bare siding. Of course, I could buy the paint and do the work myself, but why? My salary was small, and I fully intended to be Galway's best schoolmarm. Unpainted wood rots more quickly, making more expense for the school board. Blue paint would save this expense as well as white. There was no excuse for Henry's "We'll see" besides stubbornness. Or else he assumed that the start of school would wash away all my thoughts of blue.

ON THE MORNING of my first school day, I rang the bell, as I'd done so often in my dreams. Twenty children marched in, fewer than I expected. The town children had new clothes and shined shoes; most of the country children were barefoot, and would be, I'd been told, until the first frost. But they were all alike in this: the friendly, open faces at the ice cream social had vanished. Now forty eyes watched me warily.

Even Alice Burnett seemed cautious, as if we'd never met. Of course, what child wants summer to end? But what of the older boys' smirks and covert signs?

I introduced myself and announced we'd start the day with nature drawing. With Ben's help, I'd collected fantastically turned roots, stones with embedded crystals, feathers, oddly shaped branches, bird nests, and abandoned honeycombs. I set these all on a table. "Now choose a partner, pick something interesting, and draw it in your own way."

"Miss Clay always did spelling first." No face claimed the statement; it might have come from the walls. My crisply pressed shirtwaist grew hotter and smaller. I'd never imagined the first day like this.

Something moved in Horace Butler's pocket. He pulled it out and tossed it on the floor. Screams filled the schoolhouse as a toad croaked and hopped across my feet. I nearly screamed myself. How could they know I had an irrational fear of toads? *Don't show it. The rest of the year depends on what you do now.* I managed to corner the wildly hopping little beast, which must have had an equal fear of schoolhouses. I spread my skirt and closed the cloth around him. He was frantic now, thumping against my legs, and I was frantic to be rid of him. But I couldn't do this yet, even if—and this was also terrible—the children were seeing my petticoat.

"Empty the water bucket and bring it here, now!" I ordered Horace and sent Charlie Davis for a piece of glass that workmen had carelessly left behind. "Now get this thing out of my skirt, put it in the bucket, and cover it with glass."

"How?"

I wouldn't answer, only glared. Horace and Charlie managed the maneuver, mortified to be so close to me. "Now get your slates and list thirty things you notice about a toad. Don't stop until you do." The class was watching me, openmouthed, as if I were a toad-charmer.

"We'll do nature drawing now," I said. They moved meekly to the table, chose their objects, and set to work, their backs to the boys with the bucket.

By recess time, Horace and Charlie had listed ten factors of color, size, and shape. "There's nothing else to notice," they moaned.

"Twenty more. You noticed enough to catch him. When the others are outside for recess, you'll have more quiet for noticing, won't you?"

"Yes, Miss Renner," they said.

When the children trooped back, we began our regular lessons. So many reciting in a small space made a deafening noise; my throat ached from speaking when lunchtime finally came. I sent the children outside, including Horace and Charlie, whose list had reached twenty-five. Dripping with sweat, I sank into my chair, listening to their shouts and calls from the schoolyard. I'll draw them, I was thinking wearily, but not today.

Suddenly the screaming stopped. Why? I ran to the window and saw Alice Burnett rolling and jerking in the dust. The class made a gawking circle around her. Some twitched in mockery, encouraged by their friends. I raced outside. "The devil's got her!" Frances was shouting in gleeful horror.

"Devil fit, devil fit!" others chanted.

"Get back! Leave her alone!" I shouted. By now the fit had passed, and Alice lay spent, hiding her face in shame.

"Is it catching?" asked a voice behind me.

"Of course not. Charlie, take everybody inside. Lunchtime's over." I had Emma, the oldest girl, help Alice clean herself at the well. I might have predicted that the first day of school might cause anxiety. Which Jim Burnett had said could bring on a fit. I should have been more attentive to her, or given her a small task inside with me. Now all I could do was lecture the children until they hung their heads.

"Will this happen again?" I asked in a steely voice that was new to me.

"No, Miss Renner," they chorused.

Emma slipped back into the room. "Alice went home," she said. "She wasn't feeling well." Of course not. Her first day in my classroom had been mortifying.

I handed out paper from the small stock that Henry provided. "You'll each describe a time someone laughed at you and how you felt. Then you'll describe how you think Alice feels today. The younger children can draw pictures. *If* this happens again, I'll show these papers to your parents." Every child gulped. I watched them work. So this was what they'd remember of their first day at my school: a punishment.

For the rest of the afternoon I marched the children through spelling and mathematics exercises at their several levels, released them at three, and dragged myself home. I couldn't face Alice's parents. Henry had dropped off a package from my mother: *butterplätzchen*, carefully wrapped. "For our Hazel," the note read, "who will be an exceptional teacher." Exhausted, embarrassed, demoralized, I bent over the table and cried. Ben had been gone for days, driven to Red Gorge by his voices. Owls hooted outside, laughing at me. Fortunately I'd already planned the first week's lessons. I ate a bowl of cold soup and spent a miserable night. Why had I thought teaching was easy? What arrogance suggested I'd be exceptional?

Alice wasn't in school the next day. Nor were five of the older country children. After morning prayer, Emma cleared her throat and announced: "Miss Renner, we're sorry about yesterday with Alice."

"And—?"

"And about the toad."

"Thank you, Emma. I appreciate the apology. And I'm sure you'll *all* apologize personally to Alice." Silence. "Won't you?"

"Yes, Miss Renner." I promised to have Dr. Bentley explain what was known about epilepsy. I described in detail what would be done and not done if Alice had another fit.

"Now we won't talk more about what happened. We'll have Charlie and Horace tell us what they learned about toads." They did this, shyly pleased with their list. Then came spelling and geography bees, with questions scaled for each grade. I made quick sketches of the winners. Perhaps, with enough varied competitions, every child could win a portrait by Christmas. At recess, I asked Emma about the five students who hadn't returned.

She shrugged. "They always do that—show up the first day and then stay home." Apparently nothing had made them act otherwise for me.

After school I went to Burnett's Grocery and waited until Jim was alone to confess: "I'm so sorry about what happened yesterday. How is Alice?"

"She cried all night. She'd convinced herself that she wouldn't have a fit in your school, that everything would be different with a new teacher."

Instead, everything was the same. "I'm so sorry, Jim," I repeated.

"It's not your fault. No teacher can stop fits."

"I wish I could, but the children will not behave as they did. I can promise her that. You have our word."

"It's so hard to see your child suffer, and Dr. Bentley says it's just something she'll have to live with. But if the others don't torment her, that's something. I'll tell her what you said, Hazel. Now you tell me about the rest of the day." I described the toad incident, which made him laugh. It was, in retrospect, mildly funny. "And I'll bet you won't have any more trouble from Charlie and Horace. They're good boys, once you've got them on your side."

"I'm sure they are. But five country children weren't there, and

Emma said they won't come back. The parents promised they'd attend. They didn't tell me it was just for one day."

"Hazel, you're from the city. You asked a question in public. Of course they agreed. They'd be shamed not to. Besides, the older children have chores at home or on the farm. Sending them to school is a sacrifice."

"So I need to convince the parents—"

"No, you don't 'convince' these folks of anything, or tell them how to raise their children, or what's important and what's not. Do you want some advice?"

"Yes."

"Go call on them in the evening or Sunday afternoon, so you don't take up work time or market time. And don't talk about school. Just listen."

I did as Jim suggested, making hot, dusty treks on foot to cabins where I sat on porches or front stoops, hearing about bad harvests, bad knees, sprained backs, barn fires, and early deaths. I also heard the deep longing that sons and daughters would have a better life. I didn't need to tell anyone the value of school. They already knew. The question, I learned, was whether my school was worth their sacrifice. The next week, two of the five began attending regularly. A third said she'd come "unless there's sickness at home."

"Amazing," said Jim.

The next week, Mrs. Ashton walked Susanna to school. "I guess we did well to get a city teacher," Henry said.

MY PARENTS VISITED in late September. They marveled at the quiet and calm of Galway, the blue sky "like in Heidelberg," and friendly greetings as we walked through town. Over coffee and my mother's cookies on the porch, I related my new life: collecting wild foods with Ben, visiting families, preparing lessons, grading, and keeping house. Male teachers had the right to two free evenings a week for courting. How did they have time? The only drawings I did now were portraits of my students. Studying their faces, I could better judge what might frustrate or excite them. I described pacing off the dimensions of Egyptian pyramids, finding miniature geological structures in the stream that ran behind the school, and gathering objects for nature drawing.

"All the McGuffey Readers want is memorization," I complained. So much time was spent in drills: names and dates of presidents; lists of states, capitals, and principal products; books of the Bible; spelling rules; rhetorical figures; kings of England; wars and battles.

"Have them sing the lists," my father suggested. Why hadn't I thought of that? "It would be a long song, all the battles in Europe now."

"Isn't Hazel's house nice and clean, dear?" my mother prompted. "Nicer on the inside than the outside, though."

"It will be painted. Father, look how your tins catch the light."

"Did you know that Germany surrendered in South-West Africa? You hear young men talking about when America joins the war," my father noted grimly. "They think it's a party, or they want to be heroes. They don't think they'll be the ones with their legs blown off."

"Shh," my mother said. "See, Hazel made a lovely meal." I had worked hard. We had rolls, green beans and meat loaf with Ben's mushrooms, sweet and sour cabbage, beer brewed in Galway, and peach pie for dessert.

"How did you learn to cook?" my father asked.

"Watching Mother. And Ben shows me where to find wild things and how to cook them."

"They're eating roots at home, thanks to the British blockade."

Swerving the conversation, my mother asked if people here minded that I was German.

"They think I'm strange because I'm from the city, but nobody talks about Germany."

"They gave you a cursed house. You told us the story."

"It's *not* cursed. Something bad happened to the owners. That's all."

"If they respect you, they should paint your house. And blue draws good spirits."

"Get it done before all the painters go to war," my father added.

"Stop! Just stop!" my mother ordered. "I want to see the waterfall Hazel wrote us about, and we're *not* talking about the war."

We went to see the waterfall and said nothing else about "over there."

Three days of rain followed their visit. My house was a gray square in driving gray. The roof was tight, as I'd been promised, but in the cease-less drumming overhead I heard my mother's voice: "If they respect you, they should paint your house." *Did* Galway respect me? If they wanted the house to last, why not paint it? Working up to indignation, I slogged through mud to see Henry. What other schoolteacher had walked miles to visit country families? Didn't I deserve a little indul-gence? "I haven't forgotten," he said impatiently. "You can't paint in the rain, and my shoulder's acting up." His wife called for hot milk. "Just a minute, Agnes. Hazel's here about the paint."

"It's a small house," I reminded him.

"Is everyone in Pittsburgh so persistent?"

"If we don't want to be bamboozled."

"Fine, you win. I'll speak to the school board."

"Please." I walked home, drenched and discouraged.

CHAPTER 5

## *Just a Fluke*

Rain followed for a week. Ben hadn't been to his shack behind the grocery or to my house. Was he hurt and alone? Were his voices worse in the rain? Nobody knew where his camp was or cared to look, so all I could do was worry. Slogging into town, I found idle farmers sitting morosely around a Franklin stove in Jim's store, smoking and talking of rain, its costs to the chickens and crops, the rising creek, and trees falling in soggy earth. They spoke of rheumatism and arthritis, broken bones, fingers lost but phantom pain remaining, and all the aches of pushing, pulling, and dragging heavy weights. "Would any of you fellas take a town job?" Jim asked.

"Now why in blazes would we do that?"

The eighth day brought a gauzy drizzle. After dinner, I was laying out the week's lessons when a soft step sounded on my porch, followed by a gentle knock. Henry? Ben? A parent or child? I opened the door. A slightly built man jerked back as if fearing attack. His clothes, hair, eyes and slouch felt hat were gray. His face was pale, like one who lived in shadows. He seemed barely thirty, and yet had an air of constant travel, of a man unused to life in houses. "Weren't you afraid at night?" people asked later. I wasn't. He seemed as harmless as Ben, with an eerie wash of sadness and regret.

"I brought your blue paint, miss," he said, pointing to a line of covered buckets set on the porch. He shifted slightly to peer around me into the house. "Could I have some water?"

I brought him a glass. He drained it and gave it back. Our fingers never touched. "Henry McFee sent you, or Jim Burnett?" He shook his head. I took a wild chance. "Ben Robinson?"

"Nobody sent me. I just wanted to help out. It's good paint."

"I'm sure it is, but you don't know me. How did you know I wanted blue?"

"I just heard. Good evening, miss." He touched his hat rim, still looking past me into the house. The idea shot across my mind that he might melt like a ghost into the gray.

"Wait! Tell me your name at least."

"John," he said, so softly it might have been the wind that spoke. "I have to be going now." He stepped backward off the porch and hurried away, dodging puddles. He must have left his car around the bend. I heard it rattle, catch, and drive away, leaving only the sound of rain. Had I imagined the whole encounter, made dreamy by the weather? But I held the glass he'd drained, and on the porch sat five buckets with "Blue" neatly written on top and two good brushes. They were real enough, heavy and sloshing.

When had he even brought them? I'd only heard his step once on the porch. Could he have carried all five? I shivered. I'd met most of Galway and would have remembered his grayness. Why would a stranger bring paint? How did he know I wanted blue? He hadn't spoken to Henry. And even if he had, what were my wants to this man? Inside the house, his melting form seemed to hover in every corner and outside each window. *Don't be scary.* When I splashed cold water on my face, a name roared back at me: *John Foster*. I splashed more, wetting the floor. The killer of newlyweds, the preacher's kid gone wrong. His age seemed right, and there was that insistent peering into my house. Did he think to see Ethel Harding here alive? Was he crazy, far more than Ben? Surely he had no debt to me. Why serve Ethel's house if she'd never see it? And how could paint repay two lives? Of course, "John" was a common enough name, but what other John could be so sad, alone, and fixed on my house? I couldn't sleep. Gray men swirled over my bed, bathed in blue light.

Hot sun blazed the next day. I hurried outside. The buckets were still there, still marked "Blue." I opened one and saw the blue of my father's eyes. I searched the mud around my house. There was no trace of my visitor, no footprints or tire tracks, but of course rain would have washed them away.

What about the paint? Should I use it? Why not? It was a gift, however mysterious. If my visitor was John Foster, and if, for his own reasons, he felt a debt to the house or its tenant now, why not let him pay it? Besides, the paint was a beautiful blue. My mother always claimed that blue brought good spirits. I'd tell Henry what happened, and he might believe me. If he asked why I'd accepted a killer's paint, I'd say I would have accepted the school board's paint if it had been offered.

Ben came by at dusk, his clothes filthy and torn, blotched with crusted blood from scratching. "My voices go bad in the rain," he said. He gulped down a bowl of potato soup, eyeing the buckets. "I could paint your house, you know, Miss Hazel. Except—up there." Anxious eyes climbed to the eaves before dropping back to the comfort of earth.

"Suppose I borrow a ladder?"

"And hold it?"

"Of course." We settled that for painting my house, he'd have hot meals on the days he worked and I'd make him two drawings of Old Havana from his descriptions: one for his shack behind the grocery and one for his camp. We let some days pass to dry out the wood. I borrowed a ladder from my neighbors, the Allens, and he started work on a bright day in early October.

"See how the brush is gliding," Ben announced with the first strokes, "like the house *wants* to be painted."

"Hum," I said, puzzling over a drawing. When I looked up, blue was rising swiftly, leaving the unpainted boards like a little ark floating on water. For the highest swatch under the eaves, I held the ladder as Ben climbed, twitching wildly and muttering: "Stroke, stroke, stroke." Before sunset, the house was finished, all in one coat. We stood back to admire the glowing sapphire, as perfect as I'd imagined. Who could *not* want a blue house?

I set a picnic on the porch: bean and potato soup, beer, bread, and chunks of cheese. Despite his customary scratching, Ben had never seemed so much at ease. I talked about Pittsburgh, my family and friends, the factories, the boys' war games, and choking smoke. "You were right to come to Galway, Miss Hazel," he said. What was wrong with this town that they scorned Ben Robinson? When he wasn't plagued by voices, he was as comforting as a cat.

"Where did you live before Havana?" Perhaps this time he'd tell me.

"Different places. My family traveled."

"Doing what?"

"Just—traveling." He still traveled, from porches to back doors, to the woods and his camp, a man without a home and, I still believe, a man without harm. As the first owls hooted, he stood. "I'm not supposed to bother you at nighttime."

"You don't have to go. Here, let me get you more soup." I took his bowl, but when I returned, he was gone.

THE NEXT DAY, Henry knocked hard on my door. "It's blue. What happened?"

"The paint was a gift and Ben did the work." I described my night visitor.

"Was he my height, about thirty?"

"Yes. He said his name was John."

Henry's eyes widened. "John Foster. Where did he go?"

"He drove away."

"Well, that makes sense, at least. There's a warrant out for his arrest. He didn't do anything, threaten you?"

"He asked for water and left the paint. He never came inside. He was very polite."

"That's John," Henry agreed. "Timid as a rabbit. Until that night." He looked me up and down and demanded: "How did he know you wanted blue paint?"

"He wouldn't say."

"That's crazy. Why would a killer bring *paint*?"

Was *I* was on trial? I stepped back, annoyed. "Henry, I don't know. The point is, my house is painted now."

"A boy kills two people, he's gone for years and comes back with *paint*? Why?"

"I don't understand it myself. Do you want to see Ben's work?" Henry hung back. "Come around the side." He followed grudgingly. The paint shone like glass in the bright sun. "It's a good job, isn't it?" I prompted.

"Good enough."

Was it so difficult to credit Ben? Made bolder by annoyance, I made Henry touch the warm wood. "Here, feel how smooth it is. One coat. Isn't that amazing?" Was it the angle at which I held him, or that he resisted me? A tremor shot through my arm, then an ache, as when I'd been drawing for too long.

"I guess it was good paint."

"And here," I persisted, "there were knots. See how smooth they are." Again, I made him touch the siding. Henry gave up his hand freely now, staring at me. What was I doing, holding a man's hand against paint? I dropped it. He rubbed his shoulder. "I'm sorry, did I hurt you?"

"No—no, you didn't hurt me." Henry reached for the siding again, hand flat on the blue, slowly raising it higher. "Hazel," he said more softly, "show me where the other knots were."

"I don't remember." His eyes glittered. My arm ached, and his strange persistence troubled me. He could leave now.

"Show me where the knots were." I pretended to know, pointing. "No, *show me*." I should take his hand again? No, this was too much. I stepped away. "Blast it, Hazel, show me where the knots were!" Moving slowly, I held his flattened hand to a random piece of siding. Again the tremor up my arm. I tried to pull it free, but he gripped my hand.

"Yes," he said finally, "I can feel them. Like you said—good paint. Well, I'll be going now." When he finally released my hand, I staggered, dizzy from sun and strain. He walked backward away from me and jumped into the Model T, red bandanna flicking like a tail. He hadn't coughed, I thought vaguely, and he never jumped before. No, he always *climbed* laboriously into the car. My head reeled, as if I'd fallen into a dream: my night visitor, the gliding ease of paint, the tremor, and Henry's strange behavior. Soon a crushing weariness overtook me. I buttered a slice of bread, went to bed, and tumbled into black and dreamless sleep.

Henry came the next morning just as I was leaving for school. "Hazel, how'd you do it?" He might have been speaking a foreign language. I waited, as my father waited for Hungarian, Polish, Russian, or Italian customers to describe their needs by gestures.

"How did I do what?"

"How did you fix my shoulder? Look at this." He reached up, windmilled both arms, and shook them like rags. "And I hardly coughed last night. "How'd you do it?"

"I didn't *do* anything, Henry. I just showed you the paint." The slapping and shaking went on. "Crazy Ben" never behaved like this. I backed away. "I have to get to school."

"Not yet. I want to know. If you didn't *do* anything, Hazel, who did? There was just me and you here, and the house." He pointed at the blue box, placidly facing us.

"Henry, it's a coincidence."

He snorted. "I've sure as blazes felt *paint* before. Next you'll say it was Crazy Ben or special paint. Did *you* feel anything?"

"Well, sort of a tremor, but—"

Triumphant. "You see? A tremor! Listen, I've had a bum shoulder for years. Ask anyone in Galway. Now look!" He shot his arm up and down with manic speed. I jumped back.

"I see, Henry, but I don't know why."

"I feel better; that's what *I* know. And I'm not coughing, either. Some folks have power. You could have told me. Because you seem so—ordinary." He looked me up and down, measuring my ordinariness. Then he snapped his fingers. "Of course! *That's* why you wanted a blue house! Nobody in Galway has a blue house." He shook with excitement. "But you wanted one. That was the first sign, you see?"

"I just like blue, that's all."

"Think what you will. *I* know a sign when I see one."

I wanted to vanish like Ben into the woods. Sweat ran down my face. "I *don't* have any special powers, believe me. I'm as ordinary as—anybody else."

"Now listen, Hazel, we don't want folks thinking we're nuts or getting scary about John Foster coming back. Let's just keep this our secret."

"Of course." Whatever happened was unexplainable and surely unrepeatable. Why would I possibly speak of this? What would possess a schoolteacher, new in a small town, to publicly claim healing powers? More than "nuts," I'd be branded as a charlatan or a witch.

"Got a trick knee, you know," Henry added. I backed away, but not fast enough. He lunged, caught my hand, and pressed it hard against his knee. This time there was no tremor, just hot embarrassment and a flash of fear to be tightly held so close to a man. "Wait, I forgot. You need to be touching the house. That's how *it* works."

"There's no *it*! And please, I'm late for school." Henry ignored this. I was pulled to my house and made to touch the siding with one hand and his knee with the other. Never in my life had I felt so ridiculous, trapped, and uncomfortable. No tremor, just a wash of sweat. "Too bad," he said finally, "but you *did* fix the shoulder. Admit it."

"I can't. I didn't do anything!" If Henry had claimed my skin was blue or I'd just vaulted up a tree, the space between his words and what I knew as truth couldn't be more impassable. He cranked his arm up and down as if saluting and then ran a finger across his lips. "Remember, not a soul."

Finally, he let me go. Despite his assurances, Henry might tell a soul or several souls, I realized with horror. Or others would notice a change in his bearing or ask about the wild cranking of his arm. I walked faster and faster to the schoolhouse. The children were already in their seats. Did they see the same ordinary Hazel? Was my hand now writing on the blackboard the same hand as last week? Why shouldn't it be? Had I turned as crazy as Ben?

"Is there something wrong, Miss Renner?" Alice asked at recess. "You seem different."

My breath caught. "No, I'm just a little tired. You go outside. It's a lovely morning." I used recess time to grade papers and managed to shove away thoughts of Henry, the paint, and my visitor, like clothes stuffed into a dresser drawer.

After school, walking home, I flipped frantically through explanations of these days. Perhaps Henry had moved in some way that relieved pain, unblocked a muscle, or shifted a joint. He could be a hypochondriac, as his wife was known to be, in which case both his previous pain and his present cure were wildly exaggerated. Perhaps he was simply crazy, but he'd never seemed crazy before. My mother claimed I had a healing touch, but what fond mother has never claimed astounding skills for a beloved child?

What then? There is a reason for all things. This is the age of science. I'd laughed with friends at cheap gazettes blaring "proof" of ghosts or quacks selling snake oil. Vaudeville acts tricked the credulous with levitating and vanishing bodies, but even Harry Houdini said the basis of magic was trickery. All who claimed supernatural powers were by definition charlatans.

Could the paint itself have power? Houdini would laugh at this. What about the fact of Ben's painting the house? But he scratched as before and probably heard voices as before. Using the blue paint hadn't cured him. Henry said I had the touch, but in twenty years, what magical thing had I ever done, despite my mother's claims? Could she, I wildly wondered, have secretly enlisted Henry to— *Stop! Stop!* These were crazy thoughts. Some logical explanation would soon emerge. I must be patient. And practical. For instance, leveraging Henry's gratitude to get more school supplies. I should ask quickly, for in all likelihood, his pain would return. Of course, I wouldn't write home of this matter. Why excite my mother's superstitions or make my father doubt my sanity? I'd keep this mystery to myself.

Afternoon sun darkened my house to the sheen of a mountain lake. Running my hands over the slick siding, I felt no tremor. But what if, a curling thought whispered, I *was* pierced by the extraordinary? Couldn't God, for His purposes, do that? Had I been brought to Galway for some purpose? No! Remember that Henry was probably a hypochondriac. John Foster was a man with Ben's gift for watching and listening unseen. He'd somehow heard that I wanted blue paint. A "good boy" whose mind was twisted by disappointed love had conjured an absurd expiation for murder: delivering paint. The only rational response to these days was to forget them. Forget them and be glad my house was finally blue. By a force of will, I spent the evening planning lessons. Except, I thought before bed, Henry always coughed before and he didn't cough now. On the other hand, every ill has a beginning and therefore an end. My house had merely turned blue when his cough had run its course. Yes, that must be so.

The next day, walking into town, I passed Horace and Charlie on their new bicycles. Charlie swerved and fell, howling and holding his wrist. I ran to help, but when I touched him, he jerked away. "That hurts! I need Doc Bentley."

"Can you take him?" I asked Horace, who was miserably standing by.

"Sure. Come on, Charlie, the doc will fix you up." I watched them go. Poor Charlie, but still I was relieved. Henry's "healing" was just a fluke, nothing more.

## CHAPTER 6
## *The Healing Hand*

I didn't see Henry for more than a week. His pains must have returned. Probably he had been embarrassed by his own credulity. I was sorry for his sake, but relieved to go back to my ordinary life, without mysteries or extraordinary powers. The beauty of autumn sufficed. In mid-October, leaves blazed red and gold against skies as blue as my house. If the Impressionists came to Galway now, they'd have to mix new palettes for their work.

On a warm evening, I was on my porch grading papers when Henry brought Agnes to my house. His wife was a pale, doughy woman plagued, or apparently plagued, with ailments. Each one required new patent medicines. Even Jim Burnett avoided her at church, fearing entrapment by her litany of complaints.

"Agnes wants to see how well Ben's painting came out," Henry said, winking. I didn't move. He winked again, lifting an arm to scratch his head.

"You're welcome to look around. These have to be done for tomorrow." I indicated my stack of papers.

"Can you show us where the knots were?" Behind him, Agnes

whimpered a little. Despite myself, I pitied his life at home. Would it cost me so much to humor her?

"Henry, you're off your rocker," Agnes huffed as I led them to the siding.

"You can't see the knots, can you, dear? Hazel, show her, please." Behind his wife's bulk, he gestured at me to take her hand. When I didn't move, he put my hand in her moist and bloated one, pushing both firmly to the siding as Agnes huffed: "Off your rockers, both of you."

Mortified, I closed my eyes, waiting for this charade to end when just as before—or slightly weaker than before—a tremor flew up my arm. "Takes a while," Henry was saying far away. Agnes ceased huffing. We stood, frozen, until her hot hand slipped from mine. I said nothing of the tremor. Perhaps I imagined it in the heat and discomfort of the moment. But no, here was the following ache again and Henry's distant voice: "How's the heartburn, dear?"

She burrowed a hand under heavy breasts. Brown eyes widened in fleshy nests.

"My father has heartburn sometimes," I said desperately. "From pickles." They ignored me, fixed on the pressing hand.

"It's gone!" she said. "Sure as eggs, gone away."

"Perhaps Hazel will make us some coffee," Henry prompted.

"Yes, dear, I'd love some. What a treat. I haven't had a cup in years." Trapped, I ground and brewed coffee as the two sat at my table, exchanging knowing glances like parents sharing secrets from a child. "I didn't believe at first, but Henry's right."

"My wife thinks that you and the paint are touched."

Cups rattled on my tray. "Touched?"

"By angels," Agnes whispered.

"John Foster brought the paint. Are you saying—?"

"Hazel," said Henry firmly, "like I told Agnes, a murderer doesn't make miracles. He knew you wanted paint because you talked about it enough, all the time. He probably still has friends here. He thought bringing paint would make everything right. Who knows what he was thinking? He's probably half cracked after that night. It's *not* the paint! If it was, Crazy Ben would be fixed. I saw him today, still scratching like an old dog. No, it's something about *you*."

"We know that you're Lutheran," Agnes added. "But the Good Lord can choose strange vessels. Because if it is not His work, then it's Satan's, and why would *he* be helping folks?"

I pushed my coffee away. I wanted this talk to stop and my head to stop pounding. I wanted my old gray house again. "It could still be a coincidence."

"Coincidence? There's no coincidence! My husband's shoulder pained him for years. And my heartburn's gone! You have the touch, that's clear." Agnes smoothed a flowered skirt across broad thighs. "Remember, this is our secret. To protect your privacy, of course." They wanted the "touch" for themselves; that much I understood.

"And don't mention John Foster again," Henry warned. "You'll just get folks riled. One more thing: I'm getting you a globe like you wanted. Happy?"

"Yes. Thank you." Now I truly was a charlatan, paid for trickery, even inadvertent. And yet . . . Agnes *could* drink coffee. Henry *did* move easily and hadn't coughed in all this time.

After they left, I went outside to touch the paint, pry off a chip and smell it. Ordinary. Completely ordinary. I'd sworn I wasn't "scary." Living in the murdered newlyweds' house hadn't troubled me, but now I shivered. Could the ordinary daughter of an ordinary hardware store owner be a "strange vessel"? No, Agnes was a hypochondriac, easily sickened and thus easily relieved. Both she and Henry were fascinated by a lurid, small-town crime and craved the extraordinary in their lives.

Yet suppose I *was* a "strange vessel"? Impossible, yes, but the impossible had happened before to ordinary people in ordinary places. If Agnes and Henry *weren't* hypochondriacs, but actually healed, or at least helped, then perhaps I could help the more deserving: Alice, Susanna, and Ben with his torments and ceaseless itch, or the pains of local farmers. Could I help my father's agonizing visions of death? Could I even heal the piteous wounds of war, the bayonet stabs, bodies shredded by shells and bullets, and minds torn by ceaseless horror? No, that was ridiculous. Was I thinking of presenting myself at a field hospital with a blue house in tow, convincing real doctors that I could do what they could not? Was my own mind slipping away like the moist, soft hand of Agnes?

What would a logical, sane person do? Test the "touch," of course. For my sake, it would be best to avoid someone who would call me crazy or ridicule my pride and credulity. I needed someone who might accept the substance of things unseen. I waited for Ben. He came that evening near sunset with a bouquet of cattails and autumn grasses. I'd determined to say nothing of Agnes and Henry's claims but simply repeat what I'd done: the holding hands and touching wood. If Henry, Agnes, and I were only impressionable fools, then no harm would come to Ben. Or he might be helped.

I put the grasses in a Mason jar and said casually: "Ben, you did an amazing job with the paint. Nobody can see or even feel where the knotholes were. Come to the side of the house." I took him to the point where Henry stood and reached for the hand I'd never touched before. It was callused, scabbed, and scarred with scratches. He resisted. "No, Ben," I said gently, "you have to feel it." I pressed his hand against the blue and—yes! A searing tremor shot through my arm, then a heavy ache, as if bone had turned to lead. I staggered.

Ben drew back in alarm—for my sake. "Miss Hazel, what's wrong?"

He dragged over the chopping block for kindling. I sank down as he watched, the gentle face filled with compassion. "You want a drink?" Then he hesitated, for water was in my house, where he never went.

"No, Ben, I'm fine. Just a little tired. I haven't been sleeping well. There's some potato soup. Do you want some?" I got up. He hovered like a gentleman, offering his arm. Had this much time ever passed without his scratching or twitching? Perhaps not. I raced to heat the soup and bring out two bowls. "It's a lovely evening." He nodded. This wasn't one of his talking evenings. We were often silent together, but finally I couldn't hold my tongue. "Ben, does—are you always scratching?" He nodded, looking down at the piteous arms, then at his hands, lying still in his lap.

A wondering whisper, light as a breeze. "I'm not scratching. And I'm not—"

"Twitching?"

"No." He gave me his soup bowl. "Miss Hazel, I think I'll go now." And he melted into the woods. A cut of winter chill slipped through the autumn balm. I shivered. Had Ben's twitching come to me? The bowls rattled as I brought them inside. Of course, I was glad if Ben had been helped, even briefly, but what did this mean for *my* life? What was expected of me in a world of hurt and pain? Of course I wanted to help. Any pastor would say that those given gifts must use them selflessly for good. Did this mean that I must stop teaching, drawing, doing anything else but press hands to the walls of my house? Forever? Yet this power that came so unexpectedly could leave without warning or prove fickle. What would people say of me then?

I'd never been so grateful for the press of schoolwork: themes of the older students to grade, lessons to prepare, lists for the week's spelling and geography bees, Susanna's portrait to finish. I worked long past midnight, sweating freely with the effort of driving out thoughts of

Ben. The next days were a madness of rises and falls, wondering confidence and shame for this very confidence. Ben appeared with a string of fish he'd caught in Red Gorge, not scratching, not twitching. Cured? Which meant what, exactly?

Henry came to deliver the globe and an apple pie from Agnes. "Haven't told a soul," he whispered, although we were alone on my porch. "But I had some back pain last night. Let's go check the paint." That wink again. I followed him outside. He placed my hand on his hip. A hand on a man's hip—my mother would be appalled, as I would have been myself—before. We touched the paint together. Nothing. No tremor or pain for me, and apparently no relief for Henry.

"Well," he said philosophically, "maybe it comes and goes. We'll try again, right?"

I nodded, caught by opposites: my own relief to be back at the ordinary *before* and despair that the gift was so unpredictable—or temporary.

AT FIRST AGNES and Henry kept the secret of my blue house, or else those they told kept this knowledge secret. Ben still wasn't scratching or twitching. Perhaps nobody noticed changes in Crazy Ben or didn't connect them with me. Schoolwork was exhausting enough even without costumes, scenery, and masks to prepare for our elaborate pageant: "Around the World at Christmastime." At least I'd grown more adept at having the older children help the younger ones. Simple tunes that Horace and Emma suggested eased our way through the McGuffey Reader's endless lists to memorize. Even without a gift of healing, I was at least serving Galway as a teacher.

Just before Halloween, in the midst of a late afternoon spelling bee, Alice stiffened and fell, writhing and flailing on the floor. I was proud of my class. The older boys shoved benches and desks away. Four girls knelt around her, making bolsters of their bodies. A jacket was wedged under her head. Frances hurried the youngest children outside for a game of Duck-Duck-Goose. But this fit went on and on, frightening even those who had seen them often. Alice's head slammed the floor with sickening thuds. Her eyes rolled back. She wet herself. When the shaking finally ceased, she looked up, so bewildered and piteous that I took her in my arms and rocked her. Nobody laughed. I commissioned Charlie and Emma to send everyone home. "Have them leave quietly," I said, and they did.

The Burnetts had given me another set of clothes for Alice. I helped her wash and change. Then I walked her home. "It's getting worse," she moaned. "I have more fits all the time as bad as this one." Between gulping sobs, she said Dr. Bentley had warned her parents that worsening epilepsy could shorten her life, damage her brain, and at the least, close off many occupations. "I'm so afraid, Miss Renner."

My secret time was over. I'd have to tell the Burnetts about my blue house, no matter what they thought of me. Perhaps this was my paint's purpose—and now mine. "Alice, I'll try to help."

"How? You're just a teacher."

When Jim saw us coming with Alice in a different dress, bruised and tear-streaked, he closed the store, called Ellen, and brought me to the kitchen. Alice sat on Ellen's lap as I explained my night visitor, the paint's marvelously easy application, and the seeming cures of Henry, Agnes, and Ben. The Burnetts looked at me, openmouthed. "I don't know why this is happening," I finished. "I can't promise anything. And whatever it is didn't work for Henry's back. But it did help other problems."

Jim cleared his throat. "Hazel, are you telling us the *paint* on your house has special powers?" I was crazy, he surely thought, crazier than Ben, perhaps too crazy to teach children.

"We saw Ben this morning," Ellen said slowly. "He wasn't scratching. Remember, we noticed that? Henry walks different now, you said so yourself. He's not coughing, and Agnes hasn't ordered any more patent medicines."

"Yes, but . . . touching *paint*?"

"You heard Doc Bentley. The best specialist in America can't help her. Jim, what do we have to lose?"

Alice reached across the kitchen table to her father. "Please, Poppa, let Miss Renner try. I'm so scared of these fits."

"But—*paint*?"

"Jim, please. Let's just try."

He looked at his wife, his daughter, at me. "We'll bring her tonight after dark."

It was Friday, so there were no lessons to prepare. At home, I paced, I prayed, I envisioned every detail of how I'd stood with Henry, Agnes, and Ben, how I'd held their hands, and where they touched the paint. Then I sat outside and waited for the Burnetts.

They came solemnly, as if to church. We walked in single file to the side of the house. Leaves might have crunched under our feet, but all I heard was a drumming voice in my head: *Heal her, heal her, heal her.* At the spot I'd marked, we stopped. Wind whipped past us. *Heal her, heal her, heal her.* Alice's hand was given to me; I pressed it against the slick wood that glimmered black in moonlight and put my other hand on her head. As soon as I closed my eyes, the tremor began. My body shook.

"She's taking it in herself," someone said. Ellen? Another tremor. Heaviness like lead again. Alice was drawn away. An arm beat against my body. I opened my eyes. I stumbled. Jim caught me.

Held against her mother, Alice's dark eyes flashed in the darkness. "Did it work, Miss Renner?"

"We'll have to wait and see," I moved my mouth to say. "I need to lie down." They helped me to bed.

"Thank you, Hazel," Ellen said over and over. "Do you need anything?" I shook my head. "Then we'll take Alice home." I was awake just long enough to hear their car pull away.

A week passed and Alice had no fits at all, which was unusual, Jim said. "We haven't told anybody," he assured me. But word was leaking out, perhaps from Henry and Agnes. What secrets can endure in a town so small? Soon after Halloween, nets of wheel ruts began appearing in my yard. Bare spots on the wall showed where paint had been chipped off. Walking home from school, I might hear engines start or a quick "gee up."

"Folks come sneaking around," Ben said as we shared breakfast on the porch one frosty morning. I'd made him fried eggs, sausage, and coffee in return for chopping firewood. "I tell them: 'Leave the schoolmarm's house alone.' But they don't listen. Crazy Ben, they call me."

"I know, Ben. I'm sorry." Would some resent his apparent cure if my house didn't help their own ills? Would Alice's fits return? Every task—cooking, cleaning, drawing, teaching, and preparing lessons—was weighted by the matter of paint.

In this anxious time, war news brought a strange relief. My father sent a map of Europe with battles and casualties noted in his precise hand. The children gathered around, wide-eyed. "All for an archduke?" Horace marveled. "What was so all-fired wonderful about *him*?" I explained the web of alliances that pulled countries into war and described battlefields scored with trenches, pocked by mortar shells, and lumped with bodies.

"The good thing," Emma said, "is that it's not our problem."

During recess, Susanna tapped my arm and whispered: "Have you noticed that Alice hasn't had a fit lately?"

"Perhaps she's growing out of them. We can hope so, Susanna."

EDNA FULLER WAS the first to come directly to me. She'd walked five miles through the woods. She was rarely seen, but everyone knew of her husband's cruelty and drunkenness, the family's poverty, and the froth of warts on her face. I'd caught children playing "Ugly Edna." One of the younger girls reported a nightmare of Edna "sticking her warts on me." When I saw the real Edna at my door, I nearly stepped back in horror at the monstrous face pasted on a normal woman's form.

"Jacob don't give me any money, Miss Renner, but I was hoping you could fix my face for this." She thrust out a Mason jar of jam and insisted I take it. I'll have to touch that toad face, I thought, immediately disgusted by my own disgust. Suppose I was Edna, seeing others shrink from me, trapped with a man like Jacob? How could I *not* try to help?

I took her to the side of the house and touched the paint, pressing my other hand against her fleshy lumps. And the tremor came, weaker than with Alice, but constant. When I pulled away, Edna steadied me. In the dimming light, I noticed first her lithe, proud body, and only after that the few square inches of brow, cheeks, nose, and chin plagued by lumps and bulbs.

"Good luck, Edna. I hope it works."

"Bless you for trying, Miss Renner. I've got to get back now. I left my babies alone." She hurried into the woods, melting away as Ben did. Was it he who sent her to me?

Three days later at Bennett's store, I saw a vaguely familiar, faded cotton jacket from the back. When the woman turned, only the posture linked this woman to the one who'd come to my house. There were no warts or scars, just a handsome face framed by auburn curls. I stepped back, stunned. Edna had the grace to merely wish me good day, put her groceries in a basket, and hurry out of the store. By Sunday, Galway burned with news: Edna and her three children had left town on the night train, headed west. Raving about a stolen wife, Jacob had been arrested for drunk and disorderly conduct.

After church, people churned around me, softly asking when they could "come by." Parents had a sudden need to discuss their child. Others had a pie, preserves, dressed game meat, needlepoint, or flower bulbs they'd been meaning to drop off as welcome gifts. Some mentioned pains I'd never imagined behind the smiling Sunday faces.

They came all afternoon. Buggies, wagons, and cars filled my yard. The postman's wife had sick headaches. There were bad hips, racking coughs, bodies cruelly twisted by arthritis and deep pains of rheumatism. Charlie brought me his childish grandmother, tenderly prying open her burned and blistered hands. "She keeps playing with live coals."

A woman brought a young boy with a deep, suppurating wound on his leg. "Take him to Dr. Bentley," I pleaded. "Please, before the infection gets worse. Don't count on me. Your son needs a doctor now."

"I can't," she sobbed. "I don't have no two dollars." Coins passed silently up the line for her, and she hurried away.

The line curved around the house, slowly inching forward. The tremor didn't come regularly, or always with the same intensity. It seemed indifferent to the severity of cases. When it came, strength ran out of me and I sank into a kitchen chair someone brought outside. Women fluttered around, offering tea and sweets until I could stand again. Each time I felt weaker. When the tremor didn't come, some got back in line for better luck next time. I worked until dusk, when Henry came. "You all go home now, and let Miss Renner rest." The crowd left slowly, some muttering: "Easy for *him* to say. *It* worked for him." Others consoled me: "Don't feel bad, we'll come back." Henry helped me into my house, reluctantly agreed to take money left by seekers to the Galway Benevolent Society, and then turned back.

"It's yours, Hazel. You earned it."

"No I didn't."

"Well, maybe not," he said thoughtfully, "if the touch comes from the Lord, like Agnes says. I wonder what Reverend Collins thinks of all this."

"I don't know." Finally he left. I could barely recognize myself in the mirror. Was I Hazel the schoolmarm or the Lord's vessel? Did Margit Brandt, catching sight of herself in Heidelberg, Dogwood, or New York City, ever wonder: Who is this woman? I dreamt of men in scarlet jackets chasing me through an endless hall of mirrors, calling for Hilde.

Of course I came to school tired and poorly prepared, with no clever learning games or contests. We passed the day in dreary drills. "Like when Miss Clay was here," Frances whispered. I'd have to do better. The students shouldn't suffer because farmers' joints ached. Seekers did come after school, seven who hadn't been helped on Sunday, and another five. Tremors came for half of them. When night fell, I excused myself to work and stayed up late planning better lessons for the week.

The next two weeks took their toll on my house and me. Even if no "cures" were attributed to the paint alone, great patches of it were being chipped away. The boards themselves grew nicked as if gnawed by mice. In cold or rainy days, people took to waiting on my porch or in the house, tracking in mud, sometimes helping themselves to food left as gifts or to my own provisions. Those who hadn't been helped perhaps felt their pains and disappointments merited this recompense. Each day I grew more weary and drained, as if both cures and failures were sucking away my strength.

In mid-November, Reverend Collins presented himself at the schoolhouse, waiting impatiently until the last child left to announce that I was driving people from the church. "They're saying the school-teacher will cure them if the Good Lord can't. Edna Fuller abandoned her husband because of you. Is *that* holy work?" He crossed his arms as he often did during sermons, letting minutes crawl by as the congregation squirmed.

"Reverend, I never claimed divine powers."

"Never? Didn't you tell the Burnetts you could cast out devils?"

"No, I never said that. Alice has epilepsy. I noticed that Henry and Agnes felt better, and because I was so worried about Alice—"

"You told her parents you could cure her."

Put thus, of course I seemed a charlatan with claims buoyed by hysterical faith or lucky coincidence. "Reverend, I don't know what's happening or why. Sometimes a sort of tremor runs through me and people are cured, or seem to be helped. Why? Because of me or John Foster or Ben or the house? Maybe the paint? *I don't know.* I just try to —do some good."

"This is a Christian town, Hazel. Or it was, until you came. Does your power come from Satan?"

"I don't deserve that question."

Still a pastor despite his anger, he softened. "I'll walk you home, Hazel. The ways of the Lord are beyond our understanding. But consider, if these are unholy powers, you must pray for the Lord to remove them. And if they are *from* the Lord, you must pray for wisdom to use them wisely."

"Yes, Reverend." On the way home, we managed a little conversation about the Christmas program. He did acknowledge that school attendance had never been higher.

"I'm glad. I enjoy teaching."

"Well then, that might be the work you're called to do."

"Yes, Reverend."

IN THREE WEEKS, Alice had not had a fit, not even the smallest stiffening. Perhaps Edna and her children had found a better life. Ben, in the few times I saw him, neither twitched nor scratched. Henry, Agnes, and all those for whom I'd felt a tremor had not sought another touch. I assumed they still felt themselves cured. But everywhere, eyes scoured me: the grateful, the disappointed, the wary and suspicious. Henry came at nightfall to shoo crowds away, arguing that the schoolteacher needed time for the work she'd been hired to do. In this role, he was roundly disliked—for my sake.

Since the tremor came for only one in four, and then one in five, six, or more, the line of seekers took fervent interest in outcomes. "Successes" roused jealousy: *Why was she healed and not me? Why that trivial pain and not mine?* When I felt no tremor, a palpable shiver of pleasure ran through the line: *Good! Now there's more of "it" for me, for my child.* Some, I suspected, claimed healing when there was none, becoming objects of wonder themselves: "How did it feel? Can you help me?"

Tired as I was, with no time for myself, my house no longer my own, still I ached for each pain: a pitifully sickly child, a sudden weakening of a limb or crippling seizure of the back, burning in the gut, bloody coughs and sores that would not heal, the anguished mother whose babe in the womb had ceased kicking, a blacksmith whose eye had been burned by a spark and could no longer see to work. School was no escape. At recess, little Maude tugged at my skirt. "Miss Renner, why didn't you help my mama? You helped other people. Don't you like me anymore?"

*I'm sorry, Galway!* I wanted to bellow. *I can't do more!* And if I couldn't do more, where could *I* have peace? But there was no escape in a town consumed by wanting.

I'd never looked forward to Thanksgiving so eagerly. My mother celebrated with the earnest fidelity of immigrants; it was the one holiday for which my father happily ate "American." But it wasn't for food that I yearned to go home. I wanted to be unexceptional again, to have a respite from longing or disappointed eyes, even at the cost of noise, smoke, and smells, the press of war, and difficulty of navigating my parents' questions. But leaving Galway was impossible, I discovered, even for a weekend.

"Folks are thinking *it* will come back on Thanksgiving," Henry said. "Christmas is around the corner. Can't you wait?"

"But—"

"The Burnetts would love to host you. And remember, there's the pageant coming up." Henry was so unmovable that I had to write home excusing myself, make a reasonable imitation of my mother's apple pie, and walk to the Burnetts' on Thanksgiving Day. Ellen had set out her best china, and the family received me warmly.

"We can't leave the store," Jim explained. "So you're doing us a favor by coming." They asked about my holidays at home and what "my people" thought about the war. After dinner they urged Alice to announce what she'd told them, that she wanted to be a schoolteacher "just like Miss Renner." But when Alice slipped away from the table to read, they related painful gossip that they had "used up" too much magic from my house for her. Once they'd been friends with everyone in Galway. Now there were factions: the cured and the not cured. "It's hard for us, but we're worried about you, Hazel," Ellen said. Alice had heard the word *witch* floating around the schoolyard.

"But if the cures are stopping," Jim suggested, "maybe folks will forget. They *are* happy with your teaching."

"I hope so." I didn't mention that the hours of tending to seekers meant less time to prepare the slower children for county tests. The

Christmas pageant would be less elaborate than I'd planned, and I was scrambling to finish the portraits I'd promised each child.

That Sunday in the churchyard I heard *witch* myself. The word floated in frosty air. It was impossible to identify the speaker in the tight groups of townspeople turned away from me. Buying groceries, I heard *Kraut* from a woman huddled with her neighbor. More food was disappearing from my kitchen.

"People take things," Ben said. "And some get angry because I'm not scratching anymore. They say: 'How come *you* got fixed?' "

"They shouldn't say that, Ben." Could I somehow press one hand on the blue paint and one on the town's heart? I brought Ben a bowl of bean soup and we ate in troubled silence. Had Margit ever felt like this, that something in *her* had unleashed trouble on a town?

THE FIRST WEEK in December brought cold, stinging rains. Chipped and nicked, my house looked dismal against the gray winter woods, speaking more of disappointments than of miraculous healings. I had no tremors after Thanksgiving. The lines dwindled away, and Ben came often. I was grateful for his quiet, undemanding company. His skin was healing; clearly he'd once been a handsome man. But in perverse compensation, the voices in his head became more constant, disturbing even on my porch. Who could help him? Dr. Bentley dealt only with visible or palpable pains; Rev. Collins would tell him to pray away his devils. But Ben said he wasn't a Christian "after Cuba," and in any case, "they don't want me in church." Unhappily, he was right.

On the evening of December 17, Judge Ashton and his wife brought Susanna to my house in their gleaming Keystone automobile. She hadn't been in school for days. "Her fever won't go down," Mrs. Ashton said. "Dr. Bentley says he's tried everything he knows."

"It's my wife that wanted to come," the judge interrupted. "I don't hold with this idiocy about your paint. *I'd* say you're selling snake oil."

"Miss Renner isn't *selling* anything, Edgar," his wife retorted. "Every penny she gets goes to the Galway Benevolent Society. I know because I'm the treasurer."

He reddened, obviously annoyed. I'd never disliked him more. But how tenderly he held his daughter. He and I both wanted Susanna healthy. We shared this much. She brought a gentle, uplifting presence to the school. Jockeying for her favors, even the roughest boys were more polite. As Henry said, Susanna was easy to love. So for her sake, I tried to speak calmly. "Sir, I have no idea why some people are healed at my house and others not. Lately, nobody has been helped."

"Could you try?" Mrs. Ashton asked. "Maybe there's enough healing for one more?"

"You heard her," the judge said. "Nobody's been helped for—how long, Miss Renner?"

"Almost three weeks."

"Please, Edgar. Let her try."

"Yes, Father," said a small voice from the blankets, "please let my teacher try."

The judge was a man accustomed to command. To be helpless was clearly an agony. "Well, do what you can. But hurry. She shouldn't be out in this cold."

I led them to the side of my house, now patched with gray from the constant scraping and chipping. Reaching into the folds of Susanna's blankets, I touched her hot and clammy hand, and then the largest patch of blue paint. I closed my eyes, pressed, and prayed. The tremor, if it came, always came quickly. Nothing. Still I waited. Stinging sleet rattled down on us.

The judge's heavy breath filled the air. "Nothing?"

"No, sir, I'm sorry."

"So why keep a sick child outside in this weather? That's enough. Like I said, it's snake oil. Or if it's not, what's wrong with you? You fixed Crazy Ben, that slut Edna, and not my little girl? Exactly what were your intentions in coming to Galway?"

"Don't talk that way to my teacher," came Susanna's small, hoarse voice.

"She's right, Edgar. It's not for us to question the Lord."

"The *Lord* cured Ben and made my daughter sick?"

"Edgar, that's enough. Let's take her home. Thank you for trying, Miss Renner. We appreciate it. There's a specialist in Cleveland who can see her after Christmas. Maybe he can help." Mrs. Ashton shepherded them both into the elegant car and the judge drove them away.

I sat on my porch, watching sleet rattle down on dry leaves. *Was* I a fake, a charlatan, a snake-oil seller? Certainly the healing touch was capricious. I raised hopes that couldn't be met, and the good I did was tinged with trouble. I'd wanted to be an extraordinary teacher. Now I was only another Miss Clay whose children might do poorly on county tests. A faint flash of gray caught my eye. "Ben? Come out of the cold."

He took shape and appeared, dripping, on my porch. "Your house didn't help Susanna, did it?" So he'd been watching us.

"I'm afraid not. Maybe the specialist can do something."

"*After* Christmas. Susanna needs help *now*. There was a sick girl in Havana. They brought her out in the evenings for the sea breeze. Sometimes they let me give her flowers. Then they kept her inside and she died. Now Susanna's sick again and nobody's helping."

"Ben, please, don't worry. Her parents are doing everything they can. And really, it's only a fever." I'm not sure he heard me. Perhaps he heard his voices instead.

He studied my clapboards. "I did a good job, right?" Poor man, the whole town shied from him; children stepped aside when he passed; weeks might pass without a human touch.

"You did a fine job."

"Up top was hard. I'm scared of heights, you know."

"Yes, I know."

"I saw men hurt in Cuba. Some of them fell a long way into rocks. Other bad things. I couldn't help them. It's not good when you can't help."

"No, it's not."

"But people still try."

"Yes, they do."

"Can I stay awhile?"

"Of course. Let me get you something to eat." I brought out a blanket and a plate of toasted cheese.

"Thank you. You can go in now, Miss Hazel."

So his voices had come, and he needed to be alone with them. I went inside and drew Susanna walking in a meadow; Susanna winning a geography bee; Susanna and Alice jumping rope. And then, remembered images: grand rooms, a table set with silver, men in scarlet livery, a garden. Perhaps that world would tell me why, like Margit, I had found myself in a place that first seemed so good for me and now was so difficult and full of pain.

When I went to check on Ben, he was gone, my blanket neatly folded, and the empty plate beside it. I'd never see him again. If I'd listened more closely, I might have stopped the terrible engine set in motion when I demanded blue paint for my house.

## CHAPTER 7
## *Crazy Ben*

**W**hy wouldn't you help my Ernie?" Mrs. Ramsey demanded at the grocery store. A ring of women surrounded me.

Finally Charlie's mother spoke: "Wilma, there's *nothing* wrong with Ernie. He's just one year old. Doc Bentley said he'll walk when he's ready. Lydia walked early, but every child is different. Ernie will be smart as a whip, just like his sister."

"*She* fixed Edna," Mrs. Ramsey countered.

"Well, so what if she did? Didn't that poor woman deserve a normal face and something better than that drunk?"

"I suppose so."

Pressing her advantage, Charlie's mother turned to the assemblage, smiling broadly. "Hazel was hired to be a *schoolmarm*, and she's doing that just fine. If she's supposed to work miracles for everyone in Galway, we'd have to pay her more." A few twitters loosened the air. Mrs. Ramsey's neighbor engaged her in a conversation. I eased up to the counter where Jim put bread, onions, potatoes, and beans in my basket. "Let me talk to them," he whispered. I slipped out, determined to stretch these rations as if I lived behind the Allied blockade. Coming to town was a mistake. But there was no escaping the jealousy and resentment my house and I had brought to Galway.

The next day in school, as we were practicing the Christmas pageant, whispers and glances toward Lydia Ramsey built until I had to ask: "Lydia, do you have something to share?"

She stood up. "Yes. *Are* you a witch, Miss Renner?" Winter light frosted a sharp-edged face, the image of her mother's. Yet just last month, Lydia had shyly confessed how much she loved drawing and unfolded a deft self-portrait in pencil. I'd held her hand in mine to demonstrate how shading could highlight her deep eyes and sleek hair. She'd held her breath in wonder. Now I wouldn't dare touch her.

"Who says I'm a witch?"

She looked out the frosty windows. "Some folks."

"What do *you* think?"

She scuffed the floor, a child again. "You're our teacher."

"And that's *all* I am, Lydia. That's what matters now. We have our pageant in two days. Shall we practice?"

"Yes, Miss Renner," said the chorus.

"Good."

"Susanna is my partner," said Alice. "Will she be coming?"

The class was silent. Did they know about the Ashtons' night visit and my failure? "I hope so. But meanwhile, who can take Susanna's part?" By now most of the children knew every part of the songs we'd written to cover the geography, history, and civics topics they'd need for the county tests.

"I can," said Lydia softly.

"Thank you, Lydia." *Thank you, thank you.*

We were practicing "Christmas in South America" when the Ashtons brought in a chill blast of air that ruffled our papers. The judge didn't wipe his feet as even the youngest children had been drilled to do. Mrs. Ashton closed the door. Her face was ashen. The judge's was red. The deep voice boomed: "Where is Susanna, Miss Renner?"

Susanna? Her absence was suddenly palpable. "Because she's not here and she's not home." His words filled the little room. The children looked from him to me, their stricken faces crying: *Explain this, teacher. Tell us what happened!* I felt my mouth open slightly and then close.

"She was so hot," said a thread of Mrs. Ashton's voice. "I had her on the sunporch and went to speak with the cook. I came back and Susanna was gone." *Impossible.* In an utterly normal town, a child vanishes. Was some terrible magic at play?

"Miss Renner, what do you know about this?" the judge demanded. Jerked by the rope of his words, I was on trial.

"Sir, I've been here all morning with the children."

"That's true," said a voice. Charlie's, gathering strength: "I came early to help with the stove. She was here."

"Judge, did you search—"

"Naturally, my wife, the maid, and the cook searched the house and outbuildings before calling me. I searched as well. She's gone. And something else: Ben's gone."

Ben, poor Ben, why did your voices call you away this morning, not yesterday or tomorrow? "He often disappears. It could be just coincidence."

"*Coincidence*, Miss Renner? *Coincidence?* It's nobody who wants money because there's no ransom note. I've seen him spying on my Susanna. I've seen his crazy eyes."

I'd never seen "crazy eyes." I'd seen kind eyes, frightened eyes, eyes filled up with remembered horror. Yet now I remembered with horrible clarity his voice from our last, cold night on my porch: "Susanna needs help *now*." And I told him not to worry. *Not to worry?* I said that to a man daily tormented by horrors seen nearly twenty years ago? Crazy Hazel.

Mrs. Ashton spoke, her soft voice broken by anguish. "All we want is Susanna back safe. We think she's with Ben because he was sneaking around our house yesterday, watching from the woods. The judge warned him, but this morning we found footprints."

I backed against the slate board. Why hadn't I listened? Because I was ruminating on my own failure to help, I hadn't seen a sign waved in my face as clear as any flag. Ben would never hurt Susanna; I knew this with utter certainty. He'd give his life for hers. But what did I know of his voices? And if he had her, a feverish child, how could he care for her in this blustery cold?

"Where does he hide? Where's that camp of his?" the judge demanded.

"I don't know. I've never been there, It's 'up there' is all he ever said. But he might not be at his camp. And he might not have Susanna." Yes, I had to hang from this spider thread. There might be another explanation. Susanna might be—somewhere else.

"We'll find him. Dick Morgan's bringing his bloodhounds. We're watching the roads, and the sheriff's telegraphing police all over the state. Now that Ben's stopped scratching, thanks to you, he could have taken her anywhere and looked normal. On the train, for instance."

"But if the stationmaster didn't see her, she's still in Galway. And Ben has no money. He never wanted any."

"That's true," Horace volunteered. "My father tried to pay him for splitting wood, but all he'd take was an old jacket." Around the room, heads nodded.

"Is Susanna dead?" Alice whispered.

"No," I said loudly. "Of course not. She's just—somewhere. We have to find her."

The judge sank into my teacher's chair as if his legs had melted away. The spectacle of this fearsome man so reduced terrified even older children. The younger ones whimpered. Realizing his effect—or mortified to reveal weakness—he pulled himself up, his face icy white. "We'll find Ben, and when we do, we'll find my daughter. Search parties will start from my home. We can use every boy over thirteen and any girl who wants to help. School's over for the day, Miss Renner." Then he was gone, his arm around his wife. "We'll find her, Martha," were the last words we heard.

Facing the schoolroom, I knew what the children wanted: their old Galway back, where no child disappeared. How could I do that? Who had that power?

"Maybe she's in Pittsburgh; she always wanted to see a big city," Horace said. The others brightened. However huge, Pittsburgh was a *place*, and any place can be searched. Except that Susanna would never go alone to Pittsburgh. She'd never gone alone into Galway.

"Nobody would hurt her," said Charlie, who adored her.

"I think it *was* Crazy Ben," a low voice muttered.

"He's not crazy," I said sharply, "just different, but now we have to find Susanna. Some of you older ones can help, like the judge said. Make sure you have warm clothes. You younger ones go home now." They needed to be with their families, not here feeding on each other's fears. "Susanna *will* be found and we *will* have school tomorrow and the pageant the next day." The children scrambled to their feet, gathered their coats, and were gone. Not even Alice looked back. I was Ben's friend; they all knew that. Now Susanna was gone, and if Ben had taken her, in these children's eyes, and in Galway's eyes, how could this *not* point back to me?

*Find her, find her. Think only about that.* I banked the fire and left the schoolhouse unlocked, for Susanna might come, or she might be brought here. I went home. Nobody was there; nothing had been disturbed, and the only footprints to or from the porch were mine. I hurried to join a gathering crowd at the Ashtons' house. Sheriff Wilkes had come from the county seat with a roll of maps.

Dick Morgan arrived with two young bloodhounds. "Where's Heddy?" the judge demanded.

"She just whelped. She's not strong enough for a hunt. But Jiff and Daisy here are good trackers," Dick promised.

"They better be. Let's go." The hounds were given Susanna's nightgown to sniff before charging into the house as we waited outside.

"There's the schoolmarm," someone whispered. "I bet she knows something." Another man: "We should have kicked Ben out of town long ago. That crazy loon isn't fit to associate with decent folks." The man caught my eye and stopped.

Charlie appeared beside me. "Never mind them, Miss Renner." He signaled his friends and they gathered close.

"Thank you, boys," I whispered. A cold drizzle was turning to sleet, like the last night I saw her. Sick as Susanna was, how long could she endure outside? And would the dogs have more trouble finding her now?

"Do you want to sit down, Miss Renner?" Charlie asked. No, I'd stand. *Send my strength to Susanna. And Ben, bring her back, send her back and then run, far away from the judge.*

Dick appeared at the front door, leading the dogs. They sniffed the grounds earnestly but aimlessly, circled the empty gazebo, and then looked quizzically up at their master. "It's the cold and wet. My Heddy could track—"

"But Heddy's not here, is she, Dick?" the judge snapped.

"Let's get organized," Sheriff Wilkes announced in a gruff, military voice that gave everyone comfort. "Dick, you take the dogs to Red Gorge with some men. Fan out and search the woods. Whistle three times if you find her. Some of you start with Ben's shack by the grocery and then search every house and every store in town. There are two roads out of Galway. We need every car stopped and searched. Doc Bentley and you women, go to the church and set up a first aid station, coffee, and sandwiches. Burnett, can you help?"

"Sure. Tell me what you need. I'll bring it from the store."

I joined women making sandwiches while boys and fleet-footed girls ran between teams and back to the sheriff, who marked the searched zones on a map of the township. My house and the schoolhouse got a black X and then another sign that I took to mean they'd be searched again. Mrs. Ashton sat frozen on a chair. Women brought her mugs of coffee, exchanged for new ones as they chilled. Nobody spoke to me or touched me or worked close to me.

Sleet became snow as afternoon wore into dusk. Teams staggered back, weary, cold, and empty-handed. They ate, warmed themselves, and went out again. Jiff mangled his paw in a fox trap and had to be taken off the search. Daisy began sniffing in circles. Roadblocks ringed the town. No one answering Ben and Susanna's description had been seen on any train in Pennsylvania.

Search parties began reporting injuries on snow-covered trails, frostbite, and exhaustion. "We have fathers and sons out there. Some-one's going to break a neck," Sheriff Wilkes announced. "We'll go out again at dawn." When Judge Ashton protested, Wilkes snapped: "I'm in charge here. Dan, call 'em back." The barrel-chested deputy who'd been an army bugler sounded recall. Answering whistles sounded in the darkness. The teams began returning, soaked and shivering.

"Sorry, Judge," many said. "We'll find her tomorrow." They wrapped frozen fingers around mugs of coffee. Ice chunks fell from their jack-ets, melting in pools at their feet. Women watched silently, thinking of their children. Slowly the crowd disbanded.

Back home, still in coat and boots, not bothering to light a fire, I sank into a chair, barely thinking beyond a dull repeat: *"Lord, bring her home safe."* And Ben. Why hadn't I seen his signs? How could I have been so blind? Once I'd blandly assumed I'd bring only good to Galway. I'd be the marvelous teacher. Now two innocent souls were in peril. And wasn't it my blue house that brought Susanna and her parents to me, fanning poor Ben's memories of the sick girl in Havana he couldn't save, swerving his broken mind to *this* sick girl whose father would now hunt him down?

PAST MIDNIGHT, TERRIBLE chill led me to the stove. I was blowing embers back to life when a gentle rapping sounded at the door. The wind? It came again, more persistent. To satisfy disbelief, I opened the door. There she was, shivering in an ice-caked man's jacket. "Susanna, Susanna, you're safe!" Dizzy with relief, I carried her to the stove, took off the jacket, tore blankets from my bed, and wrapped them around her. "Are you hurt?" I asked over and over until she warmed enough to answer.

"No. Just tired and a little hungry." Joy, joy. She wasn't hurt, just hungry. With trembling hands, I heated pea soup, cut bread, and poured a mug of hot cider. She took it with one red-mittened hand.

"I lost the other mitten. Mother will be angry."

"No she won't. I promise." *Ask!* "Susanna, who brought you here?"

"Ben." I closed my eyes. *My lost and gentle friend, who can save you now?*

"How did he—why were you with him?"

"I was on the sunporch and he came to the window." She dove into the soup, bowl to her mouth. When it was empty, she wrapped the blankets around herself.

I took the bowl. "Ben came to the window? And then?"

"He asked if I'd like to go up to his camp. Maybe it could help me.

He said he felt better there. So I said yes." When my house couldn't help her, he'd offered his own.

"Why didn't you tell your mother?"

"He said not to. He said the camp had to be secret. That's how it works."

"I see." I sat at her feet, my legs weak.

"Ben didn't do anything wrong, Miss Renner. Don't think that."

"He took you from home, in the cold."

"He carried me the whole way in this jacket. He made a big fire and gave me tea from roots. He had me touch his house."

"He thought it could heal you?" My stomach knotted more tightly with each revelation.

"Yes. He said voices told him to."

"What else about the voices?"

"Nothing. He said he did a bad thing once in Cuba and now he wanted to do a good thing. We're alike, you know. My sickness comes and goes. His voices come and go. He said fresh air helps. That could be right, don't you think?"

"I suppose so."

"And look, the fever's gone. Feel my forehead." She was right. The fever had gone. "Ben's a little strange, but he's nice," she said dreamily. "Maybe he can visit me sometime."

"Maybe." *No, he'll never visit you, ever.* "Where is he now?"

"I don't know. He brought me here, and then I looked around and he was gone."

"Yes. He does that."

"I'm so tired now." Her head dropped into blanket folds; her eyelids fluttered down. Whatever I thought, whatever I felt or feared, I had to get her home. Of course I had no telephone. I decided to keep her wrapped in blankets, sit her on the old bicycle Jim had given me, and walk her to the Allens' house, which was closer than her own. The snow had stopped. Moonlight slicked the road.

The rest happened quickly, like the sudden end of a one-reeler. Mr. Allen called the judge, who came with Mrs. Ashton, their Keystone roaring over frozen ruts. "Ben didn't hurt her," I repeated as Susanna was checked for injuries and peppered with questions she was too drowsy to answer. "He only meant to—"

"Kidnap her," the judge snapped. "And might do it again." He wrapped Susanna in a fresh blanket, putting mine aside.

Susanna peeked around him. "Thank you for the soup, Miss Renner."

"Sleep now, darling," her mother said. "We're taking you home."

"I'm calling Sheriff Wilkes," the judge told Mr. Allen. "We'll start at eight o'clock tomorrow to finish the job." *Finish the job.*

"Good idea."

When the Keystone pulled away, Mr. Allen hoisted my bicycle into the back of his truck and drove me home. "It'll be a miracle if the whole town doesn't get pneumonia after a day like this," he said. "You make a good fire and rest, Miss Renner. They don't need you at the church. Stay home."

"Ben only meant to help. And Susanna wasn't hurt. You saw her. She even looks better. There's no fever."

"That won't matter to the judge," Mr. Allen warned. I nodded bleakly. "And frankly, if it was my little girl, it wouldn't matter to me, either. But she's safe now. That's the important thing."

I stayed inside until Mr. Allen's truck rounded the bend and disappeared. *Finish the job* roared in my head. Jim Burnett once said that in Judge Ashton's courtroom, even the innocent blurted out confessions. What Ben did was foolish, even crazy, but the judge would surely impute malice. Then "justice" would trample a fragile and innocent soul.

I rode my bicycle to Ben's shack behind the grocery. It had been searched, of course. Muddy pawprints and footprints covered the floor, which was strewn with his few possessions: my sketch of Havana, a few penny postcards of Cuba, cheap prints of woodland scenes, a cup, plate, fork, cans of beans, bags of roots, a sack of coffee, and a cracked vase with dried flowers. If I left a note, it would be found. I rode home. His camp could be anywhere. How could I find it in the dark when dogs and search teams had failed? But they'd find it soon. The judge would wrest from Susanna enough sense of distance and direction to narrow their search. My only hope was that Ben would come to my house and I could persuade him to leave Galway by some secret route. I waited all night. He never came.

At seven thirty, I was in the church, the only woman in a murmuring crowd of weary men. All had heard of Susanna's safe return, but the news only enraged them.

"Ben's got to be close, we'll get him."

"That little girl's lucky to be alive."

"Don't need his type in Galway."

Nobody acknowledged my presence. Was I invisible? Had Ben felt like this? Had this, in his tangled mind, prompted his spying? Did he assume that he'd be as unnoticed in the brush around houses as he was on the streets?

At eight precisely, the judge entered with Sheriff Wilkes, cutting through the now-silent crowd. At the front of the church, he spoke briefly to Wilkes and then faced the men. Some stepped back slightly, straightening rough jackets. Then I knew with sickening certainty. They knew. Ben was dead. The judge had "finished the job" alone. I wanted to leave this place and mourn my friend alone, but I owed Ben to hear his end, to walk his last steps with him.

"Wilkes, tell them what happened," the judge said. "I'm going home to my family." We watched him leave by a side door. Then all eyes swiveled to the sheriff, whose customary stolid calm had deserted him. He shuffled his feet as my boys did before recitations and rubbed his hands. I looked out the window and listened.

"Just before dawn, Judge Ashton called and said he meant to take Red Gorge Road and look for Ben. I asked him to wait for me, but he said it was his right to go." A murmur of assent ruffled through the crowd. "He did find Ben. He was twitching again, walking along and talking like there was somebody beside him, looking rough, as if he'd slept outside. What the judge testified in my office just now is that he stopped the car and told Ben he'd have to come in for questioning. They were on the bridge at that time."

"What did Ben say, Sheriff?" one of the men called out.

"He was rattling on about Cuba, not making sense. The judge tried to get him in the car, but he ran away. The judge ran after him, but Ben climbed over the railing and jumped. You all know that bridge."

We did. Red Gorge Bridge arched fifty feet over the Monongahela River, now swollen with icy water tumbling through boulders. Any fall would be fatal. Ben's body, once recovered, would be too battered for signs of what happened before his fall. No, it was no fall. He was pushed.

Didn't everyone know the judge had lied? Ben was terrified of heights. Why would he jump or even look down off the bridge? But there were no witnesses. I imagined the men's thoughts: *I'd do the same if it was my daughter.*

Hot and breathless, I squirreled through the crowd and out the door to the icy steps. I pictured Ben hungry, cold, confused, and frightened of the judge, pulled toward the black car. His voices roar. The judge is a big man. How can Ben resist? He hears crashing water. He's dragged to the railing. He sees distant, jagged rocks. A struggle, a lift and push.

Ben falls. His screams echo down the gorge. Then silence. The judge drives away. The job is finished.

If I hadn't saved Ben, could I at least save the truth? He meant to help Susanna when everyone else failed, when my house failed, when he feared a specialist would fail. Surely some would believe his innocence and the facts of his death. The church door opened and Jim Burnett emerged, hands jabbed in his pockets, walking grimly past me. I ran to catch him. "Ben never jumped," I panted.

"I know."

"He didn't hurt her."

"I know. I've seen him with my Alice."

"So we have to do something. Judge Ashton is just—"

Jim stopped walking, speaking softly. "Hazel, you can't judge the judge. And he owns half the town."

"But—"

"What do you expect? That someone will testify against him? There were no witnesses. Why would people listen to you? Or do you think Judge Ashton will confess?"

Deep cold settled in my stomach. "Ben was a good man," I said finally. "He just wanted to help."

"He was. I don't know what's happening in this town anymore." He looked at his watch. "But it's time to open the store. Go home, Hazel, and get some rest." Be out of sight now, he must have meant. Don't remind people of what they were being asked to forget: that an innocent man had died.

I trudged home, boots crunching, remembering evenings with Ben on my porch, his stories and woodland gifts, how he watched seekers come to my house, stand in lines, pry off chips of paint, or help themselves to my kitchen when I was gone. He watched Susanna. He ached for a little girl in Havana. He wanted to help Susanna and me, perhaps. For this he lost his life. If I'd helped Susanna, Ben would be here. If I'd helped nobody at all, Ben would be here. If I'd never asked for a blue house, Ben would be here.

In the blistering cold, I considered my balance of help and hurt in Galway. It swayed against me. A few healings. But more who'd gone away uncured. Jealousy had caused the Burnetts to lose friends. Yes, some children had been excited by lessons and came eagerly to the school, but now so much tainted me. "Are you a witch?" Lydia had asked. If not a witch, I was surely dangerous. See what happened to Ben after spending time at my blue house?

How long before a small town's great wrath turned against me? There'd be no need for Red Gorge. There are many ways to expel a stranger. Stares can rake the skin. Talk at home can poison children against their teacher, making some give up a long trek to school. The dutiful would endure lessons, waiting out the days until June. I'd be just another Miss Clay. For whose sake should I stay here?

We had the Christmas pageant. Lacking rehearsal time, many players missed or fumbled their lines. Fathers who had spent long hours on search teams coughed and wheezed. After polite applause, parents hurried their children home, each with the portrait I'd finished. "Merry Christmas, Miss Renner. Thank you for the picture," they said dutifully. In the tense and wary air, nothing felt like Christmas.

THE NEXT MORNING I was packing when Jim and Ellen Burnett knocked on my door. "We wanted to see you before Henry McFee gets here," Jim said.

"About this?" I showed them my letter of resignation. I wouldn't be back after Christmas. "Isn't that what Henry's coming to say, that Galway needs a different teacher?"

"Yes," Jim admitted. "The school board met after the pageant. Ellen and I are sick about this. You were the best teacher we ever had. I'm on the board, but they voted against me. They felt it would be 'better' if you left." He set an envelope on the table. "This is the rest of your year's pay. It's from us and Charlie and Emma's parents. We want you to have it. Ellen and I will never forget what you did for our Alice."

"And please," said Ellen, "don't think too much about the troubles here this fall or about Ben. It's over. He's at peace."

I nearly cried for their kindness after the terror of these days. I took the envelope. "Thank you, and please thank the others for me. Who'll teach now?"

"The pastor's niece just got her certificate. She'll come after Christmas. If you teach someplace else, we'll be happy to recommend you."

"I'm not sure I can teach right now." I poured coffee. We spoke a little about Alice's future and even shared a few stories about Ben.

"Write to us," Ellen said. "And Alice wants to write to you." I gave them my parents' address and said I'd let them know my plans. When they left, winter silence wrapped my house.

When Henry took me to the train the next morning, we passed men carrying crowbars and sledgehammers. I asked where they were going. Henry coughed. "The new teacher will board with the pastor."

"I see." My blue house didn't serve Galway anymore. People would see it and think of their unhealed pains, of a young girl stolen, and a troubled soul dead in Red Gorge. I imagined stories about me and my house winding through the town, whispered as warning, embellished, or twisted to suit the teller: a teacher who once had a healing gift and lost it. "What happened to her?" strangers might ask. "She went back to the city," someone will say.

CHAPTER 8

*Looking for Margit*

Where does one go when dreams turn sour and promises become pain? Of course I went home, if only to gather strength for leaving again. But if someone on that train had asked who I was, I wouldn't have known how to answer. Healer, fake, teacher, witch? One who came to a peaceful town and found no peace? Had Margit done the same?

Did I even fit in Pittsburgh? What did our quiet flat know of frightened children, bloodhounds, bodies smashed on rocks, or houses torn down? It was Christmastime. My mother would have made her festive cookies: macaroons, cinnamon stars, *butterplätzchen*, ginger-rich *lebkuchen*, and anise-spiced *pfeffernüsse*. Rich and heavy loaves of *Christstollen* would be ripening for friends and fortunate customers. On Christmas Eve, we'd walk to midnight service, lit with candles and sacred with ancient story. We'd pass the kiss of peace and pray for peace in our Fatherland.

Why should I poison these solemn days with my story, or churn faithful hearts with what I'd done and the black unknowing of what lay before me? My father would already be anguished for the terrible war

losses this fall. Nobody dared hope that the magical, spontaneous soldiers' Christmas Eve "armistice" of 1914 would be repeated this year;
there would be no singing of "Silent Night" across No Man's Land,
each side in its own tongue, no soldiers climbing out of the trenches to
share photographs of home, cigarettes, wine, and chocolates with men
who would be enemies in the morning but *that* night were comrades.

No, I'd wait until after the New Year to confess what I'd done in
Galway. Perhaps by then I'd know where I must go next to repay the
damage done by pride and ignorant innocence.

"We're so glad they painted your house, Hazel," my mother said as
we sat at the familiar table, waiting for my father to close the store.
"That shows they respect you, doesn't it?"

"Yes, I suppose so." I swerved our talk to the schoolchildren: our
pageant, Alice's grave manner and clever mind, how Charlie's eyes
flashed when he solved a difficult problem in fractions.

She spoke of war. "Your father says poor Bulgaria is surrounded by
Allies. He worries about every town in Germany. And I worry about
him. How much sorrow can one man take? I hope you can distract him."

"I hope so, too." Once it seemed I held the pain of Galway, but that
was a little town. My father carried the weight of millions.

"Could you do your magic on my shoulder, Hazel? The cold makes
it worse." She couldn't know the pain of this request or the desperate hope for one last tremor of healing. I tried. Nothing. She grimaced
when I moved her awkwardly. So I'd even lost the solace of massage.

"What does Dr. Edson say?"

"That I might feel better in the spring. Meanwhile, just be patient."

Patience, yes. Could I have been more patient, not pushing for a blue
house, not hurrying to "fix" the scratching and twitching that may have
somehow calmed Ben's voices? Why hadn't I sought the help of those
whose true work was healing? Rev. Collins and Dr. Bentley were rooted

deeply in the town. I was an outsider. "Don't tell people how to raise their children," Jim had warned. Visit. Listen. Let parents *choose* to trust me with their children. Suppose I'd been as patient with my house?

My mother stopped these fruitless cogitations. "Never mind, Hazel. Just sit with me. It's good to have you home." I choked back a sob. She spun around to grip my hands. "Hazel! What's wrong? Tell me."

"I can't. I'll tell you after Christmas. Please, don't ask me now."

She wouldn't ask, but what pain this waiting must cost her. At last my father came upstairs. I remember that first home meal, the clean warmth of potatoes, tang of onions, and savor of sausage. My father spoke of war contracts and workers from the South flooding into Pittsburgh, where making bullets paid far more than farming, mining, or any work of peace.

The next days passed quietly. I helped in the store, shopped with my mother, and visited Luisa, saying little about my work or plans. Early on Christmas Eve, my family exchanged gifts: my drawings of Galway, a fine hand-turned wooden bowl made by Horace's father, jars of my fruit preserves and apple butter. They gave me a muffler and mittens, a plaid woolen dress, an illustrated history of European art, and a newly hammered tin of a forest scene titled "A Quiet Kingdom."

Then, as always, we walked to the midnight service, afterward milling on the sidewalk, exchanging greetings and Christmas plans in that soupy mix of German and English that Saturday school teachers dismissed as "Germish." But it was familiar and comforting, nothing one would hear in Galway. Friends asked about my first months away. Did I still love teaching? Did I "fit" in a small town? Was I happy to be home for the holidays? Yes, I said to every question. Yes, of course.

Long past midnight, I slipped between freshly ironed sheets in my spotless room and watched a full moon dig through Pittsburgh's eternal clouds. Sleeping lightly, I was awakened before dawn by thuds, a smash, a ruffle of laughter, and running feet on the sidewalk below. I dressed and slipped downstairs.

Broken eggs smeared our big store window facing the street. Plastered to the glass was a poster of a great foot poised over a running man in a spiked helmet. "Stamp out the Hun!" red letters screamed. "Kraut!" was scrawled below the new sign: "John Renner, Quality Hardware." An American name for an American store, but not American enough. A small window was broken. Were we to note the "courtesy" of sparing the big one? Or was this a warning: "Next time we'll do worse." If my father did what? Stop being who he was? Stop coming from his country?

I ran upstairs for a sponge, bucket, and broom. My father was in the kitchen. "Again?" he whispered.

"Yes."

He pulled on his jacket and followed me to the street. We washed away the egg and soap, swept up shards, and covered the hole with flattened cardboard. "How many times has this happened?"

"Several. But they never broke glass before." His letters hadn't mentioned vandalism, just as mine never mentioned my troubles. "Don't tell your mother."

"Again, Hazel? On Christmas Day?" my mother whispered as I set out breakfast plates and my father shaved. I nodded. "Poor man. Don't tell him I know." Nor did he know of hisses she received on the street or in streetcars: "Kraut, Kraut, Cabbagehead." Turning quickly, she'd see only a bland face or pair of snickering children. Once she'd been pushed and fell on an icy sidewalk, scattering her groceries.

We all kept our secrets and tried to be jolly for Christmas dinner with Uncle Willy and Tante Elise. My mother diverted talk of Galway for my sake, and my father changed the subject when Uncle Willy mentioned vandalism of a nearby German store. So we spoke of new contracts in Pittsburgh, the difficulty of supplying troops on every side of Germany, and the terrible efficiency of the British blockade. The men took out their pipes. "Finally we got Serbia," Uncle Willy said. "And we'll get Montenegro and Gallipoli soon."

"Small places," my father muttered into his stein. "And our men are tired. England has an empire to draw from. When Americans come in, they'll be fresh."

"And we'll be the enemy. I'm so afraid of that," said Tante Elise.

"You don't *have* to stay in Pittsburgh," I began, but stopped as four startled faces turned to mine. Their homeland gone, of course they'd stay in this city that first received them. They'd dig down like soldiers in trenches and endure. A memory from a year ago came bounding back. I'd taken a streetcar to the Carnegie Institute and sat near two sleekly dressed young couples.

"Like I'm telling you, Hank," said one man, "a few divisions of Yanks could finish the job."

"You bet. Whip those Krauts to Kingdom Come. Forget trenches. Burn the cities down like General Sherman did in Georgia. Then bomb the rest to smithereens."

I had to speak: "It's German *civilians* who'd suffer—children, women, old people."

The second man turned to me. "Once the Kaiser surrenders, all the little Krauts will be safe."

The red-cheeked girl beamed at him: "You're right, Lewis. It's the German *people's* fault, my daddy says. They shouldn't have voted for the Kaiser if they didn't want war." Useless to explain that Kaiser Wilhelm wasn't elected. I got off before my stop. "Bye-bye, fräulein," voices called. "Give Wilhelm our regards."

If America joined the war, soon Hank, Lewis, and their prim companions would have fallen friends and family to avenge. Then in every streetcar, store, and workplace, adults would play out the bitter games of our empty lot. Tante Elise was right that we'd be enemies, watched, feared, and unwelcome. In Galway, I was a witch. Where could I simply be Hazel?

In the days after Christmas I wanted only deep tunnels of sleep without memory, but had nightmares instead. Dream classrooms hosted pageants of witch trials. I drifted between benches of moaning, bloody children of war I couldn't help. My blue house was bombed. I walked out of Burnett's Grocery into a gauntlet of glaring faces. Ben appeared and disappeared in frozen forests. I was with him in Cuba, pushing men off cliffs. Walking by the sea together, we passed invalid girls wrapped in blankets, each small face a festering mass of warts.

In daytime, lines at shops were lines of seekers at my house, their silent faces asking: "Are you saving *it* for me?" Crossing any bridge in Pittsburgh, I imagined twitching Bens falling like rain. "When are you going back to work?" my mother asked when days passed after Christmas and I still hadn't spoken of return. I told her the holidays were longer in the country. She didn't press me.

Yet slowly, as roots begin to waken even under frozen earth, I was beginning to know what I must do next, where I had to go. Not Galway or any new, exotic place. Certainly nowhere in Europe now. I had to find where the strains of healing and hurt kinked together, where Hilde was made and how she became Hazel. I had to follow my bloodline back to Margit, in Dogwood.

On Epiphany, January 6, when my parents' anxious, guarded glances at each other became unbearable, I told my story after dinner. Outside, snow fell fast, dampening the distant clang of factories and wail of freight trains carrying munitions east.

"All the houses in Galway are white, but I wanted mine blue," I began. They listened, my mother with her mending, my father with his pipe. I told them about John Foster, my night visitor, and how Ben painted my house. I'd written briefly of Ben before. I told them more. "Please believe me. It happened this way." I related how Henry and Agnes were apparently cured, Ben's scratching and Alice Burnett's fits stopped, and Edna's warty face transformed. I described the growing lines of seekers at my blue house, the chipped paint, and glaring, jealous eyes. My father put down his pipe; my mother's threaded needle rested in her lap. Their eyes widened. *Our daughter did this? Our Hazel?*

I explained how suspicions gathered as my tremors ceased and "witch" was voiced around me. Then the last, terrible week: Susanna gone and returned, Ben's fall, and the school board's vote against me. Crowbars pulling my house apart. Yes, I'd been "extraordinary." All the early signs of my healing touch were true in ways that none of us could imagine. Who could have seen the tangled consequences in a peaceful town? My mother reached across the table for my hand. Our windows rattled. The mystery brooded like another being in the flat, a stranger to us all.

My father cleared his throat. "Hazel, what you just told us is nothing we can understand. All I know is that it isn't your fault." My mother nodded.

Of course they'd say this. They loved me. They didn't want to think that with or without "fault," my coming to Galway had turned one wheel that turned another and finally killed a man in Red Gorge. They scrambled to crush mystery with practicality. I should speak with Pastor Peterson. No, I knew him too well. "Pray for understanding," he'd say. "Learn from the Gospels." But he'd never tell me how to do that, and he'd never, never believe me. I'd be a witch *and* a liar in his eyes.

Pittsburgh was full of jobs, my mother noted. I could help in the store. Or get a higher teaching certification. Did she realize how mined with dangers teaching was for me now?

"No. I need to go to Dogwood." Our kitchen clock ticked heavily as I tried to explain why I had to see where my story began. In a little town like Dogwood there could still be faint traces of Margit Brandt. I'd find them. And more: I'd learn why each new land, each chapter of her life defeated her or proved insufficient, why Heidelberg's ancient charms were as empty for her as Pittsburgh's booming growth was for me. I couldn't go forward without first going back. This much I knew, even if my parents couldn't follow the path of reason that brought me to this certainty.

"But you don't have to," my mother said. "You're nothing like my sister Margit." Except that she had voiced exactly this to Tante Elise.

"It's like—" I strained for higher authority. "Like Martin Luther said: 'Here I stand. I can do no other.' I *have* to go."

"For how long? A few days?"

"I don't know." And truly, I didn't. I saw myself in Dogwood, at a train station, on the street. I didn't see seasons pass. I didn't see where I'd live. I imagined myself asking strangers about Margit. "I might stay awhile. I have some money of my own." I explained the Burnetts' gift. "I could find a job."

"Not teaching."

"No, not now."

My father sighed. "Well then, it's time to give her Margit's letters." He pushed back his chair and stood up. Slowly, as if he'd rehearsed this walk a thousand times, he went to their room and returned with a small, flat box. "They won't make you happy. But you'll learn something about her." It was past midnight. "We're all tired, Hazel. Let's go to bed. We'll be here in the morning." Yes, they were my solid ground that now was not enough to hold me.

I TOOK THE box to my room. No letter was more than a page, written large in a childish hand. "New Jersey is so dull," one declared. "Farms, woods, fields, and boring little towns. Worse than Bavaria." Other letters complained that "He"—I assumed her employer—was demanding and hard to please. Only days off brought pleasure. Men's names sprinkled the pages: Chester, Pat, Bert, Arthur, Emil, Jack. They took her to Atlantic City and dance halls in New York City, all "great fun." Some letters ended: "How is the child?" Nothing else about me. No regrets, concerns, or great curiosity. No plans to visit Pittsburgh. The last announced: "I'm going to New York! Jack found me a job!"

A large envelope was addressed in a different hand, with a note inside: "These were found in Margit's room." I set the note aside and gasped at a stack of pen and pencil sketches: young men with eager eyes, a stone archway, and a woodland path. In one, a small child is seen from behind walking past rosebushes. Me? The figure could be any child or simply there to balance the scene. Margit struggled with perspective, but her lines revealed the weight of stone, the lightness of petals, and the warmth of a young face. I'd never heard that she drew. Perhaps this seemed too close a link to me. Perhaps it was her secret pleasure, for she hadn't mailed the sketches. They'd been sent after her death by someone who wanted no trace of her left behind.

I meant to leave for Dogwood right away, but sickness kept me home. Like everyone in Pittsburgh, I'd had a mild cough all my life. It was too common a condition to note, like sweating in the tropics. After a month in Galway, when I could speak whole conversations without disturbance, I'd thought this fact was extraordinary.

The night after telling my story, a heaving, hacking cough left me panting, my chest aching and throat raw, as if torn by brambles. Had the clean country air weakened me? Or, I thought wildly, was this the consequence of saying what should not have been said? In any case, within a day, I could barely speak. "Don't try," my mother said, producing a pad and pencil to express my needs that grew steadily simpler: water, broth, blanket.

Nothing helped, not soups, teas, or steaming pots of herb infusions I breathed at the kitchen table, my head under a Turkish towel. Dr. Edson didn't strain my voice with questions, only listened to my chest and said to raise a hand when his gentle probing brought on pain. Then he cradled his trusty stethoscope and diagnosed bronchitis that must run its course. I'd also cracked my breastbone with coughing, which would take time to heal.

"It hurts." I scribbled.

"I'm sorry, Hazel, but there's no magic cure. Just rest and good hot broth." If Dr. Edson noted how we all stiffened at "magic," he gave no sign. "You must be patient. Once the wet cough stops, you'll have to stay home another week to be completely cured. Otherwise you'll infect others. You don't want that, do you?" I moved an aching head from side to side. No, I wouldn't bring infection to another place.

My sickness dragged on and on. At least my parents were healthy. But because of me, they couldn't receive friends in our flat. My mother shopped, then hurried home. "I'm sorry," I wrote on my pad. "Tante Elise?"

"I can visit her. The problem is, Elise's cakes are much too heavy." She talked about baking, which always gave her pleasure. For her sake, I scribbled questions: *Why? How much? How long?* There was little else I could do. Even reading was exhausting. Coughing jarred my hand too much for drawing. Dr. Edson had prescribed five circuits of my room daily to keep my legs from weakening. Even this was difficult. Sickness was another land unimagined by the strong and healthy; now I knew how seekers at my blue house rankled when others whose pain seemed insignificant were rewarded with a miracle.

It was early March before Dr. Edson declared that we could safely have guests at home. Finally recovering my strength, I helped my mother disinfect every surface with Lysol. We washed curtains and linens, capturing the rare, bright blue day to throw open windows, beat dust from cushions, and boil, dry, iron, and fold away the cloth squares I'd used for coughing. To celebrate, we invited Uncle Willy and Tante Elise for Sunday lunch. Since I said nothing of the Galway troubles, everything about my Dogwood plans was inexplicable.

"You'll teach?" Tante Elise asked.

"No. Not now."

"But you'll work?"

"I hope so."

"This is because of Margit? You do know that some things are better not examined."

"She's going," my father declared. "There's nothing more to discuss. As Martin Luther would say: There she stands; she can do no other."

Tante Elise bristled at the secular use of her hero. "Well then," Uncle Willy soothed, "we won't discuss it."

In the depth of my sickness, closed in my room, I'd been removed from my father's brooding fixations on the war. He'd just bought cases of nails from a new supplier. "If every nail was a man," he announced, "they wouldn't make a week's casualties at Verdun. They say the battle could last for months." British conscription had swelled the Allied ranks. "Where will *our* new soldiers come from? Already every healthy man is in uniform. Will we start taking little boys and old men? How much more blood can we lose?" My mother pressed his arm as if to draw away pain. Where was *her* blue house?

"Maybe the best thing *would be* for America to join," said Tante Elise. "Just to end things quickly."

"All for an archduke," Uncle Willy said, echoing my students.

"It's a beautiful day," my mother announced. "Let's take a walk to celebrate Hazel getting better." We did that. Emboldened by the sparkling air, we walked up to Shadyside to enjoy the views and luxurious distance from war plants. After weeks in my room, every color, every new shape and vista was a gift. The moist earth revealed by melting snow promised springtime. The men walked together, smoking their pipes. Tante Elise, my mother, and I linked arms. These were my people, and this was my city, for all its difficulties. If only I could stay. If only I weren't like Margit, drawn away by longing for something *different* or *other* or *more*. Yet if I didn't find myself, then any other place on earth, any great city, flowered paradise, or exotic Eastern land would soon prove false to me and I to that place.

At breakfast, my mother picked at the crust of her rye bread. "It's a long way to New Jersey. What should I make you for the train?"

I gripped the chapped hand. "*Lebkuchen* with hazelnuts. I'll help." We baked, speaking of only cookies, cinnamon buns, and strudel. She brushed flour from my face. I tied her apron when it loosened.

"Hazel," she said quietly. "In her own way, Margit must have loved you. She just didn't want to be a mother."

"And you did."

"Yes. I did, very much." We stood close together, shaping cookies. From the store below came the *ping-ping-ping* of my father's hammer. Her face clouded. "He spends so much time on those tins now." She put the *lebkuchen* in the oven and sat beside me. "When peace comes," she said dreamily, "whoever wins, I'll make cookies for the neighborhood. Then we'll close the store for a week and borrow an automobile." She looked out the window. "We'll drive until the sky is blue. Your father will be happy like before. Won't it be wonderful, Hazel?"

I took her hand. "Yes, it will."

The night before I left for Dogwood, I crept barefoot to their bedroom door as I'd done so often as a child, listening to voices filtered through oak. "It's so far," my mother was saying. "The other side of Pennsylvania."

"Katarina, we came from the other side of the ocean."

"But we had each other. She has nobody."

"You know, we *could* have stayed in Heidelberg. It's more beautiful than Pittsburgh. All our people were there, and I had work. Why did we come here?"

"Because—we wanted to. We were young. We wanted a place of our own."

"Exactly, we wanted to. Hazel's young. She wants a place of her own. At least she'll be safe." The bed creaked. "There's no bombing in New Jersey."

"Oh, Johannes, don't think about the war. It only makes you sick. Come, come close."

I slipped back to my room, where my suitcase stood in a patch of moonlight. I had some money, clothes to be decently dressed for work if I found it, a few drawings, and three of my father's tins. Besides these things, I'd packed the hope to untangle the lines of hurt and healing that ran through Margit and into me.

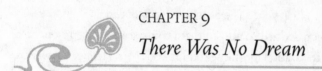

A stubby conductor recommended a boardinghouse in Dogwood and warned me when the stop was coming. The town was larger than Galway, a ruffle of shops and homes set in modest hills. I'd expected worse from Margit's description. The roads were freshly paved; a new brick school and public library stood near the station. Well-dressed townspeople bustled by. Newsboys hawked headlines of baseball, state scandals, and local taxes. Nothing here spoke of war. Windows sparkled. The air was sweet and clear. Nobody looked at me oddly. Perhaps these people were accustomed to strangers. Why couldn't Margit have been happy here?

As I soon discovered, the owner of the boardinghouse was the train conductor's sister, but Twin Oaks was clean, comfortable, and modestly priced. A brisk young Italian maid who spoke bits of English showed me to a room. She couldn't have been in Dogwood long; she'd know nothing about Margit.

I washed my face and hands, brushed travel dust from my clothes, and took a walk down Main Street. A sign on Henderson's Drug Store announced its founding in 1895. The tinted photograph in the window showed a handsome, beaming man and guarded young woman framed by bunting on what was surely opening day. Inside, an older version of this woman, more rounded and at ease, was busy dusting shelves.

"Mrs. Henderson?"

"Yes. May I help you?" The dusting never stopped.

My mission seemed so absurd that I could scarcely keep from bolting back to the station for the next train west. Mrs. Henderson waited, dusting more slowly as I composed myself to ask: "I'm wondering if you knew a Margit Brandt. She lived in Dogwood about twenty years ago." The puffed face hardened.

"Yes, I knew her. Why?" Mrs. Henderson glanced into the back room, where a still-handsome gray-haired man stocking shelves must be the proud owner in the photograph. Perhaps his was also one of the flitting names in Margit's letters. Perhaps she caused Mrs. Henderson's strained and wary look in the photograph.

"Margit had a child named Hilde. My name is Hazel Renner now, but I was that child." The duster stopped as she studied my face and body. I added quickly: "My father was from Germany, someone she worked with."

Mrs. Henderson's voice dropped to a whisper. "Why did you come here? Everything's good now." Stepping back, I bumped a table. Glass rattled wildly. Could trouble start so soon?

"I just wanted to learn a little more about my mother, that's all."

"Like what?"

"Well, she went to New York. Do you know why?"

"No. She left and nobody heard from her again." *Good riddance,* the tone said. "She probably didn't like the city. She didn't like anything for long. She was beautiful and charming, but she made trouble for other people."

"I'm sorry."

She studied me again, perhaps gauging how much of Margit's bad blood had passed on. Tante Elise could be right that some things are better left unexamined. I was about to leave when Mrs. Henderson put aside the duster. "Well, it wasn't your fault how she was. We heard Margit gave you away."

"Yes, to her sister and her husband. They raised me in Pittsburgh."

"You were a nice little girl," she conceded, straightening a pyramid of bath salts. "Anna was heartbroken when you left. I'm sorry, Miss Renner, I shouldn't talk badly about your mother. But it looks like you found a good home."

"I did. Who's Anna?"

"She worked with Margit at the castle."

I jumped. *Men in scarlet. A banquet hall.*

"What castle?"

"Don't you know?" Did every little New Jersey town have a castle? "Baron Georg von Richthofen owns it. We just call him Baron. It doesn't sound so German."

"Why would a baron come to Dogwood?"

Mrs. Henderson bristled. "Why not? It's beautiful."

"Yes, I'm sure, but why build a castle?"

She shrugged. "He wanted to and could. They say he had family troubles back there. He pays a lot of salaries in town, one way or the other. And better a castle than a dirty factory, right?"

"I agree, but Margit didn't like living in a castle?"

"Not if she had to clean it. Or act decent with the help." The swath of damage had been wide. Where could reparations begin?

"Ginny, look at this tonic." I spun to face Mr. Henderson. "Oh, excuse me, miss." The eyes widened.

"This is Hazel Renner," I heard behind me. "She was Hilde Brandt. *Her* daughter."

"Just visiting," I said quickly.

"Well, enjoy your visit, Miss Renner." He seemed about to say more, but didn't, moving toward his wife and holding out a blue bottle. "Did we order this tonic?"

I backed away. "Thank you for your help, Mrs. Henderson. Could you just tell me where the castle is?"

"Walk north on Main. When you see towers on your right, take the next street to a big iron gate."

"Thank you."

"Good-bye, Miss Renner," they chorused, huddled tightly over the bottle. As I hurried north, older men passing on the sidewalks glanced at me. Did my face recall former pleasures, pains, or broken promises? Margit was my age when she trounced Dogwood's peace. She'd had me carelessly and thrown me away as she threw away men like broken toys. Was there so much difference between us? Many in Galway might be thinking now: *Good riddance to that woman.* I'd been extraordinary as was Margit, in her way. Now my healing course was to become ordinary. How strange that my journey would begin in a castle.

Even forewarned, I gasped at the sight of turreted stone towers after blocks of tidy shops and wooden houses. I walked faster, finally reaching an enormous width of wrought iron. Elaborately fretted letters spelled out *Mein Königsberg*. My Königsberg. Surely this was the castle gate, yet the juncture of two halves was barely visible. Did the inmates never leave? Margit must have felt imprisoned. I peered down a drive framed by meticulously clipped evergreens to an arched stone entryway. The castle was gracefully proportioned, with decks of high, diamond-paned windows. Pittsburgh boasted mansions built by steel, coal, and railroad barons whose gaudy excess announced: "See what new money buys!" But these walls could have stood for centuries. A Grimm Brothers' tale might be set here. Yet, wasn't the entry arch familiar? Yes, it was in Margit's sketches, and this cobbled drive as well, framed by these trees, much smaller when she drew them.

My face was pressed to the gate when a wolf bounded at me, snarling. I jumped back, fell, and scrambled to my feet again. Such a beast might crack iron bars like old bread. A man's voice shouted: "Lilli, down. Sit!" As if bewitched, it sat, great eyes pinning me in place. The man appeared from between the evergreens, an ordinary-seeming American, despite his astonishing powers. He had neat work clothes, an open, ruddy face, and tweed cap barely restraining black curls. Just a man. "Do you have business at Mein Königsberg, miss?" Anyone could be cordial with a tamed wolf at his feet.

"I'm looking for—" What, exactly, was I looking for? "My name is Hazel Renner. I live in Pittsburgh. I came here because my mother, Margit Brandt—"

The wide face broke open, beaming. "Hilde! Sorry, *Hazel*. You came back! How wonderful." He fumbled with the lock. "Do you remember me? I'm Tom Jamison. I was ten when you left. I carried you around."

"In a garden?"

"Yes, yes, in the rose garden and here, on this path."

"I'm sorry. I only remember being carried."

"Never mind. It was a long time ago. But come in, come in." The great gate opened wide enough for a carriage. I didn't move.

"The wolf," I reminded him.

"The— Oh, you mean Lilli? She's a German shepherd. You've never seen one? It's a new breed of working dog," he explained proudly. "There *is* a bit of wolf bred in for strength and intelligence. They're wonderful animals. Look: Lilli. Friend. Up." She scrambled to her feet, long tail wagging. "Hazel, come closer and hold out your hand.

She's perfectly tame." Under his spell, I inched forward. The tail never stopped as she sniffed me solemnly. "You can pet her. Steady, Lilli." She froze. My palm hovered over the head. When it didn't flinch, I touched the dark velvet between silky ears with my fingertips and moved down the coarser pelt of neck, marveling at my courage. "See? She likes you."

"How do you know?"

"From her stance. Don't you have a dog?"

"No. I never even touched one before."

"You never— Really? Ever? Well, that's so—*extraordinary*." Tom's somber shock, the great tail waving like a flag, my hand half hidden in fur, all this made us laugh. Suddenly, incredibly, I was at ease with this man and his wolf-dog. "So you live in Pittsburgh?"

"Yes, and you live in a castle?"

"I'm the head gardener, driver, carpenter, and picture framer. The baron keeps me busy."

"You were born here?"

"No. I wasn't." The answer seemed to guard a private pain, a door shut tight. He threw a bent stick into a pile of branches. "Fetch, Lilli." She leapt away and began diligently searching the pile. "She'll find it. Come, I'll show you the rose garden, although nothing's blooming now, of course." Lilli bounded back with the same bent stick. "Good girl. Drop it." She did. "Heel." She flanked him, precisely matching her pace with his. As we walked, I briefly explained how I'd discovered that my "parents" were in fact my aunt and uncle and described my plan to learn what I could of Margit. "And then get a job until the war ends. After that, I'll go to Paris," I finished with a flourish. There: a plan fit for a castle. Did it sound in any way credible?

"Of course." In those two syllables, a wedge of warmth slipped through the late winter chill. "So here we are: rose garden, much bigger now than when you left. Over there, the kitchen garden, cutting garden, orchard, and meadow. You should see them in springtime." I had, in Margit's sketches.

And inside, would I find the mirrors, banquet hall, and men in scarlet, proof that my memories were no dreams? Could I also find here some redeeming quality of my mother? We reached the grand entry, but now Tom stopped, looked up to a tightly curtained window, and shook his head. "The baron's having one of his headaches. They last for days. He stays in the dark and receives nobody. I'm sorry, Hazel, but I can't take you inside without his permission." He truly seemed sorry.

"Is there an Anna who works here?"

"Yes, the cook, but it's her day off."

"I see." So close, and now shut off. I wanted to see the mirrored halls *today*.

"I was just a child then, but I can tell you a little," Tom offered.

"Mrs. Henderson didn't have a good opinion of Margit Brandt."

"No, I don't imagine she would."

"Tell me about my father." Was his memory as dark and distasteful?

"His name was Emil." One of the names in her letters. One of many. "He had your eyes and hair. He was the baron's master cabinetmaker, a genius with wood. I was just a kid, but he taught me about working with grains, joining, carving, and finishing each kind of wood." Tom glanced at me. "That's not what you want to know, is it? You want to know about Emil and Margit?"

"Yes."

"I think they were happy at first. I know the baron was annoyed at how much time they spent together. Then they had a fight, and Emil left Dogwood before you were born."

"He didn't come back or write?"

"No."

Not to see or ask about me or leave me any trace of him. "Do you know where he went, or if he's alive?"

"No, I'm sorry. I don't."

"And my mother?"

"Just that she died in New York. Maybe the baron knows more." We were circling the castle.

"Tom, could you ask the baron if he'll see me now? Just for a few minutes. Or tomorrow, if he's feeling better."

"He'll say no, I'm afraid. These attacks can last for days."

"Tell him," I added recklessly, "that sometimes I can help headaches." The little ease I gave my father as a child, perhaps I could still do this. And perhaps—who knows—the touch might come back.

"He's tried every pill and powder and gone to the best doctors. But I'll ask. Stay here with Lilli." He disappeared through a doorway half hidden by ivy. I waited on a stone bench. Without orders from her master, Lilli wandered away. Breezes scuttled dry leaves across the lawn. Rosebushes bared their thorns. Cold seeped from the bench into my legs. If there was any good to be discovered about Margit, it would likely come from the baron. But if he wouldn't receive me now, why would he promise tomorrow? If I came back in a week, he could easily be having another attack. Or he could simply decline an interview.

Tom appeared, astonished. "He'll see you for ten minutes since you came so far. Speak softly and don't move much. Motion makes him ill. The room's very dark; he can't stand light."

"I understand."

Tom led me to the great front arch, three times my height, of thick wood braced in iron as if to keep out barbarian hordes. The handle was a finely rendered wolf head. When it was turned, the door swung open with the faintest whisper, revealing a paneled hall larger than our flat, circled by marble statues of Greek gods. So many. We could be in a museum. I stopped, frozen like a statue myself.

"This way, Hazel, he's waiting," Tom said, shepherding me up a lustrous grand stairway. "Emil made this. He turned the wood." My father? Each step was a marvel. Exquisitely carved vines circled the newels; every baluster invited a lingering touch. "On sunny days, the stained glass windows—"

"Make a rainbow light. I remember." My mother walked up and down these stairs. Perhaps she carried me. I stopped, tracing a vine. Tom cleared his throat slightly and I hurried on. We reached a wide hallway, paneled in wood and hung with tapestries. There was no sound but our footsteps.

"How many people live here?"

"Only three: Anna, the baron, and me. The gardeners and the inside help come from Dogwood. The housemaids work at night; they wear felt shoes and are to be very quiet. I used to think magic elves cleaned the castle. Quiet now. Here's the library." A leaping stag was carved into the door. "Emil's last project," Tom whispered. "The baron wanted another for his office, but Emil left before the wood was even ordered." So Margit made trouble even over doors. The stag was magnificent, artfully shaped in the swirling grain. A long neck swelled to sleek flanks and a perfect arch of rump. The antlers swept back and up, graceful and fierce. Touching them, I felt a velvet warmth. Had Emil won Margit with his art? Did she want the hand that worked this wonder? But even this art wasn't enough. As Mrs. Henderson said, nothing satisfied her for long.

Tom knocked softly, mouthed "good luck," and opened the door for me. I stepped into gloom. A Persian carpet silenced my tread, as if my body had lost all substance. In a shadow within shadows, I made out a tall, slender man in a wing chair with a cloth pressed against his eyes.

"Hazel Renner who was Hilde Brandt?" said a voice in heavily accented German.

"Yes, Baron von Richthofen."

"*Baron* is quite sufficient. Stand there. Please." He pointed to the palest slice of light leaking through nearly drawn curtains. The cloth must have moved, for I glimpsed the whites of his eyes as he regarded me top to toe. I stood still as a marble statue. "You want to know about Margit?" I could make out wide gold cuff links and a heavy ring.

"Yes, Baron."

The whites disappeared. "She was a lovely woman, even her detractors admitted. However, she had a difficult character and created problems. Do you, Miss Renner?" How to answer? "An unfair question, forgive me. You speak German?"

"Yes. Would you prefer—?"

"Not particularly. I find English more restful. The mind works strangely, does it not?"

"Yes." In the schoolyard once in Galway, three boys cornered a rabbit that sat motionless until I made them let it go. I was the rabbit now. Perhaps he sensed this.

"Would you take some wine?" His ring glittered toward a decanter and crystal goblets set on a nearby table. A lady never drinks alone, my mother said, but the query felt like a command.

"Some for you as well, Baron?"

"Now? No." As if this should be obvious. "And then sit please." So despite my mother, I poured a little red wine and took a chair some paces from his own. "So, the Renners raised you in Pittsburgh. They loved you and so forth."

"Yes." Had anyone ever loved this man "and so forth"?

"Good." He pressed the cloth to his eyes with a muffled groan.

"If you'd rather wait—"

"No, you're here now, and there's not much to say. My cook, Anna, was fond of you and was distressed when you didn't come back from New York. Margit said only that a sister had taken you. However, she quite carelessly left behind letters with this sister's address. I had contacts in Pittsburgh determine that your situation was satisfactory. Anna was relieved."

"I see." So we'd been watched. He seemed to feel this was his right.

"Your father's hardware store does well, I presume."

"It does, thank you."

"Pittsburgh is also doing well, selling arms to the Allies."

"To *both* sides."

"To both sides then."

In the few minutes I'd been granted, did we have to speak of war? "Emil—" I began, but the baron groaned. When I half rose, he held up an arresting hand.

"It will pass."

"Would you rather be alone?"

"No. At the moment you are—distracting." No way to answer this. "And German."

"Yes."

"So you may understand what Tom can't. I'm torn asunder by this war. My homeland bleeds. America has made me rich, given me a home. Yet I'm an enemy here. As you are, Miss Renner?" I nodded, thinking of broken glass at our store and mocking couples calling me *fräulein*. His forehead glistened. "When the last soldier lies rotting in a French field, who'll farm for Germany? Who'll paint, and write, and compose our music?" A white hand flicked toward bookcases and a grand piano looming in the corner. "Who'll be our new Hegel, Goethe, Bach, Wagner, or von Beethoven? Who?"

"I don't know, Baron."

"Rinse this for me. Please." He held out the flannel cloth. Coming closer to take it, I nearly gasped at my first clear sight of his face. Like Michelangelo's *David*, his beauty ensnared the eye. Only a master's hand could shape the smoothly arched brow over deep wide eyes, fine straight nose, square chin, lightly cleft, full and shapely mouth, and lush chestnut waves of hair faintly streaked with silver. He must have been stared at all his life. He cleared his throat. "Miss Renner, you must understand that a person's physiognomy, however appealing to the observer, is an artifact of nature, a confluence of heredity. If I were grotesquely deformed, would you not feign indifference to this fact?"

"Yes, of course." Chastened, I rinsed the cloth in cool water and wrung it out, trying to imagine an ordinary-appearing man approaching middle age, to think only of the pain he was enduring. "Baron, my father had headaches and sometimes I could ease them."

"You had the touch, as they say." Did he see me flinch? "You may try. Nothing else has helped. The pain is here." Elegantly manicured hands indicated his temples. Yes, the blue house was far away. I hesitated before touching his beauty, as I had before touching Edna's warty face. Then I took a long breath and began. No tremor ran down my arm, but I copied the steady, circling pressure that once helped my father. "Remarkably better." Relief and fear. What would he expect of me next? How long before I disappointed him? "No, don't stop. Distract me. Talk, but softly."

Of course I couldn't speak of Galway. "What should I talk about?"

"It doesn't matter." So I described how I discovered the secret of my birth. He said nothing but "Go on." I spoke of my father's anguish as the war continued, how he counted the dead and beat out his tins.

"This war will have its way with us. Water, please." I found a pitcher by the wine and poured him a glass. He drank and regarded me again. "You wanted to learn more about Margit Brandt."

"Yes."

"She was difficult, as I said. I would not have kept her so long if not for certain skills."

"Skills?"

"Laying out gardens, not the work, but the envisioning of them. She was quite unschooled in design but had a surprisingly fine eye for interiors and the placement of art. Her dalliances in town hardly concerned me, but the servants disliked her, and she distracted Emil, whose skill I needed."

"Then he left."

"Then he left, which was infuriating." What about his leaving Margit? Of no concern, apparently. "Emil was an artist in wood but jealous, quick to anger, and given to gambling. He left debts in town and work undone here. Your parents had gifts, Miss Renner, but their lives were careless. At first, Margit seemed softened by the prospect of motherhood." So she wanted me, or wanted a child at least. "However, the reality was less enticing. Your care largely fell to Anna."

"I see."

"Then Margit found another solution for you and one for herself in leaving Dogwood. As you have no doubt learned, she died soon after in New York."

"Tom said that you might know more."

"I don't. I only knew that she died because she'd given this as her last address."

"You didn't ask—"

He sighed. "Miss Renner, you are very young. One does not search out particulars of a departed employee whose service has been, on the whole, problematic." No, I supposed one does not. "I sent on to Pittsburgh some drawings she'd left here along with the news of her death. Your aunt and uncle, apparently, also chose not to investigate. Or couldn't. So the trail, as they say, is quite cold."

"I see."

"You saw her drawings, I presume, before this journey?"

"Yes."

"They showed talent, however raw and undisciplined, like much about her. I regret that this little story is so incomplete and in some ways tawdry." Yes, it was tawdry. And yet, Margit had talent. She'd linked herself with an artist. She'd been happy at first with the idea of motherhood.

The baron closed his eyes. "My pain is eased. I thank you for this, Miss Renner. However, I'd like to be alone now."

"Of course, but could I see the rest of Mein Königsberg?" Perhaps I could find signs of her that weren't tawdry?

"I can't oblige, obviously. Have Tom show you around. You're lodging in town?"

"Yes."

"Then good evening, Miss Renner. I hope your journey was helpful. If you stop by tomorrow, Anna would like to see you. Now please excuse me." He must have somehow signaled Tom, for in retracing my steps, I soon encountered Lilli, closely followed by her master.

"You were there for an hour," he said in wonderment.

"Apparently I was distracting."

Tom laughed, patting Lilli's head. "Distracting. What do you think, girl? Is Hazel distracting? So far, the only other person he could bear during these attacks was Friedrich."

"Who was he?"

Tom hesitated. "His—assistant. You'd like to look around?"

"Yes, very much."

"Come." The castle was huge, yes, but more astonishing were the galleries filled with paintings by Corot, Turner, Constable, van Dyck,

Dürer, Breughel, Goya, Cézanne, and Monet, all exquisitely framed. A Gauguin and a Rubens lay on a long table. *This* was a dream, a fable.

"The baron owns all these?"

"Not all of them. He's a dealer in paintings, sculpture, coins, crystal, and books. Some of this he's selling for Europeans who need ready cash. Some he's storing until the war ends."

"It must be amazing to live here and see all these treasures every day."

"It is, yes, but the baron is very precise. You can't make mistakes." Tom bent over a Corot landscape. "You see where this frame was repaired, here on the gilt?"

I looked hard and saw only a smooth wash of pale gold. "No. It seems perfect."

Friedrich did it. He was an upholsterer before he came here, but his repairs were magical. The baron bought this oil from a French collector who needed cash. The baron gets a commission which he uses to support all this." A sweeping arm engulfed the gallery, the castle, gardens, himself, and the "elves" that cleaned at night.

"Where did the baron come from?"

"Prussia."

"Why did he leave?"

"I don't know. Come." In fact, the baron's past meant little to me now. The greater the mass of an object, I'd told my students in Galway, the more it tugs on you, as the Earth's gravity tugs us to her. I moved slowly through each room, stunned by the gravity of this splendor that was tugging me in. Imagine living here, walking daily in these rooms. And Margit wasn't happy here? With her "surprisingly fine eye," she didn't want to stay?

The baron had furnished the castle over time, Tom explained, churning profits into stained glass, carpets, bookcases, furniture, and walnut wainscoting. "This was added just before you were born," he said, opening a door to a sight so unexpected and yet familiar that I gasped: a gallery of mirrored walls. "As soon as you could walk, you'd find your way here." Rows on rows of reflected Toms, Hazels, and Lillis stretched left and right, before and behind us. Deep in the infinite reflections was there still a tiny Hilde? "We were playing tag here once before a dinner party," Tom was saying. "The footmen made us leave. They said we might have broken a mirror."

"Footmen? There were footmen?"

"Dogwood men, really. Sometimes he'd dress them in red jackets."

"With gold braid?"

"Yes."

"Were there musicians and a grand table set with crystal?"

"Yes, for banquets."

So it *was* here, everything I remembered. No dreams but memories. Here, too, was confirmation that I'd been given away like a dress she didn't like. *Don't think of this.* "Does he still have banquets?"

"No, not since before Christmas, when Friedrich left."

"Where did he go?"

Tom's glance strayed out the dark windows. "To fly for Germany with the baron's cousin, Manfred. They'll down a lot of Allies." As we left the mirrored galley, the rows of us dissolved one by one.

"And Friedrich—?"

Lilli turned her head. "It's the baron's silent whistle. Normal ones pain him. I'm sorry, Hazel, I have to go. But come for breakfast to see Anna. Will you do that?" He reached for me as if we were still children in a great house and then dropped his arm. "It's amazing, after all this time, you here, all grown up. Distracting, as the baron said." Lilli whimpered. "I have to go. Can you let yourself out? Go left at the end of this hall, then straight."

I found the great door and walked back to Dogwood, churned between Margit's tawdry story and all the castle's marvels. At the boardinghouse, I picked at veal stew and baked beans as a salesman for Happy Days washing machines described his wares to an insurance agent who stopped the pitch by asking what brought me to Dogwood.

"I'm—visiting old friends."

"Give them my card, miss," the salesman interrupted. "Life's better with Happy Days machines." I excused myself, leaving my stew for the agent, who'd been eyeing it.

"Excuse me, Miss Renner, did you meet the baron?" the cook asked as I passed the kitchen. "I was at the drugstore this afternoon. Ginny Henderson said you were going to the castle."

"Yes."

"And?"

"He was very cordial, but I'm tired now, ma'am, and going to sleep."

I didn't sleep. Wind puffed through trees outside my window, bobbing branches. I pictured the morning: I'd go back to the castle and meet Anna. She'd exclaim over how I'd grown. Likely she'd have her own poor opinion of Margit. Perhaps I'd see Tom and Lilli again: his smile and the bushy flag of her tail. Suppose I found work in town? What was I thinking? Would women whose men had known Margit welcome me? Mrs. Henderson hadn't. Would men she'd enjoyed and cast off be glad to meet her daughter? My mother's spirit did linger in the castle, not wholly for the worse. She might have helped shape the mirror gallery, or inspired the great stairway. She might have wandered in the galleries, dreaming on the landscapes.

Could I build a better, different Hazel there? I'd be no Friedrich, but

I might be somehow useful to the baron, disappointing nobody, disturbing nobody. I could be a better Margit. My blood began here. If the healing touch returned, this time I'd speak with those who might help me understand and guide the gift. If it never returned, surely it was a tangible good to save great art from war.

Wind whipped harder outside. In Pittsburgh, my dear, practical friend Luisa would bat away every part of my plan. She'd point out that the baron might not receive me again. Even Tom hadn't voiced the slightest option of my staying at the castle. I was simply invited to meet Anna and ease her old concerns. But night can breed boldness. I would come out of my trench and claim this piece of Dogwood that once was mine.

## CHAPTER 10

## *Rembrandt's Lady*

A different gardener opened the gate for me. "Anna's in the kitchen," he said gruffly. "Side door." Then he was gone, slipping behind a hedge. Light snow frosted the gravel and dusted trees. The castle loomed, cold and unwelcoming. At least the kitchen windows glowed. The man silhouetted inside was surely Tom. Lilli barked; the door flew open and a dumpling-soft woman with gray curls burst into the cold, arms outstretched.

"Hilde, you came back!"

"Not Hilde. I told you. She's Hazel now," Tom called from inside.

"Of course, my dear, come in where it's warm. You've had breakfast?" The encircling warmth felt like home.

"Yes, at Twin Oaks."

"Hah! That's not breakfast. *Now* you'll eat. Let me look at you, all grown up. Do you remember your Anna?"

"Yes, I think so." And I did dimly recall a kind, attending face that could not have been my mother's.

"*Here's* breakfast," Anna declared, marching me to a sideboard laden with breads, butter, honey, cheeses, liverwurst, salami, sausages, blackberry and cherry jam, oatmeal, boiled eggs, pickles, herring, fresh and dried fruits. Then she bustled to the oven, pulling out a tray of sweet buns. "Tom's favorite," she said over her shoulder.

"Anna's, too," Tom commented to his newspaper. "Sit down, Lilli." She sat.

"The baron kept you for an hour, even with his headache! Amazing." After setting down the sweet rolls, she studied me as if I were a fresh sweet roll myself. "I can see her in your hair and eyes. And you have Emil's chin. Not their character, I hope."

Tom cleared his throat, rattling the *New York Tribune*. "Verdun is becoming a death machine," he announced. "An air war, that's what the Allies need. Quick and fast."

"Stop it. That's what Friedrich said," Anna snapped. "Then all you get is young men dying on land, sea, *and* sky. Meanwhile the baron sits in the dark, like a body without a soul. Friedrich should have stayed. One pilot more or less for the Kaiser, what good does that do?"

I gathered this was a familiar debate. "Friedrich felt he had to go. And besides," Tom continued wistfully, "imagine flying free, like a knight in the air."

"Shot on the ground or in the air, dead is dead, young man. But never mind that. Hilde's here. Tell me—" A buzzer and two flashes of light from a bank of bulbs made both their heads swivel. Even Lilli looked up. Tom and Anna turned to me, astonished, as if I'd caused this marvel.

"What is it?"

"He's in his office," Anna explained. "The attacks *never* end so soon. And he wants breakfast. That's his sign, two flashes."

"Let me take it to him."

"Tom always does; he brings breakfast and gets the day's orders. Stay here for a bit, after all these years."

"Let Hazel take it," said Tom. "I'll get my orders soon enough." Grumbling, Anna set a Spartan meal on a heavy silver tray: black coffee, toast, butter, a pot of jam, and an apple sliced in eighths.

"Lilli will show you the way," said Tom.

"Really?"

"Trust her," he said cheerfully.

"Don't spill the coffee, not even a drop," Anna warned.

"Just keep telling her to find the baron," Tom repeated. "Anna, you can talk to me."

"Talk to *you*? What's special about that?" A dishrag hurled across the room brought a rolling laugh from both of them. The castle kitchen was a warm and easy place. It hadn't suited Margit Brandt, but it might suit me. The first step was to create work for myself.

"Find Baron," I told Lilli. She assumed her task with eager purpose, darting down a hallway, stopping, turning, waiting, mounting another grand staircase, and waiting at the landing as I carefully ascended. Anna had set the silver tray with a white linen cloth that would betray the slightest spill. I followed Lilli down another hallway toward a wide, plain door. Was this the one that Emil hadn't carved? But another issue was more pressing: how to knock while holding a tray. Surely one does not kick for entry to a baron's office. I needn't have worried, for a niche by the door held a small inlaid table, exactly the size of my tray. The sight of it chilled me. What would it be like to work for a man so exact? I could still retreat: deliver the tray and a polite pleasantry, spend some happy hours with Anna and Tom, and go home on the afternoon train. No, as my parents had remade themselves on East Ohio Street, here was the place where I'd remake Hazel Renner. I set down the tray and knocked. Lilli trotted off.

"Come in, Tom."

I entered. The baron didn't look up. An identical inlaid table stood next to his desk. When I set down the tray, he turned, perplexed. "Miss Renner?"

"Yes, sir, I brought your breakfast."

His Adonis-perfection was even more stunning in the wash of morning sun. *Don't stare.* But how could I not? He was exquisitely dressed in a fine woolen jacket, necktie knotted with military precision over a snowy linen shirt pressed smooth as an icy lake. Close as we were, he seemed strangely distant, as if behind glass. "You'll excuse me. These attacks blur the memory. You came asking about your mother." I nodded. "You were helpful in reducing my pain, for which I am grateful."

"Thank you."

"I presume Tom showed you Mein Königsberg and you met Anna, who must have been glad to see you." He pronounced "glad" carefully, as if testing its sense. When I asserted that all this had indeed happened, he began attentively buttering his toast, clearly a sign that I should discreetly withdraw.

*Say it. Step forward.* "Baron, I would like to assist you in your work here."

If Lilli had spoken, he could not have looked more astonished. The silver butter knife hung in the air; sunlight glinted on its edge. "Assist me? You seem like a pleasant, well-brought-up young lady, but what makes you think yourself capable? You have experience in my work?"

Friedrich began as an upholsterer, I might have noted. "Perhaps I can't do everything or even part of what—your former assistant did, but there is much that I *can* do, or learn to do." The beautiful face hadn't moved. "I appreciate art." This sounded ridiculous.

"You appreciate art." The words rattled like dry stones. "Meaning what, precisely?"

My voice slid up and down as I spoke of my hours in the Carnegie Institute, the sculptures I'd sketched, landscapes I'd studied, my drawings in Galway, the faces of children and how I'd chosen pen, pastels, or pencil according to the nature of each child.

When I'd finished, when my throat went dry, he precisely positioned a cup and saucer on the tray. "Miss Renner, I am a dealer in fine art. Perhaps Tom told you this? I arrange importation and consignment of valuable objects to collectors. I don't see how sketching children prepares you to assist me. If you taught school, why not return to that worthy enterprise?"

"Because—it's impossible now."

"Why?"

"I can't say, sir. I mean, I can't tell you." Of all that I had said, this fact seemed to intrigue him most. I pushed on, a soldier advancing. "I would not be costly." Scanning the neat stacks of documents, indexes, and maps, I hazarded: "I could file for you, write letters, make copies, help Tom in some way, and then, at the end of the war, you could find someone more experienced, from Europe perhaps."

"The end of the war," he repeated, turning away, his profile a pale relief against the wooden paneling. "And when might that be?"

"Soon, I hope."

"*Soon* would be advantageous. And this assistance you offer without experience would not be costly, you say."

"No. I would like to learn the—business of peace." A fine brow arched up in inquiry. "Helen Keller spoke of it, sir. She said many are involved in the business of war, but few attend the business of peace. To preserve art is part of the business of peace, I believe."

"And you want to pursue this 'business' here, in Mein Königsberg?"

"Yes. Here."

"I see. Your ministrations did save me some hours of pain, for which I am in your debt." He studied the paper before him so long and intently that I wondered if another "attack" had begun. He squared the paper on an ink blotter. "Well then, we will see if you are suited. Take a seat, Miss Renner." There were two other desks in the office, one marble-topped like his, with an elegant antique chair, upholstered in tapestry. Perhaps it was Friedrich's. The other was oak, with a sturdy, rush-bottomed chair. I sat there. Nothing happened. Was this the first test, how long I could endure silence? Finally the baron crossed the gulf between us and set a file on the desk as gently as if it were a holy relic. "Begin here, with—my assistant's records of a collection we bought and dispersed. Let me know when you've reviewed them."

Pages of script in a meticulous hand described a group of Albrecht Dürer engravings, listing the provenance, history, and specifics of each, auction bids, and correspondence. "FW" neatly inked in every corner must be Friedrich's initials. The file included envelopes ordered by date, steamed open, not slit. No wonder the baron found my presumption astounding. Who could work to this standard? But I wouldn't retreat now.

I closed the ledger and cleared my throat. "What would you like me to do next, Baron?"

He pushed back his chair. With precise economy, he selected a folio and came to my desk. His posture and pace, the very precision of his gait, bore a military economy of gesture, a relentless, unspoken force. I couldn't move, trapped between terror and fascination. "I'd like to sample your writing skills, Miss Renner, and test your eye, since, as you say, you 'appreciate art.' That established, we could proceed to the more typical aspects of potential employment: filing, copying, and so forth." I nodded, afraid my neck would crack from strain. "Good." He set the folio on my desk and opened it to reveal a print of an oil painting depicting an older, clearly wealthy woman with a seventeenth-century headdress gazing out from a darkened space. "The artist is?"

"Rembrandt." Not a difficult question, but hard to answer with my throat so dry.

"Precisely. The original Rembrandt is owned by an Italian banker near Trieste. You know the current conditions there?" I nodded. Pin-pricks for the endlessly vacillating battle lines in northeastern Italy made lace of my father's maps. "The banker wants to move to Switzerland. He's selling this Rembrandt and other objects of his collection and believes that American collectors will offer advantageous prices."

"But how will he get them out," I blurted, "with U-boats in the Bay of Trieste? It would take a miracle."

The marble face warmed, and I glimpsed, as through a veil, a man who might once have laughed. "In a sense, yes, a miracle. However, Miss Renner, war never occupies *every* man, even in a battle zone. The task is finding agents willing to take risks, for a price, of course. How else can art survive? *Your* job is to write an offering letter describing the portrait to a collector in New York." He indicated a second sheet. "Here is additional material regarding its condition, place in the artist's *opus*, and provenance. You'll find paper and pen in the desk and a sample offering letter in the Dürer folio. Draft your version and tell me when it's done."

A Swiss clock with fantastically looped numerals chimed half past ten. I read Friedrich's work, quickly wrote a similar letter in my best script, and brought it to the baron, who scanned the page and returned it to me. "Miss Renner, please understand that what you call a miracle must be funded, which requires a motivated buyer. And don't ramble on; he's a busy man."

I took back my page and studied it. Yes, I could describe the portrait better and intimate the difficulties of acquiring it. I did this and brought my revision to the baron. Surely he'd be pleased. When he turned away to read, I saw only the ordered waves of chestnut hair, starched collar, and the edge of my page. He returned it without a word, as if spurning infection.

I went back to my desk, sweating in the cool room. The slight scratch of his pen filled silences between the clock's solemn ticks. Possible wordings collided and smashed into jumbled phrases. My own pen slipped and clattered on the desk. Each start proved no better than the last. The wastebasket filled with crumpled pages. Desperate, I studied the reproduction. Why would anyone open a wallet for this dough-faced old woman in a starched, ridiculous headdress? "Start by observing," I used to tell the children. "See the lacy veins in a maple leaf." I saw how light played on the woman's net of wrinkles. Slowly, her beauty unfolded. How delicately Rembrandt had suggested a lonely, restless soul. In the wistful eye I saw her considering her own mortality, inviting us to consider our own. Word by word, I rebuilt the letter. This portrait *must* endure. I ached for the dangers it faced from Trieste to America. My back, arm, and right hand cramped; sweat smeared the desktop.

When I set a clean copy before the baron, he didn't look up. "Is this your best, Miss Renner?"

A soldier climbs out of his trench, fully exposed. "Yes. It is my best."

"Then I'll read it carefully." Minutes passed as I stared, immobile, out diamond-paned windows. He put down my page and turned to me. "You can use a typewriter?"

"I never have."

"I'm sure you're quite capable. You seem tired. Offering letters can be difficult." I dared look at his face, more open now and less fearfully beautiful. "Anna will have lunch prepared. I'm sure you'd like to inform your parents of your new employment."

"I'm hired?" He might have been speaking another language which I only now understood.

"Yes. You will be engaged in 'the business of peace.' Welcome to

Mein Königsberg, Miss Renner." He held out a manicured hand, surprisingly warm. "It will be convenient for me if you live here since your hours will be long and sometimes unpredictable. That would be acceptable?"

To live in a castle? "Yes."

"Would twenty-five dollars per week, with lodging and meals, be sufficient?"

"That's very generous, sir."

"Not particularly. You'll earn your salary. We begin at eight precisely tomorrow morning. I'll have a room prepared. That's all for today." As I left, the handsome face turned toward Friedrich's chair.

On my way to the kitchen, every bolt of sunlight, every shadow and sheen was delightful. I was here "for the duration," as people said of the war, here among the masterworks, here where I'd begun. My parents should be pleased or at least intrigued that I was working with an actual baron and vaguely "in the professions." Perhaps they could visit. Nobody would ask if I was a witch.

By the time I'd reached the kitchen, somehow Anna knew I'd be staying. Setting out sliced pork, potatoes, green beans, pickles, and fresh bread, she said Tom was on his way to collect my bags from the boardinghouse. Tilda, the housekeeper I'd rarely see, would prepare my room. How quickly news flew through these hallways. "I'm so glad to have you back," said Anna, stroking my hair with the authority of one who'd washed my first curls. In that intimacy, I asked what Tom wouldn't tell me and I couldn't ask the baron.

"Why did he leave Prussia? The Hendersons said there was family trouble."

Anna closed the kitchen door and glanced out the window. Then she pulled a chair close to mine and spoke softly in German, her hand on my arm. "They gave him a pot of gold and suggested he go to America.

They wanted to give their castle in Prussia, the *first* Mein Königsberg, to his younger brother, who would preserve the family line."

"I don't understand."

The voice dropped. "Our baron wouldn't marry the princess they courted for him, or any other princess, baroness, or merchant's daughter."

"Why not?"

Her glance said this was a childish question, too innocent to answer. "Because he wouldn't. That's all I can say."

"How do you know all this?"

"We sailed on the same ship from Hamburg. He was in first class and I was in third, but I met a woman who knew his family. She didn't like them, but our Baron Georg was a gentleman, she said, worth the lot. I got work in Newark, but when I heard he was building this castle, I came to Dogwood, cooked him a good meal, and stayed ever since."

"Friedrich?"

"Was his assistant," she said shortly. Here the tale ended. With a great bustle she began chopping cabbage, saying loudly, "Everybody loves my sauerkraut."

I saw the baron's chill and astonishing beauty differently now: softened by the sadness of exile. The kitchen filled with the sweet, remembered tang of cabbage. I began a letter home, describing Dogwood and the castle, why I'd chosen to stay, and my new job. "Many here remember Margit," I added, not specifying what was remembered. I wrote of Emil and the scarlet jackets that were no dream. "Please visit me soon" I finished.

I pictured my father reading the letter and discussing it with my mother in the quiet kitchen as she rolled out spaetzle for Sunday dinner. Would they be happy for me? Would they visit? Since coming to Pittsburgh, they'd never been more than fifty miles from its center. This much I knew, that after reading the letter, my father would reach for the *Volksblatt*. The pages would crinkle as he read war news aloud. My mother might cajole him to speak awhile of store business, their friends, the price of meat, or a new Charlie Chaplin film they might see. But soon enough, he'd reach for his tin tools. My mother would take up her mending, stealing anxious glances at the beloved face. Could I help her if I still lived there? No, I might distract him, but only peace in Europe would bring back the cheerful man I once knew.

"If you leave now, you'll catch the afternoon post," Anna was saying. Yes, I'd do that. Outside, the taciturn gardener I'd met at the gate was pruning a rosebush.

"So you'll be staying, miss?"

"Yes. I'll be working with the baron."

"Working with the baron," he repeated, circling the bush.

"Yes. Do you know when Tom will be back?"

He shook his head, cradling a bent branch. "Kurt's doesn't talk much," Tom would say later. "But he'd go through fire for the baron—or his roses." When I took my leave of Kurt, he nodded, still studying the bush.

I'd been in Dogwood barely a day, but from the quick glances and frank stares in town, it was clear that somehow everyone knew that I'd be staying. Tom's getting my bags from Twin Oaks had been proof enough. I caught wisps of phrases behind my back: "Margit's girl . . . Pittsburgh . . . German . . . the castle." On Main Street a woman leaving McClellan's Bake Shop was the first to address me. "You'll be working with the baron, Miss Renner?"

"Yes."

"Well then, welcome to Dogwood." She volunteered no more and hurried away.

"Still doesn't make him a regular guy," whispered two men at the post office. They hushed when I passed. Outside Henderson's, teenage boys sitting on a Ford muttered, "Krauts taking over the town." A gleaming wad of tobacco-streaked spittle landed on the sidewalk. I ducked inside.

"Lazy louts, a disgrace to Dogwood," said Mrs. Henderson, beating on the window until the boys slid languidly off the Ford, only to lean against it. "Don't worry. They're all bark. But now that you're here, could you bring these headache powders to the baron?"

"Yes, of course." I dawdled in the shop, waiting for the louts to amble away. Then I hurried back to the castle. If only it had a moat and walls high enough to keep the war away.

"Tom brought your bags," Anna said. "Come see your room." It was on the third floor, facing north, with a window overlooking a wide lawn, orchard, and rolling fields beyond Dogwood. A poster bed with a thick comforter filled a corner. The long table would be perfect for drawing. And for reading, I surmised by a stack of books on art history clearly placed for study. A small etching hung on the wall: a Rembrandt. I had a Rembrandt in my room.

"It's perfect," I told Anna.

For the next week I rarely left the castle grounds, organizing papers to the baron's meticulous orders and studying Friedrich's letters to tease out his methods. Workdays ended with tedious practice at a Remington typewriter, hunting letters and finding a rhythm that would keep the evil keys from jamming. "How did Friedrich learn all this?" I asked Tom on one of the evening walks that soon became our practice.

"Not in the first month." Every day revealed the baron's astounding competence: recognizing forgeries, evaluating collections, determining fair or possible prices, packing and shipping methods, and weighing safe routes that shifted with blinding speed. My own daily work was mundane: filing, copying, culling prices from ledgers, and preparing invoices. But the baron insisted on a broader education in art. "Study this tonight," he might say of a treatise on Greek and Roman hairstyles useful in dating classical sculpture. Yet this work suited me, and it wouldn't risk betraying gentle souls like Ben's or raising expectations I couldn't fulfill. I was content in the castle, feeling the warmth of Emil's woodwork, and imagining that certain plays of color, the set of vases on long tables, or the curve of garden paths showed Margit's hand. In late April, I wrote to the Burnetts, hoping Alice was well and briefly relating my work with an art dealer in New Jersey. I didn't ask if Ben's body had been found, or say that still, before sleep, I imagined us on my porch, easy with long silences before he slid into the woods.

In May the baron went to New York for business. While I had a hefty list of tasks, the longer afternoons left time for sketching: Anna working by a sunny window, Kurt in the kitchen garden, or Tom building a gazebo to be covered with climbing roses.

"I'm using Friedrich's plans. He loved roses," Tom said as I worked. "He and Kurt spent hours talking about them. Friedrich would have built this himself if he hadn't gone to be a pilot."

"And the baron—"

"Tried everything to make him stay." Tom consulted a careful sketch. "But in the end, all he could do was have his cousin Manfred get Friedrich in a good flight school. Germany has great pilots and the best planes." Tom looked up through the half-made gazebo into a blue bowl of sky. "They're the enemy, of course, but magnificent. Like hawks sparring in air."

"Flying is so dangerous. I read that British pilots—"

"I know. Most don't survive the first week. What do you expect if you send boys up with less than a day of instruction? But imagine a *trained* pilot, skilled in every weather, a master of his craft, matched with a fine machine. If America enters the war, wouldn't it be better to fly and not be a trench rat?" Tom stood straighter now, eyes glittering. Even Lilli looked up. "Whatever they say in town, there's no finer gentleman than the Baron von Richthofen, but his country's tearing the world apart. Even he knows the Kaiser is a beast, leading an army of beasts. He must be stopped."

I stepped back. Didn't he realize that I was one of *them*? "You're busy. Perhaps I'd better go."

Tom turned so quickly that Lilli jerked to attention. "Please don't, Hazel. Perhaps you could—sketch Lilli for me. Here, on the grass." At Tom's command, Lilli sat. *Let it go. He's American. He can't help thinking as an American.*

"I'll have to try some angles."

"Sure. We have plenty of time, don't we, girl?" he asked Lilli. "And we won't talk about the war."

I sketched Lilli's ears and muzzle, legs, haunches, and luxurious plumed tail. With the last of the sun, I secretly drew Tom's high cheekbones, dark froth of curls, and strong fingers gripping a carpenter's pencil.

"What kept you?" grumbled Anna when we came late to supper. "I hope you're hungry." Yes, we said like bad children, we were hungry.

The baron's "some days" in New York stretched beyond a week. A constant flow of telegrams and terse telephone calls directed my work, but still I had time to finish the study of Lilli and begin a series on textures: folds of velvet curtains, ornate picture frames, and sunlight on marble busts. With every sketch, I thought, I'll root my peace in this place. Still, watching from my upper room as night mists rolled over the orchard, darker images came to me: Ben's face when his voices called, jealous seekers at my house, and children leaving the schoolhouse, never looking back.

"I'm sorry, but we can't visit Dogwood," my mother wrote. "Your father's afraid something bad will happen to the store if we leave. Thank you for the pictures of the castle. We're glad you found good work." Yes, they were happy for me, but what anguish surrounded that happiness? I saw my father seeing distant trenches; I saw my mother's anxious watching, longing for her old Johannes. Come when you can, I wrote back. Come any time. I promised to visit them soon. At least we could have a picnic, walk up to Sunnyside, or watch the Keystone Cops. There must be some distraction.

The next morning, Tom stopped by the tower office to say that the baron had returned very early and gone straight to the library, asking not to be disturbed.

"One of his headaches?"

"Yes, but something else, I think. I've never seen him like this before." Hours passed. In the vast castle, we spoke in whispers. Even Lilli seemed distressed, refusing food. Finally Tom knocked at the library door and asked if the baron needed his powders. No answer.

"*You* try, Hazel," Anna concluded at sunset. "He hasn't eaten all day. He hasn't even asked for water."

"But you know him better."

"Exactly. He's not used to you." Over my protests, she and Tom shepherded me upstairs with a bowl of ice water, a flannel cloth, and a vial of headache powders. Curled outside the library, Lilli scrambled to her feet at our approach. We knocked. No answer. Anna opened the door wide enough to gently push me in.

## CHAPTER 11
## *A Constable in Pittsburgh*

The baron was deathly immobile in his darkened room. "Baron," I whispered, "it's Hazel. They—we're worried about you." The bowed head turned slightly as I set down the bowl, towel, and powders. He was holding a white envelope. Others lay scattered at his feet.

"Should I pick them up for you, Baron?" The chin declined a fraction. I knelt to gather the envelopes. They were all from the baron to Friedrich Stein at various German military addresses. Each had been steamed open; each had a letter inside. Why do people return letters that have been so carefully tended and kept? In anger or—I looked up at the baron's stricken face—in death. Someone in his fighter squadron, perhaps the baron's own cousin Manfred, had gathered and returned Friedrich's letters after he'd been killed in action.

I hadn't grasped the depth of the baron's ties to Friedrich. I'd thought they'd merely worked well together, complemented and enjoyed each other. No, they loved each other deeply. How could I not have seen this? Once again, I hadn't read signs. Friedrich's leaving was an agony, and now he was dead. "I'm so sorry, Baron." A tiny *ping* hit the envelope on his lap. He didn't turn away. This supremely private man had let me see him cry.

Another's grief calls up the desperate, futile urge to do or say something, to busy oneself on the mourner's behalf. "Would you like some water, Baron?" No answer. I wedged a glass in his hand. It didn't move. Not to seem hovering, I stepped back. He was deathly still, as if the soul had drained away, leaving the solid body behind. An idea shot through me. I had Tom bring Friedrich's chair from the tower office and set it near the baron.

The barest murmur: "That was *his*."

"Yes. Would you like to sit in it? Come." He hoisted himself up, took a wooden step, slowly bent into the tapestry seat, and folded forward, head in hands. "Would you like to be alone?" A slight shaking of the head. The pendulum clock had been stopped. "He was shot down?" A nod. "It must have been quick. He couldn't have suffered."

Now a sharp retort: "Quick? Falling from the sky, flesh burning?" Of course. Why offer absurd condolence? Hot and burning myself, I stood by, miserably helpless. "This was our room. He was here. Once." Haunted eyes turned to me.

"Should I—draw him here?" The slightest nod. But how? I'd never seen an image of Friedrich or heard anyone describe him. I drew two men talking in shadows. At first my pencil's passage over rough paper seemed to soothe him.

Then he murmured: "Why move art around? Why bother anymore?"

"Because art is important. We're keeping it safe."

"For what? Europe will be filled with cadavers. Who'll be left to look at art or make it?"

"Stop talking that way!" My normal voice was startling in the quiet room. He raised dark-ringed eyes to mine. I crossed the gap between us and pressed the damp flannel to his brow. He leaned back. We didn't move. Precisely now, his work *had* to matter. A man can't live in a darkened room. An idea bloomed. Unlikely, but worth trying. "Baron, do you remember John Constable's landscape of Normandy, the one you're shipping to Pittsburgh?" A pale hand waved off the matter. "No, it *is* important. Mr. Carnegie's agent expects it soon, and I'd like to visit my parents. We could take the train and deliver it ourselves."

"No."

*Say it, say his name.* "You and Friedrich worked hard to get that oil out of France. You said yourself that John Constable paints peace. Art must go on. You said that, too."

"You take it."

"If you talk to Mr. Carnegie's agent, he might be interested in other pieces. And it would be good for you to—"

"No. Leave me alone."

"But—"

He waved me away. I left. Tom and Anna were waiting in the kitchen. "Friedrich?" Anna said.

I nodded. "Shot down."

"I was afraid of that," said Anna. "And the baron?" I shook my head. "Will he eat?"

"I don't think so. I thought we might take a painting to Pittsburgh."

"What did he say?"

"To leave him alone."

"Shot down," Tom repeated. He whistled softly for Lilli. She came and without any order, put her head on his thigh. His large square hand dug into her fur.

I brought a breakfast tray to the library and retrieved it at noon, untouched. The baron did not leave the room that day or the next. He issued no work orders. Silence seeped like smoke under the library door and drifted through the castle. Even in the kitchen, we consulted in whispers. Lilli curled in corners, refusing food.

"In town, they think he's dying," reported Polly, a young housemaid lately hired. "I told them he's sad 'cause his friend died. They say he deserves it."

"Clean the west gallery next," said Anna tartly. "Then the hall of mirrors."

The next morning I found a note on my desk, evidently left at night, saying that he'd inspect the Constable in the library. If its condition was satisfactory, we would take it to Pittsburgh by train. I was to review "his" procedures for transporting large oils.

Anna was ecstatic. Tom and I brought the Constable to the library, where the baron meticulously examined the canvas and ornate frame. But his shoulders were sloped and his voice toneless, a man gauged out by sorrow. Friedrich's chair seemed both empty and full. "When will we leave for Pittsburgh, sir?"

"Friday. Telegraph the agent." And to Tom: "Prepare a crate and padding." Then he waved us away. Each morning, there were new instructions on my desk. In a flurry of special delivery letters, telephone calls, and telegrams, constantly reviewing Friedrich's notes, I arranged the baron's hotel and special handling for the crate, set a meeting with Carnegie's agent, prepared an invoice, and told my parents to expect me.

He was silent as Tom drove us to the station. I might have been transporting *two* oils. He sat immobile on the train, refusing the dining car and barely glancing at rolling hills that Constable would have loved. Halfway across Pennsylvania, he did concede: "We went to Chicago once by train." A little later, waving slightly toward the window: "Prussia looked like this around the military academy."

"How long were you there?"

"Too long. The officers get in your bones; they shape you. See?" He pointed to his legs, precisely parallel, feet flat on the floor. "They make marionettes to send other marionettes to war." This was his longest speech in days. He rubbed his bezel ring and returned to his silence. What would Mr. Carnegie's agent think of this shell of a man?

But when the conductor passed, calling "Pittsburgh, Pittsburgh," the baron snapped to attention like a soldier to a bugle call. He straightened his jacket, smoothed his hair, and escorted me from the train. As we entered the station's bustle, a milling crowd gave us space. One man whispered to his neighbor: "Must be some Brit for the munitions plant."

Languid porters scurried at his crisp commands and pocketed discreet tips. He rejected the first cart; they brought another and carefully edged Tom's wooden crate out of the freight car. The truck I'd ordered was waiting, as well as a Packard and driver to the Carnegie Institute. I'd hoped to go with him, to see offices behind the galleries and meet the agent, but when the baron stepped ahead of me at the Packard's open door, I understood he meant to go alone.

"Thank you. All the arrangements were very well done. I appreciate your help, as always." His first direct praise of my work. Disappointment flew away, and I was glad for every recopied letter and twice-checked invoice, every late evening's work, and tedious care with the packing. Here was the prize of his people's loyalty: the slight smile, the warming blue of wide eyes, and quiet pride in having pleased him. "Miss Renner, may I have the pleasure of calling on your parents tomorrow?" Calling on us? A baron in our walk-up? Surely his "contacts" had described the simplicity of our flat. It could easily fit in his kitchen. A light rain was falling. The driver coughed slightly, impatient to go.

"They'd be delighted, I'm sure." Anna's last instruction to me had been: "Try to make him eat." He'd turned toward the Packard door. "Perhaps you'll come for dinner, Baron. My mother is an excellent cook. We eat at seven."

He hesitated before bowing slightly. "With pleasure. Assure your mother that nothing out of the ordinary is needed." I was about to give him our address when he interrupted: "Renner's Hardware, on East Ohio Street. At seven tomorrow." The heavy door closed behind him.

I made my way home. So little time had passed, but I felt myself a stranger, remembering just in time to remove my muddy shoes before mounting the steps to our flat. The kitchen smelled of *butterplätzchen* and *apfelkuchen*. Tulips filled our prize Wallendorfer vase. My mother fluttered and fussed over me, yet the air had thickened in our flat. At closing time for the store, she warned: "You can hear in how he climbs the stairs if someone talked about Huns today. So much upsets him now. You'll see."

Apparently it was a quiet day; we heard my father's customary quick, even step. Yet his smile was tentative, testing my shoulders before a quick embrace, sitting slowly in his chair as if it might splinter with his weight, reflecting carefully on the simplest question about Uncle Willy and Tante Elise or business at the store. When I asked about the neighbor boys, he stiffened. "They call little Herman the 'Kaiser's rat.'"

"I'll talk to them."

"You can't. They won't listen."

"Shall we eat?" my mother interrupted. "Everything's ready."

At dinner, dishing out potatoes: "Do you know what they're eating in Berlin?" *Say something. Do something,* my mother's eyes cried.

"The baron asked to call on us. I invited him for dinner tomorrow. He doesn't expect—"

Our big spoon clattered in the potato pan. "Baron von Richthofen is coming *here*? For dinner? Hazel, how could you?"

"He wants to meet you and Father. Everything you make is fit for a prince, let alone a baron. His cook's *apfelkuchen* isn't half as good as yours."

She had to smile. "He's from Prussia?"

"Yes, near Königsberg."

"So meatballs with herring and white sauce with capers and potatoes. I could make *faworki*, their fried biscuits."

"He's related to Manfred von Richthofen the pilot?" my father interrupted.

"A cousin."

"Every Allied pilot wants to down him. We're losing our best men on land, at sea, in the air." He closed his eyes. "Excuse me, a headache."

I cooled my hands on our ice block and pressed them to his temples, making the slow circles that once helped. He covered my hands with his. "Hazel, it's so good to have you home. But I keep seeing bodies, thousands dead for each yard of miserable earth. And the *earth*, have you seen pictures after battles? Shredded, pitted, littered with bodies, nothing living." I pressed harder, praying for a tremor. Nothing. Nothing for those I loved the most. Still, I held my hands to his head, cooled them, rubbed, and cooled them again. "Thank you," he said finally. "Let's finish dinner."

We had veal for dinner, more tender than Anna's, or perhaps it was the home taste I'd missed. I told them about Lilli, the gardens, the new gazebo, and how Tom packed marble busts for shipping—easy subjects far from war. When the dishes were washed and dried, I brought out my father's tin plates and tools. "Suppose you make a beautiful landscape and I'll draw one. We'll show how the earth can be." We worked all evening, while my mother prepared sugared mounds of *faworki*.

The baron's crisp knock sounded precisely at seven the next evening. My mother hurried to open the door. For once her natural hospitality failed. She stepped back. I hadn't warned her, but how could even "he's a very handsome man" have suggested such preternatural beauty?

I stood for introductions, but he had already bowed to my mother and presented a bouquet of yellow roses. He congratulated my parents on their daughter whose services he had the "honor and pleasure" to employ. Dazzled, they couldn't have noted the curve of his shoulders.

He never betrayed the slightest notice of the plainness of our flat. He admired the "vista" from our front window and exclaimed over my father's tin of the Neckar River flowing past Heidelberg. We showed him others: women gathered by a well, a street musician, lovers on a stone street, a woodland path. "Peace was so long ago," he said.

"Dinner's ready," my mother announced. She moved us to the table, set with our best linens and dishes, and filled our plates with roasted potatoes and meatballs in creamy sauce. At his first mouthful, the baron sighed. "*Königsberger klopse,* the pride of Prussia. I've never tasted finer." He ate slowly, with such clear pleasure that my mother blushed. We did not speak of war, but of Heidelberg and a walking tour of Germany the baron recalled in fond and avid detail. The halves of my lives folded together. Our bonds of custom and culture bridged the great gap of wealth. Everything American that marked us as foreigners was far away. My father joked as he once did, and my mother recited a poem by Goethe, solemn as a schoolgirl. I shared one of the patter songs we invented in Galway about Europe's great rivers. How easy we all were then.

After dinner, over coffee and *faworki,* the baron drew a photograph from his wallet, holding it by the edges as if it were a tiny Rembrandt, and set it gently before my father. I leaned over to see a man reading in the rose garden. Who could it be but Friedrich? "Could you make this in tin, Herr Renner? You'll be well compensated." Deep eyes warned me: *Say nothing.*

My father studied the photograph. "I'll try." We drank schnapps in crystal glasses that had never in my memory left our glass cabinet. The baron briefly recounted his success with the Constable landscape.

Carnegie's agent was pleased and might buy a series of Dürer etchings and a jeweled medieval chalice just recently available. "Tell us about the Constable," my father said. The baron described how land rolled into sea, the stark tree, the great sky—and here he stopped. What else did he see? A burning man falling, a plane spinning, an Allied fighter arching up, triumphant at his kill? My parents were silent. They must have known.

"A friend died three weeks ago," the baron said. "I happened to be at our embassy when the telegram came. He was a pilot. The body was—unrecognizable."

My father refilled the baron's glass. "We're losing our best."

"How many for you, Herr Renner?"

"Three cousins in Tannenberg, two in Gallipoli. Another lost both legs. Ten nephews are dead or missing. Five women from bombs. Twelve children. Of friends and their sons, nearly thirty. Seven crazed from shell shock." My father looked away. Did he see a regiment filing past him, all the dead, wounded, and lost? "And you, Baron?"

"Nearly fifty from my academy. Of my relatives, eleven. If we were over there, Herr Renner, we might both be dead." Now both were helpless bearers of guilt and grief.

Our clock struck eleven. The baron waited out its chimes before pushing back his chair. "Herr Renner, it is said that pain shared is pain halved. We are brothers of a bleeding land." He grasped my father's hand for a long moment before turning to my mother. "And Frau Renner, you have given me a taste of Prussia and a welcome in your home. I sincerely thank you for both." He kissed her hand.

"Miss Renner, a car will be here at nine on Monday morning. We'll meet at the station." He shook hands and left. From the baron's metronome tread, I knew the academy had put this in his bones as well: how to descend a stairway.

After the dishes were washed and dried, as my father sketched drafts for the baron's tin, my mother took me to the front room, where she kept family photographs from Germany: weddings, birthdays, baptisms, Christmases, and outings in the country. She slowly turned the yellowing pages. Tiny black crosses hovered over many heads. "Killed?" I whispered.

"Yes. And look." She opened a wooden box of crude tin faces with a name under each: Erich, Franz, Clara, Gretchen, Bernard, Harald, Horst, Max, Peter, Otto, Ludwig, Hilde, Sophie, Ernst. Many showed children. Beneath them lay stacks of blank plates. I put my arm around her. She leaned against me.

"Now he's hammering someone else's dead. Come back again soon, Hazel. He needs you." We went quietly to bed, but my father stayed up, hammering late into the night. Even if I came back, what relief could I bring him in a city that thrived on war? "We're the arsenal of the world," many boasted. Two hundred and fifty war plants beat out munitions. Those who didn't smell factories or hear the laden trains rumbling east saw smoke curling like huge snakes into the air day and night. Even if my touch returned, could it reach and lift a sorrow like my father's, so deeply sunk into a soul?

We went to church on Sunday, had a quiet family dinner, and walked up to Shadyside. In the evening, at my mother's insistence, we saw the new Charlie Chaplin film. We laughed and stamped our feet at the Little Tramp's misadventures. "You two should come more often," I said on the way home.

"We will," my mother declared. "Even if I have to drag him. And we'll visit you in Dogwood. Everyone needs a vacation."

"Perhaps," my father said. "We'll see."

In the morning, I took leave of my parents in our flat and hurried down to the waiting car. Holding their faces before me all the way to the station, I wondered if Margit had known their capacity for love. As her own dreams and plans bloomed and burst, did she trust that Johannes and Katarina Renner would keep faith with each other and with me? Yes, I'd done right to search for her in Dogwood. At least I'd discovered this: Margit had taken some care in her plans for me.

On our eastbound train, as the baron read from a leather-bound volume of Goethe, passengers turned to stare at him or found reasons to pass us in the corridor. I imagined their thoughts: *Who is this handsome, foreign-seeming man? An actor? Someone important?* How wearisome to be a constant sideshow attraction, a beautiful freak of nature. As we drew near Dogwood, his shoulders stiffened and he sat erect, facing the next battle.

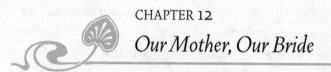

CHAPTER 12

## *Our Mother, Our Bride*

My father's finished tin of Friedrich arrived and disappeared into the baron's suite, which only Tilda entered. She was a gaunt, fierce-eyed woman who pressed herself against walls when I passed and returned any greeting with the briefest syllables. "Tilda's not a talker," Anna said when I remarked on these encounters. "That's why she cleans his rooms." The potato peeler's *click-click-click* said the subject of the baron's rooms was closed. "There's a letter for you on the table."

It was my own letter to Susanna, returned unopened in an envelope from the judge. He didn't trust me not to speak of Ben—that was clear. He didn't want me, letters from me, or any memory of me in Galway. Anna discreetly made no comment. At least the Burnetts kept our friendship. I'd sent them a postcard of Dogwood and Alice wrote me back. The new schoolteacher was nice but a little boring. Some country children had stopped coming. She was reading *Great Expectations,* by Mr. Dickens. It was good. Her mother was having a baby; she hoped for a baby brother. They were all so excited. She was feeling well and hoped I was the same.

Alice remembered me, but what of the other children? How many had been told to forget about the witch, the fraud? My blue house was gone. My drawings on the schoolhouse walls must be gone and perhaps my collection of feathers, rocks, and dried flowers. *Never mind. You're here, in Dogwood.* The baron required only diligent, meticulous work. When the war ended, peace would surely heal my father. The children had a teacher, perhaps boring, but causing no trouble.

"Even if you aren't Friedrich, you're useful to the baron," Tom said when we returned from Pittsburgh. "You could stay after the war, you know. There's nothing wrong with Dogwood." That was true. It was also true that Tom's own gentle, steady presence was weaving itself so tightly into my own life that it was hard to think of leaving.

Still, I couldn't help musing. Suppose a healing touch *did* return? Then, my fantasy followed, shouldn't I take it where the need was greatest, to the Western Front? Could I ease trench fever, suck out poison gas, calm the shell-shocked, and patch up bodies ripped by guns, grenades, and bayonets? But the need was boundless over there. Each "success" in Galway had brought dizzying weakness. Could I survive one ward of wounded men? And what of the civilians blasted by bombs or starved by blockades? I walked through the mirrored gallery, making infinite regiments of Hazels, left, right, ahead, and behind. Would all of us suffice to heal the wounds of war?

The *New York Tribune, New York Times, Newark Star-Eagle, New Yorker Staats-Zeitung,* and *Philadelphia Demokrat* brought casualty counts. Every two-reeler that Tom and I saw at Dogwood's Palace Theater began with newsreels of soldiers scrambling out of trenches, poison gas alerts, and Red Cross nurses feeding broth to men with bandaged faces. A Wurlitzer organ played triumphantly over scenes of Allied victories in the forests of Mametz, Orvillers, and Trônes. Troop trains steamed out of London. How many men in last week's films were dead or maimed by now? When the Battle of the Somme began, we watched Allied troops furiously digging trenches, and then relaxing with cards and coffee. Only newspapers reported the carnage. There were sixty thousand British casualties on July 1 alone. What of their families?

And German families? The baron was helping the National Relief Fund Committee for the Wounded and Destitute in Germany and Austria-Hungary slip food and medical supplies through the British blockade. "Germany is our mother, America our bride," committee members fervently declared, swearing that loyalty to the bride could never discount compassion for the mother's plight. Yet with the committee suspected of arms dealing and some banks refusing its accounts, members began raising funds through private sales of artwork, jewelry, and antiques.

On a hot August day, I helped Tom pack crystal goblets from the baron's collection for an auction house in New York sympathetic to the fund. "It must be hard for him to be so caught in the middle," Tom was saying.

"It's hard for *all of us*. Him, Anna, Tilda, me, my family. You know what we're called: 'hyphenated Americans' Huns.'"

He stopped packing. "Oh, Hazel, nobody thinks that about you."

"No?" I told him about my father's soaped and broken windows, the streetcar sneers, and the "louts" at Henderson's Drug Store.

"I'm so sorry. I wish I could help."

"You do. Just by—" Just by his broad smile in the morning, his whistle that came floating up to our tower office, our walks, his steady loyalty to Anna and the baron, and the warm, rolling, infectious laughter I needed more each day. "Just by being here," I finished, "and not talking about 'over there.'"

"Then we won't. We'll pack crystal and I'll talk to you about—flying." He held a goblet in the sunlight, spraying rainbows across the room. "Did you know that I'm taking lessons?"

"You are?"

"Yes, I haven't told Anna or the baron. They'd be worried."

"Of course, after what happened to Friedrich."

"It's New Jersey. There's nobody shooting at you. And it's magical. You're free. You're an angel, a bird, playing in clouds. So far up, everything you see is beautiful, like—a Corot landscape. You have no body, only soul. I know that sounds crazy, but it's true." He took my hand. "Hazel, come up with me. You'd be perfectly safe, I promise."

I looked out into a vast blue sky. How could it hold a mortal body? And who could fly *here* without imagining pilots *over there*, hunted, falling, burning, or shooting, bombing, pouring down death? If America went to war, and if Tom flew like Friedrich, wouldn't he be as vulnerable as Friedrich, a flimsy soul in a man-made flying box?

He must have read my mind, for he held up a warning hand. "Don't think about that. We'd just see the castle, farms, woods, orchards, and little towns. You can't imagine how peaceful it is."

"No. Please, Tom, I don't want to go." He didn't ask again. We finished packing, speaking of Lilli's new tricks and how well she could find any of us now, inside or outside the castle.

THREE LETTERS CAME from my mother in one envelope, written a week apart, as if she'd been reluctant to say, "*This* is what's happening." In the first letter, my father was leaving their bed before dawn. He'd slip down to the store, where she'd hear him hammering tin. In the second letter, he was spending whole nights there. "He says people might put signs on the windows if he's not around. Even Uncle Willy's worried." The third, hastily written, said: "I found a stack marked 'Battle of the

Somme' with names I don't know. I think he's inventing them. Please come home and make him forget the war."

That night my wastebasket overflowed with balled-up versions of "Father, don't think about sad things." No, I couldn't insult his grief with banalities. But perhaps, hard as it would be to leave Dogwood now, a long visit home could give my mother some relief.

"The baron needs you here," Anna said whenever I spoke of leaving. "He hasn't had a headache for months, even after Friedrich died."

"Not because of me."

"You don't know that. And besides, you like the work, and you like being here."

"Yes, of course."

"So? You should stay." She was blanching cabbage leaves to stuff with her jealously guarded mix of chopped meat, breadcrumbs, spices, and "extras." Next, she'd tend her beer barrels brewing in the cellar. In midafternoon, she'd knit socks for an orphanage in Newark. Anna never doubted her place in this world. My life would be easier if I could only cultivate her calm "So?"

EACH WEEK OF war brought new complications to our work. When Italy joined the Allies, our agent in Venice refused to work with Germans. The tightening British blockade complicated every shipment from the continent. Even moving work out of neutral Sweden was "a job for Harry Houdini," the baron said grimly. More and more, we bought and sold for American collectors.

In late September, I was preparing a file when the baron stood so suddenly that I looked up. He dropped a newspaper on his desk and left the office, the polished shoes dragging as if he pulled a great weight.

What had he read? I crossed to his desk. The *New Yorker Staats-Zeitung* was reporting on the Battle of the Somme, now in its third month:

"Somme. The whole history of the world cannot contain a more ghastly word." The corpses couldn't be retrieved quickly enough; they piled in trenches and carpeted No Man's Land, attracting rats. Half a million German soldiers might die in the mud of the Somme, the writer de-clared, and as many Allies. A million casualties. All for a tiny slice of the Western Front.

The baron's desk was private; that went without saying. But I saw correspondence regarding clandestine food shipments across the Baltic Sea and into Prussia attached to a list of items I recognized from his private collection. There was an early Rubens, a Roman bust of Alexander the Great, a Paul Gauguin lately acquired, and two Ming vases. Would these be sold for Prussian food? What pain he must feel for the land that expelled him and yet starved as he ate, destitute as he lived in comfort behind an ocean. Was some of this food for his own family? I carefully replaced the newspaper and returned to my desk. When the baron hadn't returned by noon, I went downstairs for lunch.

In the kitchen was another letter from my mother. "He's so worried that new customers will hear his accent and go away that he hired an American clerk named Frank." My father spooled between home and store as if under fire. He gave extra weights in nails and screws and tested every item, as if he might be arrested for a bent nail. "Dr. Edson says it's like he's shell-shocked, even if he's thousands of miles from the front. What can we do?" Looking up, I saw Tom and Anna watching me with anxious concern. I translated the scrawled page.

"Invite them here," Tom suggested.

"I already did. My father won't leave the store."

"Ask again, or have the baron invite him. This Frank can manage for a week. And since the baron's in his library and you don't have anything to do right now, you can come apple picking with me."

"Go on, Hazel," said Anna. "I need the apples and you're working too hard."

I went. It was a warm afternoon with the slightest hint of cool in puffs of breeze. We filled baskets with windfalls for cider, applesauce, and apple butter. I climbed a ladder into the dappled shade and passed down perfect red globes for eating. Sunlight splashed on Tom's upturned face. He caught fruit like baseballs, jumping and diving. Lilli watched, first perplexed, then bored. She stretched out on the grass to sleep.

"I could still carry you on my shoulders," Tom said.

"You're sure?"

"Yes."

"But—"

"Nobody can see us. Kurt's in the rose garden." I eased from the ladder onto Tom's shoulders. Memories came rolling back. Yes, I was like this once, high and safe, looking down on flower faces. He carried me to an apple tree with a low-hanging branch. When I grabbed it, he slipped out from under me, held my waist, and gently let me down.

We stood close together in the charged silence, warm wind ruffling our hair until, with slow-coming thought, I managed: "Anna's waiting for the apples."

"I suppose she is." We carried the bushel between us. Lilli trotted ahead, looking back for orders. A hawk circled overhead. A question flew out of me: "If America joins the war, you wouldn't go, Tom, would you? Because—the baron needs you. You're so necessary here."

He threw a stick for Lilli and she bounded after it. "If there's a draft, I'd have to go, but let's not worry about that now." *Let's. Let us. Us.* We didn't speak all way back to the kitchen. Let me, let *us* stay in this island of peace, cloistered, disappointing nobody, causing no damage or pain, just . . . picking apples.

Anna took the bushel and we snapped apart; Tom had an errand in the next town and I went to my room. The baron still hadn't left the library or given new orders for work. My mind flicked restlessly to the orchard with Tom, to Pittsburgh with my shell-shocked father, and to the peaceful early days in Galway. Then I saw the Dogwood station and a train taking Tom away. In the autumn sun, maples, birches, and aspen sparkled in reds and yellows. A bright leaf fluttering down took me to Ben falling. Friedrich falling, burning. Tom falling, burning. *Other faces, draw other faces.* I drew Alice, Susanna, Charlie, and Emma. I drew my father with his pipe and my mother with her mending, both of them telling me stories of the Old Country long ago.

Anna and I ate alone, for Tom hadn't returned. I read after dinner, or tried to. After midnight, Lilli scratched at my door. When I opened it, she walked a few steps, turned, and waited. Someone must have said: "Find Hazel." Surely it was Tom. I dressed, brushed my hair and hurried after her, but she led me instead to the tower office door, framed by a leak of light. I knocked.

"Come in." The baron was at his desk, head in hand.

"Do you have a headache, sir?"

"No. This war defeats me, Hazel." *Hazel.* He'd never used my first name before. "I appreciate the late hour, but—"

"I can work now, Baron, if you need me." I went to my desk, expecting a task. But there were no instructions set out for me. He gave no orders, just faced the dark window.

"Germany our mother, America our bride," he said finally. "When our bride goes to war against our mother, as she surely will, can we stand by? And if not stand by, do what? I was wrong when I said war can't be everywhere or affect every man. Sometimes I think I should go back to Germany and enlist. Perhaps I can—"

"No," I said too sharply. "Aren't there enough bodies? You have to stay here. Think how much art has survived through so many wars, protected by the work we're doing now, by people like you." He drummed his armrests. "And you're helping the fund with your Ming vases, and the Gauguin." The chiseled face turned to me. "I saw papers on your desk, sir. Under the *Staats-Zeitung.* I shouldn't have looked."

"Which goes without saying. However, you did look. And it's true. My mother is suffering." His country or his blood mother? The set face deflected questions. "I was trained to be a soldier, but you're right. What good is one more dead body?"

"So then," I ventured carefully, "since I *did* look, did you want to sell the pieces on your list?"

"Yes, as quickly as possible. Shall we begin?"

We did. I prepared an offering letter for the Gauguin that was acceptable, even "good" by the second draft. As I typed, the baron disappeared, returning with wine, cheese, ham, pickles, bread, butter, and a linen cloth he spread on the marble table.

"I seem to be hungry. Perhaps you'll join me?" What would my mother say to dining alone and so late with a gentleman? But how solemnly we toasted Germany the mother and America the bride in the silent room, sharing the secret intimacy of those who worked as others slept.

"I haven't had a headache since—Friedrich died," the baron said. "Strange, isn't it?"

"Yes, sir. It's as if he took your pain with him."

"Perhaps. But there are other sorts of pain, are there not?"

"Yes." I related my father's "shell shock" and our anxious hope that a visit to Dogwood might relieve or at least distract him.

"Tom came to see me regarding this. I suspect he's concerned that you might leave us, which would be a problem to me as well. He suggested that I invite your parents here myself. If you like, I'll do so."

"Thank you, sir. I would be grateful."

"Tell me about growing up over a hardware store."

He leaned back, crossing his legs like any civilian, resting a wine goblet on his knee. Memories came and came, astonishing in their detail. I described the smells of our flat, the cinnamon and soap, warm bread, beer, floor wax, and fresh flowers managed by many small economies. I recounted Sunday dinners with Uncle Willy and Tante Elise, how the store was closed for my school recitals, how my father sat on my bed at night and told tales, changing his voice for bears, witches, princesses, and woodsmen. I described the kitchen table where I did my homework, where my mother prepared meals and sweets, my father did his store accounts and made tins, and where we talked about our days.

The baron listened as if to a fairy tale. "My brother and I ate with the governess. She brought me down for interrogations."

"Interrogations?"

"Before we were old enough for the military academy, we were tutored in fencing, gymnastics, Latin, and German history. My father tested our progress. He did not sit on beds and tell stories."

"He was proud of your progress?" I ventured.

"Moderately, at first. I was a better scholar than Erich. However, a family needs heirs, and when I would not provide one by marrying properly, even for show as an uncle had done, it was suggested that I establish myself elsewhere."

So Anna's story was true. "Your brother—"

"Erich will, weary of his dalliances, marry, and inherit the castle, even if he despises 'that old pile.' However, if he survives the war, which is likely as an attaché behind the lines, he may lose everything to gambling debts. Absurd, isn't it, that to preserve his patrimony, his chief pride, my father chose the son least likely or inclined to do this?"

"Yes, it is—absurd." I considered which question might be least aggravating to the baron's melancholy state. "You correspond with your family?"

He shook his head as if at a preposterous notion. "Rarely. An agent keeps me informed. You are more fortunate in your acquired parents."

"Yes, sir. I am." Had I ever repaid that good fortune?

"And your mother, if she comes, could be induced to make her meatballs?"

"Yes, I'm sure so."

"Good. And now, refreshed, shall we return to work?"

Hours later, when violet streaks announced the dawn, we slipped our documents into an envelope that would be taken by messenger to New York. "We'll resume tomorrow," the baron said. "I've imposed on you enough for today. I will telegraph an invitation to your parents." Buoyant with sleeplessness and the intimacy of that night, I went down to the kitchen, where Anna and Tom curiously compared the dark circles under my eyes with the airy lightness of my step. I even let Anna bring me oatmeal, which she always offered and I always refused.

"Finally. People who don't eat oatmeal dry up before their time."

"If you'll eat oatmeal, will you go flying with me today?" Tom asked. Barely thinking, I agreed.

Anna turned on him. "So you've been flying? Since when?"

"Three months."

"And keeping it secret all this time. Now you're taking Hazel up. Suppose—"

He put an arm around the broad shoulders. "I promise I'll bring her back. And I'll take you up someday if you want."

"No, not me, not ever." She laid a hand on his cheek. "Be careful. I didn't fuss after you all these years to have you fall out of the sky like Friedrich."

"I know, Anna."

She turned away. "Well, go then, and come back safe."

"We will. Hazel, let's leave before you change your mind."

Anna's wide, anxious face filled the window as we left. "She's like a mother to you," I commented.

"Of course."

"Did you—"

"Let's go. The airfield is twenty miles away." Airfield. It seemed a great joke. A field of air. Tom drove quickly over the country roads, earnestly explaining how air could hold us up. I was strangely calm until we parked, rounded a corner hedge, and I saw three airplanes, fragile as dragonflies, their wings bobbing in the breeze.

I pulled back. "No, Tom, I can't."

"I know. It looks impossible. That's the miracle I was telling you about." A miracle. I wanted one in my life now. A magical, lifting touch.

A gangly mechanic appeared from a shed and raised his cap to me, beaming at Tom. "So I guess I owe you five dollars. How'd you get her to say yes?"

"Timing, Steve. She'd been up all night."

I stood aside as they checked instruments and maps, speaking of gauges and speeds. Birds swirled overhead. After all my life on land, I'd be joining them. The idea was stunning enough; the reality left me breathless as I was helped into the cockpit, given a helmet and goggles, and heard the last shouted bits of advice from Steve as we bumped across the grassy field: "Throttle . . . north, northwest . . . the curves . . . thirty minutes, don't forget."

Tom's face, as fixed and calm as when he trained Lilli, took the full morning sun. "About to lift off!" he shouted. "And now . . . up!" I closed my eyes.

Before that minute, "up" was jumping; "up" was a park swing or the inclined railroad in Pittsburgh. This was the *up* of angels. The day's warmth turned chill against my face; my clothes flapped; my heart pounded. "Look where we came from!" Tom cried. I looked down and gasped. The airfield was a green cloth. Small as a puppy, Steve waved at us. Houses were toys; trees were lumps of russet and gold. A Constable landscape spread below us. Sun glazed Tom's goggles. His words flew at me: "Beautiful, isn't it?"

"Yes!"

He pointed: "Newark . . . Pittsburgh that way . . . and over there, behind us is Philadelphia. Let's go see the castle." We put the sun behind us and yes, in a minute, there was Dogwood and the castle's slate roof and towers, lawns and gardens. "Orchard!" Tom shouted in my ear, pointing to the grid of apple trees where we'd stood so close together. The war was nowhere. I opened my mouth, breathing in sky. Air field. Air plane. Air woman. Air man. The pure joy of air.

"Will you bring my father flying?" I called over the wind.

"Yes, of course." Tom pointed to a hawk considering us. Were we his larger cousin, a great eagle? We swerved over a ribbon of water, a farm, and another village. Far away, on the airfield's green cloth, I spied Steve waving a red cloth.

"We've been up thirty minutes. Time to land." Thirty minutes! Unbounded by earth, I thought we'd escaped time as well.

We bounced to the ground. Steve helped me from the plane. "Well, Hazel, do you like flying?"

"You owe Tom five dollars."

Steve paid. They spoke again of wind, gauges, and a slight wing imbalance as I looked up to the empty sky. We'd been *there*, looking down *here*. As we ran to the car, wind lifted my undone hair as if we were flying again. Tom turned to me: "You understand now?"

"Yes, oh yes."

We went to the airfield twice more, each flight more spectacular as autumn spread her tapestries below us. Then no more.

A fire broke out on the airfield, destroying every plane. Newspapers blamed Stefan Bauer, a German-American mechanic, alias "Steve Banks," claiming that he'd acted on the Kaiser's orders. "It wasn't Steve," Tom swore. "He's as American as I am." Steve even had an alibi. On the night of the fire, he'd been seen in a tavern far from the airfield. Still he was charged with arson and espionage and taken "elsewhere" for trial. At the courthouse, Tom was told that no more information was available. "And considering who you work for, Mr. Jamison," a clerk warned, "it's best not to be overinterested in Stefan Bauer."

That night, looking out into the starry, moonless sky, I recalled my first flight, the magical "up" of pure freedom, away from earth's troubles and fears, the glint on Tom's goggles, and flying with the hawk. More and more, through the next months, as America drew closer to war, that hawk became an enemy plane bearing down on us, shooting fire. What could protect a craft of wood and metal sheeting? Suppose an attack came from behind, invisible against the sun, or burst from covering clouds? A stunning jolt, the craft shudders and falls into the terrible earth, spinning and burning.

CHAPTER 13

*A Million Tins*

I want to visit you," my mother wrote, "and I'm sure your father does as well, but he keeps saying: 'We'll go later.' Or: 'It's too far away. I can't leave the store.' Can you help?" Twenty years ago, my father left Heidelberg for America. Now a train trip across Pennsylvania overwhelmed him. The baron gave me leave to get my parents and bring them east to Dogwood. Tom drove me to the train station with Lilli sitting primly between us. I was about to board when she cut through the passengers and shepherded me back to the car.

"What's wrong?"

"She knew we forgot something." He leaned close and kissed me. "Isn't she clever? You better go now. There's your whistle." I hurried to a seat by the window in time to see Tom waving, beaming, and Lilli wagging her tail. My cheeks burned.

"Is that a *wolf*?" a passenger demanded.

"No, it's a dog, a German shepherd."

"Krauts and wolf-dogs: perfect fit." He snapped open his newspaper. I took out a history of famous book collectors and we passed the next hours in silence, broken near Harrisburg when my companion observed: "If Woodrow Wilson thinks he'll sail through the election and keep us out of war, he has another think coming. We need a fighting president."

"The election will be close."

"Close as a cat's whisker."

Full dark had come when I reached Pittsburgh. The station's bustle of Americans, businessmen, wailing children, and porters' shouts of "Stand clear! Stand clear!" brought a comforting anonymity. Nobody whispered as they did in Dogwood: "She works for that Kraut at the castle."

My father greeted me warmly and then edged back to his tins, drawn like a drunkard to his drink. My mother brought me to the front room. "I've packed and paid the bills. He still hasn't given Frank the store keys. Yesterday, I said: 'Remember, Johannes, we're leaving tomorrow.' He just went back to his tins. That sound is making me crazy. Hazel, do you really think a vacation will help?"

"It will. There are no munitions plants in Dogwood. He'll breathe clean air and nobody will talk about war." She gripped my arm, trying to believe over the hammer's tap, tap, tap.

I brought Frank the keys. He was a good man, taking time to understand customers' problems and needs in any language, miming, drawing, or recruiting others to help with translations, just as my father had always done. The caramel jar was still there by my old stool. Frank's wife was "expecting," he admitted shyly. Soon another child would be looking for "the best and sweetest" candy.

"Congratulations."

"Thank you, Hazel. And a good rest is just the thing for Mr. Renner."

"He's been—"

"Preoccupied."

"Yes, I know."

With my father's indifferent assent we offered Frank a raise for the two weeks he'd run the store and a bonus if profits rose. In the morning, Frank brought down my parents' heavy suitcase and then left us to open the store.

"Hazel's arranged everything. We'll relax and have a wonderful time. Isn't that right?" my mother prodded.

"Katarina, I never gave you a proper vacation." *Katarina*. He'd actually used her given name in front of me. Was this an oversight, or had I passed out of childhood and become an adult in his eyes? So soon? Because I'd grown, or because now he needed me more?

"What's in the suitcase, pal? Grenades?" the huffing taxi driver demanded.

"Books," I said sharply. "Can you get us to the ten thirty eastbound?"

"Sure, lady."

An hour later, the city's stain was far behind. My father read his *Volksblatt* inside the *Pittsburgh Post* and then slept. My mother steadily quizzed me about Dogwood, the castle, its people and kitchen, Lilli, and "that Tom you write about."

As we left Pennsylvania, my father sat up, dazed as a child awaking in a new place. "Katarina, remember Gunter, the one-eyed baker?"

"In Heidelberg?"

"Yes, of course. Do you think he's safe?"

"Of course. They wouldn't draft a one-eyed man." She stroked his hand.

He peered out at the rolling fields. "New Jersey looks like home—before."

Tom met us at the station. They fell silent at the first glimpse of Mein Königsberg's looming bulk. "It *is* a castle," my mother said finally. "Just like you wrote. Just like you remembered."

My father asked only: "Hazel, are you happy here?"

I glanced at Tom. "Yes, I am. Very happy." My father smiled.

Anna had prepared a light supper: sausage and potato soup, cheeses and ham, pickles and dark bread. Lilli performed her many tricks, delighting my parents. The warm soup filled us. Tom told jokes. My father relaxed enough to describe an addled customer who had confused his hardware store with a bakery, demanding hot buns. Anna said she'd prepare *Schäufele* the next day, a tender pork shoulder my mother loved. As we toasted my parents' visit, I thought yes, it was good to bring them here.

Within days, Anna and my mother were like sisters, four hands in the kitchen, ending each other's sentences, their faces twinned in the steam of cooking pots. Both had pleasant singing voices, harmonizing with cheerful ease. I'd never seen my mother smile so easily or move so lightly. She must have been lonely in our walk-up flat, I realized with a guilty start. Cleaning, shopping, cooking, and mending for one man and one daughter, how could this have been enough for her?

She and Anna challenged each other's recipes, creating ever more tender strudels and sweetbreads, fragrant stews, cabbage rolls, and Prussian meatballs that made the baron sigh. "Try this," one or the other would urge as we passed the kitchen. Usually so grim, Tilda beamed when sent home with packages of golden potato pancakes like crispy little suns. The baron said smells wafting from the kitchen would tempt any hermit. He even took some meals with us in the small wood-paneled dining room that he and Friedrich once used. "This could be a Heidelberg tavern," my father said. "You never want to leave."

My mother beamed. "He's happy," she whispered to me. "Look at his face. And he's not talking about *over there*." At the end of the first week, she won first prize at the school fund-raiser with her *Schwarzwälder Kirschtorte*, labeled in English as "Black Cherry Cake."

"It's really German," another contestant grumbled. But Mrs. Mc-

Clellan drew me aside: "If your mother lived here, I'd hire her in a minute for my bakery. Good is good and folks want good."

My father quickly found his way to Tom's workshop, put on an old apron and began sweeping, ordering, and sharpening tools. The next day, he was helping to build shipping crates and marvelously repaired a small chest. A week later, the baron asked if he would consider staying longer to work with Tom.

"We actually don't have to go back right now," my mother said. "The store's doing well. And he's doing better, don't you think, Hazel?"

"Yes, I think so. I heard him whistling this morning. Remember how he used to whistle?"

"Yes. It was good to come here, just like you said." Of course it was. Every sign showed that my father enjoyed working with Tom, the dinners in company, and comforting distance from war talk. Sometimes he even played card games with us in the evening instead of slipping off to his tins.

We made easy arrangements with Frank to manage the store for another month, send us weekly accounts by special delivery, and take his agreed salary. His expanded section of "kitchen gadgets" was drawing more customers. In fact, it was my mother who managed their correspondence. "Good idea," my father would say, or "If that's what Frank thinks."

"It's strange," I told Tom.

"But everyone's happy this way." We were walking into town on a cold Saturday afternoon. Our breath puffed. Bundled against wind, we walked close together, shoulders touching. I dared bring up a subject he'd always avoided: "Tom, you know my family now. Could you tell me about yours?" Our steps echoed in the brittle air. "Do you mind my asking?"

"No. It's just hard to talk about it. I wanted to tell you when it was time. Perhaps this is the time." He looked down, as if drawing strength from the frozen pavement. "I came over with my parents from England when I was two. We ended up in Newark. My mother died soon after of pneumonia. Then it was just my father and me. He was a handyman. We had to keep moving when he drank up our rent money. We'd come home and find everything we owned on the street."

"I'm sorry."

"I hated that. And I hated him for letting it happen. But on good days he let me tag along on jobs and hand him tools, count nails, and sand wood. He made blocks for me and I built things. But evenings when he drank, I had to wait for him in our rooms."

"Were you afraid?"

Years blew away from Tom's face and I saw him in those rooms, a small child alone. "Yes, I was afraid and cold and hungry and wondering if he *would* come back. If our room had a window on the street, I'd watch men I imagined were fathers going home to their children. I wanted to be them or sometimes just not to be at all. When I was six, he didn't come back one night. And then he didn't come back the next day. I finished all the food and went looking for him. A man at a tavern said he'd gone west. Someone had told him there was good work in California. He was drunk."

"So he just left you?" I pictured the six-year-olds in Galway, their open faces, delicious laughter, warm hands, and eager hearts. A man could walk away from one of these?

"Yes, just like that. I decided to go find him. I was six, remember. I had no idea where California was. So I went to the station and slipped into the first train I saw, which actually was headed east. The conductor put me off at Dogwood. He said the stationmaster would call my parents. But there was nobody to call, so I just walked out to Main Street, sat on the curb, and waited, I'm not sure for what. Then I started crying." I slipped a gloved hand into Tom's.

"Anna saw me there, brought me to the castle, filled me up with meatballs, gave me a warm bed, and sang me to sleep. I felt like I'd walked into a fairy tale."

"I can imagine."

"She and the baron made inquiries, but of course nothing came of that. There was talk of an orphanage, but somehow Anna convinced the baron to let me stay, go to school, and do little jobs to be useful. I was happy to sleep in the same room every night, have plenty to eat, and be with people who cared about me. I learned about gardening and carpentry from Kurt and Emil. Anna was good to me, and the baron was always fair."

"You never heard from your father?"

"No. But as Anna said, there was no way he could have known where I was. He wasn't much of a father anyway. So that's why, when Margit was—like she was, I felt so close to you. When you went away, Anna said I couldn't write because you had a new family and had to forget about us."

"As if you were all just my dream. Or I was yours."

"Yes." Arms linked, I felt his skin through layers of our clothing as close as when he'd plucked me from the apple tree.

"So we're both orphans," he said. "Yes. Or were. Now we've got each other." Words fell away. We simply walked, pressed together, north to the edge of town, west toward the lumberyard, and then back to the castle, completely forgetting our errand for Anna. Three times now, my life had shuddered from its path, spun, and reshaped itself. The first time was on the stairs when I learned the secret of my birth, and then when my hand on paint brought healing. Now the words "we've got each other" erased the path before me. I'd thought of Dogwood as a way station, a place to find myself and then leave, not the place to fix my life. Yet even here, war was bearing down on us like a train, scooping up young men and taking them away, erasing every private plan.

"Don't go, Tom, please don't go."

Of course he knew my meaning. "America's still neutral. Let's not worry now. We have this time together."

He was right. *Think only of now.* From the long gravel road to the castle, I saw a light in the workshop. *Think about my father.* "Tom, when you work together, does he talk to you about the war?"

"No. He talks about what we're doing. He says we need a better lathe."

"Does he tell you how he's feeling?"

"Does he tell me how he's *feeling*?" Tom's astonishment made me laugh.

"I guess men don't do that."

"Not much, no. Not like your mother and Anna. He likes having you close by, though."

"He says that?"

"Well, not exactly. But he looks better after your walks. You're good medicine for him. Or for anybody. You have the magic touch."

"Tom, don't say that. You don't know what happened before I came here."

"Tell me."

Yes, I'd have to. Suppose he didn't believe me or found me tainted by the story? But he'd trusted me. I'd have to trust him. "Let's sit in the gazebo." Wind whistled through the lattice frame in the gathering dark. I began. "Before I came here, I taught in a one-room schoolhouse in a Pennsylvania town called Galway."

"Yes, we know."

"But there's more." I told him about the "scary house" that I wanted blue, my night visitor, the tremors and first astounding healings, the lines of seekers, followed by disappointments and accusations. I described Ben and his voices, how Susanna was taken, and how Ben was killed. That I left town just before being sent away. "I don't understand what happened or why some were healed and others weren't, why my power came and why it left. Poor Ben was killed when he only meant to help. It was so strange, and then so terrible. They called me a witch. Do you want that in your life?"

"I'm so sorry, Hazel." He took my hands in his, sheltering as a bird's nest. "You did good in Galway and some took it badly. Terrible things happened that weren't your fault. It's strange, that's for sure. But you know—" That familiar, crooked, perfect smile broke over his face. "If this touch never comes back, if you're just ordinary Hazel forever, that's wonderful enough for me."

"But—"

"Hazel, you asked if I want 'that' in my life? I want you." The wind was bitter now. The kitchen door opened. Anna apparently gave Lilli an order, for she trotted down the gravel path, sniffing. "She'll find us. Watch." And yes, she was heading to the gazebo. "Our chaperone. All right, girl, we're going inside." Lilli led us back to the kitchen, to mugs of hot cocoa and our people. But I was already warmed, glowing like fire inside.

THE NEXT WEEK brought early snow and blasts of war news. My father began walking into Dogwood to get the morning paper and relating the news at breakfast. "Let's not talk about that," my mother would say.

But my father couldn't keep silent. "One million casualties at Somme," he announced when the Allies claimed victory. "More than any battle in human history. One million. *One million.*"

"Please," my mother said softly.

"What? We can't talk about *one million* casualties?"

"Perhaps it's the last big battle," Anna suggested.

"You really think so?"

The next Monday, taking letters to the post office, I passed my father on a bench in the churchyard, rocking slightly. I hurried to sit by him and take his hand. He shook his head. "Remember the Bible verse yesterday: 'How long must I take counsel in my soul and have sorrow in my heart all the day?'"

"I remember."

"You and your mother wanted me to come here, so I did. But it doesn't help. I have sorrow in my heart all the day because there's too much pain over there. Hazel, one million dead. We thought Tannenberg was terrible, but think of the bodies at the Somme: a thousand wide, a thousand deep. Look." He pointed down the icy street. "Imagine them here." Yes, with his eyes, I saw a blanket of death. "And how many of those bullets were made in Pittsburgh?"

I put my arm around his back, shaking him slightly. "Let's go home. The baron needs more packing cases."

He stood heavily. "How many of our customers back home worked in those plants? How many—"

*Think of something.* "Would you like to stay here until the war ends?"

He shrugged. "If Katarina does."

I asked my mother. "If *he'd* feel better and the baron agrees, I'm sure we can make arrangements with Frank."

I asked the baron. "Tom could use the help," he said.

"You don't mind, sir?"

"No, actually I don't. I appreciate the company after—" He squared a page on his desk.

"After Friedrich's death?"

He nodded. My mother was jubilant. She astonished us all by hurrying into town and returning with a job at McClellan's bakery. She'd start before dawn and return by midafternoon in time to help Anna in the kitchen. The next day, she presented herself in the tower office and told the baron that she and my father would now pay rent.

"Frau Renner, considering your help in the kitchen and your husband's with Tom, rent is quite unnecessary. In fact, I propose paying you both."

"That would be welcome, but rent is necessary for *us*. We will not be beholden." She stood immobile, arms at her sides. I knew that she'd win.

"I see. Then you may set a rent that seems appropriate. I will expect it on the first of each month."

"Thank you, sir. However, I'll need Hazel's assistance to settle our affairs in Pittsburgh."

"This is a difficult period, Frau Renner." She didn't move. "Very well. Will three days be sufficient?"

"Yes, sir. I'd like to start tomorrow."

When she left, the baron shook his head. "A remarkable woman."

"Yes, she is."

"It would be remarkable to have such a mother." He cleared his throat. "However, we were discussing other matters, were we not?" This was my first glimmer of the Baroness von Richthofen. She was nothing like Katarina Renner.

By the next afternoon we were in Pittsburgh. My mother offered our flat to Frank and his wife, charged against his salary. Frank was delighted; they'd been living in his parents' cramped three rooms. "When the little one comes," he said, "I'll have my family right overhead."

He showed us how he wanted to rearrange the store, putting common items in the back so customers would have to pass displays of newer tools and gadgets. For women he'd offer better toasters, egg beaters, can openers, and irons. He proposed installing brighter lights and changing the window displays every Monday. My mother agreed to everything. "All Mr. Renner's personal things are here in boxes," Frank said. "I put his German newspapers in the closet."

"Good. One day he won't have to hide them."

We spent the evening with Uncle Willy and Tante Elise, who listened with wonder to tales of the castle and with concern that my father had measured off the dead in the Somme. "We miss you, but he's better off away from Pittsburgh," said Uncle Willy. "We've stopped speaking German on the street. It's come to this."

"We can hope for peace in 1917," Tante Elise said. "And that we'll all be together soon."

In the morning we packed a trunk for the months ahead. I'd thought my mother would be slowed by memories, but she moved purposefully, gathering clothes, her mending basket and German scissors, my grandmother's spaetzle maker and cookie press, a venerable cookbook that was a wedding present, our cuckoo clock, and best beer steins. Then we cleaned the flat for Frank and his wife, scrubbing out weeks of coal dust and grit. When we'd finished, my mother took off her apron. She didn't shake it out the window as she always did, but crammed it in a garbage pail we'd take downstairs. "It's been so good not to wear that thing every day."

"You don't *like* cleaning?" I asked in astonishment.

"Cleaning is what you *do*. Cooking is what I love. You didn't know that?"

How could I? She'd never shared such thoughts with me. "Will you miss the flat?"

She looked around at our oak chairs, satiny with use, the worn floors and shelves for her few treasures, and the door to their bedroom. "I'll miss the good times, but right now, it's better for your father in Dogwood."

"I hope so."

"Well, let's go," she said briskly, not once looking back.

IN DOGWOOD, ONE of the baron's clients had commissioned a pressed tin ceiling for his music room. My father worked early and late on the project. "The tapping makes me a little crazy," Tom confessed at breakfast.

"At least it's not pictures of the dead."

"That's true. If he gets more commissions, he might not have time for the dead. Anyway, come and look outside. There was an ice storm last night." We peered through a diamond-cut window at sunlight on ice-coated branches under a sheer blue sky. With the scene before me and Tom at my back, all was beauty and peace that morning.

At the bakery, my mother gave American names to her German Christmas cookies, delighting customers with hazelnut macaroons, almond crescents, and angel eyes. At home, she helped Anna bake loaves of fruit-studded *Christstollen* for the castle and the baron's friends in New York. Mrs. McClellan said she couldn't risk selling stollen: "It's too German." She'd offer only English fruitcake.

"Which nobody will eat," my mother predicted. "How could they?"

Gentle snow enfolded us after the candlelight service on Christmas Eve. If only this peace would circle the world. In the small dining room we feasted on roast goose and potatoes, kale, Brussels sprouts and cabbage, bread, trays of cookies, and *Christstollen*. Flushed with wine, the baron was almost jovial. "King George of England would gladly trade his fruitcakes for a slice of your stollen, Frau Renner."

In our put-together family, we sang and my father told a country tale, creating voices for witches and young maidens. I translated for Tom. With this slight excuse, we moved our chairs close together; our shoulders sealed as I whispered in his ear. Snow swirled outside, but inside we were safe, warm, and far from trouble. Up in the tower office sat a beautifully bound edition of Martin Luther's writings, just arrived, a lovely Monet watercolor, and a Corot landscape in which palpable sunlight stroked folds of earth as soft as flesh. In the museum where it was bound, hundreds would find comfort here. Surely we were doing the work of peace.

But that night in my room, my head spun with rich food, red wine, and schnapps. Wind blew icy snow against the window like pebbles. In their room down the hall, my father would hear this rattle. Would he count the pings on glass and compare them to casualties? Wandering in the mirror gallery as he often did, was he imagining infinite rows of soldiers marching to their deaths? How simple I'd been to think the castle gate could shield us from the war. Faintly, behind the rattling snow, were those drumbeats bearing down on me as well?

On January 31, 1917, Germany announced unrestricted submarine warfare against U.S. ships. The baron was utterly silent at his desk and I could barely work myself, making endless mistakes in copying until my wastebasket was full of paper wads. Four days later, Wilson severed diplomatic relations with Germany.

"*Now* things will change," people said downtown. "*Now* the Kaiser's met his match." In fact, soon after, German troops withdrew to the Hindenburg Line along the Western Front. This was a "tactical" and "planned" maneuver, the German press claimed. "A shorter line is easier to defend," the baron interpreted for me, "especially if you're conserving munitions." He looked out the window. "The Capodimonte is ready to ship?"

"The crate's made. I'm helping Tom with the packing this afternoon."

The massive bouquet of delicate Capodimonte porcelain flowers would go by train and then truck over rough roads to a wealthy, eccentric widow in northern Michigan, an insatiable buyer of silk, porcelain, and painted flowers. "I wish she'd buy paintings," Tom said. "Breathe on this wrong, and it breaks." As we nudged the centerpiece into place and began the tedious work of padding, we couldn't help speaking of the Hindenburg Line.

"A shorter line *is* easier to defend, but also easier to break," Tom said thoughtfully. If he left Dogwood now to break it, how could I protest, after millions of women from dozens of countries had watched their men march off? If Tom was an unlikely soldier, so were these men. Some, like him, once held carpenter's tools. Now they used machine guns.

"Let's break the straw into shorter pieces near the petals," I suggested.

"Yes, good idea." Digging his hands into our straw, he found mine. Our fingers braided together. "Shorter pieces," he whispered. "They're so much better." That moment of pleasure in straw was a precious memory in the coming weeks. My father had tacked a large map of Europe to the workroom wall. One afternoon I found him standing in front of it, transfixed. I wrapped my arm around the thinning waist. "What do you see?"

"Forests, rivers, gardens, castles, churches, orchards, villages, children playing, trenches, bodies blown apart, rats, craters, wasteland."

"Perhaps you don't need to read the paper every day."

He looked at me in astonishment. "It's my country."

I sighed. Stacked beside us were the client's finished ceiling plates. They were beautiful, some with musical instruments, others with flowers and vines. But my father's eyes were fixed on the map. In the hall outside, Lilli barked, coming closer, with Tom's boots clattering behind. She bounded in and sat at my feet, evidently fulfilling the order: "Find

Hazel." The great tail swooshed with pleasure. "Good girl," said Tom. "We started in the meadow and she found you here." His cheerful energy felt so foreign, so American.

My father and I turned from the map like guilty children. At that moment, for the first time I noticed a pair of wooden crates stashed near my father's workbench, brimming with tiny bits of tin. "What are they?" I asked. He didn't answer and I asked again. They weren't just scraps. Something here was too meticulous.

"Casualties from the Battle of the Somme," he admitted. "I want to see what a million looks like. It's not a million yet. I'm not finished. I may never finish."

"Do you—"

"Yes, Hazel, I have to. It's my penance for being in America."

"Johannes," said Tom quietly, "the client wants the plates today. Do you have the chart for installing them?"

"Yes, it's here."

"He has to be busy," I told the baron. "Is there anyone else who might want ceiling plates?"

March 3, 1917. Through morning fog, I saw my father coming toward the castle, newspaper in hand. The baron was walking with Lilli. When they met, my father gave the paper to the baron. Then the two men walked out of view, shoulder to shoulder. At breakfast, we all learned that the German foreign secretary had made secret attempts to incite a Mexican attack on the United States. "It's coming," the baron said. "President Wilson *has* to respond. Watch." I watched. America was a huge ship being launched from dry land. Supports are shifted, a pathway eased, and the great weight of the ship draws it into the water. Nothing could halt the slide to war.

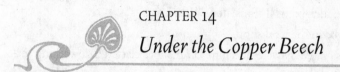

## CHAPTER 14

*Under the Copper Beech*

In the next weeks, I tried to stay close to my father: taking walks, pulling him into discussions about new projects, or taking my drawing pad to where he worked. Passing his chair in the kitchen, I'd grip his shoulder. At the table, I brushed his hand when bringing coffee. Walking, I kept my hand on his arm, wanting every touch to say: "Whatever happens *over there*, I'm *here,* with you."

April began with astonishing warmth. On April 5, I showed him the meadow that Tom had planted last fall with golden crocus, daffodils, and lapis-blue hyacinth around a copper beech tree. Flowering crab apples rimmed the clearing with frothy white. He stood still, breathing deeply. "A man could rest here and forget the world."

"Let's do that." We sat on fresh grass, ringed by the golden cups, brushed by hyacinth perfume. I leaned against him. He seemed to breathe more easily. When a late afternoon breeze crossed the meadow, he set his hand on my cheek. "Thank you for bringing me here. But we should go back. Your mother will be worried." We walked home together on our last day of peace.

At 3 A.M. on April 6, 1917, Congress declared a state of war against

Germany and the Central Powers. My father left the newspaper in the kitchen where Anna, Tom, and I found it. My mother was already at the bakery. "What's this?" Tom asked. A card had fluttered to the floor. Scrawled in pencil were two words: *Zu schmerzlich.*

"Too much pain," I translated. "Where is he?"

"Maybe in the workshop."

"Let's go. We have to find him." Our shoes clattered down long corridors. He wasn't in the workshop. On his bench lay one crudely etched tin of a man's face, thin like my father's. "Tom, I'm so afraid."

"We'll find him." He whistled for Lilli, a piercing note I hear even now, answered by galloping paws. Tom held my father's apron to her nose: "Find Johannes!" Perhaps he was asleep upstairs, or in the mirror gallery. But Lilli ignored the door leading back into the castle. My heart pounded. The bakery? Sometimes he'd stroll there in the morning, arriving as the first sweet rolls came out of the oven. Lilli took us outside, but not on the gravel drive to the gate.

"We'll find him," Tom repeated. *Zu schmerzlich.* Where would a man go to escape too much pain? Then I knew. Lilli must have known as well, for she was running past the rose garden. *A man could rest here and forget the world.* I'd brought my father to the meadow and he'd returned. To do what? To sit in peace and forget? Yes, yes, just this. Lilli reached the woodland path. Tom held my hand as we followed, faster and faster, through the greening brush. The path branched, left to the orchard, right to the meadow. Hope bloomed again. Lilli stopped and sniffed. But I knew. We plunged right.

If anything had blocked my view of the copper beech, I might have had another instant's hope, but the great tree stood alone in a skirt of flowers and green. My father's feet hovered over grass, an angel suspended. *Zu schmerzlich.* Too much pain. Not true. Not possible. I touched his hand. It was still warm.

Tom cut him down, pulled the rope away, and laid my father gently on the ground, his head in my lap. A thick bruise circled his neck. I pressed my hand to his heart. I was so far from the blue house. No tremor. Nothing. "Get the baron!" Tom was telling Lilli. He may have said other words to me I didn't understand before he ran after her.

Now we were alone. It wasn't grief I felt at first, only wonder. Alive, he was my father. Dead, he was one of millions: fathers, sons, husbands, and brothers. I touched his face, head, shoulders, arms, calling back the Johannes Renner who once held me, coached my reading, listened, walked with me, and first taught me how to draw a human face. How was *that* man now *this* man, unmoving in my lap? By his own hand, he'd rid himself of torment. His was a fatal healing touch. A breeze shook the crab apples, showering us with petals. I rocked with my own pain. I never truly understood this man or grasped the depth of his anguish. I didn't read the signs.

Moving my hand over the motionless chest, I felt a lump in his pocket and reached in. One caramel. He must have known I'd find him first. In his despair, he'd thought of me. "The biggest and juiciest for my Hazel." At my first gasping sob, birds flew up, squawking. I tore away the waxy paper and crammed the candy in my mouth. Warm tears trenched my cheeks; sweet juice ran down my throat, every drop a memory. No other fathers mattered now, no body stiffening, only this man who took me, fatherless, whose somber, loving kindness filled our flat, whose "Well then?" began my true education and gave me strength for my own journey. Sadness beyond sobbing, tears coursing down.

One by one, the birds returned. A robin scuffed the grass where Tom had cut the rope. That robin lived. The grass lived. I lived. But Johannes Renner was heavy in my arms. I brushed back the graying hair. When had his brow grown so furrowed, or this lace of wrinkles begun to circle his eyes? I hadn't noticed. I would notice everything now, before other hands took him away. Here was the blue work shirt, still crisp from my mother's iron, the hands spotted with calluses, the belt notched tighter, the lips and fingertips turning gray. One silvered edge peeked from his trouser pocket. At my touch, a palm-sized tin slid out, showing a line of trees with the towers of Heidelberg above them. Had he gone home at last? I hugged him until my arms ached. "Enough," I whispered in the chilling ear. "You've suffered enough." But what about me? My pain had just begun. Hadn't he thought of this, or of my mother's pain? Or had he marched off like a soldier, not daring a look backward to the women who loved him, afraid to weaken his resolve.

Lilli came first, then Tom, Kurt, and the baron, panting. They'd brought a linen sheet. That was wise, I thought, for I was shivering. Instead they wrapped my father. "We'll take him now," they said, as they lifted the body out of my arms and carried him away. Anna and Tilda met us on the path and walked beside me, one on each side, holding tight.

Kurt offered to drive me to the bakery, but I wanted to walk. "She's in the back," said Mrs. McClellan, barely looking up from the bread she was slicing. My mother had just taken a tray of hot cinnamon rolls from the oven. Even now, cinnamon is my scent of sorrow.

"Hazel, what a nice surprise!" When she saw my face hers went pale. "What happened? Is he—?"

"Yes. I found him." Her tray crashed down, scattering rolls across the floor. I kicked them aside to reach her.

"How?" she whispered. I touched my neck. She gripped the table. The gold of her wedding ring gleamed through a dusting of flour. I told her about the note. "Johannes, Johannes," she groaned, "you had so much pain." She laid her head on my chest, shoulders heaving.

Mrs. McClellan found us thus. "Your father?" she mouthed. I

nodded. She untied my mother's apron and gently brushed flour off her dress. "Go now, Katarina. Let Hazel take you home."

"The rolls."

"Never mind the rolls."

It was past nine. The streets were filled with people speaking of war, loudly comparing when they'd first seen it coming, how quickly we'd win it, and what our boys would show the Kaiser. My mother and I walked slowly through groups that parted as we passed. Two boys on skates curved to a stop, watching us. "What's wrong with them? Don't they read the papers?" one asked the other.

Anna was at the castle gate, tying on a black ribbon. She folded my mother in her arms: "Katarina, my dear."

Her face was a mask, her voice flat. "There's so much to do."

"Mother, don't think about that."

"Hazel," said Anna firmly, "some things must be done, however you feel."

I wanted to curl in my bed and cry. But as I learned in the next hours, the ministrations after death brought their peculiar solace. First there was the washing and dressing of my father's body before he stiffened. Then they'd dye my mother's lavender dress black. We'd need a casket. "Tom could make one," I suggested.

"Yes," my mother agreed. "That would be best."

The families in Germany must be informed, a difficult task now that we were at war. "The baron will find a way," I said.

"Telegrams to Uncle Willy and Tante Elise," my mother added, "Pastor Peterson, the Schmidts, the Hesses, and the Schwartzbaums." This pale, composed woman was not my mother who cried over sentimental songs and shook at thunderstorms. "We have to make the funeral food."

Anna hesitated before "of course." Why? There would be a funeral. Didn't that go without saying?

It didn't. The baron pulled me aside. "I just called Pastor Birke. He says he can't perform one or bury your father in the churchyard."

"Why not? My father was Lutheran all his life, baptized—"

"I know, Hazel, but he took his own life, which in church doctrine is murder."

"What? He suffered and then he couldn't suffer any more. He wasn't a murderer. He *has* to have a funeral. He was my father." At the word *father*, I choked, unable to speak.

The baron waited. "It is a gift to be able to mourn such a man," he said finally. I believe Birke is wrong, but it's his church and the choice is his. I can find you a pastor from New York or Philadelphia who's willing to give the service."

"No. My father died here. This was his last church. Pastor Birke *has* to understand."

"He may understand, but he won't change his mind."

"Then I'll have to change his mind for him. If he can at least do the church service, could we bury him here, in the meadow where we found him?"

"Yes, of course. But I suggest that you prepare yourself before speaking with Birke." The baron handed me a copy of *Tischreden*, Martin Luther's collected sayings. I spent an hour with the tome, gathered some of my father's tins, and went to the church.

Pastor Birke was in the sanctuary with the sexton, who backed away as I approached, as if I carried my father's sin. "My deepest sympathy to you and your mother, Hazel," the pastor began. "However, I deeply regret, as I explained to the Baron von Richthofen—"

"Yes, he told me your church does not generally perform funeral services for suicides."

"Actually, never that I know of since our founding in 1782."

"Pastor, you are familiar with Martin Luther's thoughts on the subject?" I read from the *Tischreden:* "I don't have the opinion that suicides are certainly to be damned. My reason is that they do not wish to kill themselves but are overcome by the power of the devil." I closed the book. "In his case, Pastor, would you not agree that the 'devil' which overcame my father was this war?"

He pressed his hands together, clearly troubled. "You understand, Hazel, that I am responsible for the congregation of this church and the message our actions convey? To perform the funeral is to condone the act of taking a God-given life. Doing this may encourage others to follow his path."

I looked into the limpid blue eyes until they blinked. "Would you be condoning the *act* or showing Christian compassion for the *man*? This is what my father wrote before he took his life, when he knew his countries were at war." I held out the card.

"*Zu schmerzlich,*" the pastor read. "Yes, I know of his pain."

"Do you know how deeply he took upon himself the pain of those dead from this war? He honored their lives." I spread out tins on the pew. "These are men he knew: Karl, Thomas, Georg, Heinrich, Peter, Wilhelm, Otto, Hans. There are boxes more, friends and strangers. My father mourned them all. You saw him on the church bench. He looked for comfort; he ached for consolation. He came to Dogwood to find peace when Pittsburgh became an arsenal of war." I took a breath. "This war ripped him in two. Can't the mind be tormented like the body? Do you deny Christian burial to the sick?"

"Of course not, but I can't encourage others in despair to doubt in the Lord. And what is suicide but absolute doubt?"

My voice echoed in great space. "Of course he doubted! After one million casualties in the Battle of the Somme, who wouldn't doubt?

Who wouldn't despair? Can't he have rest at last?" The pastor was silent. "You know that I was adopted by the Renners when my first mother couldn't keep me? Shall I tell you what kind of father Johannes Renner was?"

"It's not necessary, Hazel."

"It is necessary for me. If you deny his funeral here, I'll give his eulogy now." I did. The pastor didn't interrupt as I spoke of our talks in his shop, the credit and aid he gave to so many in our neighborhood, his love for my mother, the many skills he brought to the baron's work, even the caramel he left for me at his passing. Then I stood. "Baron von Richthofen has offered to bring in a pastor from New York or Philadelphia. We can have a funeral at the castle and bury him on the grounds, but for the little while that he was in Dogwood, my father was in your care, at your church, and it would give my mother great comfort to have you perform the last rites for him."

"I will pray on it."

"Thank you, Pastor." I left him in the sanctuary, head bowed, and walked out into the lawns bright with daffodils and speckled with robins. Everywhere tiny plumes of leaves unfurled. How could my father be gone on such a day? Halfway down the street, I heard the heavy tread of one unused to running. Pastor Birke's black jacket flapped at his sides like wings.

"Hazel," he panted. "You know I can't require the choir to sing."

"I understand. But you will perform the service?"

"Yes." He leaned against a tree, breathing heavily. He was a good man. In my anger I hadn't seen that or counted what this change of heart would cost him.

"Thank you, Pastor. I understand that some in your church may be angry."

"Indeed." He smiled slightly. "Some will be *exceedingly* angry and not reticent in telling me so." However," he drew himself up, "*I* am the pastor of this church. It occurred to me that your father was Dogwood's first casualty of this war. He will not be the last, I fear. I'll call on your mother this afternoon. You'll need a coffin. Shall I send over one of the Harris brothers? They have a good selection, reasonably priced."

"Tom will make one for us. My father would have preferred that, I believe."

"Of course." We determined that the funeral would be in two days to give Uncle Willy and Tante Elise time to come from Pittsburgh. Then, with a slight bow, he returned to the church.

"Well done, Hazel," the baron said at my news. "He's risking an angry congregation. Your father is ready, if you'd like to see him."

The body had been washed, dressed, and laid out in the small dining room. "We had to pull the collar up to hide his bruises," Anna explained. "Stay with him as long as you like. I'm helping your mother with the funeral dress."

She led me to a chair and I sat. Was this my father's ashen face? This stiff, somberly dressed form couldn't be the man I held in the meadow. I thought of bodies in No Man's Land, blown apart, eaten by animals. Men like my father. Other women's fathers. Once he had judged how many blocks of East Ohio Street would be filled with the dead. Now he was part of that paving. I got up so quickly that the chair toppled loudly on the wooden floor, bringing Anna at a run, her hands dyed black from rinse water.

"Hazel, come to the kitchen with us. We'll all sit with him later."

"No, I want to be outside."

"But not alone." So Tom took me to gather daffodils, hyacinth, and sprays of pussy willow and crab apple blossoms. With his arm around me and Lilli brushing my leg, I could feel the ground again, even if shadows dangled from every tree.

Pastor Birke called on us in the afternoon. Mrs. McClellan brought a tray of almond cookies. The Hendersons came with their lanky son, Geoffrey, who had been away at college. Mr. Finkle the postmaster and his wife brought a gift of black-rimmed handkerchiefs. My mother accepted them graciously, only later muttering: "I don't need black handkerchiefs to remind me that I'm a widow." She wouldn't wear black after the funeral, she'd decided: "Why make a show for others? Your father knew I loved him with all my heart. I'll miss him forever. It doesn't matter what I wear."

Uncle Willy and Tante Elise came on the last train, bringing the gift of their presence. Oblivious to the castle's grandeur, they took bread and cheese in the kitchen, listening, nodding, never speaking of war.

"Let's go sit with Johannes," my mother said after they'd eaten.

Startled, I caught Tante Elise's eye. She had noticed the change as well. It wasn't: "Let's go sit with your father." From now on it would be "Johannes" or "our Johannes" in my presence. I had joined a sisterhood of loss.

We went into the room where he lay. Tom and Anna had set out chairs and put our flowers around the body. "Johannes was alone too much," my mother said. "I was always at the bakery."

"And I made him come to Dogwood. Perhaps he should have stayed in Pittsburgh," I added.

"No, this place was good for him," Uncle Willy insisted. "And it was good that you worked, Katarina. I know he was proud of you. And he had some peace here. He wasn't around war factories all day."

"But I could have—" Done what?

Uncle Willy took my hand. "Hazel, the pain that was too much for him, that pain was who he was, a man who ached for every loss a world away, whose heart was large enough for that. Did you want to make him less than such a man?" Did I? Was it arrogance or selfishness that I had thought to "heal" his crippling compassion? The father who gave me caramels felt for *all* the fallen fathers. Mourning him hurt so much. But he had mourned millions. Who could do this and live?

"Johannes, my friend," said Uncle Willy, "you were the best of us."

We held hands together and breathed the flowers. Then very slowly, the stories began. We talked about old times in Pittsburgh and the Old Country. At last, we even laughed together, as my father would have wanted.

Tom worked all night on the oak coffin, cutting and fitting, sanding and waxing until it glowed like amber. He nailed a cross on top and below it two of my father's tins: a woodland scene and the Old Bridge in Heidelberg.

"It's beautiful, Tom," I said when he brought me to the workshop.

"It's my best work," he said shyly. "But it'll be buried, so I made these for you and your mother." He held out two palm-sized boxes with tiny flecks of tin and a miniature cross. "I only knew him a little while, but it feels like I've lost my own father." I have the little coffin still, the crisp edges worn by a thousand touches. In each touch I've felt my father's heart and the caramel sweetness of his time with us.

All the castle staff came to the funeral, Mrs. McClellan, the Hendersons, the Finkles, and some of the bakery customers who were friendly with my mother. The choir wasn't there but with the doors thrown open to spring air and sunlight pouring through the high windows, we were embraced by peace. Anna and Tante Elise sang "A Mighty Fortress Is Our God." When Pastor Birke spoke in German, I translated for Tom. My mother never moved, only closing her eyes when the deep bell tolled my father's soul to rest. I thought of poor Ben, who'd had no such bell.

The baron had ordered a black coach with black horses to bring the coffin home. We walked behind it, carrying flowers for the grave. It was a Monday morning, the streets busy and American flags fluttering on many windows. "Crush the Kaiser!" read a banner outside the barbershop. We passed a group of young boys. "Another Kraut gone," one said. Pebbles hit the carriage. "Should I do something?" Tom whispered. I shook my head. We walked in silence, broken by rustling whispers on the street: "Huns . . . one of *them*." Pebbles hit the horses, making them lurch. Captain Neal, the town's portly policeman, came out of Delia's Café just then and quietly joined our procession. The pebbles ceased.

"Thank you, Captain," the baron said at the castle gate.

"I can't stop the war, sir, but I'll be damned if I can't keep the peace in Dogwood."

Tom, the baron, Kurt, and Uncle Willy carried my father to the meadow, where a grave had been dug. Pastor Birke said a brief prayer. We buried him and laid flowers on the turned ground. I felt weightless as we walked back, as if I'd left my own body behind. Tom held my hand.

"Now we eat," said Anna. *Now we eat?* Since we'd cut my father down, food had turned to sawdust in my mouth. "Hazel," she said firmly, "it's time."

We gathered in the small dining room, fragrant with apple cake and Mrs. McClellan's gingerbread. Tom opened a keg of Anna's beer. There were meatballs in cream sauce with the crispy fried potatoes my father loved and onions sautéed to sweetness in fresh butter. Tante Elise's tangy sauerkraut banished the scent of grave dirt that hung around us. We ate and ate, filling our emptiness.

"Frau Renner," the baron said over apple cake, "you are welcome to stay with us as long as you wish."

"Yes, Baron, I'd like to." So quickly she'd decided. I was happy, of course, but surprised. She'd said nothing to me. Was this how she'd felt when I announced my plans for Galway or for Dogwood?

"Good," said Anna. "We'll try to make you happy here."

Hazed with beer, I pressed close to Tom, needing the warm weight of his presence. With America at war, how long would he stay in Dogwood? In these few days, my world had changed. My anchors were breaking away.

In the last nights, my mother had shared my bed. Now she'd sleep alone. "I have to start sometime," she said. Two days later, as we walked to the meadow, she announced: "I'm selling the store to Frank."

"Are you sure?" She had deliberated for weeks over buying a Victrola.

"Yes, I'm sure."

"When did you decide?"

"Yesterday. I spoke with the baron. He knows an accountant in Pittsburgh who'll oversee the inventory and help me draw up papers."

"You won't want to go back sometime? You've lived there so long."

"No. You're here, for now. I have work, clean air, and friends. I'll miss Elise and Willy, but Johannes is everywhere in Pittsburgh. I couldn't bear it, and I don't want to manage a hardware store."

"I see. But can Frank afford to buy it? And suppose he gets drafted?" I stopped, not to overwhelm her with issues. But she'd thought of everything.

"I'm not in a hurry; he can pay over time. We worked it out yesterday."

"You spoke to Frank yesterday?"

"Yes, I called him. He said he has asthma and flat feet, so the army won't take him. He'll get a bank loan. That shouldn't be hard. The store is doing well." This was a new Katarina Renner, changed before my eyes.

"Well then, it's settled. And when the store's paid for, what then? You'll buy a bakery?"

"Perhaps."

I stopped walking, amazed. "You thought of that?"

She took my hands. "Hazel, the truth is, living in Pittsburgh or Dogwood, selling the store, buying a bakery, are all little things. How to live without Johannes, *that's* the big thing, *that's* what I have to figure out."

We reached the meadow. We knew we'd see his grave. Yet the sight of bare, mounded earth took our breath away. He was underneath, in a wooden box. "*Zu schmerzlich,*" my mother whispered. "Hazel, it's going to be so hard."

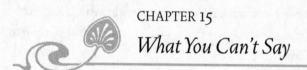

## CHAPTER 15
### *What You Can't Say*

As swiftly as spring came to Dogwood that year, America was changing. Now I was the one who walked to town early for the morning paper, each a louder drumbeat calling us to arms. "Once lead this people into war," President Wilson had said, "and they'll forget there was ever such a thing as tolerance." He was right. Hatred of Germany and the Central Powers was being manufactured and sent through the air like factory smoke, blowing into homes, stores, schools, and churches, fanned by legions of "Four Minute Men" who commandeered theater stages before every show to rouse a fighting spirit.

"There is something fundamentally wrong with the Teutonic soul," intoned Professor G. Stanley Hall, the psychologist my normal schoolteachers so admired. The great evangelist Billy Sunday preached: "It is Germany against America; Hell against Heaven."

In taverns, Tom said, many patriots swore off German beer in favor of corn whiskey. Poppy, the town drunk, was arrested for disturbing the peace after careening down Main Street, screaming: "Drink American, everybody! Drink American!"

In New York, the baron was handed a flyer. He showed it to me, holding the paper by its edges as if it might corrode his hands. I read: "The hideous Hun is a fiendish torturer and sadist who thinks no more of raping a 10-year-old girl than of sweeping priceless treasures from the table to make room for his feet in the French chateau commandeered as his headquarters." The baron raised an anguished face: "*This* is what they think of us?"

Stopping in the public library, I noticed gaps in the shelves. "Those were German books," the librarian said primly. "They have to go." I saw a copy of *Heidi* on a stack marked for discard.

"Heidi was Swiss," I reminded her.

"But she spent time in Frankfurt. Our children have plenty of American and English books to read, don't they, Miss Renner?"

"Yes, ma'am, I'm sure they do." In Galway, children sang a verse of "Silent Night" in German for the Christmas pageant. They wouldn't do this now. In every public place, we had to censor our speech. New laws forbade criticism of the war, the Constitution, the American government, the flag, the Red Cross, the YMCA, the uniforms of the United States or any ally. Obstructing the sale of war bonds or any "disloyal, profane, scurrilous, or abusive" remark about any aspect of the war effort could bring a ten-thousand-dollar fine or twenty-year prison sentence. The post office would not mail periodicals criticizing the war effort. We could not say "sauerkraut" in public: it was "liberty cabbage." Hamburgers were "liberty steaks." German measles were "liberty measles." Lilli was an *Alsatian,* not a German shepherd, and dachshunds were now "liberty pups."

At the bakery, Mrs. McClellan staged furious battle against houseflies after hearing that German scientists had infected them with deadly germs. "It *could* be true. That's the kind of thing they'd do." When some customers took offense at my mother's accent, Mrs. Mc-

Clellan sadly said she'd have to stay in the kitchen and please refrain from singing German songs as she worked.

"Hazel, what's happening to people?" she demanded. "People still want my cakes and cookies, but they don't want *me*. A little girl came into the kitchen to watch me making rolls and her mother snatched her back as if I had the plague. But I'm sure it's no better in Pittsburgh."

"I know, Mother. I'm sorry." Even if I looked, dressed, and talked like any true American, I was known to be from the castle and therefore stared at in town, just as I was in Galway, a stranger and suspect. What would they have done to my father, with his strong accent and the Old World cut of his jackets?

America must be saved from people like us: Huns, butchers, Teutonic beasts. Eating must change for the war effort, declared Herbert Hoover, the nation's food administrator. Through "voluntary rationing" we were to keep wheatless Mondays and Wednesdays, meatless Tuesdays, porkless Thursdays and Saturdays, and heatless Mondays to conserve coal. We began seeing Ford automobiles pulled by horses as "real Americans" saved gasoline for the war effort.

Geoffrey Henderson was the first in town to enlist. I saw Mrs. Henderson red-eyed as I filled a prescription for Anna's heartburn. "He was in college, so they promised to make him an officer. Maybe he'll be safer that way."

"He *will* be safer," Mr. Henderson called from the back. "Right, Hazel?"

"Of course. Everyone says the war will end quickly now." *Yes, quickly, before more young men go.* Alice Burnett had written me that a recruiting officer came to Galway and five country boys signed up. "They said the army had to be better than farming. Horace and Charlie tried, but they're too young." Of course they were. They were schoolchildren, playing tag at recess. How could they be soldiers?

We must send millions of men "over there," newspapers cried. "Bang! Bang! Bang!" cried little boys running down Main Street with toy guns. Recruitment posters bloomed everywhere. "Join the Air Service!" said one in the Hendersons' window. In the bakery: "Be an American Eagle." By the theater: "Come on, boys! Do your duty!"

I watched Tom training Lilli to go left, go right, sit, stand, wait, fetch, and find. "Stay," he'd command, and then busy himself with other tasks while secretly timing her stay. *Tom, you stay, too. The trees stay, the rose garden stays.* But walking with him, sitting in the meadow, seeing him follow a bird across the sky, I knew that war would soon suck him away.

"I couldn't bear it," I told my mother.

"You'll have to," she said quietly. As she bore my father's passing. That went without saying.

I ceased making plans. To stay in Dogwood, leave Dogwood, go or not go to Paris after the war, what did my plans matter now? This war was a vast whirlpool, churning plans apart. The one million dead at the Somme all had plans, and so did those they left behind. Cities bombed to rubble had plans. The earth, the forests, farms and fields, the growing things where now was wasteland had plans. My mother meant to grow old with her husband. So did the baron and Friedrich, I assumed. Even Ben had yearnings that drew him on. Who was I to think that my plans were inviolate?

Work, just work. We had just acquired a set of watercolors by J. M. W. Turner of storms at sea. Here was the appropriate scale of plans for these times: helping the baron create a list of possible buyers.

NOTHING UNUSUAL HAD happened the day Tom enlisted. I'd walked back from town with the morning paper as always, and he met me at the gate as always. We walked slowly to the castle as always, arms entwined, slipping between pines for hidden kisses. At breakfast, our feet met beneath the table. Anna lamented the latest rationing. I watched Tom balance his bread, as always, in a tangent on his plate.

"What's wrong, Hazel?" Anna asked. "Did you see a ghost?"

"No, I just remembered something for the baron."

That afternoon, I found Tom straightening his tools. "You enlisted." He looked up. A hammer wavered in his hand. "Is it true?"

He put down the hammer. "Yes."

"When are you leaving?"

"Not right away."

"When?"

"Saturday."

A band squeezed my chest so strongly that I had to sit. "So soon?"

"Hazel, they need trained pilots."

"You knew you'd do this."

"Yes. I didn't want to spoil our time together."

"Spoil our time," I repeated dully.

"I'll come back."

"Don't promise. Just come back."

"*You* came back to Dogwood. Now it's my turn." I stepped toward him. I smelled his shirt, his skin, and the sharp bite of sawdust. Without words, we went to his room, to his bed. Now there was no space between us, no leaving, no gravity, no time. That long afternoon, we flew in blue air.

For months I'd known he'd leave. Even the fact of our meeting here after so many years, our ease and pleasure in each other, the thrill to be close, all this was pure chance, not in my plan, nothing to do with searching after Margit. That chance had yielded a great gift. I should only be grateful. And yet, to not see Tom in the morning, to not walk together in the evening, hear his laughter, or feel his solid presence in the dark times, how could I endure this pain, even if I knew that I must?

In his last days at the castle, Tom put in a bench by my father's grave. He took long walks with the baron who had been so much to him for most of his life. He sat with Anna in the kitchen as she plied him with presents of knitted socks, a vest, and a scarf to keep warm "up there." He walked my mother to the bakery and talked with Tilda as she worked. He met with Kurt in the rose garden. In the lengthening afternoons, he and I took blankets to the meadow and lay together, as close as skin.

"This beautiful place," he said, "and you here. How can I not return?"

"We could meet in Paris, afterwards."

"Yes, we could do that. The war won't last long now. Remember, the German supply lines are stretched thin and they've had heavy losses. Americans will come in fresh; the Brits have airpower and the blockade. We can help the French. It won't be long now."

"Suppose you have to fly against his cousin Manfred, the one they call the Red Baron? He's downed fifty Allied planes already."

"Don't worry, Hazel. If I say I worked for his cousin, they'll send someone else." A pretty lie, but I'd think of it often with comfort. "Remember that the Capodimonte porcelain piece we packed arrived without a single broken petal. And I'm not made of porcelain. I'll come back safe. Besides, since I know how to fly, they might make me an instructor."

"I hope so." An instructor far from the front, that would be best of all.

We ate in the banquet room the night before he left. The baron invited everyone who ever worked in the castle. There were speeches, songs, and gifts. I'd made a sketch of us together. "It will fly with me," Tom promised. We were all so brave, knowing full well how many such dinners were being held all across the country.

Early the next morning, the baron, Lilli, and I walked to the train station with Tom. "Take care of yourself," said the baron, kissing him on both cheeks.

"I'll be back, or I'll be in Paris," Tom said to me. "Stay," he told Lilli, took his bags, and was swallowed in a pool of men leaving Dogwood.

We walked back to the castle. Lilli lagged behind us, looking constantly over her shoulder. The baron rested a hand on my shoulder. "Hazel, I promise to keep you busy until the end of this madness." The polished shoes took measured steps on the gravel walk. I tried to match his pace, to soldier on like him.

THE BARON KEPT his promise. The next months passed in a wash of work as summer mocked us with lush beauty. The gardens bloomed wildly. The orchards dripped with fruit. Songbirds rejoiced in the abundance of food. In the long twilights, my mother and I often walked out to "visit Johannes," sitting on Tom's bench as shadows crept over us. Once in Pittsburgh, she'd noted with mild disdain: "Those Italians are always touching each other." Yet now she put her arm around me or leaned against my shoulder. She brought no handwork to the meadow, which was unusual. She'd always been busy cooking, cleaning, dusting, mending, or keeping books for the store. Even while reading with me, she'd be knitting, winding yarn, or peeling potatoes. Now her very stillness seemed a concentrated activity.

Tom wrote weekly, with two letters in each envelope, one for me and one for "my friends at Mein Königsberg." The latter I read in the kitchen and then gave to the baron. Even Lilli listened, curled in her bed on one of Tom's flannel shirts that she'd confiscated. "I'm older than others in my flight class," he reported, "but I'm keeping up." Once "over there," American pilots would join Allied flight squads, until more American planes arrived. Every letter carried less war news. He wrote of a rose

garden he'd seen, an idea for packing large vases, incidents in the barracks, quirks of his comrades, books from the base library, a stray dog
he'd adopted. I knew his purpose was to ease our worry with normalcy,
but these letters, by turns droll and thoughtful, only made me miss
him more.

We all lived by letters in those months. We shared them, wrote
them, and carried them in pockets and purses. Letters fanned the war
as much as posters, parades, flags, war bond sales, and speeches. Ginny
Henderson posted careful copies of Geoffrey's letters in the drugstore
window. "Nobody knew he could write so well," she boasted.

"Mrs. Scott's son read Geoffrey's letters and went straight to the
army recruiter," my mother said at dinner. "Soon there won't be any
more boys left."

In fact, they were being drained away like water from a sink. Luisa's
two brothers had enlisted together. Her husband was safe from the
draft, for he was now the sole support of his newly widowed mother,
Luisa, and their twin baby girls, both sickly. "I don't know what to
hope for," she wrote. "If they get better and I can work, I lose Tony. If
they don't get better, I'll lose my mind." More and more boys were en-
listing in Galway, Jim Burnett wrote. "You can't believe how this town
has changed."

Everywhere, brutality was seeping into civilian life. At the machine
shop where he'd worked for twenty years, Uncle Willy was suddenly a
"hyphenated American," a Hun, a possible traitor. Because he would
not crawl across the shop floor to kiss the American flag, he was
shunned. "They can't fire him," Tante Elise wrote, "because he's their
best mechanic, but nobody talks to him. They leave ugly notes. He's an
American citizen, Katarina. He's godfather to some of their children.
It's happening all over town to anyone who has an accent."

Broken beer bottles littered our driveway. When Lilli sliced her paw on a shard of glass, we kept her inside for days, fearing poison. I wrote nothing of this to Tom. He shouldn't be worried. He should just think about coming home safely.

Kurt organized paper and scrap metal drives in town. His wife, Ilsa, rolled bandages for the Red Cross. "We have to" was his explanation. I discovered why. Their landlord had threatened eviction. When he walked downtown, boys followed him. "Swine," they whispered. "Kaiser's swine."

In Pittsburgh, boys had played war games in our empty lot. Now adults attacked each other, vandalizing foreign-owned stores, ruining businesses, and firing employees with "un-American" names. In once-peaceable towns, mobs beat their neighbors. Some were tarred and feathered. "My sister in Illinois saw a man lynched," Anna reported. How naïve to think the Atlantic could so neatly divide war and peace. If young men were learning to plunge bayonets into enemies' faces and bellies, then shouldn't their parents, their little brothers and sisters spit, poison dogs, and wrap hateful notes around rocks and throw them through our gate?

On a bright fall morning I unwrapped one that said: "Go home, Kraut!" in childish scrawl. The baron had lived in Dogwood for twenty years, but how many children knew him? A handful. Very few had ever spoken to him. The next morning I launched a proposal: "Baron, we could invite a class here to see some paintings."

He looked up, startled. "Why?"

"People don't know what you do here. My mother hears people talking in town. Some think you deal arms or train spies in the woods or create new kinds of poison gas that nobody can detect."

He put down his pen. "Go on."

"Well, there are children who have never seen you. Most have never spoken with you. Imagine what they think about you."

"Meeting me might not improve their opinion. I seem to be an acquired taste, not yet acquired uniformly, even after two decades." A wistful sadness veiled the beautiful face. Sadly, he was correct. What would children see, even if their parents let them enter what some called "the Hun's lair"? Here was a man wholly unlike their fathers, unnaturally handsome and impeccably attired in vaguely foreign cut, formal, even pedantic in speech, unmistakably German in accent and cadence. His military stance, crisp and measured stride, and precise turns might all be frightening. The grandeur of his castle would surely intimidate. Fed by fairy tales and local gossip, would they wonder if the paneled walls hid secret passageways to dungeons where stolen children might be kept?

They wouldn't see the man who opened his home to an abandoned boy, and an "unsatisfactory" servant's illegitimate baby girl. They wouldn't feel the kinship he shared with my parents, how he welcomed them, shared our grief, and honored my father's passing. If they knew of his love for Friedrich, they'd be repulsed. They wouldn't know the man who earned our loyalty or how his unyielding standards pushed, prodded, and drew us to levels of work we could not have imagined for ourselves. No, classrooms in the castle would not clear the poisoned air of Dogwood. "Could I at least take some paintings to the school and talk about them? It might help make people less suspicious. I'm sure the children would be interested."

"Really? In fine art?"

"They could be." I told him of the books I brought to school in Galway, how the children peered at etchings of Notre Dame, marveled at the shading in Da Vinci's paintings, and were first contemptuous and then intrigued by modern art's fractured images.

He studied me. "Apparently this is what *you'd* like, to have some contact with the school?"

"Yes." Yes, I missed this in my life. I also feared it, but what harm could come of such a small project? "There's a new Cézanne landscape and the Gauguin prints. The children might like to see them."

"*Children*," he repeated, as if speaking of an exotic tribe. He'd hosted me as a baby, I reminded him, and raised Tom. "Yes, that's true, but children in the abstract are so inexplicable."

"They wouldn't be abstract children. They'd be like Tom was once, or you yourself."

"No, not like me, I assure you. But if you're so convinced, I'll provide a few pieces. Kurt can bring them to the school, not to be handled by children, abstract or otherwise."

"Of course not, Baron. Thank you."

I spoke with Lena Hardy, a young teacher I knew slightly from church, earnest and enthusiastic, precisely as I'd been in my first months at Galway. She was delighted. She'd heard of the castle's treasures but thought them as inaccessible as any prince's holdings. We fixed a date in September. I dressed carefully, prepared my notes, and had Kurt pack a small Cézanne still life sketch, a French garden scene by Watteau, reproductions of works by Corot and Gauguin, and a Chinese watercolor of misty mountains sheltering a farming village.

Then I was in a schoolroom again with the familiar smell of books and chalk, rows of jackets, printed alphabets, a flag and globe, and all the sounds of children. I'd be speaking only to fourth graders. How quickly I'd grown accustomed to the jumble of a single room and all that one could do and not do with young and older children learning together.

Lena had elaborately prepared her students to see "real art that's going to great museums." I was "an actual artist" who worked with the

Baron von Richthofen, who was "an internationally known collector." They must appreciate this rare opportunity. Kurt and I set up the pieces as twenty-five children watched, wary, intrigued, suspicious, and unsmiling. Of course. I was a stranger. Why would they welcome me? I shared how I'd started drawing at their age, how all peoples, in all cultures found pleasure and meaning in art.

"Are these Kraut pictures?" a red-haired boy interrupted.

"How much did they cost?" asked the girl beside him.

"Who'd pay money for *that*?" another boy demanded of the Cézanne. The "Chinese thing" would be nicer in color. Was Gauguin a castaway in the South Seas or did he go there on purpose? Why didn't Corot have more horses and people?

"Gloria, what do you see here first in the garden scene?" Lena asked.

"A girl on a swing."

"Why?"

"She's pretty."

"The man and the dog are looking at her," said a somber boy with shiny brown hair. "We look where they look. And there's the arc of the trees framing her." He also noted that Gauguin's colors were "simpler" and his shapes "fit together like a puzzle."

"Maybe he just can't draw, Waaal-ter," one boy scoffed.

"Well, *I* think it's interesting," Walter maintained. "And look over there." He pointed to the Corot. "The white clouds have blue in them."

"Clouds aren't blue, you dope."

"Pete," said Lena sharply. "We don't use such language."

I invited Pete to come closer and examine the brushstrokes. He marched up, peered, and conceded: "Yeah, there's *some* blue."

After this small victory, I had the children examine brushstrokes on the other canvases, Cézanne's "crazy angles," and how the Chinese artist made a few lines suggesting a laboring farmer. Walter noticed

Corot's "silky water" and Gauguin's mild perspective. Our hour flew. Lena released the class for recess.

"They're pretty pictures, Miss Renner," said Gloria, the last to leave. "Too bad they're locked up with a Hun."

"Huns lived a long time ago. People from Germany are Germans."

"Well, according to my dad, they're Huns."

"It's recess, perhaps you'd like to join the others outside," Lena suggested. Gloria darted off. "Hazel, I hope you'll come again. Walter, especially, was so looking forward to this."

"He has a good eye."

"He does. Hazel, it's true what you told Gloria, but you must know that people are suspicious. The baron is all shut up in that castle, like he's hiding something."

Searching for a quick and easy answer, I found only: "He's busy with his work."

"Well, we appreciate the art. Please thank him for me." Nobody could blame either Lena or Gloria, I thought, as Kurt drove me home. The baron *was* "shut up in that castle." He wasn't a "Hun," but he also wasn't part of Dogwood.

"He doesn't want to be disturbed," Anna warned when we came back. Late that night, peering out my window, I saw the baron walking Lilli by moonlight, their charcoal shadows making slow circles on the dark velvet lawn. Some days before, he had sent me to the Hendersons for sleeping powders. Evidently they didn't work, for restless promenades continued, even under a steady autumn drizzle. At work he was distracted, repeating questions, strangely uncertain, checking and rechecking figures. I sometimes saw him in the workroom, studying my father's map of Europe, gently touching the pinpricked swath of Prussia.

Each week brought shorter, more ragged letters from Tom. He was "somewhere in Belgium," behind the lines, but close enough to hear the bombs and see the endless flow of corpses. He was a flight instructor, safe for now, but safety brought him grating guilt: "My men get shot down, sometimes on their first raid. We can't even get their bodies back. Tell Anna that I'm wearing her scarf. It's always cold here and hard to sleep. The bombs never stop. Johannes was right. We're making a hell here."

## CHAPTER 16

# *A Child Like You*

On a clear winter night, when moon shadows lay crisp as silhouettes on the ground, I dressed and joined the baron, coming so quietly across the lawn that Lilli merely turned to watch my approach. "Ah, Hazel, you can't sleep, either?"

"No."

"You've heard from Tom?"

"Not for a week. In the last letter, he said they needed pilots. They'll be sending him up."

The baron looked over the trees. Moonlight iced his face. "I just heard that my brother Erich was killed. It was not in battle. He was driving back from town very late, quite drunk. He stopped to relieve himself and was hit by a sniper. There is no military honor for such a death."

"I'm sorry, sir—"

He held up a hand. "I don't mourn him, particularly. I never had a moment's pleasure in my brother's company. He despised me from the first."

"Despised? But—"

The baron nodded. "I know it must seem strange to you, Hazel, this lack of familial sentiment."

It was. He might have been speaking of another species. All I could think to ask was: "You have this news from your father?"

"I've had *no* news directly from him in years. I rely on other sources. Apparently Erich's death, or more particularly the inglorious nature of it, was too much for him. He had a stroke and is bedridden. There is no competent doctor nearby; all are dead or gone to war. It's left to my mother and the cook to nurse him."

We walked on. Nighttime made me bold, and mystery drew me on. What deep well of hurt was covered by his calm? "Could you tell me about your parents?"

He looked into the pines. Our boots crunched on needles. "My mother's family were inconsequential landowners, but she was quite beautiful. In his single moment of weakness, my father married her. He never let her forget how far he'd stooped to do so. Ultimately, this hardly mattered. His tireless service to the Kaiser was rewarded by a noble title and a large estate with a crumbling castle."

"The first Mein Königsberg."

"Yes, precisely. I was eight when we took possession of what Erich termed 'that old pile.' Legions of workers were hired to restore and expand the 'pile' to appropriate grandeur. Then, of course, it must be filled with fine furnishings and portraits of fictitious ancestors. This became my task."

"Yours? How old were you?"

"Thirteen. A professor at the military academy had let me explore his library and modest art collection, my only happy hours there. That summer in Vienna, I went with my father to an art dealer to buy, as he put it, 'old things.' I picked some true treasures from the dealer's jumble and he congratulated my 'natural eye,' comparing it to young Mozart's natural ear."

"And your father?"

"He would have preferred other skills, but this one was useful, at least. He had the purse and I had the eye. Soon his collection was noted in our circle of petty nobility. Of course, my agency was never mentioned. It wasn't a matter of family pride."

"And your mother?"

"She was an adornment herself. She loved me and didn't want me to leave for America, but she had very little power in that household. However, on my last night, she gave me this." He took off his familiar ruby bezel ring and opened it to reveal a young woman's face, a hauntingly delicate version of his own, with the same deep eyes, high cheekbones, and exquisitely sculpted mouth.

"Your mother? She was very beautiful."

"Yes." He closed the ring. "She promised to write to me in America and did so briefly. Then either my father discovered the correspondence and disliked it or she simply stopped writing."

"I'm sorry."

"Hazel, you have the gift of mourning a father *after* his death. I've mourned the one I never had all my life."

In the slightest shifting of his voice and stiffening of stance I read, as I had learned to read in these months, that the subject of his family was closed again, like a curtain pulled shut. Yet because he kept walking with me, I broached a new subject. "There's a child like you at the school. He has a natural eye. His name is Walter." I described the boy's keen observations of color and form.

"A child like me." The baron touched a rosebush, all thorns and bare branches. "He'll have troubles, I'm sure."

"Perhaps you could help him or encourage him in some way."

"Perhaps." The moon had dipped below the castle's bulk. "For now, I'll walk awhile, if you don't mind. It may induce sleep." So I left him. Later, from my room I watched the erect, solitary precision of his march, like a sentry never relieved of duty.

A LONG LETTER came from Tom. He was flying reconnaissance. Every place name had been inked out, but the censors had let stand evidence of a man's soul shaken like a rag by months of war. "Even back here in the airfields, the blasts rattle your teeth. We have beds and decent food, not like the poor devils in the trenches. You think about them all night. You can't sleep. I flew today. Up there, it's quiet. There's a bit of green in the distance. I could pretend there's a real world somewhere that war isn't. I've got an English pilot friend named Colin who was a gardener back home. He has a cure for rose mites. We wouldn't mind some mites. All we have here are lice."

The next page was written a week later, crumpled, as if it had been started and stopped many times. It began: "Colin was blown up today. He was walking to the barracks. All he ever wanted to do was grow roses. A grenade blew him into pieces." The writing faltered. "I made the medics find them. The pieces. We'd had tea ten minutes before. If I'd just said, 'Colin, let's have another cup,' he'd be here today. You try not to think like that or you go crazy like the boys they send away with shell shock. Tell Kurt to varnish the bench by your father's grave and plant more pear trees. We took ten prisoners. One might have killed Colin. But Hazel, they were pitiful. You can't imagine how hungry & scared those Germans were, like kids with old men's eyes. One said in English: 'A whole potato. For me?' It spins your head around. How are the roses? All that's here is mud and blown up earth, dust & burned things. War takes color away.

There's just dust, mud, and rock. Only red when boys are bleeding. I keep thinking about Colin. One more cup of tea and he'd still be here. They're getting the mail now. Tell Anna I'm wearing her scarf. I'll see you soon. This can't go on. Love, Tom."

I read the letter aloud in the kitchen, letting each sheet fall on the table. Afterward we sat in silence. A breeze lifted the stack, scattering pages on the floor. Lilli whimpered when one flew at her. "Every day he's alive is good," my mother said finally.

"He'll be better once he gets home," Anna added.

In the meadow Tom's soft skin and yielding flesh had pressed into mine. I felt his bones. He folded around me. How could this body withstand shells that shook the earth until it bucked? How could a plane of sticks and metal sheeting block machine-gun fire? Why would he *not* be one of the millions dead before peace ever came? And what of the mind that seemed so firm? His letter lurched from bombs to pear trees. Would it, in lurching, shake loose the Tom I knew? "Hazel, you look pale," said Anna. "Should I tell the baron you're not feeling well?"

"No, we need to work." I climbed to the tower office with Tom's letter in my pocket. I meant to share it until I saw the baron leaning against a window frame, a telegram in his hand, folding and unfolding the yellow paper. I'd never seen him do this. He disliked creased paper. The marble face was very pale. I stopped at the door. He gestured for me to come in.

"Bad news, sir?"

"My father died three weeks ago. The baroness told nobody. Perhaps she was afraid of creditors. My agent only now learned of his death."

"I'm so sorry. First your brother and then—"

He went on folding and unfolding the telegram. "You've finished the latest offering letter, Hazel?" For the first time, I truly pitied the baron.

"Yes. It's on your desk."

I thought he might speak more about his father as we worked. But the beautiful face was marble, the back rigid. Was this how we must all endure the war? Tom must fly, not thinking of Colin or soldiers in the trenches. The baron and I must work, he not thinking of Prussia, and I not thinking of Tom. I pulled my chair forward, my back straight and feet pressed hard into the floor.

"There may be a good market for our Voltaire letters. Could you re-search it, please?" We worked steadily through the day. By the dim-ming afternoon, Tom's letter was so heavy in my pocket that I had to take it out and share it with the baron. He read slowly, holding each page by the edges like a rare manuscript, setting it down carefully, and finally reassembling the letter neatly and handing it back to me. "No good will come of this war. None. And our Tom's in the midst of it." He looked out the window. His hand strayed to the telegram of his father's desk. He was utterly immobile for so long that I asked again if I should leave. He nodded.

THE NEXT MORNING, the baron left for New York to meet a collector. A note on my desk listed a Dutch still life, Greek vase, and J. M. W. Turner watercolor I could show the schoolchildren. "You may be right. We could do some good here and hurt nobody. Have Kurt help you pack them." I ran for Kurt, relieved and happy for the distraction.

Lena was pleased as well and quickly organized another session. This time she assigned Jud, one of the larger boys, to help us with the easels, a punishment for being "obstripus," he said.

"Obstreperous?"

"Yeah, I guess."

Jud's interest flared briefly for the Greek vase with scenes from the Trojan War, but dimmed when Walter pointed out recurring patterns of black between the red warrior figures. "Sort of a rhythm," he suggested, ignoring Jud's theatrical yawn.

Louise studied a Dutch still life of a laden table and concluded: "They didn't have food rationing." Walter, bolder now, pointed out that the artist used perspective "even on apples and eggs." I looked closely. He was right; the shaping was subtle, but there.

Jud dubbed the Turner "messy." At least he wasn't yawning.

Walter, staring at the landscape, commented: "It's *not* messy. Look how he mixed the blues, different for water and sky."

"You know what, Waaal-ter?" Stan announced. "You're really strange."

Walter shrank, shoulders curling in. A pretty girl named Alma asked loudly, "Miss Renner, did the Trojan War really happen?" Susanna would have done the same, neatly parrying a bully's thrust. I gave her a grateful smile. My tale of Heinrich Schliemann's excavation of Troy launched a spirited discussion of Indian villages that might lie under Dogwood. When bells rang for the lunch hour, children sprang from the room as if they'd been launched.

"I hope we can do this again," Lena said as we folded the easels. Muffled cries brought us racing from the schoolyard, where Walter was being jerked like a doll between Jud and Stan as they repeated: "You wanna be a still life? Do you, Waaal-ter, do you?" Lena and I grabbed both culprits by the collars. Walter crumbled between them, holding his head.

"Jud, why are we fighting in Europe?" Lena demanded.

"To defend the American Way," he parroted from a dozen posters, pamphlets, and Four Minute Men's speeches.

"Is the American Way about respecting the other guy and not being a bully?"

"I guess so."

"Good. Then help Walter up and go eat your lunch." In answer to pleading looks, Lena conceded: "I won't tell your parents, but no more fighting in school. There's too much of it going on over there."

"Thank you," Walter said after Jud and Stan darted off. "I should just keep my mouth shut."

"You shouldn't have to," I said. "Walter, do you draw in your free time?" He turned to me, startled, as if a secret vice had been discovered, and nodded cautiously. "Could I see some of your work?" He shook his head and excused himself, disappearing around the corner of the school.

"He's shy," Lena said as we walked back to the classroom. "Maybe next time we'll invite only the interested children." But there was no next time. Some of the parents had complained about "Kraut art" being shown to the children. Walter's mother wanted no more excuses for her son to be beaten up. We might try again after the war, Lena suggested, when "things are quieter."

But I'd seen Walter's head snap back and forth and said only, "Yes, perhaps."

IN THE NEXT weeks, I looked for Walter when I passed the schoolyard; on Sundays, when most of Dogwood walked to church; on Main Street; and in the library, where Lena said he often passed his afternoons. Perhaps he was avoiding me.

So many in Dogwood were avoiding each other now. The local casualties had begun. A Dogwood man died in Flanders. The Sandersons lost both sons in one week near the Hindenburg Line. The war had been so remote, and the soldiers' leaving so festive, with flags and songs, many calling out that they'd be back by Thanksgiving, or Christmas at the latest. The whole town shuddered when the first black buntings draped doorways. Those who had lost men and those whose men were safe for now did not speak to each other, looking away, hurrying along on the streets, huddled with their kind after church.

I found cards with names of the dead tied to the castle gate, fluttering in the wind. "Satisfied?" someone had scrawled. I pulled off the cards, but more came. "Stop the Hun!" they might say or "Smash the beast!" Pastor Birke walked my mother home one afternoon when boys were following her on the sidewalk, hissing. Captain Neal went to speak with the boys' families. The hissing ceased, but now Kurt drove her to work early and picked her up at the back door. When I went into town, I was constantly asked what the baron thought of the latest war news.

"He hopes for peace, as we all do," I always said.

"You don't have to go into town," Anna observed. "Kurt can get what you need."

But Dogwood was my town for now, and the war encased us all. Weeks had passed since my last letter from Tom. I drew daily courage from knowing that other women wanted a letter as much as I did, that they also longed to touch paper that their men had touched. We shared a silent sisterhood in that endless spring.

Despite constant losses, the Allies steadily advanced, fueled by fresh American troops, new tanks, and ceaseless air strikes. In April, jubilant headlines announced the downing of Manfred von Richthofen, the Red Baron. "He was your baron's cousin, wasn't he?" I was asked outside the Hendersons' store. "One less flying ace for them. What does *he* think about it?"

"Manfred was his cousin, as you said."

"And our enemy."

"Yes." Manfred was my enemy, for he might have flown against Tom. Now Manfred was gone. So I should rejoice. But how? Manfred and our baron had been like brothers despite their difference in age. They took walking tours together. Until the baron left Prussia, Manfred had been his strongest ally in the family.

Kurt brought newspapers covering Manfred's death and extraordinary funeral. The Australian Flying Corps buried him with full military honors, with a wreath inscribed: "To our gallant and worthy foe."

"Full military honors," the baron repeated. He circled the tower office as I read accounts of Allied officers carrying his casket, led by a chaplain in his robes, an honor guard, and a final salute. "Should I be comforted, do you think, Hazel, by this display of military courtesy? Nearly medieval, is it not?"

"I'm not sure."

"Exactly. You remember what Shakespeare said of honor? He called it 'air. A trim reckoning. Who hath it? He that died o' Wednesday. Doth he feel it? No. Doth he hear it? No. 'Tis insensible, then? Yea, to the dead.' Now Manfred is dead. So let's not speak of honor. War is death and destruction. Nothing more."

He was wrong, I soon discovered. War was also void. It was not knowing. Jud, Walter's tormentor, worked for Western Union now, delivering telegrams in a crisp uniform that made him look far younger and wiped the brash confidence from a now-earnest face. On a Saturday morning in early May, when the lawns were bright with tulips, Jud brought my telegram: Thomas Alan Jamison was missing in action after a flight over enemy lines in Belgium. The words danced, meaning nothing until I read them aloud.

"So he's not dead yet," said Jud. We were in the kitchen. I was standing by a window. I wavered; I pawed at space. Jud brought me a chair and snatched off his cap. They probably told him at the Western Union office: *Show respect. Always remove your cap inside.* "Maybe Tom got captured, you know, Miss Renner. Although, if the Krauts can't feed their own soldiers, how in blazes can they feed prisoners?" He went on, his voice growing shrill. Why couldn't he stop? "Or if he was a pilot, that's another thing. When planes get shot down, sometimes they don't know who it is because the bodies are all—" Anna came in from the kitchen garden, saw the telegram in my hand, and heard the last of Jud's words.

"Young man," said Anna quickly, "Miss Renner needs to be alone now."

"Just a minute, Jud," I managed, my voice as flat as paper. "How many telegrams have you delivered this week?"

The face crumbled. "You mean the 'killed in action' kind?" I nodded. "Three so far. Mrs. Casey was the worst. She's that way." The grubby hand shaped a pregnant belly. "Fell flat on the ground, bang! Bang! Right in front of me. I had to help her up. I hate this job but my folks need the money. I'm sorry, Miss Renner. Tom was nice. He gave us wood for our forts. I hope he comes back."

"So do we," said Anna. "But you run along now, Jud." She gave him a quarter and eased him out the door. Then she pulled up a chair and gathered me in her arms. "You were smaller the last time I did this," she said softly. "When Margit left you at night, you'd tug on my apron and I'd hold you." Pressed into the starched cloth over the soft and yielding chest, my body remembered the warmth, the scent of sugar and soap, and the broad hand patting my back.

"Missing in action. Where is he? Why won't they tell me if he's safe? He could be a prisoner or burned up, like Jud said. Or lost." My shoulders heaved. Anna held me tightly.

"Hazel, I've been worried about that boy since he came here. Is he eating right? Fevers, nightmares about his father, boys making fun of him at school. Will he fall out of a tree? Moving heavy things for the baron, will he get hurt? Love is worrying about somebody. There's no way out of it."

"But this is different."

"No, it's not different. You can't help him right now. You just have to bear it." Still patting my back, she began singing so softly that the song seemed to rise out of my own mind: "Muss Ich Denn." My father sang it to me when I was small, holding my hand as I drifted to sleep. Coming back from the bakery, my mother found us sitting together.

"I know," she said. "Jud told me."

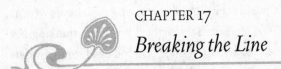

## CHAPTER 17

## *Breaking the Line*

M issing isn't dead," the baron said. "One must have the courage of patience." Of course. And what right had I to be crushed by this one telegram, when he'd received so many: Friedrich, his father and brother, friends, family, and scores from his academy? Manfred's death had been shouted in headlines. Yes, I must be patient; I must sleep at night and not stare at the traitorous sky that had not held him aloft and safe, flying with hawks, circling green fields. I must follow the war news attentively. I must be concerned that with Russia's force occupied by the Bolshevik Revolution, German forces could leave the Eastern Front and strengthen the Western Front along the Hindenburg Line.

"Yes," I said mechanically to the endless debates on this point. "That could be terrible."

"Pure bunk," Mr. Henderson announced when I came for more of the baron's sleeping powders. "We'll break that line. Our boys are fresh. You've heard of the Hundred Days Offensive? We'll have peace before Christmas." *Peace before Christmas*. People said that in 1914, four years ago. Didn't he remember? Suppose the war went on Christmas after Christmas, the missing never found?

"Any news of Tom?" Mrs. Henderson asked.

"No, not yet. And Geoffrey?"

"He just wrote. I'm sure they'll both come back." Her eyes were as shadowed as mine. Did she watch the night sky as I did, thinking: *Are you covering him, too? Are you keeping him safe?* "Do you need some powders yourself, Hazel?"

"No, thank you." What was the use? Waking or sleeping, I imagined Tom a prisoner of war or lying in No Man's Land, burned beyond recognition. I saw him fallen in a forest, his body left for a hunter years from now to stumble upon, or lost to himself and us, one of the legions of shell-shocked casualties of war. Was he missing by intention, having deserted a battlefield more horrible than hell? Had he deserted me as well?

A Western Union boy rode past the store, head down in a misty rain. "Your heart stops when you see one coming," said Mrs. Henderson. "Then he passes and you live again."

But was this boy Walter? The slight, strained form was exactly Walter's. His parents blamed him for being mocked in school, Lena had said. Was this their plan to make him tougher? If so, I'd done my part to put him in that horrible uniform, condemned to bring death news.

I watched him pedal away and then turn right. Toward the castle. Now I was hurrying after him, with barely a word to Mrs. Henderson. Did Walter have a telegram correcting the first one? Was Tom not missing, but killed in action? Walter's classmates mocked and shook him. Wouldn't I shake him if he was my messenger of death? Stop! We received dozens of telegrams at the castle. Why should this one not deal with some trivial matter of a Rembrandt or the wildly rising market for Gauguins? I walked faster. Then ran. But nobody was at the gate. Walter had pedaled on, bringing death or trivia to another house. "Then he passes and you live again," Mrs. Henderson had said. Panting with relief, I stopped running, suddenly grateful for "missing in action"—a message of promise and hope.

"Miss Renner?" a child's voice whispered. Walter and his bicycle were pushed into the deep shade of pine trees. He beckoned me closer. Fear surged back: he'd give me the telegram in private. But no, he was holding a rolled sheet. White, not Western Union's sickly buff. "I wanted to show you my drawing."

I smoothed open the paper and gasped. Despite a web of creases, the work was stunning. Beginning with a simple-seeming house and garden on a cloudy day, sunrays made skillful rhythms of light and dark. Subtle distortions menaced the country scene, drawing one to look deeper, learning more.

"Walter, you have incredible talent." Pride lit his face; gladness poured through me. Just a wonderful drawing, not a telegram of death. Joy made me generous and eager to help.

A thin finger hovered over the paper. "There wasn't really a tree here."

"You put it in for balance?"

"I guess so."

"I'd like to show this to the baron. And you can see the castle."

The brown eyes widened; he pulled back into the pines. "No. People say there's mad scientists in there who catch boys and make them weak. It's the Kaiser's plot so that when he invades us—"

"Walter, stop. You can't believe that nonsense." He shrugged. "What about Tom? He was strong, right? And he lived in the castle for years. Come with me. I promise to protect you from mad scientists." A tiny smile. "What do your parents say about drawing?"

"To stop doing it if boys make fun of me."

"They made you take this job?" He nodded. "And you hate it?" Nod. "Walter, maybe I shouldn't have brought those pictures to school."

"No, I'm glad you did. When I draw or think about drawing, I'm happy."

Through the gate, I glimpsed the baron walking with Lilli. "There he is. You don't even have to go inside. He can come out here and see your drawing."

Walter peeked through the gate and jumped back in alarm. I knew why. "Walter, it's a *dog,* not a wolf. Her name is Lilli. She's very gentle. She's a—we call her an Alsatian shepherd now. And the baron is very kind. You have to believe me." I took Walter's silence as assent and signaled the baron to join us. Walter stood closer to me as they approached. His hand barely moved from his body as I introduced him, so the baron bowed slightly to grasp it.

"Walter Baines. Miss Renner has spoken well of you."

Walter was mute. "Let's have Lilli show you her tricks while the baron looks at your drawing." I handed over the wrinkled page and had Lilli sit, shake, lie down, and fetch for the slowly warming Walter.

The baron cleared his throat. "Miss Renner has not exaggerated your skill, young man." He returned the drawing as if handing over a Leonardo. "She showed you a watercolor by the English painter J. M. W. Turner?"

A whisper: "Yes, Mister Baron Sir."

" 'Baron' is sufficient. Turner was the greatest landscape master of his time. His work at age twelve was remarkable, as is yours at age—"

"Ten."

"Ten. As I say, remarkable. You might study his work." He noted Walter's uniform. "Yours is a difficult job in these times."

Still a whisper: "People hate me. They scream at me to go away." The beautiful face surveyed the small one. He offered no advice, no wisdom or encouragement. He simply laid a hand on the thin shoulder. Walter raised his eyes and said in a normal voice: "Thank you, Baron. You can keep the drawing." He retrieved his bicycle and was gone, pedaling frantically back to town, looking over his shoulder at another boy on a bicycle far down the road.

"Next time we could show him some Turners," I suggested.

The baron sighed. "There won't be a next time." He was right. Walter never came back. Jud had seen us with the baron and reported this fact to his parents. Lena told me that Walter seemed daily more timid and withdrawn. His parents had taken away his drawing pencils. "They said it was for his own good. When he's not working, he should be playing baseball with the other boys."

But not even Jud had time for baseball now. Headlines trumpeted Allied victories on every front, but Western Union kept receiving death notices. On a rainy spring day, I saw Walter for the first time in weeks, riding down Main Street in uniform and ignoring my greeting. Alma happened by, long pigtails bobbing as she skipped between puddles. I asked her how Walter was doing in school.

"Not so good. He brought the telegram to Billy's house. Now nobody talks to him even if it's not his fault the Huns got Billy's daddy."

"But Jud's a Western Union boy. Do his friends still talk to him?"

"Yeah they do, but I have to go." The long pigtails swung away. I followed Walter's path. It was easy in a small town. His first deliveries were innocuous. He slipped in and out of stores, usually pocketing a tip. Then he turned into a neat yard, passing Gloria, who stopped her game of jacks and followed him, stiff-legged. The front door swallowed them both. A woman inside screamed: "Go away! Get out of here!" Walter ran out to the curb and bent over, vomiting. I reached him and held the shaking shoulders.

"I can't do this," he sobbed. "I can't. I can't. I can't."

"No, Walter, you can't. It's not fair to ask a child. I'll do something."

"But my father says I have to keep this job."

"Then we'll change the job. Come, I'll deliver the rest with you." Fortunately there were no more death notices that afternoon. When we parted on Oak Street, he turned to me with hopeful trust, like seekers at my blue house. "Thank you, Miss Renner. I know you'll fix this." How? By ending the war or stopping Dogwood men from dying? By magically causing survivors to receive these telegrams placidly?

Back at the castle, I explained my predicament. "Be careful what you promise," was the baron's advice. He wouldn't consider secretly matching Walter's salary. "Obviously his parents would suspect me. Please, Hazel, be reasonable." It was my mother who suggested I take my problem to Pastor Birke.

"To talk about it?"

"Of course not. To fix it." Dubious, I went to his office and found him surrounded by piles of clutter, a surprising contrast to his studied public matter.

"I'm a bachelor," he explained, "and sometimes I just can't organize—but sit down, Hazel. Here, let me clear you a space." He moved stacks of journals from two chairs, sat by me, and listened to my story of Walter and Jud. "And Katarina thought I could solve this problem?"

"Yes. She sent me here."

His eye strayed to a map of Europe on his wall—apparently pastors had them, too. "So this is what we do," he said. "Men my age create wars. Young men fight and die in them. Then we send out *children* with the news. It's a sin, Hazel. Let me think." We sat in silence. "Yes, this could work. Charlie Snead runs the Western Union office. He's a parishioner. I think we can keep children from doing this work in Dogwood." He stood, hunted for his hat, and led me to the office door. "Give my respects to your mother. Her cinnamon rolls are from heaven. Truly."

That Sunday Pastor Birke took me aside to say that he and Charlie Snead had contacted Dogwood's two other pastors, the priest, and the rabbi. All had agreed to help. Starting immediately, when a death notice came in, Charlie would have one of them bring it to the family. If no clergyman was available, Charlie would go himself. Jud and Walter would continue delivering routine telegrams.

"You can be proud of your part in this," the baron said warmly. And I was proud. It was a small thing, but wholly good. Pastor Birke also began giving the names and addresses of the grieving families to Mrs. McClellan, who had my mother bring a loaf of fresh bread and cinnamon buns to each home. Often I went with her. "In the midst of sorrow," she'd say, "the salt and the sweetness of life remain. One must eat."

LATE IN THE summer of 1918, I came upon the baron studying his map of Europe. Like my father's, it was a lace of pinpricks. Blue pins showed the Allied advance, constantly pushing back red pins of the Central Powers. "The Hindenburg Line is breaking," he said. "We're losing the Balkans. Germany our mother, America our wife. What happens when the wife is strangling the mother?" He walked to the window, turned crisply, and came back. "When Germany's utterly defeated, how will my mother survive?" I took the question as rhetorical. German's postwar troubles were beyond me. More insistent: "Hazel, *how* will she survive?"

"You mean—"

"*My* mother, the Baroness von Richthofen. My brother and father left massive debts. The Poles will take Prussia back. Then what? Even in peacetime, my mother was like a child. She's never been in a bank. She couldn't manage an estate, even if she's allowed to keep it. Which is impossible. When the war's over, vandals will come. Tenants, townspeople, and soldiers will strip Mein Königsberg. Perhaps they'll burn it. Who knows what they'll do to her. They hated my father." He turned to me, wanting help. This was as strange and nearly as frightening as when he judged my first offering letter.

"She let your father send you away. But she's an old woman now and helpless. Is that what you're thinking?"

"Yes. For years, I hated her weakness. Yet, as you say, she's an old woman now and helpless." He turned his bezel ring.

"She could live here."

"*Here?*" Startled, he turned to the office door, as if imagining the baroness coming in.

"Isn't this like her home in Prussia?"

The question clearly made him uncomfortable. "Yes, somewhat." He wrote a line on notepaper, perhaps an option: The baroness comes here. Then he crossed it out with a neat stroke. "Impossible. She was always terrified of water. Even crossing bridges made her panic."

"I see. Is there someone in Germany she could live with?"

"A sister in Berlin." He wrote another line. Considered it. "Aunt Elka always needed money. Discreet monthly payments could be arranged, which might make her more hospitable. I have an agent in Berlin."

"Would the baroness be happy there?"

"They always fought. Aunt Elka hated my father and said my mother was a fool to marry him."

"Well then."

"Yes, well then." He crossed out the "Aunt Elka" line. For moving delicate art through war zones, the baron was an endless font of alternative methods, agents, and routes. This project defeated him. He put the fine pen in its holder. The square shoulders slumped.

"After the war, you could go over yourself and bring her back," I suggested. "The baroness might be less frightened if she's with you." He didn't lift the pen to write: "Go to Prussia."

"The Allies will be everywhere. As soon as I open my mouth, I'll be another enemy. Why would they let me through?"

"Can you leave her in Prussia?" The question hung in the air for so long that it took physical shape between us. When he lifted his pen, it seemed weighted. He set it down.

"No, I can't leave her there. She's an old woman now and helpless."

"Well then."

And for me, Hazel: *Well then?* Didn't I owe him help, now that he, too, was helpless? If I went, I'd be an American in an Allied zone and a buffer in the surely tense rapport with his mother. I could be useful, perhaps essential. Yes, there might be danger, but millions of men had faced far worse. Tom had faced worse. Here in Dogwood, I was only waiting for Tom. In Prussia after the war, I might find news of him or at least be close to where he might be, or where he might have ceased to be. "I can go with you, Baron. I can be your ally."

He looked at me as he rarely did, head to toe. "In Prussia?"

"Yes."

A slow, wry smile crossed the beautiful face. "We could pretend to be a couple."

"Yes, that might help."

"We could even pretend for my mother."

"We could."

He crossed the space between our desks and extended a hand to mine, bending crisply at the waist. "When the war ends, we'll go. And I thank you, Hazel."

"When the war ends." And so I began a new stage of *when*. *When* the war ended, I'd go to Prussia with the baron. *When* Tom was found, joy would begin. *When* he was known to be lost forever, I'd begin imagining my life alone.

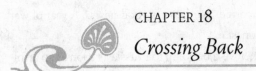

# CHAPTER 18

## *Crossing Back*

Through the summer of 1918, Allied forces pushed deeper into German territory. The Hindenburg Line wavered and cracked. German sailors revolted. Soldiers mutinied and deserted, first a trickle, soon a steady flow. Yet when Kaiser Wilhelm II was informed that his military situation was hopeless, he refused to abdicate. The generals kept fighting. Bombs still pounded the wasted land, mustard gas poured into trenches, and men were thrown against machine-gun fire all along the Western Front. Everywhere civilians starved. We waited for the end, as when a dying man struggles on until the anguished family's hearts cry out: *Let it go, stop fighting, there's nothing left to win.*

In Dogwood, the terrible telegrams kept coming. People drew their curtains when clergymen appeared on their street: *Go to another house. Keep walking. Keep driving. Go away.* Would a somber man in black come to our gate with a new telegram regretting to inform me that Thomas Alan Jamison, formerly missing in action, was now confirmed dead? I whipped between fear and hope. Without news of his death, Tom might still be alive. But each day that he was lost, unidentified in a field hospital or imprisoned by a starving enemy surely brought him closer to death.

"Any news?" Lena asked when I saw her in town.

"No."

"I'm sorry." She spared me "No news is good news." A year of war had made us all more honest.

When I told my mother we'd be going to Prussia as soon as an armistice was signed, she was horrified. "Don't. Hazel, please don't."

"I have to." We'd be back in a month, I assured her. If there was news of Tom while we were gone, Anna would notify the baron's agent in London.

"But it will be dangerous. And the baroness might not even be alive when you get there."

"Mother, I have to go. I have to help him." She and I spent more time together. As I'd done with Tom, I made the most of our *now*.

My vague plans for Paris after the war had turned murky. If I still meant to go, the baron advised, better to wait until the city settled, a year, or six months at least. But Tom might look for me there. I wavered daily. After Prussia, where should I wait for him? And how long should I wait? Every "after" was unknowable.

I wasn't alone. "After the war . . . After our boys come home," was the only talk in town. Even when "our boys" came home, would they be the same as those who marched gaily away? Would arms or legs be missing? Would they wobble and twitch from shell shock, scream and hide at loud noises, or seem to see, like endless nickelodeon loops, enormous rats eating the bellies of their comrades?

Even my mother struggled with her "after." Rationing had cut bakery supplies; there were fewer weddings and parties. Sales dropped steeply; debts mounted. Mrs. McClellan spoke of closing the shop. After so much death, would people ever be happy and wanting sweets?

Meanwhile, in the tower office, we worked frantically. By circuitous routes, the baron let his mother know that he was coming and that she must pack a few necessities for the voyage, which he had his agent assure her would be "mostly by land." We sent out inquiries to potential buyers of certain family treasures, "assuming they weren't sold to pay off my brother's debts," the baron noted grimly.

Grumbling loudly about our folly, Anna began listing supplies we must bring to "the wasteland" we'd find in Prussia. She packed tea, chocolate, soap, hard biscuits, dried fruit and meats, jams, and sauerkraut. "These things never go bad," she argued when the baron reminded her that we'd be traveling light. "Do you think you'll find stores over there? Believe me, some people will give their shirts for sauerkraut."

"We'll take it all," I interceded. "Thank you, Anna." Beneath her fussing was pure panic. I overheard her and my mother reeling out the dangers of land mines, bandits, demobilized soldiers spoiling for revenge, starving and desperate civilians with nothing to lose, poisoned wells, ruined farms, and nowhere any food. Most of all they feared the baron couldn't protect me. A fresh-faced young woman, unspoiled by war, I'd be any man's prize.

"He'll take his pistol," Anna reminded my mother.

"And use it against his own people? They won't even be *people* anymore. They'll be animals."

This kitchen talk, Kurt's dour "Are you sure this trip is wise?" and the Hendersons' warnings of perilous ocean crossing filled me with anxious dread. But I couldn't retreat now. At least I wouldn't be trapped in trenches or foxholes, bombed or gassed. Nobody would force me "over the top" into barbed wire and machine-gun fire. By the simple fact of my sex, I'd been spared death, maiming, shell shock, and the ceaseless sight of maimed bodies. Why *shouldn't* I confront the world that was Tom's? No, I must go forward like any good soldier.

Kaiser Wilhelm II abdicated on November 9, 1918. Two days later, on November 11, Anna, Kurt, Tilda, my mother, and I joined a raucous crowd on Main Street to hear the glorious news. An armistice had been signed at 11:11 a.m. in a railway car in France. Church bells ran. The firehouse whistle blew. Car horns blared. The Hendersons gave out scores of toy horns; children blasted them up and down the street, chased by wildly barking dogs. My mother and Mrs. McClellan passed trays of "victory cookies" made from the last of their sugar reserves. I caught a glimpse of Pastor Birke helping with the trays.

Those who had hissed and whispered "Hun" behind our backs now included us in rounds of kisses, hugs, and giddy congratulations. Still, some asked: "Where's the Baron von Richthofen? Couldn't show his face today?" When I didn't answer, they drifted off.

Coming upon Walter and his parents in the swirling crowd, I risked: "Your son has a great talent for art. I hope you can encourage it."

In the flow of good feeling, they both nearly smiled. "Well, perhaps. Now that the war is over."

When they turned away, I whispered to Walter, "Come by the castle whenever you want."

"Maybe."

THE BARON ARRANGED our cabins on a hospital ship steaming across the Atlantic to collect the dead and wounded. Kurt drove us to the ship in a car piled with supplies that Anna and my mother had packed for us. We'd get a car in Antwerp, the baron said. We might even, he suggested wryly, need a second one for the sauerkraut.

We were barely out of the harbor when I managed to corner a Red Cross nurse to ask if a pilot reported missing in action might in fact be among the wounded. "No," she explained, as if to a child. "Then he'd be on our wounded lists."

"But what if he was so wounded he couldn't identify himself?"

"We can read their names on medals around their necks. So he'd be on our lists."

"And if he was a prisoner?"

"Then he'd be on our prisoner list," she said less patiently. "I'm sorry, miss, but I'm on duty now."

"The lists aren't perfect," I suggested to the baron at dinner. "Or someone could have read a tag wrong." Tom could be in a hospital, healing, or with a jubilant band of prisoners just released.

"Yes, that's possible." He was pale and complained of a headache. "I'm sorry, Hazel. I'm going to lie down. I dislike ocean travel." He didn't leave his cabin all evening and didn't appear at breakfast.

Wandering alone that morning, I met a Chinese sailor who spent his free hours constructing elaborate flowers out of cord. Sam had been a houseboy in San Francisco before running away to sea. "My boss say I only to understand orders, not talk, always be silent. But everything she say, I say to myself. So I learn English." Proving this stolen fluency, he told Chinese folktales as his fingers twisted, looped, and tied obedient cord into a full-blown rose. "Nice American lady, this is for you."

"Thank you, Sam, but are you well? You look flushed."

He shrugged. "Little fever. But I drink tea and don't worry. I'm strong."

I didn't see Sam the next day. "He's sick," another sailor said. "Good thing it's a hospital ship."

"What's wrong?"

"You heard the ditty, miss: 'I had a little bird. Its name was Enza. I opened up the window, and in-flu-enza.'" Yes, I'd heard reports of influenza racing through army camps and larger cities. It had even passed lightly over Dogwood; both my mother and Anna had been briefly sick, but nobody in town was seriously ill. Our wholesome air and situation protected us, Mayor Woodruff claimed. Influenza news hovered in the far back pages of newspapers. With peace coming, why worry about sick people in distant places? "Tell Sam I hope he feels better."

"Can't tell him nothing, miss. He's quarantined, spitting blood." Sam had been slightly flushed the day before, just that. Could influenza chase down ships? Should I have tried a healing touch at least? But what would he have thought of a Western woman pressing a hand to his brow? And what about the baron? No, no, he was merely seasick, he insisted when I visited him. And tired. Of course he was tired. The war had exhausted us all. I was tired myself and mildly dizzy, perhaps a little seasick, too.

That evening at sunset, Sam was buried at sea with the first mate, also dead of influenza. I panicked for the baron, now feverish and attended by a private nurse. Sam's knotted rose was in my pocket. And here was his body, wrapped and weighted in sailcloth, the ship stopped under a violet sky, the chaplain reading scriptures, the bugler playing taps. Two boards tipped; the bodies slid feetfirst into dark waves. Two splashes. The ship seemed to buck, pushed up by the mass of their bodies? My head spun. Coughing, I gripped a post.

"Are you sick, miss?" said a voice nearby. "Orderly, get this one to the infirmary."

"No!" But they were already carrying me through a dark passage.

I AWOKE ON a narrow bed in a line of beds separated by white curtains. "The Baron von Richthofen?" I asked a passing nurse, her face covered by gauze. They all wore masks, I noticed, as if their mouths were gone.

"He's in another ward." Where? I struggled to sit. "No, no, miss. Lie back." So hot. Was this my breath, so loud and wheezing? And what held down my body, making me so weak?

"Do I have influenza?"

"Yes."

"Will we get better?"

"I hope so. You've lasted three days. That's a good sign." Her eyes were smudges. "We haven't had more than two hours' break in days," she admitted. The nurses had begged the captain for sailors to help in the wards. "He refused. I can't blame him." Coughing racked my chest, as terrible as bronchitis. My body ached. *I need a healing touch,* I thought.

Later there was someone nearby, lifting my head, wiping my mouth. "Mother?"

"No. I'm a nurse. Try to sleep."

I slept. I woke. "No blood in the sputum yet," a man's voice was saying. "That's good." The baron had been moved back to his cabin, I was told. They took me to a different ward, much quieter. "You're with the lucky ones," a nurse said. I was fed, washed, and woke without fever. Someone sat near me. I craned my neck and saw the baron masked and reading. His eyes were clear and back erect.

"You're alive." My voice was hoarse; each word grated.

"Quite." He closed his book. "As you are."

"How long was I sick?"

"Four days. We'll be in Antwerp soon. We'll find influenza there, but apparently surviving one attack gives some immunity." Every sailor taken on in Boston had died, he said, ten more after Sam, three nurses and a doctor, all gasping for air as bloody sputum filled their lungs. "First the war and now influenza from China to Africa, and all across Europe. Eskimos are dying and cannibals in the South Pacific."

"The newspapers didn't say it was so bad."

"No, of course not. They didn't want civilians worried. But everyone knows about it now. There are mass graves in Philadelphia." I jerked up. He gently pressed me down. "Dogwood's safe so far. They let me telegraph the mayor."

"Pittsburgh?"

"Very bad." *Luisa. Uncle Willy. Tante Elise. All my friends.* "Rest now. The next part will be difficult."

WE DOCKED IN Antwerp and entered a wasteland. In the cold rain, we passed fields of rubble. Tom was right: war takes color from the earth, leaving only mud, dust, charred wood, bone, and the ghastly gray of death. From houses with broken windows came coughing, coughing, coughing. A farm wagon dumped bodies in foxholes, convenient for graves. Walking skeletons surrounded us. Returning soldiers and desperate civilians stripped and looted where they could. We bought a battered Peugeot from a man who'd lost his family in the last days of war. "Where am I going now?" he said. "What kind of peace is this?"

Moving east into Prussia, threading rutted roads, we bought what food we could to supplement Anna's rations and share along the road. Lines of refugees shuffled on, walking, limping, pushing laden bicycles or wagons, leading bony horses, every face a blank of sorrow. Was Tom somewhere on these roads?

We gave as many rides as the Peugeot could bear. "We're going home," some said, or simply "away from here." Everywhere land was scored by trenches and scooped by bombs. Everywhere we saw black sentinel trees, endless coils of barbed wire, and nothing moving in the fields but vultures, dogs, rats, and wolves.

When we came upon an American unit, I left the baron in the car, calling him "my driver." The soldiers suggested routes that might be passable. I asked about Tom. "A pilot missing in action?" repeated a lanky sergeant. "Behind enemy lines?" He glanced at my face. "Well, don't give up, miss. Takes a while to get things sorted out."

How could all this be "sorted out"? A giant hand had shaken the earth, flinging men across Europe, knocking down cities like blocks, scattering families. We passed nuns shepherding children to an or-phanage that might receive them or might already be destroyed. We gave a potato to each child. They were instantly devoured, like pebbles dropped in a well of need.

When we ran out of gasoline, a passing British convoy gave us more. "It's good to travel with an ally," the baron said. One-legged men on benches and weary women examined us. We were close to his old home now, the baron said. Perhaps these people remembered him, or perhaps we were only notable in seeming unscathed by war. The bakery was gone. "Russians did it," an old man told the baron. "Or Poles. Or one of ours. There's no bread anyway."

"How do you eat?" The old man shrugged. We gave him the last of our potatoes. Pale eyes under bushy gray brows studied the baron. The baron studied him as well, peeling back years. "Ensel the butcher?"

The old man nodded. "And you are one of the von Richthofens? Erich died heroically, we heard. So you are—?"

"Georg, the oldest son."

The man jerked back, raising a wrinkled hand. "No, no. Don't play tricks on me." He reeled into one of the gaping doorways.

"The war does strange things," I said finally.

"It does. Let's go. The castle is just ahead."

A wrought-iron gate hung open. A line of stumps stood where chestnut trees had been cut, probably for firewood. "There's our cemetery." He led me to a clearing with ranks of marble headstones overgrown by weeds. "Men like my father came here two hundred years ago, sent by Frederick the Great to civilize the 'vile Polish apes,' who of course hated my ancestors. Now the Poles will take back what's theirs."

In a corner we found his father's grave, crudely marked with a wooden plaque. The baron's polished boot edged aside a clot of dirt, revealing the coffin. "So shallow. I wonder who buried him." Another wooden marker had been jabbed in the sod:

ERICH WILHELM VON RICHTHOFEN
1872–1918
DIED FOR THE FATHERLAND

"Apparently the body wasn't returned. And they didn't care to write: 'Died drunk, with his pants down.' The honor of the von Richthofens, honor above all," the baron said bitterly. It was only when we turned to go that our eyes caught an older marble headstone, elegantly carved. I grasped his arm. He blinked, as if the words were a mirage. He touched them. They were real enough:

GEORG HEINRICH VON RICHTHOFEN
1869–1890
DIED AT SEA

No wonder Ensel the butcher had turned away; he thought he'd seen a ghost. "So they buried me. So much easier. So many awkward questions avoided if Erich was the only heir. I wonder how elegant my funeral was." He stood at attention, his own honor guard.

"Should we go see your mother?" I asked finally.

"Yes. Even if I'm dead."

## CHAPTER 19

# *Wasteland*

Dogwood's castle outshone its Prussian parent. A slate-gray sky and bare trees added to the gloom, but neglect was everywhere. Ragged ivy crawled up walls and curtained windows. Great vases by the entryway had fallen over and shattered. Garden walls had crumbled. Only one of many chimneys emitted a trail of smoke. "Mein Königsberg," the baron murmured, his face so filled with memory, regret, and private pain that I turned away.

He took out a polished key. He'd kept it all these years. We pushed open the heavy door and entered a dusty chamber. High wooden walls bristled with mounted heads of wild boar, deer, and elk. I turned and found myself face-to-face with a bear's head, the mouth open to show gleaming teeth. I jumped back. The baron managed a smile. "That was the point, of course, to declare the von Richthofen men as hunters. All others are the hunted."

"Some of these trophies were yours?"

"Yes, I was an excellent shot. With a gun in hand, I made my father proud." Our footsteps echoed. "Now we're hunted by creditors, it seems." Clean squares on faded walls showed where paintings had been removed. Marble pedestals stood without busts; china cabinets were empty; light patches on wood floors once had fine carpeting. From a distant room came rattles and thuds. He smiled. "That's Lotte, the noisiest cook in Prussia. She'd be old now. I loved her kitchen. She always had apples for me."

Echoes followed our footsteps like ghosts as we drew near the kitchen and quietly entered. A coal stove barely warmed the cavernous room. There were no apples. Sausage hooks dangled free. The flour barrel was nearly empty, as were rows of pantry shelves. Still, with the slightest trick of the eye, I could imagine a young baron with cheeks red from the cold, looking for treats in a warm and fragrant place. A solid woman with steel-gray braids banged a wooden spoon around an iron pot. The few bobbing dumplings must have taken most of the flour. "Lotte, it's Georg. I've come home."

She jumped and spun, eyes wild. "Go away! Go!" She raised the spoon and then another in a cross. "Georg died at sea. We had a funeral."

"I'm sure you did. I saw my grave. But 'death at sea' gave Erich my birthright, didn't it? A clever fiction, since, as you see, I'm quite alive."

She edged toward his proffered arm and touched it tentatively, gripped his shoulder, and finally clapped work-reddened hands to his cheeks, as she must have done to his boyhood self. "Georg, Georg, yes you're alive. No wonder the old baron acted so strangely at the funeral, hurrying it along. And here you are, a grown man and still so handsome." She touched his temples. "Just a little gray. Where did you go— after you didn't die?"

"To New Jersey. I built a castle called Mein Königsberg. I deal in fine art."

"Ah, you were always the clever one, the determined one." She noticed me. "And this is your lovely—"

"Fräulein Renner."

"I see. Well, welcome to Mein Königsberg, fräulein, That is, to the *ruins* of Mein Königsberg."

"Thank you, Lotte."

The strangeness of our presence in her barren kitchen struck her now: "Did you come for your inheritance? There's nothing here but debts and nobody left in Prussia but old men, orphans, cripples, and thieves. You can't defend the castle and there's the fräulein to think of."

"I'm here for the baroness, Lotte. I'm taking her to America."

"She said someone was coming, but I didn't believe her. So *you* are that someone?"

"Yes, I am that someone. You can help Fräulein Renner prepare a small trunk for the baroness, just what she'll need for the journey."

Lotte cleared her throat. "I have my own packing to do. I'm going to Hannover. My daughter's there." I nudged the baron, indicating a traveling bag half open on the floor. A silver candelabrum peeked out. Silver candlesticks sat nearby. Lotte's eyes followed ours boldly. "I haven't been paid in a year. I can't go to Hannover like a beggar. And I didn't leave when the old baron died."

"You're leaving now. If I hadn't come, would you have abandoned the baroness?"

Lotte stepped back from the frosty voice, but still hers rose. "All the others left. You don't know what we've suffered here with the war, the Russians, the blockade, your brother's debts, the old baron dying, and the baroness turning childish. Then it was just me and Minna, the kitchen maid, and her little bastard boy. Influenza got her yesterday. If I stay it'll get me. Or the Poles will kill me. Have you heard? In one town, they nailed a German woman to a barn door and did what they wished to her. I *have* to leave."

The baron sighed. "Lotte, take the silver. I'll pay your wages. Just make us dinner and stay until we leave. Will you do that?" She nodded, wiping her nose on a threadbare apron. The baron offered a linen hand-kerchief. She stroked the fine surface. "Keep it. But go help Fräulein Renner pack for the baroness."

Lotte pocketed the handkerchief and backed away. "I can't."

"Why not?" She turned to her soup. And so I knew. We both knew. The baron's voice rose. "Lotte, does the baroness have influenza?" She nodded. "When did it start?"

"Two days ago."

"Is she coughing?" Nod. "What have you done for her?"

"I leave soup at the door. I can't help her. The fever comes and you die. There's no doctors left, even if there was money to pay one. Everyone's dying. Everything's ruined. I'm alone here." The wide shoulders shook. Anger turned the baron's face to white marble. When he took a step toward Lotte, she cowered.

I stepped between them, touching his sleeve. "Baron, let's go to your mother."

"Don't!" Lotte cried. "You'll catch it and give it to me and we'll all die. The Allies bombed germs on us. They'll—"

"Stop!" said the baron so sharply that her mouth snapped shut. "The fräulein and I were sick and recovered. We won't get it again. We'll tend the baroness since you're unwilling."

He spun on his heels and left the kitchen. I followed him up a curving staircase as massive as his in Dogwood, but cruder without Emil's artistry. On the upper floor, coughing led us on, the same desperate fight for air we'd heard on the ship. We walked more slowly, not speaking. Our footsteps clattered. "There were Persian carpets here. This was my room," the baron was saying, pointing to a closed door. "And this was Erich's . . . There were Italian landscapes along this hall . . . my father's study . . . his dressing room." We turned a corner. Paneled walls changed from walnut to oak. The coughs grew louder. "My mother's quarters," the baron recited, "her sitting room . . . her dressmaker's workroom . . . her bedroom." He knocked at a wide door.

A hoarse voice responded: "Lotte, is that you?" The baron's grip on the handle loosened and tightened. He slowly pushed the door open. Sickroom smells rushed out at us: stale air and stale linens, sweat, dried blood, and somewhere a chamber pot. In a corner stood a large curtained bed. Around us, thickly carpeting the room, were decades of a noblewoman's finery. We stepped gingerly through tangled mounds of Belgian lace, stacks of silks and furs, billowing heaps of evening gowns and day dresses, some from the last century with mutton sleeves, crinolines, and puffed bodices. Baskets held corsets and yellowing bustles. Here was a tower of open hatboxes spewing feathers. I saw a tea service and ponderous soup tureen, a bearskin rug, enameled beer steins, a French mantel clock, table linens, down comforters, shawls of lace and wool, gloves of every length, a jumble of ivory elephants in various sizes, toiletries and jewelry boxes piled like blocks. A terrarium under a glass dome. In a corner sat two large trunks, absurdly small for the mass around them.

The baron passed a hand over his forehead. "Lotte's right. She's like a child."

"Lotte," gasped a hoarse voice from the bed. "Where were you? You haven't done the packing." We waded through lace to the baroness.

"It's Georg. I've come to take you to America."

"Georg. At last."

Yes, she was sick, wrinkled, and old, shrunken in foul, sweat-stained linens, with wiry strings of gray hair strewn across pillows. But still faintly visible was the beautiful young woman of the baron's bezel ring: the elegant profile, high cheekbones, sculpted lips, and perfect chin.

She stretched a white hand to him. "Georg, you've come to take me away."

He moved a spindly French boudoir chair to the bedside and sat down slowly, rubbing the thin armrests. Had he sat in that chair before? "Yes, we're going to America."

The baroness squinted through reddened eyes. "What a pretty young lady. Is she your American wife?"

He glanced at me. "Yes, this is Hazel."

"I'm glad you finally—" A fit of coughing overtook her. The cloth she pressed to her mouth came away bloody. When the coughing ceased, she had forgotten me. I busied myself with sickroom services: opening windows to relieve the foul air, shoving the bloody cloths in a sack, and ripping linens for new ones.

"Lotte doesn't come. She's impossible. And that Minna—"

"Mother, I saw my grave. Lotte said there was a funeral." He pointed to a black satin gown frosted with black lace as the bitterness of years came rushing out: "Did you wear that for me? Did you cry when people said what a promising young man Georg was, what a pity he died at sea? Exile wasn't enough? You had to kill me?"

She writhed in the great bed, whimpering: "I'm sorry, Georg. I didn't want to, but your father said it was the only way to keep people from talking when Erich inherited. And you were in America. You weren't coming back." She coughed, jerking up, and then collapsed against mounded pillows, gasping. "You don't know how terrible it's been. Lotte and I had to bury your father ourselves. We had to make a wooden headstone. *Wooden*, Georg. What will people think?"

"Nothing," he said quietly. "They won't think anything. There's nobody left to think."

I'd found a fresh nightgown and bed linens in the jumble. "Baron, she might be more comfortable in these. Would you excuse us?" He did, bowing slightly to his mother as must have been his custom.

"You'll find me in my father's office," he said, stepping around the elegant rubble.

I changed the nightgown, looking away from her shriveled body. Then I helped the baroness into a chair, remade her bed, and threw the old linens in a corner. Rummaging in her toiletries, I found lavender water to sprinkle on the bed.

"Ah, that's good," she whispered. "I've always loved lavender." She was feverish. I filled a bowl with water, laid a wet cloth on her brow, and held the waving hand. No healing touch could reach her now. Death was near, hovering by the door. "That's better," she whispered, pulling her hand free. "Leave me, dear. Go to my son. I want to rest."

A leak of light took me back to the old baron's office, a chilling parent to the warm retreat in Dogwood. The baron sat at a massive desk before a stack of letters. "The baroness wanted to rest."

He nodded. "Unfortunately, you'll have to take the interrogation post." He indicated a rush-bottom chair dwarfed by the desk. "Imagine being a child defending the various ways you offended the honor of the von Richthofens."

I looked up at the baron, crowned in gaslight, with crossed spears and a coat of arms above him. "Intimidating," I agreed.

"Of course. As are these creditors' demands. In theory." A smile lit his face, so broad it might have been borrowed from another man. "They can't be paid. That's the charm. Because I'm dead, you see? As are my father and brother. You won't find my mother's name on any title. So from whom can these creditors collect, assuming they survive this second war with influenza?" He picked up a bone-handled hunting knife that must have doubled as a letter opener.

The smile faded. "Strange. For years, I bided my time, alone and then with Friedrich, waiting for Erich to come to ruin and my father to die or relent. We had plans for remaking this castle. So many plans. Now Friedrich's gone and the Prussia I knew is gone. Mein Königsberg will fall to other hands. But I'll take some treasure home. I helped my father acquire all this. Look."

He brought me to a long table, astonishing even after all my time with him. Here was an illuminated Psalter from the court of Charlemagne, a silver buckle reportedly made for the Holy Roman Emperor Frederick Barbarossa before his last Crusade, the elaborately worked helm of a Viking sword, a jewel-encrusted gauntlet, a Roman brooch set with sapphires, heavy signet rings of Renaissance princes, and a cup of ancient coins.

"How did all this survive?"

"Because my father hid it from Erich."

"But not from you?"

"He trusted me not to gamble his treasures on a horse race. He was convinced that with age, Erich would become a model of sobriety and prudence. Then he'd reveal the secret."

"Perhaps he hoped you'd come back."

"Why, if he buried me? I was his art buyer and sometime hunting companion, nothing more."

It was difficult to grasp the dark twists of a family that had buried a living, faithful son in favor of a wastrel. But was my baron so wholly despised? In the jumble of ancient coins, I spied a bright bronze disk of recent stamp and fished it out. "This is from 1882. It looks like a school medal."

He dropped the gauntlet he'd been examining and reached for the disk, lightly touching the crossed pistols, silent for a long minute. "My marksmanship award from the academy."

"He kept it with his treasures."

"A minor gesture of affection, considering that he buried me."

"Minor, perhaps, but real."

"Yes, real." He turned the disk over and over. Then he put it in his pocket and looked toward the sickroom. "She won't make it to America, will she?"

"I don't see how. She's coughing blood. But you can speak with her." He didn't move. "She loves you."

"In her way, yes."

"Well then." But he didn't move. "I'll go back with you, Baron, if you like." He nodded.

The coughs had subsided. The baroness struggled to lift her head as we entered. "Tell me about America," she whispered. "Will I like it?"

He reached for the brittle hand. "Mother, it's just the same as Prussia, with farms and fields, the sea close by, and many forests. People speak German."

She smiled. "That's good. Where do you live?"

"In a castle just like this one."

"We had a rose garden. Nobody takes care of it now."

"Never mind. I have a rose garden, and kitchen gardens, and an apple orchard." She smiled. "There's a grand staircase, paintings, and a gallery of mirrors."

"American food?"

"It's exactly like ours: meatballs with herring and white sauce, potatoes, *faworki*."

She lurched again, gagging. He held her. "*Faworki*," she sputtered.

"Sauerkraut and good bread."

"Lotte?"

"She'll help you pack later. Rest now." Her breaths gurgled slightly. The faintest blue tinged her lips and fingers. "I'll stay here awhile, Hazel. Go have some soup."

I found my way back to the kitchen. Lotte had set a simple table. "The baroness?"

"He's with her. He'll be down later."

She put three beer bottles on the table. "Those are the last ones." We were about to sit when the outside door creaked open. "Beasts," she hissed. "Get back, fräulein." She seized a poker and swung it over her head.

A child slipped in. I screamed as the poker whizzed past his ear, clattering on the floor. He couldn't have been more than three years old, painfully thin, with a pinched face and enormous blue eyes. He stood so calmly as Lotte retrieved the poker that I ached to think what his little life had been. "It's David, Minna's boy. She had him by a Russian soldier. There were no other kitchen maids around, so the old baron had to hire her, even with the bastard."

"Who cares for him now?"

"I feed him. Sometimes he goes away. Maybe he eats somewhere else." Like a stray cat? I took bread and cheese from my knapsack, gave him some of my soup, and pulled a chair next to mine.

"And when you leave for Hannover, what happens to David?"

"I'll—take him to the priest." We'd passed the bombed church in town. If there was a priest there still, would he accept the child? Or would David be sent wandering in search of the last unbombed orphanage? A thin hand crept into a fold of my skirt and wrapped around my heart. *Don't, don't. Don't raise your eyes like that to me.*

From a bulge in his cloth jacket, he pulled a battered wooden horse, which he cradled in grubby hands. "It was Georg's," Lotte explained. "I found it in the nursery and gave it to him."

"That was kind of you."

"David is a good boy," she admitted. "It's too bad."

Too bad that he'd die? No, David would *not* die in Prussia and he'd join no mass of starving, homeless children slowly moving through Europe. I'll take him, I decided suddenly. Then my certainty faltered. Could I? We'd been lucky so far, but no match for any band of soldiers or civilians. A child would slow us down. We couldn't guarantee his safety. Once in America, suppose he longed for his old world, ruined as it was? Suppose he felt ripped from his land? I couldn't go to Paris with an orphan boy in tow. Or could I? Well-meant choices in my past had come to pain. But if I did nothing now, this child would have no chance at all. Johannes and Katarina had not refused an unwanted, inconvenient child. The huge eyes fixed on me. He set aside the wooden horse and set a feather-light hand on my skirt. I took it in both of mine. And we were joined.

"It looks like the baron's staying up there," Lotte said, clearly uncomfortable with David's presence. "I'll bring him some soup." She had just filled another bowl when the baron appeared and slowly sat.

"She's gone." A spoon clattered on the table. "It happened so quickly. She couldn't get breath." His eyes were faintly rimmed in red. "She wanted to see America."

"I'm sorry, sir." I touched his sleeve and he laid his hand on mine, an extraordinary gesture.

"This is no world for the baroness," Lotte said quietly. "It's nothing that she knew. Even if she wasn't sick, she couldn't have endured it." The baron nodded. Lotte slipped into the pantry and emerged with a dusty bottle of schnapps. "The last of the old baron's stock." We drank to the memory of the baroness. There was no time or spirit for long stories as we'd done at my father's wake, but Lotte did recall being a kitchen maid when the baroness was a young bride, very beautiful and shy.

The baron looked far away. "When I was fifteen," he said, "she and I danced together at a fancy dress ball."

"We servants watched," Lotte confessed. "In all Prussia, there wasn't a finer-looking couple." She refilled our glasses.

But that was all the time we had for memories. "We have to bury her," the baron announced.

Lotte stiffened. "There's no time. And the priest died last week." Her eyes caught mine and flicked away. So how could she bring David to the priest? Clearly, she'd had no plan besides leaving him behind.

"The baroness will be buried with my family. I'm not letting the vandals have her."

Lotte finished the last of the soup. "If you prepare the body, fräulein," she said finally, "I'll help the baron with her grave."

"Well then." For the first time the baron registered David pressed against my side, his head barely grazing the table, wide-eyed through this conversation. "Who's that?"

"His name is David. His father was a Russian soldier. He's the orphan child of Minna the kitchen maid and needs to go to America."

Appraising eyes measured the small figure. "He's a *child*."

"Yes," I said in English. "A child. Not a child in the abstract. A child who will die if he stays here."

"Hazel, what difference does saving one child make? You've seen Prussia. Imagine all of Germany, all of Europe now. There are millions of orphan children." Like my father, he looked away, seeing bodies stretched to the horizon.

"It will make a difference to *this* child. We can make a miracle for him."

"What about Tom?"

"When he comes home, he'll find a little boy." David watched our faces avidly, surely guessing that his fate was being weighed in our mysterious words.

"Getting back to Antwerp will be hard enough for us. And far more difficult with a child. It's not a good idea," he finished, as if I'd proposed an unworkable plan for shipping fine crystal.

"No, it's not. You would have brought the baroness back."

"He doesn't have any documents, I assume."

"No. We'd have to create them."

"I see. You want to be responsible for this child?"

"Yes."

"You've considered the complications?"

"Yes."

"Just now, so quickly?"

"Yes." Like my mother in her arguments, I didn't move.

The baron studied David's grip on the wooden horse. "When that was mine," he said finally in German, "I called him Bucephalus, after Alexander the Great's war horse."

"Bucephalus," David repeated, cradling the horse's bare rump.

"He had a tail of horsehair once."

"Maybe I can make him another one."

"Maybe you can." He cleared his throat as he did before any formal negotiation. "David, what Fräulein Renner and I have been discussing is the option of—" He caught my eye and began again. "Would you like to come to America with us?" The child's eyes widened. Had he heard the horrors about Americans that our children heard about Huns?

The great blue eyes fixed on me. "Is there food?"

"Yes."

"And children?"

"Yes."

"Are there—" He looked out the dark window.

"It's safe. There's no war in America."

"Will you die?" Of course he asked this. His mother had died. Who knew how many corpses he'd seen? Wagonloads of bodies must have been as familiar to him as milk trucks in Dogwood.

"We'll be very careful."

"Can Bucephalus come?"

"Yes."

"Good." He bent over the horse, whispering, his face hidden by straw-bright hair.

"Well then," said the baron. "We're taking a child." He stood. "Hazel, will you prepare the baroness?" It was full dark. Lotte got a lantern and followed the baron outside, her stride matching his.

"Where are they going?" David asked fearfully.

"To do some work." I didn't ask if Minna was buried. Perhaps her body was simply left in whatever narrow space had housed her bed. "You and Bucephalus stay here while I—see the baroness." I moved him near the stove. Then I found a bucket, soap, and sponge, and went upstairs to wash the body. I would rather have helped dig the grave. I'd never washed a corpse before. *Hazel,* I heard my father say, *certain things must simply be done.* I did this job, brushed the thin hair, put her in a clean shift, and wrapped her in a sheet.

Past midnight, the baron and I carried his mother to the cemetery in a wheelbarrow we found in a storeroom. The grave was very shallow. Lotte had fashioned a cross. We covered the body as best we could, put rocks over the mound to discourage dogs, and said some verses. David watched, gripping my hand.

"Now I'm the last von Richthofen," said the baron, surveying the three graves, each cruder than the last. "You were always the clever one," Lotte had said. He was also the most faithful.

The baron and I brought our bags to his father's office and packed the treasures. We'd have no protection against determined thieves but might confound casual rifling. The Psalter fit in a hollowed-out geology text. The baron's false-bottomed suitcase held the gauntlet and sword helm. Coins, smaller objects, and the best of the baroness's jewelry we hid in the lining of our coats, hats, and heavy gloves, and the hollowed-out heel of the baron's boots, adapted for this purpose. "Take some of her furs," he advised. "We'll need them for the child."

"David's documents?" I asked.

"We'll get them made in Antwerp. There isn't time now. We have to get out of Prussia." We had a quick parting with Lotte. At daybreak, she'd join one of the streaming groups of refuges, making her way to Hannover. We made a nest of furs in the back of the Peugeot for David, who was feverish with excitement.

We'd started down the long drive when Lotte came panting after us with a gift for the baron. It was the last of the apples. "You were always my favorite, Georg. God keep you in America."

As we reached the main road, David curled around his horse, never looking out the window. "By morning, the vandals will know that we've gone," the baron said quietly. "They'll take whatever Lotte leaves behind. Whether they move in or burn it for spite, I can't go back." The certainty seemed to comfort him. "How's the child?"

"Asleep."

"Just as well. He doesn't have to know. He's lost enough. "

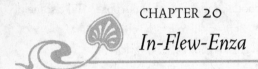

## CHAPTER 20
## *In-Flew-Enza*

We reached an American camp just after sunset. My "husband" was mute from shell shock, I explained to the sentry. His uniform and all our identification were stolen. I began explaining how we'd come to be in Prussia with a child.

"You're Americans, and he fought with us. That's enough. But all we've got is tents."

"A tent is fine, isn't it, dear?" I asked. The baron stared ahead.

"We've got a lot of shell shock," the soldier said kindly. "Maybe he'll come around. It's funny how there's guys who never saw the inside of a trench, never set foot in No Man's Land or saw their buddies blown to bits, and they're wandering around with their minds shot up just the same." *Could Tom be wandering somewhere, his mind "shot up"?* I was glad David woke up then, whispering for water. "Go get something to eat, you folks. The boy must be hungry."

Soldiers swarmed David as we ate our rations. A few reached to touch him. "Hey, Jack," one called out. "Look here, a little kid. Isn't yours about this size?"

"Should be," Jack said, limping closer. "Hey, buddy." David drew back from the haggard face. "Cat got your tongue?" Behind Jack, I nodded. David copied me. "Well sure. All us strange guys. You got yourself a horsey?" He pointed. David edged closer to the baron. "You take care of that horsey."

"Did you know Tom Jamison, a pilot?" I interrupted. "He went missing in April. He was—my husband's best friend."

"Tom Jamison" ran through the crowd. No, nobody knew him. "We were infantry, though, ma'am," Jack said. "But missing since April? That's a long time."

"Thank you," I said quickly. "And we appreciate you letting us stay here."

"You don't wanna mess with Huns at night, soldiers *or* civilians. They're all animals. Come on, fellas, the kid's tired." They wandered off, some looking back longingly at David. *An American family,* they might be thinking. *How strange in this wasteland.*

A cold mist swept over the camp. When David started coughing, I hurried him into our tiny tent and put him between us for warmth. "I saw a map," the baron whispered. "There's a British camp we can reach tomorrow." We devised two stories: one for the road among Germans and another for Allies. On shipboard, we'd be an American family, and David must start learning English.

David was murmuring to Bucephalus. I risked a kiss on his sweaty thatch of hair. He didn't turn away. "Good night, David."

"Bucephalus says good night," a small voice whispered.

The baron wished them both good night and then: "Good night. Hazel."

"Good night, Baron."

A pause. "Georg. Please."

"Good night, Georg."

David's warm hand reached for mine. He coughed himself into restless sleeping.

THE AMERICANS ADVISED an alternate route that might avoid minefields, but the sights were fearsome. Forests of scorched pine trees scraped gray skies like giant needles. Bloated corpses lined the road, scavenged by feral dogs, their snouts dripping blood. Charred houses were everywhere. I saw a woman being raped as other soldiers waited their turn, rifles drawn to guard their spoil. "I can't help her," Georg said. "They'd get me first and then go after you and David." The truth of this was a sickening thud. In the minutes he'd left us to drain gasoline from an abandoned truck, a wild-eyed man had stalked me. Georg fired a shot that grazed the man's head and made him run away. The woman's screams tore my ear.

"Lotte was right. It's just as well my mother isn't here," Georg said. "She'd lived inside those walls so long that she hardly knew the world in peacetime. How could she endure all this?"

"I hope he doesn't remember any of it," I said in English, glancing at David, whose head was pressed against the window as the horrors streamed past us. We tried diverting him with games and English words, but his attention steadily flagged; his brow burned. "Georg, could it be influenza?"

He didn't answer. He didn't have to. Influenza filled the castle and the village. The child was already starving. What resistance would he offer? Georg moved bags to make space for me in the back. David's pulse was racing. His eyes grew red and weeping. "I hurt all over," he moaned. Two days in my care and the child was slipping away. My chest ached with his. As quickly as influenza had seized his body, love had seized my heart. *Get better, get better,* each of my breaths implored.

I pressed my hand to the burning brow. No tremor. Nothing. *Save him. Put my strength in him.* I prayed, knowing full well that thousands of mothers were fighting me for the world's small store of miracles. I was like the desperate seekers at my house whose mute eyes screamed: *Don't waste your force on them. Save it all for me!*

When the road passed a fast-flowing stream, we risked stopping to wash David in cool water and perhaps bring down his fever. Working quickly, I barely noticed a rustling in the brush. Then so quickly they seemed simultaneous I saw a gray blur leaping at us from the right, heard a pistol shot, and felt a thud beside us. I screamed. David only stared.

"A wolf," said Georg, calmly. "Going for the child."

"You got him in the air, with one shot. How—"

"My father disliked making animals suffer. He had great compassion for his prey. But let's go now. There may be another. They hunt in packs."

We hurried David to the car. When Bucephalus fell from his sweaty hands, I tucked it in his shirt.

We reached the British camp after dusk. The sentry said we couldn't stay, directing us to an American camp "somewhere" farther east. "We have a child," I protested, hoping David wouldn't cough. But he did, the little body bucking and thrashing.

"A child with influenza. Sorry, ma'am. Orders."

"If we're on the road at night, you know what happens. *We're* not sick. My husband and I had it and recovered."

"The child won't leave this car," Georg said, although we'd agreed that he wouldn't speak.

The rifle clicked. "A damn Kraut."

"He was an interpreter for the Allies," I said frantically.

"As you see, sir, our documents are in order," Georg continued smoothly, handing over a sheaf of papers. The soldier's eyes widened.

With a glance over his shoulder, he pocketed the banknotes and pointed to a rutted field where we could pass the night.

Georg stayed with David as I searched for a doctor. I found only an exhausted Red Cross orderly. Weary eyes peered over a soiled gauze mask. He said he'd worked nearly forty hours straight. "The infirmary's full," a toneless voice declared. "More than full. Two in a bed until one of them dies. We lost three doctors and a nurse. I don't even know if I'm alive myself right now."

"You don't understand. We have a sick child."

"No, ma'am, *you* don't understand. If you had the king of England, we couldn't help him. This 'flu takes who it wants, when it wants." He wiped his brow. "I've been filling caskets all day. Some of those men were at Verdun and lived; they survived four years of trenches, bombs, poison gas, mortar shells, forced marches, hunger, typhoid, dysentery, and trench mouth. They slept in freezing rain. They fought rats for food. They beat the Hun. Now they're heading home, and some damn bug gets them. You tell me, is there a God up there?" He turned away. I grabbed his arm, yanking him back.

"What should I *do*? The child's only three years old."

Wavering like a drunk, the orderly took a breath. "Try to keep him alive. Every hour he lives, you have a better chance. Warm liquids. Keep him sitting up. Don't bother with medicines—belladonna, camphor oil—none of them is worth a damn. Is there gurgling in the chest? Does he cough blood?"

"No. That's good, right?"

"It's not bad. When did the symptoms start?"

"Yesterday."

"If he lives to morning, you've got a chance."

"But—"

"Orderly!" someone called. He pulled his arm free and was gone.

I trudged to the canteen. With so many sick, the cook said, there was food to spare. I got baked beans, canned meat, a green mush of peas, squares of cheese, broth, and tea. Georg helped me make a table of sorts while David watched, panting. I pressed my ear to his chest. No gurgling. Yet.

"Georg," I whispered in English, "I'm so frightened."

"We survived, didn't we? So it's possible." I nodded. Yes, we survived. But were we limp as rags? Were our bodies like fire? Did we pant like this? Did our eyes blaze red?

"Hazel, you do understand that a ship captain won't take us if the child looks sick. So he's got to seem healthy when we get to port. With luck, that's tomorrow." We must make a deathly sick child look well. Who could command that miracle? I pushed spoons of broth between David's cracked lips and held him when he coughed. Georg and I divided the night into shifts; the next day would be long and we'd need our strength.

Near midnight, David's fever spiked. He shrieked that his mother had come for him and tried to scramble from the car, biting me to get free. I wrestled him down and tied a blanket around the thrashing body. At dawn, we left camp. Limp, feverish, coughing, wheezing, aching, the whites of his eyes a terrible red, at least he'd survived the night.

Finally we reached Antwerp. In sight of the USS Ulysses Grant, Georg turned to David like an officer sending troops over the top. "Listen to me. You must look healthy when we board. You'll wear a hat and keep your head down. You'll walk on your own and you will not cough until we reach our cabin. Do you understand?" The red eyes widened. Georg held up his marksmanship medal. Sunlight flashed on the bronze. "This will be yours if you don't cough." David gulped and nodded.

Georg went to have a birth certificate made that listed David as our son. The cost was our Peugeot. "Everyone wants documents these days, and there's only one good forger left in Antwerp," he reported. "But this will get him in the country."

"Thank you, Georg."

When he smiled, years flew off his face. "I never thought I'd have a son, even a counterfeit one."

"Did Tom—could you—?"

"I telegraphed the Western Union office in Dogwood. They haven't heard anything."

"I see."

We dressed David in the best of his ragged clothes. He coughed constantly. "Everything hurts," he whimpered. At a ransacked pharmacy near port, I paid an exorbitant price for a vial of laudanum. "At least it'll make him sleepy," the druggist said.

Georg's guise as shell-shocked soldier couldn't last for days on shipboard. We'd say he'd been a civilian translator for Allied intelligence whose papers had been stolen. Discreet inquiries revealed that the captain was a weapons collector. Georg bought our passage with dollars, his pistol, and the Viking sword helm.

"Why'd you bring your family over?" the captain asked, fingering the pistol's pearl-inlaid handle.

"I can't reveal that," Georg said stiffly. "Except that it concerned the war effort."

"I see. Well, we board at 1600 hours."

We dosed David with laudanum and angled a hat over his eyes. He walked silently up the gangplank, squeezing my hand. "The kid looks tired," a sailor noted.

"Yes, very," I said. "Could you point us to our cabin?" Tucked into a real bed at last and clutching the medal he'd won, David gave himself up to a spasm of coughs. I panicked. "The captain will hear him, and there's no more laudanum."

"The captain's on deck. Once we're at sea, the worst he can do is quarantine us. Don't worry. I'll find some dinner." Georg left us in the cabin as I washed clothes and propped up David with pillows. I listened to his chest. Still no gurgling. We had a chance.

SLOWLY THROUGH THE night, David's coughing eased. By morning he could take a bit of egg in broth. When sun broke out in the afternoon, we carried him on deck. I pointed to the glinting western rim of the ocean. "America's over there."

"Is Mama in America?"

"No, David. She's not."

"I'm tired. Can Bucephalus and I go back to bed?"

The fever passed by the second morning. He coughed less and less and ate more. Slowly a child emerged whom we hadn't seen in our first, fraught days together. He roamed the ship, petted and spoiled by soldiers. A burly infantryman was brought near tears by the sight of David eating crackers. "Look how he holds them with two hands like a squirrel. Maybe you think I'm crazy, ma'am, but down in the trenches, so scared, tired and hopeless, death all around you, a man forgets what little kids are like. You forget there even *are* little kids somewhere eating crackers in peace."

The soldiers fed him English words and phrases like candy, policing each other's diction. David parroted them with grave care, he so eager to please, and they so eager to be pleased that the games lasted for hours. They taught him the rhyme of the bird named Enza and whooped when he belted out: "And in-flu-ENZA!"

I offered to translate but he wanted to learn another song from "my new uncles." At night, slotted between us, he recited: "Knee bone kineckted tu di shinbone. Shinbone kineckted tu di—di—"

"Ankle bone," I prompted.

"Ankle bone. Gud?"

"Yes, David, very good."

Next came his version of the wildly popular soldiers' ditty: "Oh, how I hate to get up in the morning," or rather the first line, before his English melted into "da, da, da," which pleased him just as much. Moonlight from the portal window splashed Georg's face, softened by delight. This must have been how Friedrich knew him.

Winter weather kept us below in the grandly termed "salon" with its battered card tables, board games, and rows of chairs. Each day, it held fewer men, for influenza had boarded with the soldiers. The infirmary filled quickly. As some died, others filled the empty beds. The captain had sworn not to bury America's fighting men at sea; he'd bring the bodies home. Card games faltered when banging from the carpenter's shop below signaled another coffin being made. "Where are my uncles?" David demanded.

"They're working," we said. "The captain keeps them busy."

"It's the Kaiser's revenge for losing the war," announced one soldier. "He sent sick men to the field camps disguised as Yanks."

"Hell no," scoffed another. "He used a germ bomb."

Had influenza taken Dogwood? The ship's wireless was not available for civilian use. We'd have to wait until we docked in New York.

And Tom? I found an exhausted Red Cross officer on a break in the salon and asked about the prison camps. Perhaps Tom was there. "They're being emptied very quickly now," the officer said. "All the Americans have been released. That's one of the terms of the armistice. So if your friend's alive, he should turn up. However, we did receive lists of prisoners during the war. Do you understand, Miss Renner, that many of the missing will never be found?"

I didn't ask, as I'd asked on our last crossing, if the lists could be mistaken. A soldier named Butch came to my table. "He's right, ma'am.

You have to understand how it was. Men got buried in bomb blasts. If one of ours died in enemy territory, he wouldn't get reported, maybe never even found. Some just walked away."

"And then?" Here was hope, just a shimmer.

"A man alone, probably shell-shocked, no provisions, pretty soon no bullets. It would take a miracle to last a day. And miracles are rare in wartime." Butch nodded at David, who was struggling to follow our English. "You've got a cute kid here. That's something." Yes, the sweet curve of cheek, the melting eyes, the now-even breath, the small, square hand on my arm all were something. More than something. And yet, could Tom be alive, trying to come home?

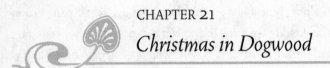

CHAPTER 21

## Christmas in Dogwood

Steaming into New York Harbor on a windy morning in mid-December, we joined a throng of healthy men on deck waving down at a sea of jubilant, jumping and cheering men, women, and children. "This is America?" David asked in wonder. "So many people! Where do they live?" We pointed to skyscrapers in the distance, but they must have seemed like child's blocks to him, stacked impossibly high.

Then came somber silence, for the captain had ordered that the wounded be brought off first. Those waiting on the dock drew back silently as a stream of orderlies carried out men on stretchers and helped others who were bandaged, limping, blind, or horribly twitching from shell shock. Finally the healthy could leave. Georg carried David down the gangplank. One by one his surviving shipboard "uncles" were enfolded into waiting arms. We found a public telephone and waited in an agonizingly long line to call home.

"Hazel, you're back!" my mother shrieked. She and Anna were healthy. Yes, influenza had passed through Dogwood. It was terrible, but over now. No, they'd heard nothing of Tom.

"The baroness died in Prussia," I said. "We have a three-year-old boy."

"What? A little boy?" my mother demanded just as the line fell.

"Let's go," said Georg. There was just time to catch the next train for Dogwood. With some difficulty, we got David into the railroad car, assuring him that it wouldn't swallow us. Seeing our bags, a dapper passenger asked if we'd been away long. I said we'd been visiting family. "Where?"

"In Canada."

"Canada. Good territory for shoes. I sell them, you see. Good thing you were gone. You missed the worst of the 'flu." He cracked his knuckles. "Sorry. Nervous habit. Can't stop myself. The 'flu was a doozy. The Kaiser's parting shot. Came through like a freight train. Undertakers couldn't keep up. They were shoving bodies in pits. In Philadelphia, they had babies buried in macaroni boxes. Am I scaring the kid? But it's the God's truth." He cracked his knuckles. "Sorry again. They said crowds spread it, so the governor closed taverns, theaters, churches, schools, all kinds of public meeting places. Funerals couldn't last more than fifteen minutes. They set up infirmaries in warehouses, schools, armories, any place they could. Terrible times, terrible. Then it was all over. Bang! Like it never happened. Except it did. Them that didn't lose a boy in war lost somebody to influenza."

"In-flu-ENZA," David repeated.

"The kid's right. Flew in like a bird. My brother lost his wife and son. He says 'Enza should have taken him. She got everything else he cares about. Well, here's my stop. Good talking to you folks." He cracked his knuckles once last time, gathered his bags, and was gone.

"What did he say?" David asked.

"That many people were sick here."

"Just like at home." He peered out the window. "But it's not like home." No, New Jersey had no bloated corpses along the road, burned shells of homes, blasted fields, or rolling coils of barbed wire. Yet under the slate sky, a somber change had come. In the stations, signs forbidding spitting and public assemblies had replaced war posters. Advertisements hawked miracle cures. Black armbands and ribbons on front doors showed where influenza had passed.

A light, cold drizzle fell as we arrived in Dogwood to be scooped up by Anna and my mother. Georg briefly acknowledged condolences for the baroness. Anna plucked David from my arms, peppering him with questions. I saw car keys in my mother's hand. To my astonishment, she'd learned to drive. She too wore a black armband. "Marjorie McClellan," she explained. "Last week." On Main Street, we passed the drugstore and the bakery, both with black ribbons on the door.

"Geoffrey Henderson died of influenza," Anna explained. "He was waiting for the troopship to come home."

Almost safe. His poor parents. "Who else?"

"Many. We'll talk about it when you're settled. But first, you tell us, how do you have a little boy?" I explained briefly. They listened, nodding, as if bringing home the orphaned son of a Russian soldier and a Prussian kitchen maid was the normal outcome of any trip abroad. Anna's only comment was "We didn't have much time to get ready for him."

At the castle, Kurt welcomed us in his solemn way. "We didn't know, sir, if you wanted a black ribbon for the baroness."

"No," Georg said quietly. "The child has seen enough black."

"Come inside, David," Anna urged. "And see what we have for you." It was astonishing. With so little warning, she and my mother and Tilda had assembled some boy's clothes, a teddy bear, Tom's wooden blocks retrieved from storage, and a cardboard tube of sticks and spools called Tinkertoys.

"Just invented," Anna boasted. It was so good to be in the warm, familiar kitchen, fragrant with baking and filled with the abundance of peace: baskets of onions, potatoes, and apples, a full pantry. We had a comforting meal of soup, breads, cheese, and cold meat. David let himself be sniffed and licked by Lilli and settled by the stove with his Tinkertoys. Lilli curled around him, her great tail swishing the floor.

"Now then," Anna said, passing a tray of my mother's *butterplätzchen*. "Tell us the whole story." We related our sickness on the crossing, the wasteland of Prussia, Georg's grave, the castle's debts and decay, the death of the baroness, and the terrible days of David's influenza.

"So you know," said Anna quietly. She described how influenza had slipped into Dogwood the day after we left. "We had a touch in the summer, but this time, there'd be one death, another a few days later, and then more and more. They put beds in the school. Then it was over, like a terrible dream." The shoe salesman had said the same, as if all of America had the same dream.

"Here in the castle?"

"Nobody, thank God, but others you knew. Your friend Lena was the first."

"Lena?" Not possible. I saw Lena in her classroom, Lena on Main Street in a swirl of autumn leaves, sharing her concerns about Walter, Lena after church in a crisp shirtwaist, smiling. Lena who was exactly my age.

"Then Captain Neal, the policeman who helped at your father's funeral. Dan Walker the iceman, and then his wife and two children. Five on Tilda's street and seven on Elm. Charlie Snead's wife and Harold Woodruff, the mayor's nephew. Ten children from the school. Some that you knew: Jud and Gloria from Lena's class."

Jud. Gloria. I saw their faces, too. *Ask it. Say his name.* "Walter?"

"He got it and survived, but he lost both parents. He's staying with the Hendersons now. He needs a family. And after they lost Geoffrey, they need him just as much."

I looked at my mother, silent through this litany. "Mrs. McClellan?"

"She was Dogwood's last. Katarina sat with her for two days and nights," Anna said. "Even Pastor Birke couldn't relieve her."

"I wasn't with Johannes at the end. I wouldn't let Marjorie die alone." We were silent around the table, listening to the rattling rain and David's murmuring patter to Lilli.

"And this came yesterday from Pittsburgh," my mother said, handing me a telegram from Ernst Schmidt, the butcher. Uncle Willy and Tante Elise were gone. They'd been found by a neighbor, lying together in bed.

"Oh, Mother." I wrapped my arms around her.

"I'm never going back. Johannes isn't there, and our friends are dead, our good, good friends. Remember all those Sunday dinners in our old kitchen?" She pressed a handkerchief to her face.

"Yes, Mother, I remember."

"David?" Anna was saying.

He'd stopped playing and was staring at us, wide-eyed. Tinkertoys clattered from his hand. He hadn't cried for his mother's death. For days I'd waited for the tears that must come. Now a stranger's grief unlocked his own. He curled against Lilli, sobbing, "Mama, Mama."

I brought him to the rocking chair. Anna wedged Bucephalus in his arms. We rocked and rocked as dusk came and he sobbed himself to sleep. "We put him in your room for now," Anna whispered.

"I'll take him," said Georg. David barely stirred as he was lifted from my arms and carried upstairs. Strains of a lullaby drifted back to us. I didn't know that Georg could sing. Anna cocked her head. "It's 'Saulika Pateka.' My mother loved that song." Perhaps Georg heard it from his mother. I hoped so.

The telegram from Pittsburgh lay on the kitchen table like a fallen leaf. As we cleaned the kitchen, my mother shared her plans, marked by the quiet certainty that had grown in the months since my father's death. Mrs. McClellan's husband died years ago; her son lived in Philadelphia and had no interest in a bakery. "She wanted me to have it. There's a flat above the shop where I could live, and the shop next door is for sale. With the money I'm getting from Frank for the hardware store, I could expand the bakery and put in a few tables for a café."

"You don't have to live downtown. You could stay here. I'm sure Georg—"

"No. If the store is going to be mine, I have to watch over it. I'm a forty-seven-year-old widow. I have to take care of myself. Hazel, you have to decide some things for yourself as well. Tom might not come back. And now you have a child."

"I know."

"Well then? Will you stay here?"

"I don't know."

The rain had stopped. I put on my coat and walked outside under the dripping pines. Once, before the war, I'd felt set apart from the sorrows of others. I had my sketchpads and plans that stretched before me; I was extraordinarily blessed. Then the war came, Galway's delusion and Ben's death. My father's passing. Tom's leaving. Prussia. David. Influenza. Life had tumbled all my plans. Paris seemed vague and indulgent now. Who needed me there? What difference could I make? The castle could provide comfort and ease for me and for David. But Georg needed someone with Friedrich's range of talents and passion for his work. The best I ever offered was earnest attention. My mother would have her bakery and her own new life. Once I'd asked my father why he had a hardware store. "I enjoy putting tools in people's hands," he said. "It makes me happy." When had I last been truly happy at work? In Galway, I realized, before my house was blue.

IN THE MORNING, I left David with Anna, filled a basket with my mother's butter cakes, and went to call on the families of Lena, Gloria, and Jud. Sitting in front rooms, I shared my few memories and listened to stories, joining a gently rotating cycle of relatives, friends, and neighbors who took turns making coffee, tending the stove, or washing dishes to relieve the mourners. I walked the dog at Lena's house and played with Gloria's chubby baby brother, now her parents' only child. Each home held a world of grief.

At last I came to the Hendersons. During the worst of the influenza, Jud's mother told me, the Hendersons kept the store open day and night and worked shifts at the infirmary. "They did everything and more for all of us. And that was after they lost Geoffrey."

Mr. Henderson was stocking shelves. I offered my condolences. He wouldn't talk about Geoffrey, only about influenza, announcing with sudden, fierce intensity: "We were all such fools. We thought modern medicine could cure everything. We beat smallpox, diphtheria, and yellow fever. But influenza beat us. Doctors couldn't help, so people ran after miracle cures: Pepto-Mangan. Pope's Cold Compound, goose-grease poultices, pawpaw pills, chloride of lime, sulfur powder, even kerosene syrup. I said: 'Save your money. It's all trash.' Minnie Reed drove to Philadelphia for Father Jim's Weed Tonic when I wouldn't sell her some concoction cooked up in a quack's kitchen. The trip wore her out and she died the next day."

Mrs. Henderson came in. "Hazel, you're back. You heard about Geoffrey?"

"Yes, I'm so sorry."

She repeated the story she must have told a hundred times. "He was in France, about to come home, safe and sound. You can imagine how happy we were. He had to wait a few days for a transport ship. In those few days, he got the 'flu and died. Excuse me, Hazel. I can't—" She covered her face and darted back to the stockroom. Her husband watched her go.

"It's like that for us. Sometimes we have to talk about him, and sometimes we just can't. You know we're taking care of Walter Baines now?" I nodded. "We'd like him to stay. We can help each other, I think."

"Is he drawing?"

"Yes. It seems to comfort him. Geoffrey liked drawing, too. He— excuse me." The anguished face turned away.

"Of course." As I left the store, I saw Ginny Henderson hurrying to her husband. The picture of their opening day had been replaced by a photograph of Geoffrey in his uniform. Next to it, propped on a little stand, was a pencil drawing of Walter's parents.

DAVID HAD SPENT the morning with Lilli, exploring the castle and gardens, and then settled in the kitchen with his Tinkertoys. "You can leave him here with me. I'm happy for the company," Anna said. Lilli watched him work, retrieving spools and rods that rolled away.

In the tower office, I related my morning's calls to Georg. "My father lost so many. I thought I understood what that would be like. But I never did until now. And it was the same for you."

"Yes, and for so many others."

"My father remembered them with tins. There must be another way, something we could do here in Dogwood, some kind of—"

"Memorial?"

"Yes."

"A memorial," Georg repeated. We sorted our mail as an idea slowly bloomed between us for a monument to those lost in war and dead of influenza. By late afternoon, we had fixed on the image of a marble eagle rising from a fountain and holding in its talons a tablet of names. We worked at the long table. I sketched as Georg watched, suggested, and sometimes took the pencil from me. Friedrich's name and my father's would be there. Marble seats would ring the fountain so all could sit, remember, and feel the healing run of water.

I studied the finished drawing, considering what I'd learned in the past months of materials, labor, and transport. "Georg, this would be very expensive. "Do you think Dogwood can afford it?"

"Perhaps not. In which case it would have to be my gift."

The next day, we called on Mayor Woodruff, a gruff, red-faced man so stuffed into his office chair that he didn't rise to greet us. "Heard you went back to Germany, Richthofen. What was *that* about?"

"Family business," Georg said stiffly.

"How are they taking it over there, getting beat by Yankees?"

"The war is over," I reminded both of them. "And we *all* lost so many in different ways. Like your nephew, Harold. I'm sorry, sir."

The mayor deflated, all bluster gone. Pudgy fingers ruffled papers on his desk. "Yes, Harold. That boy was like our own son. Fifteen years old. We were all so relieved he was too young to be drafted. Then the 'flu got him. Where's the justice?"

"I know," said Georg. "Where's the justice?"

Mayor Woodruff turned to a broad window looking out on Main Street, seeming to forget us. "I run a small town. Barking dogs, drunks, broken water mains, bridges, roadwork, house fires, the occasional sticky-fingered clerk. That's what I do. Not people sick in nearly every house, not young folks dying. Running an infirmary. You know how many towns I called, trying to get doctors here? They had their own sick, and their doctors were dead or sick or collapsed from overwork or still in Europe. We lost so many to the 'flu: men, women, and children. And then there's the boys who won't come back."

"That's why we're here," Georg said. "To find a way to honor them all." He set our sketches on the desk.

"It's a fine idea, Richthofen, but a marble fountain? This is a small town. We don't have that kind of money."

"I would fund it."

The mayor's eyes narrowed. "For some kind of reparation?"

"No. For recognition that we *all* lost in this war."

"And some," I added, "are still lost."

He looked at me more kindly. "You haven't heard any more about Tom Jamison?"

"No."

"I'm sorry, Hazel. My condolences." He considered Georg. "You must have—"

"I did, yes. Many."

The mayor heaved himself out of the chair. "Dogwood needs a monument and your offer is generous, Richthofen. Let me take it up with the town council." We shook hands and left.

On the way home, we stopped for sweet buns at the bakery, filled with a jostling, amiable crowd. Some even greeted Georg. "I rarely come downtown," he commented. "I send people for what I need."

"I know."

"Perhaps that could change."

"Perhaps."

THAT NIGHT, I wrote to the Burnetts in Galway, explaining how I came to have a child. I'd written in the fall but got no answer. Perhaps they were merely busy. Perhaps the epidemic had spared Galway. Influenza was capricious, I'd learned, skipping some towns completely, just as shells fell randomly in trenches. I sealed the letter and took out drawing paper and a pencil. Images came tumbling back. I sketched eager, anxious faces in a spelling bee. An older and a younger boy bent over a slate board. Alice and Susanna sweeping with me after school. A relay race in the schoolyard. How many of my children still lived? How many had brothers or fathers who wouldn't return?

David couldn't sleep. He hovered at my elbow, watching me sketch Charlie carrying in a pile of kindling. "Teach me to draw."

I took him on my lap as my father once took me, pushed a pencil in his fist, and held the small hand in mine. "What should we make?"

"My mama." At his direction, we made a thin woman "with pretty hair." Then we made Lotte and "the old lady upstairs." Nothing else of his past. I'd try again later. Memories were all he had from Prussia; I didn't want him to mistake them for dreams. Then he wanted scenes from his present life: Anna and my mother cooking, Lilli in the garden. "Now the room with mirrors. That's my favorite." How strange to see in another child my own small self exploring this castle. Finally he grew drowsy, and I carried him back to bed.

Christmas was days away. Our wartime holidays had been somber, but now we planned a child's-scale celebration. We chose a high-ceilinged room for the tree and locked it off from David. The Hendersons gave me Geoffrey's old tricycle, freshly painted. They'd been saving it for grandchildren. "At least now it'll be used," they said.

On Christmas Eve, the castle staff gathered in the great dining hall for a feast of roast goose and potatoes with a sideboard of my mother's sweets. "We didn't have Christmas before. Mama said Baby Jesus was scared of bombs," David announced. Now he ate and ate in spectacular abundance. Even Tilda smiled. "I think the war is over," she said, "when little boys eat like that." We cut the *Christstollen*, the finest my mother ever made, tender and rich with fruits and nuts, the taste of peace.

After the feast, Georg threw open the locked room, revealing our towering tree. Kurt had slipped away to light its candles, but David's face outshone them. He shivered with joy, demanding how a tree appeared *inside* a house, like Fairyland. Most amazing of all—Santa Claus knew he was in Dogwood. "For me?" he said over and over, unwrapping a toy train set, a stable for Bucephalus, winter boots, another teddy bear, and a set of Lincoln Logs that Georg ordered from New York. We went outside and sang "Silent Night" in the crystal calm.

"Do you remember Tom's first Christmas here?" Anna whispered to Georg. He nodded, his long arm encircling her rounded shoulder.

It was late when I cajoled David to bed for his lengthening litany of people and animals to be blessed. That night he added "Numa," explaining, "That's you, my new mama. Is gud?"

"Yes, David. It's very good."

"You're crying, Numa."

"Because I'm happy. Now close your eyes." I sang him "Muss Ich Denn" as my father once sang to me. Curled around Bucephalus, he was soon asleep. I stayed a long time in his room, looking out his window, thinking of my father, of the night views outside my dusty bedroom window in Pittsburgh, and maple trees outside my house in Galway.

IN THE EARLY days of January, I took a train to Newark's Red Cross office, where a round-faced clerk whose smile never faltered confirmed that all British and American prisoners had been released and accounted for.

"Could someone reported missing be with other Allied prisoners?"

"That's highly unlikely."

"I see."

Back home, I went to the meadow. Rain had melted the last snow and made the dark earth spongy. I sat with my father's spirit. *Well then, Hazel,* he would have said. *What now?* Buds were still tight on the copper beech. By the time they unfurled, I promised myself, I must know my path forward. From the distance came thuds on the soft ground, as David and Lilli burst into the meadow. "Tante Anna said to find Hazel," David panted. I held David close, grateful for the compact body and easy cheer. "She said when I'm big, I'll go to school."

"Yes, you'll go to school."

"Were you a teacher?"

"Yes I was." He asked about the marble marker. "My father's buried there."

"He died in the war?"

"Yes, in a way."

"You're sad?"

"Yes, I'm sad about my father and about someone else lost in the war."

"I have to go. Tante Anna might be looking for me." He scampered away with Lilli.

Who would be looking for *me*? Daily I felt more extraneous. My mother was full of plans for her bakery, testing new recipes at night and learning to keep accounts. Everyone predicted the success of Renner's Bake Shop. Dogwood was becoming her town more than it ever was mine.

Georg, too, had plunged into work. Since our return from Prussia, the haze of sadness that once surrounded him lifted more each day, as if the loss of his family had eased the weight of their rejection. Peace burst open the fine art market. Having seen the treasures of Europe,

Americans wanted them. Old families were eager to sell dusty antiques for ready cash. European ports were busy again; rail lines and roads were being rebuilt. Suddenly, moving art across the ocean seemed ridiculously easy. In weekly trips to New York, Georg met collectors and dealers, particularly a certain Anthony. Always before, I'd opened and sorted our business correspondence, but letters to and from Anthony were handled by Georg himself. There was work in Dogwood, too. The town council had approved our design for the monument, giving us a major project to oversee.

All of this should have been exciting, but the work that once entranced me was becoming tedious. I was easily distracted and made mistakes. Embarrassed by my lapses, I tried to do better, reworking dull offering letters, rechecking inventory lists, and dutifully reading texts on rare book collecting. In oblique references to the months after Friedrich's death, I gathered Georg's point: One must go on.

I might easily have been reading about Paris in those weeks, studying French, or writing to Georg's contacts who might ease my way there. But day after day, I did none of this. Instead, I returned to sketching. While David scribbled or built elaborate towers, I drew his face in many angles. I drew other children. I drew woodlands and waterfalls. I drew scenes from a place where my work had been cut short, where in a realm of four walls filled with young people, I'd known a brief joy.

ALICE'S CHRISTMAS CARD mentioned only herself and her parents, not the baby brother born last year. "We're very sad," she'd said. She hoped I'd visit soon; there was "something" to show me.

In early March, as the copper beech buds began to swell, I requested a few days leave to see friends in Galway. Georg agreed, tactfully not querying my purposes. My mother and Anna would keep David. On the way to the station, I told him once again that I'd be back soon, before he knew it, but as I walked down the platform, a shriek ripped the air. I turned to see small legs churning toward me, straw hair flying. "Don't leave, Numa! Take me!"

"I can't. I have to go alone."

My mother reached us, breathing hard. "Come, David. Your Numa will be back."

"Maybe she won't," he wailed. Passengers were boarding.

"Suppose we visit Pastor Birke and see the big church organ? And then we'll go for ice cream." David slowly loosened his frantic grip. From the train, I waved until his face shrank to a pinprick, marveling that he'd grown so huge in my life. Was it wrong to leave him even for a few days after all he'd endured of uncertainty and loss? But I had to go back to the place where so many had trusted me and lost. I had to know if this trust could be recovered.

CHAPTER 22

## *We're Not the Same*

I walked into Galway from the station in an afternoon of teasing March warmth. There had been blizzards far into April, Jim Burnett once told me, but for now melting snow was peeling back white covers from the earth. Three years had passed since I'd lived here. "You'd be surprised at the changes," Jim said in his last letter. Those who once could barely find Europe on a map now could pinpoint the sites of great battles: Verdun, Gaza, Kemmelberg, Flanders, and the Isonzo River.

I went first to the grocery store, where a tall young girl was helping Jim stock the shelves. Could this possibly be Alice? They turned at the doorbell's tinkle. "Hazel!" Cans of tomato sauce clattered to the floor. Jim called for Ellen. Alice noted every particular of my bobbed hair and the new tunic suit that Georg had brought back from New York. We all admired how Alice had grown. "She had just two small fits last year," Ellen said happily.

"Tell me about David," Alice demanded and I did. But when I asked if influenza had come to Galway, the smiles drained away.

"The 'flu took our little Freddy," said Jim. They told the story together, each managing a few words.

"We held him the whole time. He was never alone."

"He got a fever on Sunday and died on Tuesday."

"Doc Bentley said even the best city doctors couldn't help him."

"The fever broke Monday and we hoped—"

"And then it came back, and we knew—"

"It was so terrible to hear him breathe."

"None of us got it, just him."

"He tried to smile, remember? Even when he was sick."

"Hazel, I thought, if you were here, perhaps you could have—"

"Now Ellen, we've talked about this," said Jim. "How could she help? This influenza wasn't any ordinary ache or pain. Remember how fast it got Emma Grant?"

"Emma from my school?" Emma, with the wide eyes and thick black braids? "Judge Ashton too, and Henry McFee." Poor Henry, so worried about his aches. In the end, they didn't matter. The judge's vigor and bluster hadn't saved him. "What about Susanna? The judge returned my letters so I stopped writing."

They looked at each other. "He was like that. After he died, Mrs. Ashton sold the house and went to live with her sister in Arizona. She said the dry air would help Susanna. You can write to her now."

"And Agnes McFee?"

"She's staying. She got work in the new cheese factory. It does her good to be busy." Jim looked over the neatly stocked shelves. "After we lost Freddy, it was like we were dead ourselves. But we had to keep the store open. People have to eat. So at least part of the day, we weren't thinking about him. And it helps that we weren't the only family touched. Do you want to see the cemetery?"

I'd seen enough of cemeteries, bodies, and fields of the dead, but I went. Alice stayed behind. "We expect you for dinner," said Ellen. "And you're staying with us in our spare room."

Before the war, a small yard beside the church had sufficed for Galway. In the months I lived there, only two new graves were dug. Now the cemetery was half again as large, studded with tree stumps. "We didn't have time to pull them," Jim said. Crosses marked soldiers whose bodies lay in Europe. Those who died of influenza still had wooden slabs; headstone cutters were months behind.

"We couldn't even get enough coffins. Pittsburgh took the whole supply for miles around. I made a little box for Freddy. We washed and dressed him ourselves. And we put him in the box. And then we closed the box. I couldn't bear to nail it shut. Reverend Collins helped us bury him in a hole we'd dug ourselves. We filled the hole together. It was the hardest thing we've ever done."

I let him be and walked past the crosses, recognizing names of my students' fathers and older brothers. Then I stopped at a wooden marker.

CHARLES ROBERT DAVIS
JULY 28, 1901–NOVEMBER 4, 1918

Charlie must have enlisted when he turned eighteen, been quickly trained, and sent over to die seven days before the armistice. He tested me with a toad on the first day of school but stood by me when the town turned against Ben and called me a witch. Charlie, who adored Susanna and was good to Alice for her sake. Charlie who kept our schoolhouse warm.

Jim was at my side. "Hazel, let me show you something good. We wanted to surprise you if you ever came back to Galway." Threading past the wooden crosses, we reached a polished headstone.

BENJAMIN FRANKLIN ROBINSON
MARCH 19, 1878—JANUARY 11, 1916
1ST VOLUNTEER CAVALRY
THE ROUGH RIDERS
REST IN PEACE

My eyes filled. They'd done this for Crazy Ben. "Hunters found his body soon after you left. A lot of folks felt bad about what happened. Susanna spoke up for him when the judge wasn't around. The ladies started saying how respectful he always was and how harmless."

"That's true."

"Someone donated a coffin. I wrote to the army. It turns out that Ben really was one of Teddy Roosevelt's Rough Riders, just like he claimed. We put a collection jar in the store and got enough for this headstone."

"What did the judge say?"

"Nothing. He never talked about that night and never said a word about the grave. In fact, he didn't talk much at all after—what happened."

Walking back, I asked about the school. They'd had several teachers since I left; the current one was homesick and wanted to leave. Jim took my arm as a Model T came splashing through the mud. "Hazel, Galway's changed, first with the war, and then influenza. It's like we grew up. Folks want their children to know more about the world outside this town. They want a good teacher. Do you think you'd ever come back?"

Amazing how words can stroke like velvet on the soul. Still, there was so much unfinished. "Teaching here wasn't the problem, Jim, at least not at first. It was my house, what people said about it and me, how they needed more than I could do. Whatever touch I had, I don't have it anymore. It wasn't even enough when I was here. I couldn't help Susanna, and I couldn't save Ben. I couldn't even help my own father."

"Hazel, nobody expects any magic. You have a touch with children. That's enough for us."

"Let me think about it. There's David, too."

"He's very welcome here. Your old house got—"

"Torn down."

"Yes, but there's another near the school that the town rents out. It's a nice little place with two bedrooms, electricity, and even a telephone. No strange stories. Will you think about it?"

"Yes." I had dinner with the Burnetts and showed Alice how to wind her hair in the loose chignon that was fashionable now. In the morning I walked out to the remains of my blue house, and then to the cottage that might be mine. North windows would give good light. The porch looked out on broad fields and woods where David could play. Not Paris, and certainly not a castle, but perhaps a place of peace.

I WENT BACK to Dogwood the next day. My mother had just signed a loan from Georg for the shop beside the bakery. She'd pay him back with her monthly checks from Frank. Despite Anna's protests, she was adamant about moving into town. "I'm used to living over a store. We'll still see each other; you'll come have coffee with me."

"Everything's changing," Anna grumbled, but added mysteriously, "but some changes are good. Come." She drew me to the great stairway and pointed up, toward Georg's library.

I listened closely. "He's *laughing*?"

"I bet you never heard that sound before." I hadn't. "His friend Anthony is visiting from New York. We might be having parties soon."

"Then you'll need bread," my mother noted. "And cakes and pies.

See? I'll *have* to live over the store. Hazel, go up and meet Anthony. You'll like him."

I did like him. Anthony Lamberti was tall and lanky with a long nose and scooped cheeks. Nobody would call him handsome. In fact, the craggy face was nearly comical beside Georg's beauty, but he had a warm, rolling voice and the kindest brown eyes. Under his hands, the grand piano that had been silent for so long rolled out old ragtime tunes and new jazz. Lilli howled in chorus. David clambered on the piano bench to watch the running fingers, transfixed.

The sight of his pleasure shook my resolve. How could I take the child from here, or from Anna and my mother, who both adored him? And yet my place in Dogwood was shrinking. Anthony and Georg were already deep in plans to catch the booming rare-book trade. They didn't need me. Every sign pointed me west. Even beyond the matter of work, to stay here was to wait for Tom, when every voice of reason announced that he'd never return.

The next morning, I took David to the gazebo and described Galway while he rubbed and tossed Bucephalus, giving no sign of listening. When I stopped, he asked: "What if we don't like it there?"

"We could come back. Or go somewhere else."

"I'd be in your school? You'd be my teacher?"

"Yes."

"Can we have a dog?"

"When we're settled."

"But not Lilli?"

"No, Lilli lives here."

"Can we come back for Christmas?"

"Yes."

"I have to talk English?"

"Yes, but you'll learn quickly."

"Can I play now?"

"Yes." He slipped off the bench and ran to find Lilli.

At night, when I put him to bed, David solemnly announced that he and Bucephalus would try Galway.

"I'm glad." In the next weeks, I fixed the terms of my employment with the Galway school board. I'd start work in mid-April. Harriet Willis, the current teacher, couldn't wait to go home to her family in Ohio and, many suspected, to a sweetheart just back from the war. Some small repairs would be done on the house and it would be repainted. I asked for white. In the meadow, I drew my father's grave. "See?" I whispered. "You're coming with me." I'd also bring the little coffin that Tom had made, one of his wooden puzzles, and four of my father's tins.

At a going-away dinner in the big dining room, David sang songs the soldiers had taught him. Georg and Anthony gave me art books for the school and a small Constable landscape for my house. "We'll come out soon to make sure it's hung properly," they promised.

My mother grew quiet as the evening ended. The last time I'd left her, she had my father. Now she was alone, despite the bakery and so many new friends. So much had happened here. We held each other tightly at the train station. "Write to me, Hazel. Write me all the time."

"I will. And if Tom comes back, if you hear anything—"

"We'll tell you right away."

"I'll miss you all."

"We'll visit."

"Here's your lunches," said Anna, handing me a heavy sack. "Don't forget to feed the child."

David hugged Lilli again. Georg, Anthony, Anna, and my mother waved as we pulled away.

"Will we be happy in Galway?" David asked.

"I hope so."

WE WERE SO busy in the first weeks that I had no time to measure happiness, or even question the wisdom of my choice. Once again, I visited the farm families; this time David eased my way. He was learning English quickly, and children welcomed a new, exotic playmate. Sometimes returned soldiers recounted their great adventures. Others struggled to manage their old lives and work with damaged bodies. In many houses I saw young men sitting glassy-eyed in corners or heard that they'd slipped away when they saw strangers coming, even a woman and a small child.

As Jim Burnett predicted, more families wanted their children in school. Sometimes adults followed me out to the road for a confession: "I can't read or write, Miss Renner. I don't want my kids to know. Will you teach me?"

"Don't make them go to school," Ellen said. "They'd be ashamed." So I gave lessons at my home two evenings a week. Under the guise of "calling on the schoolmarm," men and women gathered at my kitchen table, learning to sound out food labels, newspaper headlines, and familiar Bible verses. Some paid with quarters. Others brought crafts or produce: bacon, eggs, jam, fruit pies, or baskets. One man made a rush-bottom chair for David; Molly Hyde sewed gingham curtains for my kitchen.

Taking over the classroom so late in the year, I didn't push the children hard. We spoke about the war as much as they wanted to, drew pictures of those they'd lost, and had spelling, geography, arithmetic, and history bees to break up the day. In September, we agreed, school would be "more regular." I planted a vegetable garden with meticulous advice from older students who marveled at my ignorance. "You're from the city," they said kindly. "Don't expect too much your first summer."

CHAPTER 23

# A Wooden Man

The evening of June 6, 1919, was balmy. In the kitchen, chop-ping onions for the next day's soup, I struggled to excite David with the wonder of what had just happened in Washington: The Senate had ratified a constitutional amendment for women's suffrage. I'd explained "voting," then "Senate," and had begun "Constitution" when a knock at the door had David bolting away. We'd never get to "ratify," I was thinking, when he came running back.

"Numa, there's a man on the porch."

New students for my evening classes sometimes came at this hour, stiff and embarrassed, slowly circling to their purpose. My hands were deep in onions. "What did he say?"

"Nothing."

"Ask him to come in."

David darted back to the door, delivered his message, and returned. "He won't. He's wooden, like this." David demonstrated, so like John Foster, my bringer of paint, that I froze. "And there's a dog in the yard that looks just like Lilli. The man has curly black hair."

A dog like Lilli. Black hair. Here. Colors in the kitchen blared; every edge turned sharper. This moment, on this plain June day, everything was changing. "He must want reading lessons. Can you go play in your room?"

"But—"

"Go on, David. You know how shy they are at first."

I took off my apron, smoothed my hair, and walked slowly to the door. After all this time, after all my giving up, after months of mornings thinking that *today* I would have news, had he come so soon? I opened the door. And there was Tom, like a simple, solid fact. There were the same broad shoulders and dark curls with threads of gray. Arms and legs whole, face unscarred. Except that he was wooden, exactly as David said. I turned wooden, too, staring at him with my hand on the door.

In all the times I'd pictured our reunion, even at this very door, I'd always seen a two-reeler romance: *My darling, you're home at last.* I leap into his arms. Organ music swells. Fingers tangle in my hair. We kiss and kiss. Not this. Nothing in this wooden man said, *"Touch me."* Everything said, *"Be careful. I might break."*

I stepped back. "Come in, Tom. I'm so glad to see you." As if he were an evening student: *Come in, Tom. I'm so glad to see you.* Did I once lie with this man skin to skin, our bodies tangled? It hardly seemed possible.

"Can Lilli come in?" I'd never have recognized this toneless voice.

"Yes, of course."

He whistled and she came at a stately pace. Even Lilli was different, fixed on Tom, staying close, barely acknowledging me. We filed into the kitchen, a stiff procession. He took a chair facing the door. When he set his knapsack down, it clattered on the floor. Lilli sat, pressed against his leg. *Say it because it's true, wooden as he is.* "Tom, I was so afraid you'd never come."

Where did that slow smile begin? Far inside, finally cracking the wood of his face. "So was I." He put a hand on Lilli's head. "Your mother said you'd be here."

"When did you get to Dogwood?"

"Two weeks ago."

"Nobody told me."

"I asked them not to. I wanted you to see for yourself how I am."

"Oh." And how was he? Like a man under a spell. Ask something normal. "Are you hungry?" He nodded. I began making coffee and cut a piece of strawberry pie.

A floorboard creaked. Tom scrambled to his feet so quickly that the chair toppled. His knapsack clattered over. "Who's that?" he demanded, his voice sharp as a rifle crack. Lilli was on her feet as well, hackles up, growling at a pale and shaking David, who was clutching his wooden truck. Tom shook his head as if to clear it. "Down, Lilli." She sat. "It's the kid from Prussia?"

"Yes, this is David." Breathing hard as if from a terrible race, Tom righted the chair. Lilli pawed his leg. He gripped the scruff of her neck.

I went to David and spoke to him softly in German: "This is my friend Tom, who lived at the castle. He was in the war. Lilli was his dog. They've come to visit."

"He's scary. Will he hurt me?"

"No. And you're not afraid of your friend Lilli, are you?"

"I don't know. She's not the same." I sat down with David on my lap.

Tom's breathing eased. Lilli lay down at his feet. "I'm so sorry, kid. Strange noises make me jumpy. Do you understand?" A careful nod. "They told me all about you. Anna said you were very brave to come to America."

A tiny voice: "You brought Lilli."

"Yes. They thought she'd help me get better. She remembers you, I'm sure. Would you like to pet her?"

"Yes."

"Go, Lilli." David slid off my lap and Lilli bounded to him, wagging, bowing, circling, rubbing and pawing him as they tangled like puppies. We watched them play, warmed by their pure and easy joy. "Hazel, I want to tell you where I've been and what happened that made me like this."

I gave him the coffee and pie. "It doesn't have to be now."

"Yes, it does." He braced himself like a student before a spelling bee's last round, when the hardest words are coming.

"Tell me."

Tom took a long breath. "I was gone a very long time. I wasn't myself here." He touched his head. "I have some good days now, but many that aren't good."

"I'm glad that you came. I missed you." I reached for his arm. At least this was the same: hard under a soft flannel shirt. He raised his other hand and laid it gently on mine. A shiver ran through me. I'd waited so long.

That same warm, wide smile—almost the same. "Wonderful pie."

"There's more. As much as you want."

He leaned back. "Peace is so good: strawberry pie, a kitchen, a little boy, a front porch, a field without shell holes, songbirds. On the front, you start thinking that all these things are dreams. You're crazy even to remember them." His gaze drifted out the window. His body, too, seemed lighter, as if it might float out as well. I had to pull him back.

"A telegram last spring said you were missing in action. What happened?"

David climbed back in my lap. Lilli returned to Tom. He stroked her velvet head. "Late April, 1918. You knew the baron's cousin, Manfred von Richthofen, the Red Baron, was shot down?"

"Yes."

"I figured I had to be next. Nobody lasts long up there, and he was the best. I was in Belgium, flying every day. You watch the other guy's plane go spiraling down and you think: *I'm next.* The last time I flew, I was supposed to bomb a railroad terminal. A fog rolled in, and I wasn't sure if I was over a village or the terminal."

"You couldn't see."

"No, and I couldn't come back with the bombs. You had to drop them. When I flew low to see better, my plane was hit. I managed to land, but I didn't know where I was. In the fog, shapes kept coming at me. I shot them. They could have been villagers."

"But if they were shooting at you, they were soldiers."

"I don't remember if they were shooting or not. Some of them fell. Then I was running."

"Where?"

"Into a forest. I ran until it was quiet and green all around me. I was bloody and my head hurt. I must have slept because I dreamed that my friend Colin came out of the fog. He said, 'Tom, why didn't you get me another cup of tea? Then I'd be alive now.' I woke up sweating and shaking. I didn't have my dog tags, and I was wearing civilian clothes."

"How did you get them?"

"I don't know. I can't remember. There was a house outside a village with an old woman named Louise. She was hunting mushrooms in the woods and found me. She took me home and bandaged my head. She was a cabinetmaker's widow. These are his tools in my knapsack. She didn't ask questions. Or she did and I couldn't answer them. In any case, I wasn't Thomas Jamison anymore. She called me Jean-Paul. I worked for her, and she fed me. I kept seeing Colin in the fog."

"You didn't try to go back?"

"No. I just worked for Louise and people in the village. I slept. If there was wine, I drank it. I'd watch airplanes and remember how quiet it was in the clouds. When my head cleared, the idea of even trying to go back seemed crazy. The front was always moving. How could I find my unit? If I did, they'd shoot me for desertion. More likely, I'd walk into a German camp. Then *they'd* shoot me. Eventually, I stopped thinking about going back or going home or even about you. I just— was there. Do you understand?"

"Like in a dream?"

"Like a nightmare. Soldiers kept passing through the village: French, English, American, German. They were all the same to me. I'd hide in the woods, absolutely still, playing dead. Any little sound could have killed me." *Like a floorboard creaking under a small boy.* "Every time they came, I expected to die. Even if I didn't move, a soldier might see my shape and shoot. Why not? I'd shot at shapes. Sometimes I thought I *was* already dead. This is what dead people do, right? They live in the woods in Belgium. Crazy, wasn't it?"

I squeezed Tom's arm. "You aren't dead, though. You're here."

"Yes. It's amazing."

"But you didn't come home after the armistice."

He stroked Lilli a long time. "No. I'd been feeling better in the fall of '18, except on foggy days. There weren't as many bombs, and I thought about Colin a little less. Louise talked about peace: '*La paix, finalement la paix.*' On November 11, when the war ended, they celebrated in town, but peace didn't change much for me. I was still lost." David whispered that he was hungry. I gave him bread and butter.

"Louise didn't want to keep me anymore. Maybe she paid my ticket and put me on a train because somehow I was in Paris. I'd had this thought that you'd be there. I'd find you, and you could put my pieces back together. Like magic."

"Tom." I held his hands tightly in mine, as if that warmth could melt the line between our bodies. Even then, nothing happened. No tremor, only my ache for his pain.

"I know. That was crazy. Nobody knows how to put men like me back together. There's no magic. They say it takes time. And maybe it never happens, or it's never finished." He stared at the table.

"So you were in Paris," I prompted.

He blinked and revived. "Yes. It was big and noisy. I jumped at every sound. I had these tools, though, so I went around to bars and cafés and fixed things for food and a place to sleep. I helped a priest whose church had been damaged. People were kind, mostly. But I couldn't find you and I had trouble on foggy days."

"How did you get back?"

"I was working in a café and an American came in. He said, 'Are you Tom Jamison?' I jumped. I hadn't heard that name in months. It was Captain Shay, my squad leader. He bought me drinks. Apparently I *had* bombed the railroad station. A few days later, he showed up with this." Tom reached in his pocket and put a bronze medal on the table. "He said I'd earned my eagle wings."

"Eagle wings," David repeated.

"Yes," he said ruefully. "I seem to be a hero."

"Then you left Paris?"

"Yes. Shay said it was time to go home, that I'd get adjusted better in familiar places." Tom stopped suddenly, looking around as if surprised to find himself with us. Lilli nudged his leg. He stroked her and went on. "He arranged a berth on a ship for New York."

"Captain Shay seems like a good man."

"He is. He asked me if I had a girl waiting back home."

My arms tightened around David. "What did you say?"

"That there was a girl, and she might be waiting, but maybe she shouldn't. He told me there's no harm in asking."

I heard myself say: "No, there's no harm."

"Can we eat? I'm *really* hungry," David demanded.

"I bet he wants me to stop talking."

I got up to make dinner. "David, didn't you say your truck was broken? Show it to Tom. Maybe he can fix it."

"Let's see." Very slowly, David edged around the table and put his truck in Tom's outstretched hand. "Hum, one wheel doesn't turn. I wonder—yes, here's the problem. There's something stuck in the axle. See?" Mesmerized, David inched closer until two heads bent over the wheel. "Now if I just had a pencil—" David scurried to get one. My heart pounded. Wasn't this the same Tom—the same patient focus on every problem, the same pleasure in small solutions? Surely he'd "get adjusted." Lilli would help. David and I could help. See, he had fixed the wheel.

An instant later, an owl hooted and Tom jolted upright, eyes wide and wild, sweat popping from his brow, gripping the table so hard that his hands went white. David seemed oblivious, happily running his truck along the kitchen floor. I went back to stirring the soup, as if I'd noticed nothing. But "getting adjusted" would be a task far beyond fixing wheels and eating pie.

Still, when dinner was ready, we were like any family around a kitchen table. Tom's speech came slowly; sometimes a question had to be repeated, but he was *here*, talking, just like people do. I asked for news from Dogwood. Anthony lived at the castle now. He and Georg had a small party with friends from New York. "No footmen or musicians, but Anthony played the piano." More and more, their trade was in rare books. "People want them, and they don't need fancy packing." Yes, of course. How hopeful the sheer normalcy of this fact that books don't need fancy packing. It's what he would have said *before*. Couldn't we build on this?

"How's the bakery doing?"

"Very busy. And the café is always full. Your mother had her hair bobbed like yours. It looks good. She brought Martin over for dinner."

"Who's Martin?"

"You know Martin Birke, the pastor. Her sweetheart."

"Her—?" I choked on bread.

"Sweetheart. You didn't know? Hazel, I may be crazy, but I'm not *blind*." He said this so deadpan, smiling so slyly, that I laughed, he laughed, and David looked between us, perplexed.

I explained the joke, but he wasn't interested. "Does Lilli have new tricks?"

Tom's smile slipped away. "Yes, I suppose. She helps me get back to myself."

"What?"

"I'll show you in the morning."

"It's late now. Tom, excuse us, please. I have to put David to bed."

"Take your time. I'll be here." *Take your time. I'll be here.* So simple. As if he'd always been here.

I tried to hurry David, but he balked, full of questions. Would Tom and Lilli be staying with us? Could Tom really fix *anything*? And finally: "He's a little strange. But nice."

"Yes."

Winding his fingers in the cloth of my shirt as he did before sleep, David pulled me close to whisper: "Bucephalus says you look pretty tonight."

"Go to sleep, now. It's late." He turned over and over in bed, begging me to stay just a little longer, a little longer. The kitchen was clean but empty when I returned. Silence all around. Was Tom gone already? Heart pounding, I rushed out to the porch. He was smoking a pipe as Lilli explored my yard. "You're still here."

"I'm still here. Is he asleep?"

"Yes." I sat on the porch, close but not touching.

Smoke drifted over our heads. "You're teaching school?"

"Yes." I didn't want to speak of David or teaching. I was afraid to touch him, but soldiers are afraid and still they advance. I dared my hand to cross the No Man's Land between us. Our fingers locked. He spoke into the moonless sky.

"Captain Shay said there's no harm in asking. But Hazel, I don't even know what to ask for. I've got nothing, just a dog and some tools. I don't even have myself sometime."

"Tom?"

"Yes?"

"I'll ask. Will you stay the night with me?"

He closed his eyes. Not even the night was breathing. Finally he stood. His voice was thick: "Lilli, come." He held out his hand for me. In my bedroom Lilli curled against the door, protecting us. In darkness we undressed, fingers fumbling. I felt scars from his flight through the woods and a tender place in his back where shrapnel lodged. But here were the arms, the legs, the chest, the scent, the touch, the whole of him, here with me was as I had imagined . . . as I'd never imagined, as if I'd been far away myself.

"There's nothing like peace," he said at last, as we stretched over the sheets. "It's heaven on earth."

"Are you tired?"

"Very. I didn't sleep for two nights, thinking about coming here." Thick clouds rolled behind the trees. We curled together. I woke in the night. Tom was shaking me gently, asking: "Hazel, are you here?"

"Yes, I'm here." His breathing eased, and I remember sleeping deeply then. My bed faced the window. I woke to fog and sat up in terror. Fog! Tom and Lilli were gone. He wasn't on the porch or anywhere around the house. His knapsack was gone. Footprints in the soggy ground led to the road and then disappeared. I sank on the porch steps, arms aching with emptiness. The ache said I hadn't been dreaming. I'd had him again and lost him.

David found me there. "Will Tom and Lilli come back?"

"I don't know."

"I liked him."

"I'm sure he liked you, too, David."

"Then why did he leave?"

"I don't know."

One hour crawled into the next. It was Saturday, without even the distraction of school. We worked in the garden, built towers and knocked them down, and walked out to a waterfall. Perhaps Tom would be waiting when we returned. He wasn't. I hung a lantern on the porch, but he didn't come at night.

In the morning, I left David with the Burnetts, who thankfully asked no questions. The Galway stationmaster remembered Tom's coming well enough. "Curly-haired man with a wolf-dog? No, haven't seen him since. I would have remembered the dog." So Tom was still in Galway. No use searching houses or roads. I knew he'd be drawn to the safety and deep quiet of the woods, as he had been in Belgium, as Ben was. Wouldn't he go to Red Gorge?

Half a dozen search teams hadn't found Ben or his camp in winter, when the hills were bare of underbrush and a man's tracks were easily seen. How could I find Tom? But still I walked to Red Gorge, crossed the bridge, and took the first trail up. Perhaps it caught Tom's eye. Ben had spoken once of cool at his camp even in the summer's heat. So it must be up. But so many hills rolled into Red Gorge. Which one was his?

The trail divided. I laid my hand on a mossy trunk and closed my eyes, imagining Tom in the apple orchard, in the airplane when we flew with a hawk, and in the forest where he hid from any soldier. If I were Tom, which way would I go? Wouldn't it be where the green was thickest and most tangled, where a man would be hardest to find? I followed the faintest trail. Sometimes I found a freshly broken branch or lightly trampled ferns. By his feet? I couldn't read the signs. I scrambled over rocks, followed a butterfly over a fallen tree, heard a squirrel scramble through dry leaves, and found another stretch of path. I wasn't lost, I convinced myself, only moving steadily upward. Sometimes I felt him so close that I wondered if he was hiding, pressed against a tree, as still as moss, invisible, so no enemy could find him.

"There's no harm in asking," Captain Shay had said. This was my journey for asking. It was near noon. Sweat slicked my body. I was exhausted and had reached the end of a fragile trail. Had I fought this far up a hill to find I was on the wrong one? Parched, I'd drained the last of my water when my eye caught a spot of red in a crease of stone. Blood? No. I came closer. It was a child's glove, finely made. A girl's glove. So tired, so hot, I sat on the rock, holding the glove, turning it over and over, trying to think why this glove seemed so significant. Yes! Susanna. When she'd come to my house that snowy night, which bare hand had reached for hot cider? The left. And this was a left-hand glove. She must have been coming down from Ben's camp when she lost it on this hill. Tom must be here, in the place that solaced Ben. One lost soldier's refuge had summoned another missing man.

I pushed through a thicket of brambles. On the other side was something scrabbling in leaves. A flash of gray. A wolf like the one that came after us in Prussia? I backed toward a tree I could climb, but now the animal was here, jumping at me, barking, circling. Lilli! I hugged her, burying my face in the rough fur. "Lilli, find Tom!"

She was patient, darting ahead, waiting, sometimes circling behind to urge me on. In minutes we reached the trail. It was rocky and steep, but clear. I moved quickly, scrambling over roots, once even holding Lilli's tail on a slippery turn. We passed through another thicket and into a clearing with a small, rough cabin. And he was there like a statue, waiting.

"Hazel! You found me."

"Yes, with Lilli."

The dark eyes swam. I looked down at what he saw: my torn shirt, scratched arms, and filthy, shredded skirt. "Come." He took my hand and led me to a rain bucket where I rinsed my face and hands. He found a sliver of soap to wash where thorns had scratched me, and gave me a shirt I recognized as Ben's. We sat on tree stumps with Lilli at our feet. A fresh breeze cooled us.

"Hazel, I can't believe you're here."

"I had to come."

"I didn't want to run away. You have to believe me."

"You heard voices?"

"Like your friend Ben? No. More like a roaring in my head, shells and shouting. I had to find a quiet place. Somehow I found this one and the roaring stopped."

"Ben's voices stopped here, too."

He gripped my hands. "Hazel, I don't want to be like this, not for your sake or David's or mine. I'd give anything to be like I was before." Our fingers knit together. "There are so many men like me. I saw them on the ship. They twitch and shake. Some can't talk at all or act blind even if doctors say there's nothing wrong with their eyes. They scream or hide under tables. Nobody knows how to help us. I jump at sounds, like you saw. I have nightmares and sweats. Fog can set me back.

Drinking tea reminds me of Colin. Being close to anyone reminds me of losing him. Hazel, do you want all this in your life? I can go back to the castle. They'd take me. Or I can go someplace else."

"You don't have to. You can stop moving. You can get better here in Galway."

Sunlight through pines struck the dark curls I'd touched two nights ago. I stroked the hands that cut my father down and held mine as we walked in every weather, the hands that fixed David's truck. He touched a jagged scrape on my arm and bent to kiss it. "Hazel, I love you. I'll always love you, but isn't it all the trouble I bring too much?"

*Zu schmerzlich.* "Yes, sometimes it will be too much. But other times it will be like this. We'll be together. You'll have good days. Fog doesn't make the land go away. It's still there. And then the fog lifts. Are you going to ask?"

"Hazel, may I go back with you? Can we try again?"

"Yes."

"Are you sure?"

"Yes."

"Lilli, up!" She scrambled to her feet. She looked at him, awaiting orders. "Find David." She bounded into the woods and led us down the mountain, back to my house in Galway.

CHAPTER 24

*The Work of Peace*

With any American child, explaining Tom's troubles might have been impossible. But David had seen dogfights in the air and flaming airplanes fall. Every field in Prussia was scored and pitted. He'd heard bombs all his life. In fact, the silence of Galway often disturbed him. "When are they starting again?" he'd ask. In our journey to Antwerp, horrors had bloomed in his fever: bloated bodies, charred houses, dazed men walking, and bands of thieves. For Tom to say "Sometimes I think I'm still back there" made perfect sense to David. But still he was wary.

"You made my Numa cry. I heard her."

"I know that. I'm very sorry."

"And her arms are scratched. I saw them."

"Yes, I know."

"You said you'd show me Lilli's tricks in the morning."

"And I didn't. I left."

David set Bucephalus on the table between them and folded his arms. Judge Ashton never seemed so fierce. Tom glanced at me. All I could offer was help in translating. Tom wiped his brow and pulled a chair closer. "It's like this, David. I'd waited for a long time to see your mother. And I came a long way to see her and meet you. But when you've been confused for a long time, happiness is strange and confusing, as if you've forgotten what it feels like. You know how sometimes at night, you remember bad things you saw or bad things that happened to you?"

David moved restlessly. "Maybe."

"Well, I do. The fog came in, and I was hearing bombs and shells. I saw a friend who died, and I had to leave. I didn't want to. I would have given anything to stay here."

"Where did you go?"

"To a hill I saw from the train. Hazel once told me about a camp made a long time ago by someone like me. I thought it might be there."

"David, do you remember what I told you about my friend Ben?"

He nodded, his eyes fixed on Tom. "Will you go away again?"

"That's the problem. I might. But I can promise you this: I'll come back."

Thick silence filled the room. David's eyes drilled into Tom's. "Maybe you won't."

Tom pulled something from his pocket and reached for David's hand. "Here are my eagle wings. I want you to have them. They're my promise that I'll come back."

"I have a medal from Uncle Georg for not coughing."

"Well, this is another." A small hand closed around the wings. "David, can you trust me to try to get better, to work as hard as I can?"

"Can you show me Lilli's tricks?"

"Yes. Let's go outside."

In the long June evening, David learned to have Lilli sit, stay, lie down, come, fetch, and speak. We took turns hiding and having Lilli find us. We watched fireflies fill the grass and darkness below the trees. I brought out a blanket and we lay together, watching stars. Very late, Tom carried David inside, clutching his medal. Then he came to get me, and we went to bed ourselves, with Lilli by the door.

A BRIGHT BLUE week followed, bringing us good days and happy plans. Tom already had a commission from Georg for a revolving bookcase. We walked into town to ask Jim Burnett for permission to build a workshop onto the house. Jim welcomed him, discreetly not inquiring of our relationship. I had brought with us the miniature of my father's coffin and Tom's wooden puzzle.

Jim studied the workmanship. "My wife's been wanting a china cabinet. Could you build her one?"

"Yes. I can, but I can't say exactly by when. I have bad days that I can't predict." He explained why.

"You make a good china cabinet and we'll get it when it's done. Come by tomorrow and talk to Ellen about exactly what she wants." We finished our shopping and were about to leave when Jim drew us aside. "Tom, other men around here had a rough time in the war. When you get settled, I'll introduce you. And Hazel, we can say he's your hired man, but you do realize that Galway's a small town. People talk. Some things have changed, but not that."

"Yes. I understand."

"Good. I'll tell Ellen she'll have her cabinet."

Our engagement wasn't romantic. "We *could* get married," Tom said as we walked home.

Infected by his caution, I added only: "Yes, we could. I'd like to."

"When I was a boy, I dreamed of you coming back to Dogwood. Then, like magic you did come back, looking for Margit Brandt. That night, I told Anna how much I wanted you to stay."

I described how my own love bloomed the afternoon of picking apples, but he didn't seem to be listening. "Hazel, Jim's right. People will talk if we don't get married right away, and I'd hate that for you. But I want you to know what it is that you're choosing. I want you to be sure. And I want David to be sure." He touched my shoulder tentatively, although we'd done so much more. "Could we stand the gossip for a while?"

We'd stand it until August, we decided. When we'd passed the last house, our bodies came together; our shadows fused. We stepped into the woods, hidden from passing cars. The next day, we called the castle to announce our intentions. "We'd like to get married in the gazebo," I told my mother. "You and Georg can decide everything else." For the rest of the summer, the castle swirled with preparations. I had Ellen take measurements for our wedding clothes. Tilda's sister would make my dress; Georg's tailor would make suits for Tom and David. Jim convinced the school board to accept a married teacher. Then I stopped thinking about the wedding. My work in those months was to learn about life with Tom.

There were night sweats and nightmares. Sometimes he woke up screaming, frightening even Lilli. There was sleepwalking; once he stumbled off the porch and gashed his head on a rock. Sometimes he was gone but close by. I'd tell Lilli, "Find Tom," and she'd lead me to him, rigid behind a tree, hiding from soldiers. He might or might not be startled by thunder, owls, twigs snapping, a distant dog, cars honking, wind slamming a door closed, or rattling windows. The slight crowds of Galway were sometimes bearable and sometimes not. David could not have toy guns. We could never have tea in the house, for tea reminded him of Colin. Once he ran out of church, having "seen" Colin beside him.

Over and over, I had to learn that sometimes—often—I was less useful, less comforting to him than a dog. More than my touch or words, he needed Lilli's cold nose on his skin, the softness of her fur, and her mute loyalty. Then there was the going away. On foggy mornings, and sometimes for causes I'd never fathom, he'd leave us. I learned not to follow, but to simply wait. Returned soldiers who shared a brotherhood of wandering sometimes found him on the road to Red Gorge and brought him back.

Wilbur Reed sought me out. "I was a pilot, too. If Tom ever needs help, just call me, day or night. And you can always talk to my wife, Gracie. Men like us aren't what you women signed on for."

"You didn't sign on for that kind of war, either."

"No, we didn't. We had no idea. But one thing's sure. Tom loves you. He'd go through fire for you."

"I know that, Wilbur, but suppose it's foggy the day we leave for the wedding? Suppose he's gone?"

"We talked about that. You send word and I'll get the guys together. My buddy Lloyd was a scout, better than any bloodhound. Wherever Tom is, in Ben's camp or someplace else, we'll find him and put him on that train. He'll have a military escort down the aisle if that's what it takes."

"What did Tom say?"

Wilbur grinned. "I won't repeat his words exactly. The gist was yes, do what you have to."

In the weeks before our wedding, the good days were very good. We planted a rose garden and laid out an orchard. Tom put a swing in the schoolyard and cut wood for a tree house he'd build with the older children. When he made a little truck that a child could sit on and steer, David was delirious with pleasure. In the evenings, we sat on the porch with Lilli at our feet until one of us said the words that brought us to bed: "Well then." In the darkness our touches eased away loneliness and pain. As David held his horse at night, I held these memories close when the Tom I knew was replaced by a stranger and Galway became his Western Front, surrounded by enemies.

IN LATE AUGUST, Wilbur took us to the station. "Looks like you guys missed your manhunt," Tom said. At the last minute, a new conductor wouldn't allow Lilli on the train. "Orders is orders. No dogs." he said. Wilbur promised to keep her until we came back, but in the crowded carriage Tom gripped my hand for hours, sweating, his eyes clamped shut. Passengers stared at the wooden man beside me.

"He'll be fine once we're there," I whispered to David. With the rattling wheels, words spun in my head: *He'll be fine. He'll be fine. He'll be fine.* Finally in New Jersey, Tom opened his eyes to the humps of green hills. "It's not Belgium."

"Not it's not."

He struggled to smile. "And Wilbur's not here with his escort."

"No he's not."

"Lilli's not here, either. I have to do this myself."

"Yes you will."

David had been pressing Tom's medal between his hands. He opened them slightly to show his treasure, like a butterfly about to escape. Tom studied the small, drawn face. "Shall we have a wedding today? Do you think it's a good idea?" The blond head bobbed. David leaned against Tom. In the last miles, we reached another peace.

My mother met us in Dogwood. "Johannes would be happy today," she said. "He was so fond of Tom." She was happy herself, looking younger than I ever remember.

The castle gate stood open; the gazebo was draped with flowers. I'd never seen Georg so handsome, resplendent in a new cutaway jacket with waistcoat and striped trousers. "We did what we could with Anthony," he said. "Tailors make him nervous."

"I'm sure he has other virtues."

"He surely does."

Tom was hurried into a fine linen suit that Georg had ordered. There was a miniature version for David, who would carry our rings. Anna, Tilda, and my mother showed me the silky cream dress with graceful folds and satin sash. It fit perfectly, and the flowers they'd chosen were perfect as well, but I kept asking: "Will there be fog today?"

"With this blue sky? Hold still," said Anna. "I'm not done with your buttons."

Lena's parents were there, Walter and the Hendersons, the Finkles and Charlie Snead, Mayor Woodruff and his wife, others from the town who were now my mother's friends, and all who ever worked at the castle. Luisa and her family had come on a separate train from Pittsburgh to surprise me.

We were married in the afternoon. A slight breeze cooled the summer heat and fluttered my dress. In the linen suit, with his dark curls coaxed to order, Tom's wide smile was pure joy. Georg walked me down the grassy aisle to the table that was our altar. Pastor Birke conducted the ceremony. I remember the soft blue sky and waft of roses, the warmth of Tom's hand in mine, and the smooth slide of gold around my finger.

We had our wedding dinner in the grand dining room with musicians playing. "Just like you remember," my mother said slyly. She sat close to Martin Birke. Yes, anyone could see they were sweethearts. A Lutheran bishop would be in town at Christmastime to marry them. We'd come back to Dogwood then, we promised. After the wedding cake and toasts, we danced in the mirrored hall that reflected thousands on thousands of us, all my people laughing, swirling and spinning, happy as if the Great War had never happened.

I would like to say that after our wedding Tom's bad times were fewer or less painful, but I can't. The nightmares, sweats, sudden terrors, and escapes to Red Gorge have slackened, but not vanished with time. Yet our good days are many and their pleasures are deep. When fog comes, we know that it will lift. Someday we may go to Paris. Meanwhile I teach; Tom works wood. David plays with Lilli's first puppy. We know there may be no end to the private battles we wage. Any truce may be fragile and incomplete, but we soldier on. And it is enough. More than enough.

# Acknowledgments

The few years between the setting of my second novel, *Swimming in the Moon* (1905–11) and the World War I years of this one made possible an astonishing range of easily available online film material for the research process: war footage and documentaries, clinical films of shell-shock victims, film and photographs of fashions, automobiles, work conditions in Pittsburgh, and the influenza pandemic of 1919. These resources are a boon for any writer or reader.

The University of Pittsburgh maintains a fine digital archive of Pittsburgh history. I am grateful to the research staff of the Knoxville Public Library, particularly Melissa Brenneman and Jamie Osborn, for their patience and sleuthing wizardry. Margaret Sudekum, DVM, helped on issues of dog training. Karen Schoenewaldt answered questions on art conservation and shipping. Jonathan Gaugler of the Carnegie Museum of Art was helpful in ascertaining which works of art Hazel might have seen in her visits to what was then the Carnegie Institute. Jane Buchholz, Gudrun Gorla, and Jeff Mellor lent expertise on issues of German language, culture, and cuisine. Gudrun generously shared her stollen recipe. Mark Loudermilk advised on banking practices and Jim Andrews on military matters. *An Iowa Schoolma'am*, edited by Philip L. Greber and Charlotte M. Wright, uses a young teacher's letters home to illustrate the joys and frustrations of one-room schoolhouse education.

On matters of the Lutheran practice, I consulted with the Reverend William Boys. Reverend John Gill and Jim Sessions unraveled other issues of theology, pastoral care, and spontaneous healing. A luminous meditation on events beyond our sense of reason is C. S. Lewis's *Miracles*. For historical perspective on American healers at the time of my novel, I suggest Linda L. Barnes and Susan S. Sered's *Religion and Healing in America* and Nancy A. Hardesty's *Faith Cure: Divine Healing in the Holiness and Pentecostal Movements*.

For medical issues and pediatrics, I consulted Leonard Bellingrath, MD, and Lisa Herron Oros, MD. There is a horrific account of one city's response to medical emergency in "With Every Accompaniment of Ravage and Agony: Pittsburgh and the Influenza Epidemic of 1918–1919," by James Higgins, in the *Pennsylvania Magazine of History and Biography*. Isaac Starr, then a student at the University of Pennsylvania School of Medicine, recalled his clinical experience in "Influenza in 1918: Recollections of the Epidemic in Philadelphia," in *Annals of Internal Medicine*. Eileen A. Lynch's "It Started in the Summer of 1918," in the *Philadelphia Gazette* was also valuable. Epidemiologist Kathleen Brown generously contrasted current and past treatment options, as well as symptoms and disease course of the H1N1 influenza virus.

The devastating distress reactions noted in soldiers after the first battles of World War I were described as "shell shock" by Charles Meyers in a *Lancet* article of 1915. The name stuck, even if soldiers not exposed to barrages of shells began presenting the range of symptoms we now term post-traumatic stress disorder (PTSD). Wendy Holden's classic *Shell Shock* was invaluable. Professor Stephen Joseph of the University of Nottingham answered queries on the variety of clinical manifestations of shell shock and PTSD. Dr. Laurel Goodrich illuminated contemporary treatment options. Dr. Ellison Mitchell, therapist and veteran, offered resources and professional insights on combat-related

PTSD symptoms and typical outcomes which helped me shape the final chapters of this book. Dr. Kathleen Sales shared her professional work in fugue states and generously critiqued Tom's account of his lost months.

Readers Rosalind Andrews, Jessica Brockmole, Gaye Evans, and Jamie Harris provided invaluable commentary. Linda Parsons Marion graciously, tirelessly, lent a poet-editor's eye to the final version. Doris Gove, Jo Ann Pantanizopoulos, and Odette Shults helped with listening, encouraging, and generally being there. Caitlin Hamilton Summie gives ongoing guidance.

My husband, Maurizio Conti, provides the patience, support, faith, pleasures, and good humor that keep my writing life afloat.

For lighting the way, calming, challenging, encouraging, and questioning, I am constantly grateful to my agent, Courtney Miller-Callihan. Amanda Bergeron, my indefatigable editor, brought steady insight and persistence in framing, balancing, focusing, and strengthening each draft. Finally, I'm indebted to her able team for shepherding this book through its many stages and placing it in your hands.

Insights,
Interviews
& More . . .

# Meet Pamela Schoenewaldt

*Photo by Kelly Norrell*

PAMELA SCHOENEWALDT is the *USA Today* bestselling author of *When We Were Strangers* and *Swimming in the Moon*. Both novels explore the immigrant experience, inspired by the ten years she lived in a small town outside Naples, Italy. Her short stories have appeared in literary magazines in England, France, Italy, and the United States. She taught writing for the University of Maryland, European Division and the University of Tennessee and lives in Knoxville, Tennessee, with her husband, Maurizio Conti, a physicist, and their dog, Jesse. ∾

# Q&A with the Author

*Your first two novels were based in
Italian immigrant communities.
You lived in Italy for a time and your
husband is Italian. This novel is based
in a German-American community.
Are there autobiographical elements
in* Under the Same Blue Sky?

Actually yes, perhaps more than in either
*When We Were Strangers* or *Swimming in
the Moon.* Like Johannes and Katarina
Renner, my paternal grandmother,
Caroline, was born in Heidelberg. She
came to America at age four with her
adoptive parents. By all accounts they
provided a stable, loving, happy home.
However, like Hazel, the fact of my
grandmother's adoption was kept
hidden, and her memories of another
life were dismissed as dreams. It was not
until her forties that a chance comment
by a family friend unraveled the truth.
In the aftershock, she created for herself
a romantic identity story: her mother
was a servant in a noble household;
her father was the titled heir. He died
young, her story went, and the distraught
mother gave the child to emigrating
friends with the idea of saving money,
following them to America, and
retrieving the child. Then, the story
continued, the mother came over,
searched for her daughter, never found
her, and died tragically, alone. That there
was scant historical evidence for any of
this didn't stop me from having my own
fantasy that one day my noble family ▶

3

would come to save me from my prosaic New Jersey life and its onerous tasks (cleaning my room, loading the dishwasher, and so forth). They would whisk me to the splendid castle and gilded life which was my bloodright. Sigh. That never happened. But you'll see parts of the story in *Under the Same Blue Sky.*

In a more general sense, in framing Hazel's home life, I drew from my own childhood and what I perceived as German-American values that "went without saying": studying hard, doing homework, respecting teachers, being on time, never ever addressing adults by their first names, avoiding "bad company" and "trivial entertainments," being frugal, not wasting food, avoiding debt, doing respectable (i.e., professional) work. While constricting at times, this net of expectations gave a certain security to me and to Hazel, even when she broke out of the net.

**Your fictional town of Dogwood, New Jersey, houses a baron's castle. Where did that idea come from?**

I went to high school in Watchung, New Jersey, which at that time housed an actual castle built in 1900 by the Danish Moldenke family, whose line could be traced back to the Crusades. With forty rooms, medieval arms, vast library, and a mausoleum, the Moldenke castle was rich ground for local fables. In 1945, it passed to a biologist of less storied family, and the original Danish owners were forgotten. Locals invented instead a German nobleman who built the castle for his homesick princess bride. By the time I was nosing around the castle grounds with friends, we had morphed the biologist into a mad physicist who did evil experiments in his laboratory. Digression: Why always "mad physicist," and not "mad civil engineer" or "mad ichthyologist" or "mad accountant"? Being married to a not-mad physicist, this question troubles me. Back to Watchung. Eventually the biologist moved away, and no buyer could be found. The castle was steadily vandalized, then sold to a developer, burned under suspicious circumstances, and was soon after bulldozed to make way for unromantic McMansions. But the image of turrets visible from school bus windows stayed with me all this time and now has a new life in fiction.

*You describe very vividly the situation of German-Americans during World War I. While propaganda vilifying the enemy is typical in wartime, what made the German-American situation at this time unique?*

German-Americans are the largest self-reported ancestry group in the United States. Between 1880 and 1890, there were nearly 1.5 million German immigrants. By 1900, more than 40 percent of the residents of Cleveland, Milwaukee, and Cincinnati were German-born. Many smaller midwestern communities had far higher percentages. German-Americans could be found in every social strata and profession. This fact undoubtedly helped maintain American neutrality far into World War I, bolstered by general resistance to "foreign entanglements," and, as Hazel saw, the incredible profit in selling arms to belligerents without donating soldiers to the cause.

As pressures for war built, German-Americans who felt emotionally bound to their country and culture of origin tried desperately to reconcile conflicting loyalties. One way of contextualizing this conflict was the widely used phrase "Germany is our mother, America our wife." I don't know how convincing or comfortable the phrase was to anybody. For some, like Hazel's father, the strain of equal and opposite pulls was truly unbearable.

President Woodrow Wilson, who argued for neutrality as long as possible, warned: "Once lead this people into war and they will forget there ever was such a thing as tolerance." When the United States joined the Allies in April 1917, overnight the homeland of millions of Americans became the evil empire, the land of Huns. Former neighbors, friends, and colleagues were suddenly potential enemies or spies. An enormous propaganda machine sprang up. As Hazel reports, standard English had to be purged of German words with ludicrous results, like changing dachshunds and German measles into "liberty pups" and "liberty measles." That was the light side. There were lynchings, beatings, homes and businesses destroyed. Many lost their jobs; families were divided; peaceful communities were ripped apart. Everywhere, for *every* American, the ▶

**Q&A with the Author** *(continued)*

Espionage Act of 1917 and the Sedition Amendment of 1918 trampled civil rights, free speech, freedom of the press, and free assembly.

While clearly these effects were later overshadowed by the internment of Japanese-Americans during World War II, the Holocaust, and ethnic wars that claimed and still claim millions of lives, President Wilson has been proved right: war is never just "out there" on the battlefield. The tolerance that binds and enriches a civil society is ripped away by war as we take its conflicts into our communities, our neighborhoods, and our hearts.

***Was your family in the United States during World War I, and if so, what was their experience?***

My family was here, but I only know one story. My maternal great-grandmother was sent over from Germany to Iowa in the late 1800s to marry her brother's friend. (I called on this fact in my first novel, *When We Were Strangers*). By the time the United States entered World War I, she had learned English. Her husband, a dour and antisocial fellow, never did. A new ruling in their little town outlawed speaking German in public. That was fine with my great-grandmother. She'd fallen in love with her new country. When her husband announced that he'd never speak English, her response was: "Suit yourself. But nobody will talk to you." Apparently, that didn't bother him.

***Ben Robinson and Tom Jamison struggle with what was once called "shell shock" and is now termed post-traumatic stress disorder, or PTSD. Like so many families today, Hazel, Tom, and David must deal with the invisible wounds of war. What did you discover as you researched this phenomenon?***

Within months after the start of World War I, armies on both sides faced an epidemic of massive proportions. With no apparent physical injury, officers and enlisted men were presenting a confounding range of symptoms: panic, almost infantile helplessness, extreme lack of coordination, mutism, hysterical blindness, bizarre gaits and facial tics, amnesia, fugue states, headaches, uncontrollable tremors, hypersensitivity to sound, rigidity, and incapacitating fixation on traumatic events. Strangely, officers were five to eight times more vulnerable than enlisted soldiers. Everywhere, the fighting force was endangered. No other war had produced these effects on this scale. Generals, politicians, and the medical community struggled to find a cause and a cure as the epidemic raged, producing casualties as high as 40 percent in some units.

In 1915, the term *shell shock* was coined by British researcher Charles Myers, assuming that the cause of these strange behaviors was neurological damage caused by passing shells. This proved false, since troops far from the front were stricken as well. However, the name stuck. Some blamed lack of moral fiber, cowardice, and simply faking symptoms to avoid combat. Suggested cures included denial, humiliation, physical punishment, and electric shocks to have victims buck up and return to the trenches. More compassionate approaches were tried and sometimes succeeded, but the sheer mass of casualties overwhelmed resources in every army. For a wrenching description of the "boys with old, scared faces, learning to walk," see "The Survivors" by Siegfried Sassoon, one of the great British war poets.

Many turned to the new field of psychoanalysis for explanation. Ernest Jones, a British doctor who worked closely with Sigmund Freud, blamed this new kind of war, unequaled in the savagery and trench conditions that soldiers endured, forcing them to "indulge in behaviour of a kind that is throughout abhorrent to the civilised mind. . . . All sorts of previously forbidden and hidden impulses, cruel, sadistic, murderous and so on, are stirred to greater activity." The unbearable inner conflict between these dark impulses and the civilized mind, Jones concluded, inevitably produced bizarre behaviors.

The Freudian analysis has been debated and refined. Other theories have been proposed. In the past century, enormous energy has gone into prevention, identification, and management of what we now call PTSD in military and civilian life. We have ▶

certainly progressed in compassion and therapeutic options, but still many survivors and families suffer. Like those who return with shrapnel deeply embedded in the flesh, PTSD rarely just goes away. Yet the loving and patient support that Tom finds in Galway (even without the magical powers of a blue house) can ease symptoms and uncover ways to negotiate a new normal. Considering the horrific scenes and situations to which we subject our soldier-agents, this in itself is nothing short of miraculous.

*Unlike your first two books,* Under the Same Blue Sky *has elements of magic realism, most noticeably in Hazel's discovery of inexplicable healing powers during her time in Galway.*

In some of my short stories I experimented with elements of the inexplicable in otherwise realistic settings. I won my first short story award with a tale of an American woman in Italy who can't get her landlord to deal with bathroom mold. When the Blessed Virgin Mary seems to appear in the mold and apparently eases arthritic pains, our heroine's bathroom becomes a public shrine. I thought there was far more to explore here. As the setting and themes of *Under the Same Blue Sky* began to coalesce, I was drawn to an intriguing "what if": What if healing powers come unbidden? Will the consequences be wholly good? Probably not. Will there be costs to the healer? Probably. What if the parceling out of miracles in a small community is not seen as "fair"? What happens when the magic stops happening? Is there a kind of "magic healing" more subtle and yet more sustained? I wanted to find out.

On this subject, I want to clarify that I have no strong position on spiritual or spontaneous healing. I'm sure that many have experienced sudden relief of symptoms that confounds medical opinion. I've seen this happen around me. I can't posit why medical miracles happen—or in other cases don't happen. There's so much we don't know about how our bodies heal themselves—or fail us, or how the mind, pure grace, and other apparently nonmedical factors influence outcomes. It seems arrogant to claim that whatever we can't explain *can't* happen, or that person A deserves to be miraculously healed while person B does not. These are complex issues of theology, psychology, philosophy, ethics, and medical science. A novel is something different. My concern was the impact of sudden and extraordinary powers on an ordinary person who did not ask for this power and is unprepared for its unfolding consequences. Beyond this question, in what other ways do seemingly magical, profound changes happen in our lives, relationships, and communities? *Under the Same Blue Sky* explores this question. ❧

# Gudrun's Stollen

HAZEL'S FIRST CHRISTMAS MEAL after the armistice includes *Christstollen*, the traditional German Christmas bread. Hazel comments that the rich, slightly sweet, fruit-studded bread becomes for her the taste of peace.

You can make the taste of peace yourself. This recipe was generously provided by my dear friend and the best baker I know, Gudrun Gorla, from Bielefeld, in northern Germany. It's just-right sweet, moist, and wonderfully satisfying. In southern Germany, stollen is typically made with yeast. This is a quicker version, using baking powder.

Gudrun uses the Dr. Oetker brand of vanilla sugar, found in many grocery stores. You can make your own, but consider the Dr. Oetker motto: "Ein heller Kopf nimmt stets Oetker" (Bright minds always use Oetker).

## Directions

*(For two loaves)*

4 C flour
1 C sugar
1 Tbsp. baking powder
1 pkg. Dr. Oetker's vanilla sugar or
    1½ tsp. homemade vanilla sugar
    (recipe below)
Pinch of salt
1 tsp. almond extract
1 tsp. lemon extract
1 tsp. rum extract
Pinch of ground cardamom
A trace of mace

2 eggs
½ C (1 stick) cold butter, cut in pieces
3 Tbsp. lard
1 C cottage cheese (drain before measuring)
½ C currants, rinsed and drained
1 C raisins, rinsed and drained
¾ to 1 C peeled, ground almonds and/or hazelnuts
⅓ C candied fruit, chopped

For brushing: 3 Tbsp. melted butter
For dusting: 3 Tbsp. powdered sugar

Sift together the flour and baking powder onto a board. Make an indentation in the mixture and put in sugar, vanilla sugar, salt, spices, extracts and eggs. Mix together with part of the flour, making a thick mash.

Add the butter pieces, lard, and drained cottage cheese. Then add, in order, currants, raisins, nuts, and candied fruit. Cover the nuts and fruit with flour. Next, working from the center, quickly knead together all ingredients to make a smooth dough. If it sticks to your board, add some flour. Cut the dough in two and form each half into a rounded rectangle. Put on baking trays lined with parchment paper.

Bake at 350°F for 50–60 minutes until lightly brown. Remove from oven. Brush the loaves with melted butter and dust with powdered sugar. When cooled, wrap tightly in plastic wrap and let age for at least a week to blend the flavors. Well wrapped, stollen will keep and improve for 3 weeks.

*To make vanilla sugar:* Split a vanilla bean and with a dull knife scrape out the beans. In a glass container, bury the pod and bean in 1 cup of granulated sugar, seal tightly, and let sit for one to two weeks. ᝈ

# Reading Group Guide

1. Hazel's mother sees signs of an extraordinary future for her daughter. While Hazel's healing powers in Galway are certainly extraordinary, in what other, quieter ways does her mother's prediction come true?

2. Discuss the nuanced nature of Hazel's sudden gift of healing. How might a similar gift impact your life or your community?

3. What roles does Ben Robinson play in Hazel's journey?

4. Hazel's choices are often driven by vivid dreams of the past and of the future. Can you compare this to your own experience?

5. Discuss how the events of the novel transform one or more of the central figures in Hazel's life: Johannes and Katarina Renner, Tom or Georg.

6. How are the qualities of air— smoke, fog, blue sky—woven into the plot and themes of *Under the Same Blue Sky*?

7. Hazel, Tom, and Georg were in various ways "orphaned." How does this fact help bring them together?

8. As Hazel discovers, her legacy from Margit Brandt is complex. What challenges and unexpected gifts comprise this legacy?

9. When Tom returns with what we would now diagnose as PTSD, what

experiences and personal qualities help Hazel accept this challenge?

10. Communities in this novel struggle with cultural and ethnic diversity. How has this struggle changed or not changed in the last century?

11. "We're not the same," Jim Burnett says after the war. How does the experience of World War I transform characters and communities in this novel? ∾

# Suggested Reading

HERE ARE SOME BOOKS I READ, reread, or remembered keenly in writing *Under the Same Blue Sky*.

*Perla*, Carolina De Robertis
*Benediction*, Kent Haruf
*Miracles*, C. S. Lewis
*No Great Mischief*, Alistair MacLeod
*Transatlantic*, Colum McCann
*In the Company of Men*, Hisham Matar
*When the Emperor Was Divine*,
    Julie Otsuka
*All Quiet on the Western Front*,
    Erich Maria Remarque
*Jewelweed*, David Rhodes
*Imagining Argentina*, Lawrence Thornton
*Personal Recollections of Joan of Arc*,
    Mark Twain
*Reunion*, Fred Uhlman

# Have You Read?
## More by Pamela Schoenewaldt

### WHEN WE WERE STRANGERS

Too poor and too plain to marry, and unwilling to burden what family she has left, twenty-year-old Irma Vitale sees no choice but to flee her Italian mountain village. Risking rough passage across the Atlantic and the dangers facing a single woman in an unfamiliar land, Irma boldly pursues a new life sewing dresses for gentlewomen.

Swept up in the crowded streets of nineteenth-century America, Irma finds workshop servitude and miserable wages, but also seeds of friendship in the raw immigrant quarters. Her journey leads to Chicago, where Irma blossoms under the guidance of an austere Alsatian dressmaker, producing masterworks more beautiful than she'd ever imagined. Then tragedy strikes and her tenuous peace is shattered. From the rubble, and in the face of human cruelty and kindness, suffering and hope, Irma prevails, discovering a talent she'd never imagined and an unlikely family, patched together by threads that unite us all.

### SWIMMING IN THE MOON

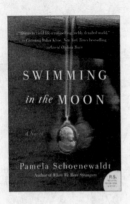

Italy, 1904. Fourteen-year-old Lucia and her young mother Teresa are servants in a magnificent villa on the Bay of Naples, where Teresa soothes their unhappy mistress with song. But volatile tempers force them to flee, exchanging their warm, gilded cage for the cold winds off Lake Erie and Cleveland's volatile garment workers' community.

With the voice of a nightingale as soaring and varied as her moods, Teresa becomes a singer on the vaudeville circuit. Clever and hardworking, Lucia blossoms in school until her mother's demons return, fracturing Lucia's dreams.

Yet Lucia is not alone in her struggle for a better life. All around, friends and neighbors, new Americans, are demanding decent wages and working conditions. Lucia joins their battle, confronting risks and opportunities that will transform her and her world in ways she never imagined.

Discover great authors, exclusive offers, and more at hc.com.